The Assembly Presents

NECESSARY MEASURES

Richard Ogilvie

Necessary Measures
Copyright © 2023 by Richard Ogilvie

All rights reserved. No part of this publication may be reproduced, distributed, or transmitted in any form or by any means, including photocopying, recording, or other electronic or mechanical methods, without the prior written permission of the author, except in the case of brief quotations embodied in critical reviews and certain other non-commercial uses permitted by copyright law.

tellwell

Tellwell Talent
www.tellwell.ca

ISBN
978-0-2288-9164-2 (Hardcover)
978-0-2288-9165-9 (Paperback)
978-0-2288-9166-6 (eBook)

To Teng,

DEDICATION

To my beloved wife, my #1 fan,
and my inspiration, Amy

So glad that I got to know you. Thanks you for the support. I hope your like it.

ACKNOWLEDGEMENTS

To all of the people who have helped to guide me through this process, please know that I would not have been able to complete this without you. To my friends and family who have supported me throughout this journey, my heartfelt thanks and appreciation. In addition, to all those that I have worked with during my time with the Federal Government, I would like to take a moment to thank you for the work that you do. So many times, you are overlooked and your contribution to the safety of the public is pushed aside. Thank you for putting your lives on the line where not too many people would dare to step.

PROLOGUE

The waiting was always the worst part. Arranging an extraction was never easy, but trying to facilitate one in a foreign city that you weren't particularly familiar with was especially stressful. The wheels had been set in motion, but now it was just a matter of time. The plan was simple enough. He was to wait in his room until a man came to get him and brought him to a taxi. The taxi was then supposed to take him to a boat that would bring him back to the United States. That was to take place at 3:15 PM. A quick glance at his watch told him that he had just under thirty minutes left to go. Much like a child waiting for Christmas, though, time seemed to be dragging.

He stood to stretch his legs. The last thing he needed was a cramp to add to the problems he was facing. He decided to grab a couple of breaths of fresh air out on the small balcony of the room he had been fortunate enough to procure. Cancun could be a veritable hornet's nest of commotion and rooms were sometimes difficult to come by. This one overlooked the street.

Once on the balcony, his senses were assailed by the myriad of music wafting up to him from seemingly all directions. Buried in the swill of "today's music", he thought he caught a C.C.R. classic fighting to be heard. He smiled to himself as his eyes wandered the street below. A couple of drunks had decided that the middle of the street was the best location to settle their differences. The police would likely be called, but how effective they were going to be was still up in the air.

His eyes travelled further and settled on the young woman who had been selling flowers the day before. It was still quite busy, but she moved in a customary fashion making it seem like she did this all the time. Her joy lit up the area around her, even as the heat of the day seemed to try and break her spirit. It was oppressive. The woman glanced up at the man on the balcony and smiled, before looking away coyly.

He returned her smile and stepped back inside. Twenty-seven minutes to go. He was about to return to the chair in the corner when something struck him as being odd. At first, he couldn't put his finger on it. It was just that something didn't feel right. He quickly replayed what he had seen out on the balcony in case he had overlooked something. If he wasn't scheduled to leave today, he wouldn't have second guessed anything. But now? Everything was important. The drunks were pervasive in Cancun. *Could their scuffle have been rehearsed? What about...? Oh shit!*

He raced over to his laptop and quickly booted it up. After the start up sequence was complete, he fished a small disk out of his pocket and inserted it. A few key strokes later and the hard drive began its demise. He snatched up his backpack and made a quick visual inspection of the room to make sure he hadn't forgotten anything else. Once satisfied, he ducked out into the hall and headed for an exit. The elevators were too constricted in their movement so he opted for the stairs. He had to act fast. There were people who wanted answers from him and people who wanted a lot more than that. The girl with the flowers was one of them, though he didn't know which. He had seen her three times in the few hours he had been in Cancun and she had never been coy. It was like she was seeing him for the first time. Something was wrong.

He thought about going down the stairs, but if he was right about what was going on, people would undoubtedly be on the way up. A meeting on the stairs would be a challenge he would like to avoid. He climbed up instead. No sooner had he reached the landing to the fourth floor, he heard heavy footsteps entering the stairs from below. He listened intently as he counted four, then five pairs of footsteps going to the second floor.

He slipped quietly out onto the fifth floor. He had studied this hotel well and knew exactly what he wanted to do. Reaching into his backpack, he withdrew a set of lock pick tools and moved to the third door on his right. It only took a few seconds to open the door and step inside. He quickly locked the door and moved swiftly to the other side of the empty room. He opened the window and stepped out on to the fire escape at the back of the building. Again, he opted to climb up. He could hear shouts coming from the alley below, but couldn't make out what was being said. He tried inching upwards silently, but the strain of his weight on the aging metal walkway sounded out his location. A shot rang out and ricocheted close to where he was standing as the voices beneath him intensified. There was no point in trying to be silent anymore. He charged up the fire escape as more shots rose from the darkened alley in an attempt to prevent his flight. He felt the walkway lurch as the weight of at least one more person was added. He was no longer alone.

He climbed even faster now as the rooftop neared. If he could get there, he would have more choices…freedom to move. Just then a dark figure appeared on the fire escape just above him. A pair of hands reached out and grabbed his throat, trying to crush his windpipe in one swift motion. Without thinking, he brought his hands together in a prayer motion and drove them up between the arms of his attacker. The force was enough to break the man's grip and knock him off balance. He thought about trying to heave this shadow off of the walkway, but instead propelled him back through the open window he had come out of. The man landed with a thud inside of the room.

With that particular threat temporarily out of the way, he continued towards the roof. He knew that there would be more people waiting for him somewhere, but he just had to keep moving. He finally crested the roof and did not stop to look back. He just kept running. It was quite a jump to get to the next building, but it was his only chance of escape. He sprinted forward towards the chasm that suddenly appeared to be a lot wider than he had remembered. It was too late to turn back now. He could hear another set of feet on the gravel of the rooftop as he neared the jump. He placed his foot on the edge and pushed with all of his might as he sailed through the air in a desperate leap for freedom and a single shot rang out in the darkness.

CHAPTER 1

The sun dipped slowly in the western sky, descending towards the horizon. The waning sunlight in August always made the world seem heavenly. It was as if the sky was purposefully setting out to inspire poets and artists. Looking out over the expanse of water making up part of the beauty of Victoria, British Columbia, Robert Seabrook wondered how his life had taken such drastic turns that would find him in this situation. Would he ever see the sun again? Would he ever leave this jetty known locally as the "Breakwater"? Would his wife be safe? And if so, would she ever understand what he had gotten mixed up in or why he had agreed to this? Would she have done the same had the roles been reversed? Probably not, he mused. But then again, she was always a better person than he had ever been. He had really lucked out when they had met.

Anna Seabrook, or Wilson at the time, had walked through the door of his high school History class (senior year) and permanently changed Robert Seabrook's life. From the moment he had laid his eyes on her, he was consumed by her beauty. He remembered the way her raven-black hair cascaded over her shoulder as her eyes swept the room looking for a place to sit. Once she had selected her desired spot, she breezed over to it as if gravity were not so much a force to strain against, but a toy to be used to make her every move seem destined. She sat down two seats over and one back from a young Robert Seabrook, whom had not been able to take his eyes off of her. As she situated herself at her desk, she did something that would forever link these two strangers - a link that would stand the test of time and distance. She looked at him. She looked right into his eyes. The look lasted all of three quarters of a second as Robert nervously averted his eyes and focussed instead on a map of the Mediterranean, which suddenly seemed very interesting. Out of the corner of his eye, he thought that he caught a smile from this beauty. He didn't dare look back. Besides, Corsica and Sardinia were presently keeping him from bursting into flames.

Over the next few weeks, Robert began what he called the "Courtship of Anna". This consisted mostly of him trying to situate himself so that Anna would be forced to keep bumping into him. Either that, or getting his friends to infiltrate her group of friends so that he'd have an excuse to see her outside of History class. In retrospect, it was quite pathetic, but what else could a shy 17 year old do to try and win the affection of a goddess. Little did he know that his attempts not only endeared him to Goddess Anna, but it was actually Anna who was trying to bump into him. Who knew that Goddess Anna's type would be a shy, nervous, 17 year old wreck with glasses that excelled at nothing but was competent in most areas? Was that her type? Non-descript? He didn't ask and he didn't care. All he knew was that by her side was where he wanted to be.

And it happened for him – for them, one Friday afternoon. After a relatively unsuccessful week of "crashing into each other", Anna Wilson and Robert Seabrook literally crashed into each other while rounding a corner of the gymnasium resulting in a shower of papers and books falling down around the unlikely pair. Without the benefit of a multi-coloured illustration of the Mediterranean (or any other body of water), Robert was forced to focus on Anna Wilson. As he stammered out his profuse apology while clumsily attempting to assist her in gathering her wayward sheets, Robert could feel himself turning an awful shade of crimson. He had the distinct feeling that due to his slight form, he probably resembled a stop sign at that moment. Cursing his luck as all of his hard work seemed to be eroding before his eyes, it was Anna who took him by surprise.

"Are you all right?" she queried. It took Robert a moment to wonder why she didn't respond to his question before he realized that it was she who had spoken.

"Uhhhhhhh…I think so" was his reply. *Brilliant*, he thought. *I steamroll the girl of my dreams and all I can do is sound like a moron.* "Are you okay?" he asked feebly.

"Oh I'm fine. I have 2 older brothers. If I can take tackle football in the backyard with them over the years, then I'm sure I can handle a dust-up like this." Was she smiling? She was already straightening her outfit and shaking off the soreness. She extended a hand down to him which is when he realized that she was standing while he was still on his knees with an armful of foolscap about to devour him. "I'm Anna" she said.

I'm yours, he wished. "Robert." All he could muster. He took her hand…and froze. Why? He would never know. Was it that when two destined souls find each other, does that moment cause time to stop? Was it that in that second, all had gone right in his life and he couldn't bring himself to break that single precious moment? Was it that he had suffered some form of freak internal injury from the collision that was preventing him from moving? All he knew at that moment was that Anna had said something else and he had missed it.

"I'm sorry?"

"I said, are you gonna propose?" she asked playfully. "Cuz you sure seem comfortable down there."

How long had it been? Too long. Not long enough. *Say something*. And then, from a well of confidence, stupidity, or brash testosterone – whichever – Robert Seabrook summoned the courage and said, "Would you say yes if I did?"

She smiled. That smile of hers - the one that cannot be described in words. The smile that seemed to reach into the very corners of Robert's existence and touch every part of his being. "Isn't that a bit strange for a first date?"

Was she toying with him? Dangling the hint of eternal happiness in front of him before snatching it away so that she and her friends could laugh mockingly at him for the rest of the year. No. Not Goddess Anna. She couldn't be. *Now or never tough guy*. "How about a movie then?" Had he just asked that question? Who was this guy and where did he come from? *Am I still kneeling?* He bolted up with that thought. Had she answered? Did he miss something else she had said? *Nice work, idiot. The girl of your dreams is standing in front of you, holding your hand, and you can't even focus enough to listen to what she has to say. Great impression. I love you, but don't say anything cuz I'm not actually listening. She'd be a fool to miss out on that!*

But she hadn't answered yet, he realized. She was just standing there, his hand in hers, eyeing him furtively. Was she assessing him? Weighing the pros and cons? *Oh God! Did I actually ask the question? Or just thought I did? Have I just been standing here waiting for her to answer a question I didn't ask? She must think I'm mentally challenged.* But the fates, and Anna's mercy, were on his side. "I'd like that, Robert."

Had a sweeter word ever graced the English language? Not that the word Robert was particularly enthralling, but it was the sound her voice made when she uttered it that made it seem mythical. Not before or at any point after in his life was he more proud of his name that when she had first said it, outside the gymnasium of Maple Ridge Senior Secondary. Robert. *Thanks Mom and Dad.* She scribbled down her phone number and handed it to him. "Call me tomorrow?"

Robert took the slip of paper from her reverently. Luckily, he resisted the urge to sniff it like he had seen in so many movies form years gone past. Some stuff just didn't look right when not in a movie. Instead, he just held the note in his hand and stared at her face – and those eyes. For the rest of his life, he would refer to them as

"Disney eyes". Eyes crafted by a master painter, a skilled animator able to create a life, body, and soul from simple cells. "I will" he finally spoke. "Looking forward to it."

"The phone call or the movie?" she laughed.

"The wedding." And he was off. What followed was the best part of Robert Seabrook's life. The movie was great. The company better. He discovered that his focus problems must have been related to his need to be with her because once he was there, he didn't miss a word of what she said. The sun seemed to rise and set with her words. He learned about her life, her family, her dreams, and her fears. Everything he could think of, he asked. And he volunteered just as much. He wanted her to know everything that he was and wanted to be. No secrets. No pretence. And she wanted the same. He met her brothers, her mother and father. And she met his mom. Both families liked each other and both families grew to love Robert and Anna. Love is not a word to describe how Robert and Anna felt about each other, though. The word has not yet been created to describe the bond they felt for each other. The bond first created in a heap in high school. Love was definitely a large part of it. But love can be fleeting. Love can be fickle. What they shared was impervious to things like pettiness or jealousy. What they shared couldn't be tarnished with envy or suspicion. Did they quarrel? Of course. They were indeed human. But what they had was an unwritten or unspoken understanding that their life together would endure and the next day would be better than the previous one.

That was until all of this, he mused to himself. What had he discovered? What had he stumbled across? It had to be pretty important to cause this chain of events to unfold culminating in this clandestine meeting with a total stranger. *Think it through, stupid. Okay. Walk it through. My patient tells me in session that he is being forced to participate in a plot to assassinate President Nieto in Colombia. Believable? Not really. He always seemed to come up with outlandish plots of espionage. One of the main reasons I was treating him. But then Nieto ends up gunned down and my patient misses his next 2 appointments – not even a phone call. So I ask around? What was I thinking? Obviously somebody found out about my inquiries. So I was contacted. Mr. Holt. Wanting to know what I knew about all of this. And what did I do? Threaten to go public? What was I thinking?*

That had not been a pleasant conversation. Mr. Holt had called his office. His secretary Janet had put the call through. "Dr. Seabrook?" the voice had asked.

"Yes this is Dr. Seabrook. My secretary tells me you have some information about Terry Philips."

"I do, indeed, Dr. Seabrook. But it's the information you may have that interests me the most, Doctor." The voice on the other end of the line suddenly seemed cold.

"What do you mean? What information? Who is this?" Robert's pulse quickened slightly as every spy movie he had ever seen raced quickly through his head.

The voice responded coolly, "I have no name at this time. But for the purpose of conversational etiquette, you can call me Mr. Holt." Now the hairs on the back of Robert's neck started to rise, as did the hair on his forearms. His grip tightened on the phone. Only then did he here the faint hum in the distance of telephone communication. Encryption? *What do I know about it? Voice modulation? Anti-tracking? I'm talking out of my ass!*

"M-Mr. Holt. I have no time for theatrics. If you know what's happened to Terry, then you need to tell me r-"

"I *need* to tell you nothing, Dr. Seabrook. What *you* need to tell me is everything Terry Philips spoke to you about in his last 2 sessions with you." Holt wasn't angry. Didn't raise his voice at all. Was that good or bad? *Probably bad*.

Robert started struggling for thoughts. How did this Holt know that Terry only spoke with him about this during the last 2 sessions? Bigger question, how did Holt even know that Terry Philips was seeing him as a psychologist? Only one defence came to him. "That's all covered by doctor/patient privilege, Mr. Holt. Surely you must know that I can't betray that." Would that be enough to deter this Mr. Holt?

"I can't get into specifics, Dr. Seabrook." Holt continued. "Let's just say that in this instance, doctor/patient privilege no longer applies."

The meaning was ominous. Robert thought back to numerous episodes of Law & Order and drew the only conclusion he could from such limited experience. "Are you telling me he's dead?" he asked, fearing the answer.

"Dr. Seabrook. What I am telling you is that I need the information you have. I need to speak to you about everything Terry Philips spoke to you about over the last 2 sessions. I am not interested in anything else he had to say. You will co-operate. I will tell you when and where we will meet. I will tell you-"

"Now hold on there, Mr. Holt" Robert interjected. "I don't appreciate being spoken to like this. You call up from out of nowhere demanding things of me you know I can't do and then start ordering me around like some sort of house pet. I have a good mind to go to the authorities and report Mr. Philips missing. Then we'll see how confident you are in your 'control' of me" he added with a slight sneer of false bravado. Did he detect a hesitation on the part of Mr. Holt? Was he regaining his composure and control of this conversation?

"You don't want to that, Dr. Seabrook" was the response.

Ha! Gotcha! "And why is that, Mr. Holt." Robert Seabrook had stood up to this intrusion like a champion. Had faced the initial apprehension and rising fear and warded it off. He felt like a true warrior. But even Achilles had his weakness. And Robert's meant more to him than any tendon ever could.

"Because Anna means as much to you as she does." And in a moment, his warrior spirit was extinguished. The lump that instantly formed in his throat felt like a watermelon. The sweat that had broken out on his forehead threatened to drown him only if the shudder that ran through him didn't snap his spine first.

"What did you say?" Robert croaked. His heart was hammering so loudly that he wasn't sure if this Holt character could even hear him.

"You heard me, Dr. Seabrook" Holt stated. "You are now a part of this, whether you like it or not. Further, your involvement has now made Anna a part of this too.

How big a part she plays is entirely up to how much you are willing to co-operate. Am I clear?

What could he possibly say to that? This kind of thing wasn't supposed to happen. Not in real life.

"I'm taking your silence as understanding, Dr. Seabrook" Holt continued. "I have no wish to see anything bad befall Anna. As far as I can tell, she's a very sweet person. Had a chance to make her acquaintance the other day while she was jogging. Very pretty. Nice house, too." The blood that had finally started to flow again through his veins, now started to simmer.

"You stay the hell away from her" he commanded. "She has nothing to do with anything".

"Oh I beg to differ, Dr. Seabrook. She has what I need the most right now. She has the power to control you. And that gives her great significance to me" the hint of a smile came through the phone line. *You sick son of a bitch*!

"I swear to God if you hurt her-"

"Can the chivalry, Dr. Seabrook. Now is not the time and believe me, you are in no position to threaten me." So true, Robert thought. "Like I said, her involvement rests entirely on you. If you do as I say, then her involvement ends here. If you try and circumvent the coming events, her involvement continues. If you try and contact the authorities…well…don't contact the authorities. Don't contact anyone. Do you understand?"

What else could he say? "I understand."

"Good. See how easy that was?" Holt couldn't hide the satisfaction in his voice that he felt from another well played game of verbal chess. He could make a career out of it. *He probably already has,* thought Robert. "Grab Philips' file and leave your office. Go to the Breakwater and wait for me at the far end of it. I will be there within the hour." And then the line went dead. So much for haggling the when and where part of it.

What the hell is all this? I didn't do anything wrong. Oh God! Anna! He picked the phone to call her. *Wait. Holt said not to contact anyone. Did that include Anna?* Surely he would have known that he would want to call her and check on her. Is that why he specified not to call anyone? *God, this is all way over my head.* He glanced helplessly around his office hoping for some divine inspiration showing him his best course of action. What was there? The certificates on the wall? No help now. The obscenely cliché leather couch that nobody even used? Not a peep. The map of the Mediterranean that he always kept as a reminder of that first day? *Oh God, what do I do?*

As if in answer to his prayer, Janet buzzed through on the intercom. "Dr. Seabrook. Your wife is on line 2."

His heart leapt with joy, and then quickly spasmed with fear. *Do I take the call? Is that breaking the rules?* After all, Holt hadn't been clear on what to do if someone contacted him. "Thank you, Janet." He picked up the receiver, took a deep breath, and accepted the call on Line 2.

"Hey babe" he said, trying to sound casual.

"Hey Robbie. How's work?" The only person in the world who could get away with calling him Robbie. It just sounded wrong if anyone else said it. But the name Robbie was hers and hers alone.

"It's work. How are things at home?" *Don't freak out, but your life may be in danger. They don't make Hallmark cards for that, do they.*

"Oh fine here." To this day, she was still the only woman he had found that meant that things were fine when she said fine. It was never "fine, but now you need to find out what's really bothering me". He had always hated that, and loved her all the more for not doing it. If there was one thing Anna Seabrook could do, it was speak her mind. If something was bothering her, she told you about it…hard. It was that trait that allowed her to cut right to the heart of the matter. "Is everything all right there?"

He paused momentarily. "Fine. Why?" he asked, hoping she had no clue about what had transpired in the last few minutes but finding that idea remote.

"I just got a phone call from some guy telling me to give you a call at work. He wouldn't leave his name."

"What else did he say?" Robert asked his wife.

"Nothing," she replied. "He just told me to call you and see how you were doing. Said you received some troubling news and could use a call from me to lighten your mood. Everything okay?"

Son of a bitch. Message received loud and clear. Your wife is fine. I have your phone number, work number, home address and am in complete control. Got it? Your wife doesn't suspect anything, so don't do anything to change that. "Yeah. I'm fine." His mind was reeling. "Just some news about one of my patients." Not a bad half-truth really.

"Anything you wanna talk about?" She had always been there for him. Always there with an open ear and a strong shoulder. He hoped he had always been there for her too.

"No, that's all right. I'll be fine." Was that a lie? A big one? He had no idea. "Listen Anna, I've gotta run. I've got a meeting to attend." Another half-truth.

"Alright. You sure you're okay, though." She could always tell when there was just something not right with him.

"Yeah. I'm fine, babe."

"If you're sure," she replied.

"I love you, Anna." He tried to hide the catch in his voice when he said it. Would he get to say it again to her face?

"I love you too, Robbie. I'll see you when you get home." With that, Robert Seabrook replaced the receiver on its cradle and said a silent prayer for Anna and for himself. He went to the filing cabinet and retrieved the Terry Philips file, took a long look in the mirror, and headed out of the office.

"Going out, Dr. Seabrook?" Janet inquired from behind her desk.

"Uh, yeah Janet. I'll be gone for a while. Just take down any messages for me while I'm out. If it's vital, Dr. Wainwright is on call." And with that, Robert Seabrook left his office for what he feared would be the last time. He didn't have a choice, really. He would gladly give his life if it meant sparing Anna hers. And it was that thought which comforted him as he waited for Mr. Holt at the end of the Breakwater armed with a file and a stomach full of butterflies. So much for his warrior spirit. *Why here? Why not some dark alley or parking garage? Why meet at a well-traveled tourist lookout?* To feign to know any of these answers seemed silly. Why? This was not his forte. Sure, he knew how to tread through the myriad twists and turns of the human psyche to help a patient discover why they did certain things or prompted their behaviours. But to ascertain the motives of a man known simply as Mr. Holt who could seemingly descend from out of nowhere and drop enough bombs that could disrupt the peaceful existence of anyone he saw fit? This was beyond the scope of a mere psychologist.

And so he waited. It seemed like an eternity, and yet time also seemed to be rushing past. He looked around nervously, trying to pick out which of the various passers-by would be, could be, the mysterious Mr. Holt. *If that is your real name* he mused. This is getting silly. *I'm starting to sound like Bond. More like Maxwell Smart.* Robert managed a chuckle as he stood at the end of the Breakwater.

"Something funny Dr. Seabrook?" a voice stated from behind him.

Robert froze as his stomach clenched harder than it ever had in his life. The voice wasn't particularly menacing, it was the knowledge of the situation and what that voice represented. *How did Mr. Holt get so close to me without me noticing? Hadn't I been watching for him?* Robert kicked himself for dropping his guard. *Well, this guy is clearly a pro.* That was little consolation, but consolation nonetheless.

"Nothing really. Just thinkin' about all this cloak and dagger stuff" he said without turning around. "It's not exactly part of my everyday life." That was true enough.

Up until about 45 minutes ago, the closest thing to the life of a spy that had entered into Robert Seabrook's life had been the time he had tried to learn the identity of the culprit responsible for rifling through his trash 2 years ago. What a disappointment that had turned out to be. 4 guilty parties. One homeless man looking for pop cans and 3 raccoons. Master sleuth indeed.

"That's understandable" Holt admitted.

Robert looked out at the setting sun. Beautiful, really. A giant ball of fire – burning gas actually. How many people have worshipped this orb? Feared it? Revered it? Hell, written songs and poems about it? And now, here is was in front of him. Was it greeting him before it dipped below the horizon? Was it saying goodbye to him for the last time? *No. If this Holt had wanted me dead, he could have done it at any time before now. Why drag me out here to do it in public? Wait a minute. Good question.*

"Why did you drag me out here? You could have come for the file at any point." Robert turned around to finally lay eyes on Mr. Holt. *Hmmm. I thought he'd be taller.* As it was, Mr. Holt stood about 5'10", medium build, white, looked to be in his 30's, black hair. White t-shirt, black shorts, runners. Non-descript. *Fantastic. When I go missing, they're gonna be looking for Average Joe. Case closed.*

"Why I chose this particular location does not concern you, Dr. Seabrook. But I'm glad to see that you are taking this seriously," Holt continued. "I see you brought the file."

"Taking this seriously?" Robert asked incredulously. "How else am I supposed to take this? You call me up outta the blue with information that you shouldn't have.

You bring my wife into this. You arrange a clandestine meeting in a public place. Aside from making sure I come alone, it's pretty much play-by-play spy stuff." Had all of that just come out of his mouth? He hoped that it was just the stress of the situation making him ramble and not some genetic defect.

Holt eyes him dubiously, then smiled slightly. "I like the way you talk, Seabrook. Clandestine? Who says that anymore?"

Robert didn't appreciate being the source of amusement for this Holt. "Look, Mr. Holt. I'm glad you're finding my awkwardness funny, but can we just get this over with? You can have the file." Robert attempted to hand the file over to Holt. Holt did not move to take it. He just stood there staring at Robert. *Assessing?*

"I need to speak with you first, Dr. Seabrook, which is why we had to meet in person. I do not trust voices over a phone line. I trust my instincts. And in order to allow my instincts to work properly, I need to meet people face to face. You can learn a lot just by watching a person's face."

Makes sense. I guess. No, wait. None of this makes sense. Robert mustered all of his remaining confidence. "Well I'm here, now. You can make whatever determinations you wish. Just take the file and leave my wife and I alone." Again, Robert tried to hand over the file. Again, no reaction.

Holt smiled again. "Dr. Seabrook. I wanted us to meet and we have. I wanted us to talk face to face and we have. I wanted you to bring me the file, and you did. I've learned all I need to know for today." With that, Holt turned, checked his pulse, and started to jog away.

"What about the file?" Robert asked.

"Already have it." Holt responded. "I just wanted to see if you'd bring it." And he was off. Robert stood there staring dumbfounded after the disappearing jogger. What had just happened? *It was a test? A test to see if the threat against Anna would produce the desired effect? And I failed. Or passed depending on how you looked at it.* And what did Holt mean, he already had it. How? The file obviously hadn't been given out. He was holding it right now. Or was he? Robert quickly opened the file to look inside. Sure enough, the file was there and appeared intact. *How the hell did he get it? It's kept in a locked file cabinet and I'm the only one with a key. Not to mention that nobody would have had access to my office without my knowledge. Except Janet. Janet? No, not Janet. Even if she went in to my office, she couldn't have accessed the file cabinet.* His thoughts were rapidly spiralling out of control. *Get a hold of yourself, Rob. Don't start jumping ahead.* His first step would have to be getting back to the office, then home.

He walked back down the Breakwater, a little faster than normal. When he got back to his car, he threw the Philips file on the passenger seat and drove away. Traffic was pleasantly light on Dallas as he drove off. His mind was everywhere and nowhere at once. What the hell had happened to the day? As he drove, he looked out over the expanse of water to the deep green of Washington State. Could he run? Could they run? His thoughts drifted to Anna. Beautiful Anna. She hadn't changed all that much since high school. Sure she couldn't pass for a senior anymore, but she definitely didn't look her age. Still no grey, though she always checked. No worry lines, though that might change when he told her about this. *Will I tell her? What will she think? God, Rob, what the hell have you gotten mixed up in?*

As he started to curve back towards the heart of the city, his thoughts bounced between Anna, Janet, and Holt. What a trio that made. The only way that a grouping of those 3 particular individuals made any sense was if it involved a situation as bizarre as the one he presently found himself. Anna; an elementary school teacher with a heart of gold and a soul of pure light who made everyone and everything around her better. Janet; a by the book secretary (assistant) who believed that her purpose in life was to keep the good doctor from losing his mind. At least that was how she acted. And Holt; who so far seemed to revel in making sure that the good doctor's mind was well and truly lost and he also appeared to have a heart of mercury. *And then there's me; the psychologist who has no idea what to do or where to go and is in this situation because I apparently completely misread Mr. Terry Philips.*

"Philips! That's where I'll begin," he said in the car. He eyed the file sitting there on the seat and contemplated pulling over and going through it immediately, but decided against it. First, he wanted to pop in and check on Janet and then home to Anna. Only then, did he realize that hadn't called her since the brief phone conversation back at the office. He quickly popped in his cell phone earpiece and speed-dialled 'Home'. It rang…and rang…and rang. Each ring increased the knot in his stomach. He could feel his jaw start to clench as his grip tightened on the steering wheel. Without even realizing it, his foot pressed down on the accelerator. After the fourth ring he was starting to truly panic. Where the hell was she? Was she okay? On the fifth ring, the phone was finally answered by a familiar voice.

"Hello?"

"Hey baby!" he exclaimed. He tried to muffle his exhalation, lest he suffer a barrage of inquiries as to why he had been holding his breath.

"Hey Robbie," Anna replied. "How was work? Everything work out with that bit of bad news?"

"Yeah. I'll talk more when I get home. What took you so long to answer? I was starting to get worried," he stated truthfully.

"I was in the bathroom. No need to worry about that is there?" she laughed. Her laugh always put a smile on his face and this time was no exception.

"I guess not. So long as you light a match," he chided.

She laughed again. "No need. I'm not you." She never had trouble finding a good comeback. It was one of the many things that he had fallen in love with over the years. Quick wit was a turn-on. Who knew? "When are you gonna be home? I can have dinner waiting if you like or do you wanna go out?"

It was comforting to hear that even though the day's events had unfolded as they had, Anna's life appeared to be uninterrupted. "I'm gonna be home in about an hour. I just have to make a quick stop back at the office before I head home."

"What do you mean back at the office? I thought you had a meeting." Damn she was quick, or was he just stupid right now.

Think quick, Rob. "I did, but Hicks and Miller wanted to grab a drink before they headed out so we finished off the meeting at the Wicket." The Sticky Wicket was an easy cover. A wonderful pub downtown on Douglas St. that the people at the office liked to frequent due to its proximity to work and the general atmosphere of the place. Hicks seemed to prefer one of the servers in particular so he was always the one pushing to go.

"Oh. Okay. Dinner at home or out?" Apparently his ruse had worked.

"At home, if you don't mind, babe. It's been a long day." So true.

"All right," she continued. "Dinner will be close to being ready by the time you get home. Hurry, okay?"

He smiled again. Even after all these years, they were both still eager to see each other again. Blessed was the word that came to his mind. "I will, babe. I love you."

"Love you too, Robbie. Bye."

"Bye, babe." And with a small click, he was alone in the car once again. His thoughts lingered on Anna for a few more minutes until he pulled up in front of his office. Now thoughts turned to Janet. Was she part of this? Doubtful. Was she all right? More than likely. "Better safe than sorry," he muttered as he moved to the door.

The office was dark. He thought that that was a little odd, but then he remembered the time that it surely must be. The sun had bid good night to this part of the world and Janet would surely have gone home by now. He unlocked the office, went inside and deactivated the alarm, and made a cursory check of the lobby / waiting area. Everything seemed in order. He proceeded down the corridor that led towards his office. He unlocked it and went inside, flipping on the light as he did so. Again, everything looked fine. "A little paranoia never hurt," he softly chided to himself. He restored the office to its darkened ways and returned to the lobby. Again, he checked the lobby just to be sure. His eye rested on something that hadn't been there when he left. A sheet of paper in his message box. His heart skipped a beat. Someone had been there. He slowly moved towards the box, fearing what he would find there. He reached out a slightly trembling hand to retrieve the folded paper. He took it gently, opened it, and read:

-Dr. Seabrook. I didn't get a chance to talk with you before I left so I took the liberty of rescheduling your 3 pm appointment on Monday to 4pm on Thursday as Mr. Williams would be unable to make it on Monday. Hope you had a good weekend. I'll be back on Tuesday. Janet.-

"Dammit," he muttered. He was really starting to hate this feeling of dread. *Right, Janet's going away for the weekend.* "See you Tuesday, Janet," he said to the walls. He replaced the note, locked the lobby, and returned to his car for the trip home. It was supposed to be a sanctuary. Now it was time to try and make it feel that way again.

CHAPTER

2

Holt exited the Breakwater and walked the short distance to his rental car. He opened the door, sat behind the wheel, and pulled out on to Dallas Rd. He quickly pulled on to the first side street he could find, pulled a U-turn, and pulled up beside the curb to wait. He didn't have to wait long. He figured as much. After only a few minutes, Robert Seabrook drove past and headed down Dallas. *Well, at least he made it that far.* Holt waited a few more minutes. After he was sure that Seabrook wasn't being followed, he turned right on to Dallas and headed back towards the Inner Harbour. He would have to leave Seabrook in the competent hands of the surveillance team he had in place, although you could hardly call 3 people a team. Such was the economy these days.

He drove back to his hotel. It should have been at the Empress, but no, Traveller's Inn would have to do. Man, things had changed. And he had only been doing this for 17 years, yet things were noticeably different. Well, at least the job itself remained intact. Sure, there were subtle differences, but the scope of the job was the same. It was just the extras (not perks per se) that had been altered. He entered his hotel room and made his usual scan for 'bugs'. As expected, nothing. This file was still relatively new so the risk of counter-surveillance was minimal. Still, one could never be too careful. He made a quick mental checklist of things still to be done, and then set about preparing for the next day. He reached into his shorts and removed the 9mm Glock from within the confines of the modified holster inside the material. No matter how much it was modified, trying to jog with a semi-automatic handgun separated from your hip by only a little bit of fabric was never an easy endeavour. He placed the Glock in the top drawer of the side table, loaded. Next, he took off his t-shirt and removed the recording device from the small of his back and placed it back in the compartment at the back of his duffel bag. Finally, he removed the wireless transmitter from his hair. *God, I feel like a walking Circuit City sometimes.* This transmitter joined the recorder in the compartment. Holt laid out his clothes for the next day and began his evening ritual: 50 push-ups, 50 sit-ups, and 50 twists. *"Used to be 100 each"*, he thought to himself wryly. But even he had to admit, he wasn't as young as he used to be. There were just days now that the thought of 100 each made him not want to do any. So 50 had been the compromise. But he still loved the job, so it was a small price to pay.

He walked to the bathroom and looked into the mirror. Not bad, he thought. He still looked young.

Well, 46 wasn't old was it? In this line of work, though? Sometimes he felt like a dinosaur. *"Even dinosaurs are dangerous,"* he reminded himself. He looked closer at the man in the mirror. He hated that he had to resort to colouring his hair to fight the battle of the grey. It made him look younger, though, and that made him feel good. Vanity. What a strange creature. It can be avoided by the lowliest of people and yet could topple even the mightiest like some cruel virus. And here he was, professional, successful, fearless, and at times ruthless, and what he was dwelling on momentarily was actually looking his age. *"Stop being an idiot"* he chided. Yet, he couldn't shake the fact that something in this image made him look "old". What was it? He leaned forward and looked closer, but he couldn't see it. The wrinkles? Barely noticeable. The hairline? Strong. It was only when he stopped looking for it, that he able to find it. *"It's the eyes,"* he breathed. His eyes carried the weight of his soul. Bore it to be more precise. The eyes that had seen far too much over the years and yet, he knew, still had much more to see. Was it the eyes that were starting to bog down? Or was it the soul itself? For that, he did not have an answer. He had been taught many things over the years, but how to spot a weary soul in one's own body hadn't been part of any of it. What a depressing class that would have been. *"OK class. Everyone take your seat and try not to kill yourself."* That thought made him chuckle. "Alright, old man. That's enough," he said to the smiling reflection.

With that, he came back into the main part of his 'suite'. He packed up the little amount of clothing he had brought and made sure that there was no trace of his occupation of the room. Fingerprints couldn't be helped at this stage. And besides, with the relatively 'young' file he was dealing with, anyone interested in tracking his movements would have the prints of at least the next 6 or 7 guests to compete with. Satisfied that he could leave within two minutes if the situation necessitated it, he climbed into bed and settled down to catch the local news. It was always nice to watch news from somewhere other than home. It somehow made it less unnerving to know that the events being reported on were nowhere near your home, even though you knew in the back of your mind that it was almost definitely happening there as well.

Plus, there was an added bonus. Every time he travelled to Canada, the news never seemed to be as bad as back home in the U.S. Either Canadian broadcasters didn't cover it as much or there just wasn't enough awful news to fill an hour. The rest was filled with the obligatory sports and weather, but there were quite a few human interest stories too. Comforted with the idea that there was indeed some good left out there, Brian Holt drifted off to sleep and tried to avoid thoughts of the things he would have to do before this file could be reassigned to the "Mop-Up Division".

———

Robert arrived home a little after 8 pm. His days usually didn't run this long, but then again his days were not usually spent meeting with strangers and worrying about the safety of loved ones. Sure, you always hoped your loved ones were safe, but those were thoughts always kept at the back of your mind. Never should you need to bring those fears to the front and be forced to focus on them so intently that no other thoughts could hold residence in your mind. At least not for an almost middle-aged psychologist with an ideal life. Pulling up to the house he and Anna shared, Robert took the chance to examine exactly how ideal his life was. Could he have asked for anything better? Anna was the greatest part of his life and one which he was permanently thankful for. He had a relatively strong practice, good friends, financial stability (even in these shaky times), and was genuinely happy. *What could go wrong?* And it was in that moment he realized that no matter how happy or comfortable you could be in a life, all it took was one person with the reason to change that and you lost control of everything you held dear. Was happiness that fragile? Was comfort just a figment of your imagination to block out the horrors that lurked behind every corner? *"That's pretty bleak,"* he thought. No. Happiness was real. Comfort was real. Unfortunately, so were people like Holt. People who seemed to resent happiness so much that they almost relished taking it from others. *"Damn you, Holt."*

Robert turned off the car and headed up the walkway to the front door. Opening it, he stepped in and was immediately greeted by the delicious aroma coming from the kitchen. *Man, that woman can cook.* He couldn't quite place exactly what she had on the go, but whatever it was had started him drooling almost immediately. *She spoils me.* "Honey, I'm home," he called, trying to sound as casual as possible. After the unusual day he had, added to the ease at which she could sense when something was troubling him, he wanted to sound as relaxed as possible.

"In the kitchen, Robbie," Anna replied with a song in her voice.

She must be listening to the radio. Anna always had music playing. Whether it was in the kitchen, the bathroom, the car for the commute to work, it didn't matter. When you found Anna Seabrook, she would be listening to music. *At least she has good taste.* He took off his shoes and stowed them neatly on the rack and placed his briefcase by the umbrella stand. He stretched quickly and tried to shake the stress of the day off before entering the house further. A quick check in the hallway mirror to ensure he was as ready as ever and then it was time to flex his acting chops. He entered the kitchen and, sure enough, Anna was by the oven "rockin out" to Aerosmith. Robert smiled at the sight, not because it was funny, but because it was right. In spite of the day that lay behind him, Anna was the same. His home was the same. And that meant that he was the same. Everything was going to be just fine. "Hey sweetie," he said as he watched her move to "Sweet Emotion".

"Hey, Robbie," she said turning around. Then she stopped short. "What the hell happened to you?" she asked somewhat worriedly.

How the hell does she do that? "What do you mean?" he replied guiltily. He thought he had made sure this time that he had kept his feelings under control, nowhere near the surface. But her eyes were drills that seemed to bore right through any shell he tried to construct. Or maybe he just couldn't act. It was probably a combination of the two, but whatever the reason, Anna Seabrook knew that something was amiss with her husband.

"I mean, you look like someone just punched you in the stomach and then stood there and made you apologize for it." She left the oven and moved towards him. "You, okay?" She had a hug on the way for him and he was more than grateful to see it coming.

"Yeah, yeah," he stammered. "Just an issue I'm having with a patient is kinda getting to me." Using the patient excuse was always a safe bet because he knew that there were some things that he just couldn't discuss with her. The specifics surrounding patients was a sure-fire way to keep the conversation on other topics. Besides, it wasn't exactly a lie. Terry Philips was, in fact, a client and this whole situation was spawned because of him. So this particular story was not necessarily a fabrication. Sometimes, the easiest way to lie is to tell the truth.

She reached him and they embraced. Even after all these years together, the spark was still there. As soon as their bodies met each other, he felt a familiar stirring inside of him; a deep yearning that called out to his primal instincts. The day long forgotten, lost within the smell of her hair that covered his face. Her body seemed to fit perfectly with his. Her body had a rhythm to it. She never just hugged him. She seemed to undulate against him like she was being controlled by some unheard Latin beat. It definitely wasn't Aerosmith that made her move like that. She sighed ever so slightly as he pressed against her. That sound alone could ensnare him instantly. She leaned back her head and stared lovingly into his eyes.

"Well I'm glad you're home now," she said with a sexy smile playing at the corner of her mouth. "Cuz now I can help you forget about your day." She reached down between them and gave him a playful squeeze that buckled his knees as she stepped away. He reached for her and tried to bring her back to his embrace, but she could tell from the look in his eyes that a hug was not what he was after. "No, no…save it for later," she said coyly. "Food, first."

But Robert was not one to give up that easily. He quickly closed the small distance between them and swept her back into his arms. She protested weakly before his lips were on hers, his tongue forcing its way into her mouth. She struggled against the force of it, but was soon giving back as much as he was giving. Her hands slid down and pulled him against her tightly as his hands explored her back. He reached up and grabbed the back of her head, forcing her even tighter against him as their kiss threatened to ignite them. They broke apart and stared hungrily at each other, breathing hard, their eyes shining with animal lust. Then she smiled that smile of hers. "Food."

Robert moved at her again, but she deftly avoided his advance with a laugh. "Food, Robbie." He let out a groan of disappointment as she returned to the stove to tend to the dinner, but he knew that he wouldn't have to wait long. She had the same look in her eyes that he was fully aware was in his own. And when Anna Seabrook got that look in her eyes, which was often, they were destined to have a great night.

Twenty years after they had first met and he still had the same yearning for her, sometimes inspired merely by thought. Was it lust? That only seemed to be a cheap description. Sure, there was a physical attraction to her, but calling it lust just didn't do the feeling justice. It was like referring to a picture-perfect sunrise as merely dawn. What it felt like was more of an all-consuming desire, not for physical gratification, but for a complete belonging; like two halves of a whole reunited for the first time. He felt that every time his eyes beheld her. It was times like these when the world just melted away leaving him satiated to the point of exhaustion, yet never so tired that he could not endure more. And at present, more was what he desired.

He moved for her once more with a smile on his face and a gleam in his eye. At the last moment before he reached her, she quickly side-stepped his lunge and gave him a playful jab in his kidney as he stumbled by her. He instinctively grabbed his wounded side and whirled around theatrically. She stood with her hands on her hips and a "don't make me beat you" look in her eye. Apart from the smile that tickled the corner of her mouth, she looked quite menacing.

"I told you. Food first," she challenged. "I didn't spend my time making us dinner so we can watch it burn."

"Alright, alright," he acquiesced. "Smells great, by the way," he admired, inhaling strongly. It really did. He had noticed it when he had first entered the house, but the aroma was even stronger now, standing over it. His stomach tightened as saliva started to fill his mouth. "What are we having?"

"Stir-fry," she answered nudging him away from the stove. It was one of his favourites, yet remarkably relatively easy to put together…for her. He had once tried to duplicate her recipe as a surprise for her birthday. What resulted could not be classified as a stir-fry. It would have barely been classified as food. What had started out as a very promising array of ingredients lovingly prepared by a very devoted husband had rapidly (alarmingly so) been reduced to a bizarre mash consisting of: burnt, yet raw beef; rice so hard that it would have been kept out of reach of small children; and vegetable shrapnel that appeared to have lost the will to resemble food of any kind. Robert Seabrook had many talents, but culinary artistry was not one of them. Thank God for take-out.

"Go grab a drink and sit at the table," she told him. "Dinner will be ready in about 5."

He tried to sneak a taste, but she quickly and deftly smacked his knuckles with the spatula. He yelped as he laughingly retreated. It was clear that this lioness was going to protect her "young" to the bitter end. Better to just wait.

He walked to the fridge and filled a glass with ice water. "Can I get you anything, babe?" he asked.

"I'll have whatever you're having," she answered without turning around.

"Well, I'm just getting water. I'll get you something else if you want." He loved her easy going nature, but sometimes felt that she sacrificed too much for him. It was minor things (like what to drink), but he was willing to get her anything she wanted…ever. She just never seemed to want anything.

She turned her head, then, as if sensing his consternation. "Water's fine, Robbie," she said. "Now go sit down." He filled a second glass of ice water, closed the fridge, and retired to the round kitchen table (the dining table seemed a little grandiose for the occasion) He sat down facing her so he could watch her kitchen ministrations. No matter what was going on, he always found solace when he watched her. Anna Seabrook. "Saviour of Souls". That was how he viewed her. He had simply been existing before he had met her and actually living every day hence. For a moment, the world seemed perfect.

"So what was with that phone call earlier?" she asked. And the reality of his present came crashing through his reverie of past and future.

"What phone call?" he replied lamely. He knew exactly what phone call she had meant. Worse, he knew that she knew he remembered. He just had to try and stall for a few moments so he could come up with something that would assuage her curiosity on the matter.

"You know what phone call," she answered plainly. "What happened today?" she asked as she began doling out their portions on to the plates.

Robert struggled for answers. Had he been talking to anyone else, this would have been easy as he was quite quick-witted. But with Anna, she could always see through his facades. "Like I said earlier, babe. It was a patient." He realized that to prevent further delving, he would have to come up with something that she couldn't sink her teeth into. As she neared the table with their dinner, he could see that she was looking for something to chew on besides the stir-fry. She placed his plate in front of him and sat down one seat over, her eyes never leaving his face. *Does she enjoy watching me twist in the wind like this?* Believing now that this would not simply go away, he continued.

"Okay. I have a patient who spoke about something that he had done during one of our sessions. He was really upset about it and now no one seems to be able to reach him." Truth IS the easiest way to lie.

"That's not good," she agreed. "You think he'd do something to himself?" she asked, growing slightly concerned.

Rather than add fuel to the story, Robert saw a way that might allow an easy exit. "I doubt it. I think he's just working through some stuff. I think he'll be back and I'm sure we'll have more to talk about." *That should be a good start to the end of this topic of conversation.* With that, he grabbed his fork and began to enjoy the stir-fry in earnest. Hopefully with his mouth full of her food, she might be less inclined to proceed further.

"You sure that's all?" she continued as she joined him in dinner.

Not quite he mused. Would this be the end of it? "Yeah. I'm not too concerned about it. I'd just like to know for sure, you know?"

"I can imagine," she agreed. He was sure he was safe, now. "But who called me in regards to you, though." *Damn!* "Can't say that's ever happened before."

He mulled that one over momentarily and then decided that, once again, it was time for another honest lie. "I have absolutely no idea who that was." He felt bad about lying to her at any time, but he really hated this. It was one thing to proffer the occasional white lie to a loved one – everyone did that from time to time – but this was all starting to strain his code of ethics. He desperately wanted to tell her the truth, but he knew her practical side and her iron will would force her to act. And then what? Notify the authorities? What could they do? As skilled as the R.C.M.P. were, what were the chances that they would be able to track down Terry Philips who may or may not be alive somewhere between Victoria, B. C. and Bogotá, Columbia? What were the chances that they could find Mr. Holt (if even that was his real name) and garner any information out of him? No. The best thing to do right now was to keep her out of as much of this as possible, no matter how much it pained him.

"Well, let's hope your patient is all right in any case," she said as she enjoyed her next bite. "How is it?"

"Sorry?" he asked bewilderedly.

"How's dinner?"

"Perfect," he stated honestly. As minor a statement as that was, it would good to feel honest with her again. The rest of dinner passed by with the usual chitchat about their respective days. Most of Anna's day had been spent going over material for the upcoming school year. She was quite excited for the new crop of third grade students who would "grace her with their presence" as she put it. She was a remarkable teacher, after all. She always strived to be better than the previous year, even though she was always the best and most popular teacher in the school. Even the parents loved her because she constantly challenged her students to shoot for the stars. Her classroom was always full, busy, and yet remained organized. And, since the day she started teaching, there was a map of the Mediterranean

Sea behind her desk. It was her way of feeling that no matter what, Robert was always behind her.

As dinner drew to an end, Robert rose from the table and customarily carried all of the dishes to the sink. If he couldn't cook, at least he could help with the cleaning. Years earlier, Anna had vehemently protested this intrusion of what she considered her domain. But over time, she had relented to his persistence. He could be quite convincing when he had to be. Besides, he did have a valid point and there were worse things in the world than having a husband who helped around the house. He began to fill the sink with soapy water as there wasn't really enough dishes to warrant a dishwasher run. She watched him with a dreamy smile on her face; the same smile that she saw on his face from time to time. The love that was shared between them was truly equal. She had never felt anything more for anyone than what she felt for him. She loved him with an all-consuming passion. It was that passion that caused her to rise from the table and sidle over to where he had begun fervently attending the wok she had used. She moved behind him, reached up, and started to massage his neck. She could feel the tension through her fingertips.

"Hmmmmm," he murmured. He stopped scrubbing and tilted his head back towards her, breathing in deeply as he surrendered to her ministrations. She stood on her toes and brushed her lips against the base of his neck, feeling the hairs standing up in response. She smiled as she felt his defeat approaching. "I have to do the dishes," he protested feebly. Turning his head to look back at her, she struck at his weakest spot. She reached further and took his earlobe between her teeth, nibbling gently.

"Leave it," she breathed. She felt him buckle at the knees. *Still got it*, she mused. "I'll do 'em in the morning."

He turned fully towards her and swept her into his arms, kissing her deeply. A mild taste of the stir-fry played on her lips as they pulled each other closer. Their bodies strained against each other, grinding together in prelude to what lay ahead of them. Their breathing rapidly became ragged. After a few moments, he broke free of the kiss that threatened to render one or both of them unconscious. Without speaking, he took her hand and led her upstairs so that they could continue their dance. All of the worries of the day vanished as they entered their bedroom. The dishes would, indeed, have to wait

CHAPTER

3

Holt woke with a start and reflexively grabbed his gun from the nightstand. He scanned the room quickly, orienting himself. It took him a few moments to remember where he was. After a few tense seconds, he was able to relax enough to move. He glanced at the small digital clock beside the bed. 5:17. Taking a deep breath to calm his nerves, he swung his legs over the edge of the bed, resting his feet on the security of solid ground. Had he dreamt of falling? Was that why the solidness of the cheap carpet felt so reassuring? He couldn't recall. Taking a second deep breath, he gradually returned his heart rate to a normal rhythm and hoisted himself off of the bed with an audible hrmmpf. *Didn't used to make that sound* he mused. Once upright, he stretched his out the kinks in his back gained from sleeping on an unfamiliar bed. That feeling was coming more and more often. He couldn't remember the last time he had truly been home. Gone were the days of being able to sleep under a bush all night while his surveillance partner monitored a subject for a while. Then again, gone were the days of simple surveillance; replaced now with covert operations, codenames, aliases, and all of the other nonsense that went with the espionage industry. Nonsensical, yet vital. *Like life*. These were the rewards of being good at your job. Ironically, it meant that you would seldom keep that job for long.

He yawned and headed for the bathroom. There was little point in trying to get back to sleep. His alarm was set for 6:00 so even if he did manage to lapse into some form of unconsciousness, he would have just been roused right around the time that it would have been worth the effort. Instead, he opted for the joys of a cool shower. After a quick face-splash of cold water from the sink, he reached over and adjusted the water temperature of the shower. Stepping in, he quickly replayed the events of yesterday and began to go through his tasks for the day ahead while keeping his Glock close at hand, resting on the edge of the shower. Vigilance never hurt, after all, but complacency could be fatal. The shower always seemed a good place to organize one's thoughts. Whether it was the solitude, the sound of the running water, or the visceral act of washing away other thoughts, it always allowed him the chance to focus his mind and identify the tasks at hand. Once satisfied that the day ahead had been well thought out (and that he was suitably clean), Holt shut the shower off and returned to the bed with his Glock. He laid it on the bed in order to dress for the day ahead. Grabbing the remote, he turned the TV back on to see if anything newsworthy had happened in the few hours of consciousness that he had been able to blissfully avoid. Nothing. Yankees won, Mets lost. *Nothing out of the ordinary.* Donning his clothes, he turned off the TV, gathered everything he had brought with him, placed his firearm securely in his holster at the small of his back, and covered it with his shirt. He made an extra check to ensure that everything was pristine, and entered the hallway that led to the front desk. 5:50.

"Morning, sir" said the morning desk clerk. She looked to be in her early 20's, very pretty, and carried herself in a very professional manner...even at this hour.

"Morning," Holt replied. "Just checking out." He tried not to sound tired, but the lack of sleep was still affecting him, despite the best efforts of the shower.

The clerk almost seemed disappointed at the news. "Did you enjoy your stay? Did you find everything you needed?" She asked as she reached for the room key that Holt offered her. He suppressed a yawn as she took it from him. He knew he was tired, but felt no need to broadcast it.

"Yes," he replied. "Everything was fine." Not exactly a lie, just nothing was extraordinary. It was a nice enough place. But affordability in this economy had replaced luxury. "Were there any messages for me?" He knew there wouldn't be as the only people who knew he was here would have known better than to contact him through the front desk. Better to keep up the illusion of normality, though.

"Lemme check for you, Mr. Upton." The clerk moved to the back office message area and checked 'Mr. Upton's message slot. Chris Upton was one of Holt's most trusted aliases. It had seen him through many an assignment without fail, though he sensed that time was slowly creeping up on him, and thus, on Chris Upton as well. The clerk returned to the desk with a rueful look. "I'm sorry, Mr. Upton. Nothing that I could see."

Is she actually upset that there wasn't a message for me? Or is she just born with the ability to emote empathy? "That's all right, Trish," he said peering at her nametag. She seemed to flush slightly at the use of her name. *So she was flirting with me. Cute.* Obviously, she was relatively new at flirting with customers or else she would have been more forthright and less flustered by his actions. "I wasn't expecting anything crucial." She smiled at that, as if he had somehow assuaged her fear of 'failure'.

"Oh good," she stated exhaling ever so slightly. "Is there anything else I can be of help with?"

Ah, if only. "No. That'll be fine," he stated with a rueful smile. Maybe in another life and with a smaller age gap he would have had the willingness to test the waters further, but there were more pressing matters at hand. He paid the balance owing on the room and set out to start the next phase of his assignment. His rental car, a green 2009 Chevy Cobalt, was due to be returned to the rental company today. It didn't have to be there until 11:00 am, so he would have plenty of time to accomplish the few tasks he had laid out for himself. He took out his cell phone and inserted his earpiece. The last thing he needed was to be pulled over for talking on a cell phone while driving. He wasn't really bothered by the 'hassle' of the relatively new law banning cell phones while driving (he always used his earpiece anyway), but he didn't like being told he couldn't do something. There was just a hint of parental scolding behind the whole thing. Nothing against the Victoria Police Department, but he felt there were more pressing concerns facing the public than a distracted driver. That thought made him smile to himself. *Sure it might not matter much to the public in general, but it sure mattered to the pedestrian who you just ran over and his or her family.* Was he becoming jaded? He hated the thought that having to deal with matters far greater than that of the 'Average Joe' was starting to make him lose sight of the small picture; the lives of the people being affected by decisions made by bureaucrats who rarely seemed to hazard a single thought to the 'little guy'.

How many people had been affected by his own actions? How many people had he killed? How many of those had been innocent? He remembered them all and, as always, he remembered one in particular. Michelle Thompson, 31. He remembered how he had levelled the gun at her (the same gun he carried now). He remembered her pleas for mercy; the verbal ones and the pleas that her eyes had made. He remembered the hesitation he had felt. After all, she had done nothing wrong other than fall in love with the wrong man. Her husband was the man who was trying to extort money from the Argentinean Ambassador. But his orders had been clear. Unfortunately for Holt, so was the memory of her lifeless body falling to the floor. His silenced Glock barely made a whisper as it extinguished the light in her eyes, forever; forced into action by his hand and his hand alone. Sure, the public had benefited from her death in so much as the extortion ceased immediately and the truth behind a large cover-up remained obscured, but did that help her family heal? Had the Ambassador been compromised, civil war very well might have broken out in Argentina and spilled over into Chile and Brazil. How many lives lost? How many lives saved? How many 'Michelle's had there been? How many more would there be?

Hopefully few, he thought as he started the Cobalt and turned onto Douglas St. It was time to meet up with the surveillance team to see if anything had turned up. With that he turned right on Pandora St. headed for the Johnson Street Bridge and its peculiar rumbling and beyond, towards the house of Robert and Anna Seabrook.

Robert cracked one eye open, contemplating whether or not to go back to sleep or to embrace the new day. His eye caught the hair of his beloved Anna spooned back into him. His arm was draped around her. He closed his eye and opted for more sleep.

"You awake?" Anna inquired dreamily. So much for sleep.

"Barely," his response. She stretched luxuriously, arching her back as she did so. This brought her shapely form in further contact with him. The desires he thought had surely been satiated the night before began to reassert themselves in the morning light. The slight prodding at her lower back gave that little secret away. Anna stopped mid-stretch.

"What's that?" she asked teasingly.

"Nothing," he grinned sheepishly. She completed her stretch and moved closer to him.

"Hmmmm. I thought you would have had enough last night," she sighed, contentedly.

"You'd think. But what can I say. You bring it out in me." He reached a hand up to move her hair from her neck so his lips could explore the delicate curves. She moaned and he felt her tense slightly as the equally powerful, if somewhat less visual, arousal began to sweep through her.

"It would appear that we bring it out in each other," she murmured. She felt his hand slide enticingly down her side sending chills that reached all the way down to her calves. She turned towards him and brought his mouth to hers. She kissed him deeply as she felt his hands lightly caressing her back. That always drove her crazy. She broke the kiss and stared brightly into his eyes. "Morning."

"Morning, baby," he replied. Just as he was about to resume their kiss, the phone rang. He cursed the timing and looked over at the clock. 7:42. *On a Saturday*. He looked back at Anna, longingly seeking advice on how best to proceed.

"Let the machine get it," she offered, pulling him back down to her. With that, he gladly resumed where they had left off. The ringing ceased after the answering machine kicked in, not so much an actual machine but the automated voice messaging service that they had through Telus. After only a few moments, though, the phone rang again.

"Leave it!" Anna urged breathlessly as they were both being swept away by the moments provided them on what was starting out to be a very promising Saturday morning.

This particular caller was relentless, though, and by the third phone call Robert had had enough. He snatched up the cordless phone by his bed, cursing the heavens as he did so.

"Hello!" he barked, perhaps a little too forcefully, but his mind was presently on many things. None of which included the niceties of polite social interaction…so to speak. Anna stifled a giggle at his harshness. He shot her a glare. Then taking note of his obvious and 'attentive' nakedness, realized what a sight he must be for her. He stifled a grin himself.

"Dr. Seabrook. It's good to hear your voice," the caller said. "Am I disturbing you?"

Of course you are. "More or less. Who is this?" And with that simple question, three things came flooding back into his memory: the happenings of yesterday, Mr. Holt, and that eerie hum in the background of an unknown phone call. The colour quickly faded from Robert's face and his 'attentive' physique wilted quite suddenly. He looked down at Anna who had fortunately closed her eyes, her hand wandering aimlessly over his pillow. He turned away from the bed so that he could hide his face from her.

"Dr. Seabrook," the voice continued. "I think we should meet."

"Holt?" Robert asked hopefully. Even while he said it, he knew it wasn't Mr. Holt he was speaking with. This voice had a sharper edge to it and seemed to be tinged with an accent.

"No. Dr. Seabrook. This isn't Holt. But seeing as how you know about Mr. Holt, then I can assume that he has already contacted you," the voice stated. "Is that correct?" Despite all of his schooling and his relatively strong intelligence, Robert couldn't think of a thing to say to this voice. He just stood and stared out the window, as if in a trance.

"Uhhh..." he finally mumbled.

"Dr. Seabrook. I don't have time for games and if Holt has already contacted you, then neither do you." Before Robert could interject anything, the voice continued. "Be mindful of what I am about to tell you, Doctor. Holt is not to be trusted. If he contacts you again to try and arrange a meeting, avoid it. Do not approach him or let him approach you. Your life could very well be in danger. I will be in touch later today," the voice said conclusively.

"W-wait a second, here...you." What else could he call him? "This is all a little much for me. Why should I believe any of this? I didn't do anything." Anna, roused from her slumber, sat up in bed looking at her husband worriedly.

The voice didn't say anything for a few moments. Robert didn't know whether to take that as a good omen or a bad one. "Know this, Doctor. You are being followed. Holt and his men will be tracking your every movement. I will be in contact shortly once we figure out a way to get to you without being noticed by him."

"Who's we?" Robert asked.

"'We' are the people who are going to try and get you and your wife through the next few days alive." And the phone went dead. Robert didn't move. It was Anna who dragged him back from oblivion.

"What the hell was that?" she demanded. Jolted out of his near-catatonic countenance, Robert turned to look at his wife. His blank stare was met with a look of alarm from Anna. She immediately moved towards him. "Robbie! What the HELL was that?" she demanded, shaking him.

"Uhhhh...nothing," he replied lamely. He didn't have to see a mirror to know that his face was a window that let Anna see the fear welling up inside of him. Besides, she would have had to have been quite aloof to miss the ominous tone of the just-ended phone conversation, despite only hearing the one side of it.

"Bullshit, Robbie!" she exclaimed, the fear he felt had seeped its way into her voice. There was no sense in shielding her any longer. She was too intelligent to try and smokescreen and too loyal to merit more fabrications. "This has something to do with what happened yesterday and I wanna know what that is!"

He grasped fleetingly for words that could possibly explain away the last 24 hours, but everything seemed either too fantastic or too simplistic. He decided, finally, to tell her as much as he could.

"Okay," he began. He took a deep breath and sat down on the bed next to her. "Okay," he repeated. "I have this patient. I can't get into specifics about who, you know that. But I will say that he is a relatively new patient. He told me about something...bad...that he was being made to be a part of. He had said some pretty outlandish things up until then, so I just figured it was more of the same." He looked up to see if he could read anything in her face, but all he saw was concern and her desire for him to continue. "I was hoping to find some cause as to why he felt the need to create these obvious exaggerations in his life. But then..." he paused. He felt Anna squeeze his hand in assurance. He smiled, a little. "Then, he missed two appointments in a row. Normally, I wouldn't have thought too much about it until that 'thing' he referred to actually happened."

"My God," Anna breathed.

"I know," Robert continued. "So I started to call around. You know, to other psychologists to see if he had gone to see anyone else. I even called the police to see if they had heard anything about him. But before I knew it, I got a phone call."

"From your patient?" Anna asked incredulously.

"No. From this guy. Real mysterious type. I think he might even be a spy or something." Saying it out loud for the first time made Robert realize how silly that sounded. "Well. Maybe not a spy per se, but he sounded like a man who lives in secrets – if that makes any sense. Long story short, he wanted to meet me to discuss my conversations with my patient."

"And is that who called just now?" Anna asked. She obviously did not like the direction this story had just taken.

"No. That's just it. The person who just called told me not to trust Holt. That's what the guy from yesterday told me his name was. He said that my life could be in danger." He looked at Anna with an expression that she had never seen before and it chilled her to the bone.

"Robbie. What on Earth are you messed up with?" she asked dubiously.

Sensing her trepidation, he spoke smoothly and confidently. "Anna. I didn't do anything. All I did was listen to a patient. Whoever these guys are, they clearly think I have information that can help them. Either that or they are worried that I have information that could hurt them." That thought placed a little more gravity on the words coming out of his mouth. What if they were concerned that he had information on Terry Philips and the assassination? Would they consider him a threat in some way? *Hell, the mere fact that Terry Philips spoke to me about an assassination that hadn't happened yet makes me a very dangerous 'loose end'.*

"Robbie….this isn't good," she admonished. "I mean, are these people dangerous?" She paused, then continued. "Better question – who the hell are these people?" Her tone was becoming increasingly hysterical. The morning's slumber had truly been obliterated now. Less than ten minutes ago, they had been lying in each other's arms, dreaming of all manner of wonderful possibilities. Now, both of their minds were spinning and filling with a lot more possibilities – some of which were too difficult to digest.

"I don't know," he answered truthfully. "But I'm inclined to believe that they are serious enough."

"I'm calling my Dad." With that, she moved over to him and reached for the phone.

"Anna!" Robert stopped her before she could reach it. "I don't want your Dad involved in this."

"But he's a cop," she protested. "I'm sure he'll have an idea of what we should do. Hell, he might even be able to look into these guys for us." She again tried to reach for the phone. Again, Robert prevented her.

"Look. I trust your Dad, you know I do. But I don't want him to know anything about this. The last thing we need is to bring a lot of attention to this, especially from the police." He hesitated before continuing. "I mean, for all we know, they just wanna talk about my patient and that will be that," he smiled wistfully.

Anna set her shoulders and cocked her head to the side, peering at him through assessing eyes. "What aren't you telling me, Robbie?"

"Nothing. I swear."

"Robbie?" she continued. "I know you better than anyone in the world and the bottom line is, you are a practical person. You of all people would be prompting anyone in this position to contact the police. Why the hesitation?"

Robert sighed with the knowledge that he would have to come clean, though he knew that doing so would only heighten her apprehension at their current situation – if that were even possible. "Okay. You know Holt?" She nodded. "He told me not to contact anyone about any of this. I don't even know if I should have told you as much as I have, but I know we don't keep secrets from each other. And I didn't wanna start."

Anna opened her mouth as if to say something, then closed it. Robert continued on. "I met with him and he told me to bring my patient's file with me. I didn't want to, but what choice did I have? When I finally met with him, he informed me that he already had the file. How could have the file? It was in my hand. But that was enough to tell me not to mess around with this. Somehow he must have gained access to my office and retrieved the file prior. Plus…" he trailed off.

"Plus what?" she inquired.

"Plus…" Robert struggled to find the right words, then decided to just dive right in. "Holt told me that he had met you while you were out jogging." He saw the blood drain from her face as she stood there, dumbfounded. "He said we had a pretty house." Robert went on. "He knows who you are. He knows where we live. He knows our phone number because he was the one who told you to call me yesterday. I didn't wanna mess with him before and after this last call, I definitely don't wanna mess with him now."

"But what are we supposed to do?" she asked. Honest enough question. It wasn't like this was an everyday occurrence. Up until this point, the toughest decision they had faced together was which house to buy. Choosing incorrectly on that one would doubtfully result in anything dire. This situation held a more ominous tone.

"I don't know, babe," he answered truthfully. "I really don't know what to do?" They looked at each other wistfully, wishing that somehow their combined bewilderment might reveal a possible course of action. Both, however, seemed to realize at the same time that their situation was not likely to improve any time soon. Then Anna had an idea.

"Wait a minute. You said this Holt told you not to talk to anyone, right?"

Robert nodded. "Right. He made that quite clear."

"Well," she continued. "How would he know if you did speak with anyone about it?"

Robert went to answer, then stopped. That was actually a pretty good question. "Uhh…I don't know. I just assumed that he'd know."

"But think it through, Robbie. The only way he could know is…what? Listen in to your phone calls? Follow you to see who you interacted with? Is that even possible?"

Robert, again, was about to answer, then he stopped. He remembered something that he hadn't thought of much since this began, and yet now seemed vital. "There was a hum," he stated simply.

"A hum? What does that mean?"

He continued. "There was a humming sound in the background of the phone calls….both of them. I didn't know what it was. I mean, I thought of things like recorders and stuff, but I put those out of my mind cuz it just didn't seem plausible. But now…."

"My God, Robbie!" She was starting to sound panicked now. "I'm starting to get scared."

"Me too, babe. Me too." He took her into his arms and held her tightly. She clutched to him and rested her head in the hollow of his shoulder. He gently ran a hand through her hair and he felt a shudder pass through her. He felt her heart pounding in her chest and only then noticed that that sound was barely audible through the pounding of his own heart in his ears. "Do you trust me?" he asked. Two days ago, he would have bet his life on knowing the answer to this question. For the first time since they had met, he worried about what the answer might be.

"Of course I do," she breathed. "But…" she trailed off, struggling to find the right words.

"We'll be okay," he reassured her. "Right now, neither of us knows what to do. So we'll wait." He saw her confused look, so he continued. "There isn't anything we can do right now except try to move on as normally as possible."

"Normal?" she asked incredulously. "You can't be serious."

"What choice do we have? All we have right now is each other. And this may sound corny, but I think that's a pretty good place to start." He gave her a small smile, which she returned, and it seemed to lighten the colour of the cloud that hung over their heads.

She took a deep breath to steady herself.

"Normal, eh?" she asked.

"Normal."

"Okay. Then help me make the bed." Her smile widened as she tried to put aside her feelings about the day's events and focussed on the previous night and why the bed was in such disarray. He smiled as well and, dutifully, helped her with the sheets and the quilt. Once the bad looked presentable, she continued to move around the room tidying up what she could. When she reached the phone she stopped. Robbie felt a chill wash over the room and looked over to her to see if she felt it too. He saw a look come into her eyes that he had never seen before – a look of sheer terror as she held the phone in her hand. Only then, did he realize that the chill was emanating from her.

"Robbie. Did you say that you heard a humming noise during both phone calls?"

"Yeah. I just figure that both phone calls were being recorded. Why?"

"Well," she continued. "If Holt is the one who is listening to our calls, wouldn't he have heard what the second caller said?" The memory of the second call flashed quickly through his head. Shortly after that, all the blood left that same area.

"We should go." With that, Anna and Robert hurriedly dressed in whatever clothes they could lay their hands on. Neither one cared for fashion or appearances. Robert grabbed a dark blue t-shirt, a pair of jogging pants, and his sneakers from the closet. Anna snatched up a red blouse, a pair of jeans, and her own runners. Robert quickly tucked his wallet and keys into his pockets while Anna grabbed her purse. They looked at each other, neither saying a word yet speaking volumes, then bolted for the stairs. He took Anna by the hand as they ran down, trying to maintain their balance as they went. They skidded to a stop just before crashing into the front door. Robert put his finger to his lips to make sure that Anna didn't make a sound Half-expecting to see Holt there waiting, Robert was a little surprised (and very relieved) to see that the entryway was empty. He cautiously opened the front door and, together, they moved for his Camry parked in the same spot where he had left it the night before. While only a few hours ago, it seemed to be a lifetime. They jumped in and, putting the car into reverse, pulled out onto the street. Robert pressed the clutch hard, slamming the car into first, and sped off. He had no idea where he was heading, but at that point in time, elsewhere seemed a better alternative. He had wanted to remain normal. It would seem that that choice had been taken away.

CHAPTER

4

Holt eased his rental car to the side of the road. He checked his watch and, as expected, was quite a bit early. It was only 8:07 and he wasn't scheduled to meet with the overnight surveillance team until 9:00. He was still a few blocks from the three-man team stationed around the corner from the Seabrook's house. Out of habit, he ran through all of the things facing him today. First, talk with the team and find out what, if anything had transpired the previous night. Then, he had to contact Dr. Seabrook again to ensure that his "suggestions" were still understood and adhered to. Finally, return this rental car to the agency and get back to Vancouver to begin the next part of this file. The ferry from Vancouver Island to the mainland was usually a pleasant trip. An occasional Orca sighting always made for a grand spectacle. Sure, you could see them at Sea World and other aquariums around the world, but there was just something about seeing a wild animal in its native habitat that was awe-inspiring. The Vancouver Aquarium was all right for a visit, but when compared to some of the larger water parks back in the States it just didn't carry the same "WOW" factor. With his thoughts unusually on other topics, Holt did not even realize that his phone was ringing until the third ring.

"Dammit," he muttered under his breath as he keyed the answer button. "Holt," he said tersely.

"Yeah, Holt," said the voice in his ear after the encryption sequence was complete. "This is O'Connor. We have a problem. The target is leaving the residence."

"What?! Any idea where he's heading?" Holt was already starting the engine in preparation to follow where this 'pigeon' flew.

"Not sure. Weren't expecting him to go anywhere… especially not this early on a Saturday morning. Headin' North right now. Looks like he's in a rush, too."

Early on a Saturday. That was a valid point, thought Holt as he manoeuvred his car towards his surveillance team. Something must have spooked him. Something more than the conversation that he had with him. "His wife with him?" Holt drove past the Seabrooks' house and headed North in an attempt to pick up the trackers.

"Yeah. They're headed towards the highway." Holt moved over to a shortcut that he had scouted the day before. He knew he had to make up some ground soon because the last thing he needed was to get pulled over for speeding on the highway.

"Okay. I'm moving to the highway now. Do you still have a visual?" he asked. He knew O'Connor well and trusted not only his judgment, but his skill as well.

O'Connor had accompanied Holt on numerous jobs, had been witness to many horrific things, and was known to do what was necessary to complete an assignment. His services had, at times, proved invaluable.

"Yeah," came the reply. "He just got on the highway. Looks like he's takin' the boat." Holt knew that this meant he would indeed be taking the ferry. Granted, it was a lot sooner than he had anticipated. But jobs, especially lately, never seemed to run the way they were supposed to. He quickly made the entrance to the highway and proceeded towards the ferry.

"I'm on the highway now. How far ahead are you?"

"We're about 10 klicks outside Sidney." That put them about 5 minutes ahead of where he was. He slowly pushed down on the accelerator, easing past a morning trucker hauling farm equipment.

"How fast is he going?" Holt asked.

"Just over the speed limit. We're 3 cars behind him."

"Okay. Keep me posted." He switched his phone off to concentrate on the task at hand. If anything unexpected happened, he knew O'Connor would contact him immediately. Holt risked going a little faster on the highway. The last thing he needed was to be separated by too large a gap at the ferry terminal forcing him to take a later ferry, especially with the weekend traffic that was sure to be there. The wait for the ferry line-ups could be nightmarish to say the least. Sidney was approaching so the ferry terminal wouldn't be far. The sign over the highway indicated that the next boat was already full and the following one was already at 45% capacity. One ferry wait. *Not bad.*

By the time he reached the line up, he was pleased to see that he had in fact made up significant ground on both the Seabrooks and their shadows. He could see O'Connor's blue Impala six cars ahead and waiting. The Seabrooks' Camry was three cars ahead of him. Holt chose a different queue to enter, hoping to make up further time. One of the lines had a large RV. This gave the impression that this line was just as long as the others, but due to the actual number of vehicles, this one made for a good chance to move up. After paying for his trip to the mainland (unbelievably they charged you for the driver of the vehicle in addition to the vehicle itself – as if there were a way for the vehicle to board on its own), Holt discovered that his calculation had been correct. He found himself 2 spots behind O'Connor's vehicle. Now, it was time to wait and see what the Seabrooks' next move would be. This early morning dash to the ferry had been unexpected. Something had gone wrong. Usually, Holt had found that if a threat was levied against a regular citizen and that threat was taken seriously, most people reacted as anticipated. Robert Seabrook was supposed to wait at home and try to live life normally until Holt contacted him again. But then, he grabs his wife and heads for the ferry and the mainland. *Did he not take the threat seriously after all?* Holt found that difficult to believe. He had been quite clear while at the same time remaining vague. It was a talent picked up and honed over the years – saying a lot while saying very little. Holt started to second guess his actions, but that only lasted a few moments.

No. Something happened. Something changed. What that change was, he was not sure. But whatever had occurred had been significant enough to drive both Robert and Anna from the assumed safety of their home and place them on the move. It had also forced Holt to alter his plans. That never sat well with him. Sure, plans had to be adjusted from time to time, but that was usually done on his terms. But this? This was someone else manipulating a situation that he felt he was in control of, and that just simply would not do. Sure, he had placed a surveillance team on the Seabrooks, but that was in case they decided to go for a drive or had visitors. O'Connor and his crew were the best and he knew that they wouldn't let him down.

Holt looked ahead and saw O'Connor and his team in their chase vehicle. Despite each one of them being deadly, they looked like a group of businessmen headed to a conference. It was a sign of a good surveillance team. He looked further ahead and saw the Seabrooks' Camry. Both occupants were looking around nervously. They didn't appear to be looking for anything in particular, but it was customary for people in this situation to try and assess potential threats. Having no idea what a threat would actually look like, though, made them appear to be foreigners in their own country. Still, something had spooked them. Spooked them enough to flee. Holt keyed his phone and dialled O'Connor.

"Yeah," O'Connor answered curtly.

"It's Holt. I'm here."

"I know. Saw you come up. Nice move with the line-up." O'Connor was definitely alert. That would more than likely come in handy in the next little while.

"Do you know what happened? Why they bolted like this?" Holt couldn't keep the impatience out of his voice. Somebody had messed up his plan and he was not thrilled at that prospect. The idea of losing even a little control, especially this early on, did not sit well. But this was not a time to let pride get in the way. Professionalism had to be maintained. He took a deep breath to settle himself while he listened to O'Connor's answer.

"They got a call. No idea what was said. Our recorders just picked up a clicking noise. We rechecked our equipment to make sure we weren't the cause, but we were fine. Must have been some kind of encryption, but nothin' like what we use." O'Connor continued. "Call lasted a few minutes, then boom. These two come racing out of the house and they bolt. We started following them and called you." He paused. "What now?"

Holt's mind raced as he struggled to process this new information as quickly as he could. A phone call had scared them. An encrypted phone call. That meant that someone else had contacted Dr. Seabrook and unless he was involved with some other critical incident, this caller also wanted information about Terry Philips. *So much for being a new file.* But who else would be interested in Philips? Who else could be? One thing was for certain. Whoever this caller was, they would be contacting Dr. Seabrook again. As he thought this, another thought ran through Holt's mind – a thought that made him a little more nervous than he was used to being.

"Keep eyes on Dr. Seabrook. His wife too if you can manage it, but he is the principle. Keep an eye out for other surveillance too. If it was encryption, there might be others with eyes on him…and us." The message was clear enough. Stay alert. We might not be alone on this one.

"Copy that," O'Connor replied. Holt terminated the call and began a visual sweep of every vehicle he could see. He knew that O'Connor and his team would be doing the same. No surveillance expert enjoyed the idea of being watched. They knew how truly intrusive it was. Being stuck in a line-up like this just made things worse because you felt like you were on display. Used to being the hunters, the role of prey was entirely disconcerting. As if O'Connor had the same thought, the rear passenger door of his car opened and Mitch Waddell stepped out. Mitch was relatively new to the team and, therefore, did most of the actual leg work. At 27, he was one of the younger people Holt had worked with in a while, though not directly. He had never actually met Mitch, but from what O'Connor had said of him, he showed potential. Waddell closed his door and stretched, shaking out his limbs from the 'business trip' he had just endured. He moved forward past the Seabrooks and headed for the terminal. It made sense, really. They had some time to kill before the next ferry and the Seabrooks might decide to have something to eat. If they had left home in that much of a hurry, they had probably skipped breakfast. Rather than following them to the concourse, Waddell would already be there. Sometimes the easiest way to follow someone without detection was to be in front of them.

Waddell strolled past the line of cars that wound its way down towards the loading area and disappeared into the terminal. Holt continued his visual scan of the surrounding cars. There were a couple that deserved consideration as possible shadow vehicles, but for the most part it seemed routine. He keyed his phone to speak to O'Connor again.

"Yeah," came the response into the phone.

"It's Holt. Eyes on the green Windstar and the black Sonata."

"Copy. Also the silver 'B-mer' and the RV that you came in after," O'Connor replied.

"The RV?" Holt didn't think that the RV was a particularly effective chase vehicle due to its size and lack of speed.

"Yeah, the RV. Seems like an easy way to disguise a mobile electronics or communications station. Great for listening," O'Connor stated plainly.

DAMN! Holt was not used to making those kinds of mistakes. He hadn't given the RV a second glance after his initial notice of it during the line-up. Hell, he had even followed the damn thing in. It had been right in front of his face. Whatever had been occupying his mind that had caused him to overlook such a potentially serious risk had to be dealt with. Or perhaps it was more than that. Perhaps he was starting to make those little mistakes that he had seen other people make. Perhaps it was a sign that he had begun to slip. Those were legitimate questions that would need legitimate answers, but they would all have to wait. For right now, though, all he could do was to try and focus his mind on the task at hand and ensure that those mistakes were not repeated.

"Any other movement?" Holt asked as he studied the RV and the BMW that O'Connor had mentioned.

"Nothin' yet. Waddell's up front and Nesbitt and I are holding here." Andrew Nesbitt was the third member of O'Connor's team. He had quite a history with O'Connor and had been partnered with him for four years. He was as skilled as any with particularly deadly aim. "So far, so good."

"Indeed. So what do you…" Holt's question was interrupted by the emergence of Anna Seabrook from her car. She looked around nervously, then leaned down to speak to her husband. From Holt's view, he could see Robert motion for her to get back in the car. She shook her head, stretched, and headed towards the terminal. A few moments later, Dr. Seabrook's door opened and he stepped out. He called out to her and she waited for him to catch up. Once he reached her, he took her hand in his and they set off towards the ferry terminal and Waddell.

"Nesbitt's gonna follow in a few minutes. I'll hang back here."

"I copy," Holt replied. "I'll stay back as well." He watched as the Seabrooks made their way to the terminal and ducked inside. After a few moments, Nesbitt stepped out of the front passenger door and moved towards the terminal. O'Connor and Holt both studied every vehicle they could see. Nobody stirred. There was no one else following the Seabrooks as far as they could tell and there appeared to be no one tailing the surveillance team which was even more good news. So they sat and waited. Sitting and waiting came part and parcel with surveillance, but never got easier. Whether you viewed it as the calm before the storm or the curse of doing nothing, rarely were there people who saw surveillance work as a wonderful thing.

But one thing that it taught you was to put your faith in others. *You can trust everyone. Trust some people to be there for you and trust others to let you down.* Either way, you just had to wait.

"Waddell."

"Heads up. Targets comin' to you," O'Connor spoke smoothly into his transmitter.

"Copy. I see 'em." Mitch Waddell took a deep breath and steadied his nerves. He was still relatively new to the actual field work as he had worked at a desk for a number of years before his promotion. While he had done a number of 'jobs', the nerves still threatened to rip him apart. He studied the Sudoku puzzle in front of him as Anna and Robert entered the terminal. Watching from the corner of his eye, he saw Anna tug on her husband's shirt and motion to the bathroom. He nodded and she moved quickly to the ladies' room. Robert stayed just outside of the door. Another woman came out of the bathroom and gave him a wary eye. He just smiled at her and looked around the area, trying to act nonchalant. Anybody with half a brain, though, could see that he was scared. Anna came out a few minutes later looking pleasantly relieved. She headed to a table while he went to the vending machine and purchased two bottles of water and two bags of chips. *Healthy choice.*

Waddell continued to monitor them through his puzzle. He didn't even hear or notice Nesbitt approach him and was startled when he sat down next to him.

"Jumpy?" Nesbitt said as a satisfied smirk crept over his face. As the 'new guy', Waddell was the target in a lot of the ribbing that went on.

"Fuck off," Waddell laughed. He knew he was wound a little tight, but there was no harm in being tense.

"What are they up to?" Nesbitt prodded. He picked up a Vancouver Province and began reading the business section.

"Nothin'. Just a quick bite and a drink. She used the restroom, but that's all."

"Right on. O'Connor and Holt are waiting back at the cars. I can keep watch if you wanna head back." There really wasn't much point in both of them staying here. After all, with the Seabrooks' car in the queue, they had committed to the ferry. There wasn't much chance of them going elsewhere.

"No. I'll stay. You never know, they might separate." Waddell didn't like the idea of leaving even if he had been told that he could. His task was to keep an eye on the Seabrooks and that was what he intended to do.

"Suit yourself," Nesbitt muttered as he made a notation in the business section. He passed the paper to Waddell so he could what he wrote. "See? Told you the TSX would bounce back," he exclaimed loud enough for people at the next table could hear him.

Waddell smiled at the subterfuge and dutifully looked down at the paper. *FUCK YOU, NEWBIE* was scrawled in bold letters over the business page. He smiled, in spite of himself. He had taken a liking to Nesbitt and could take a joke. He looked over at him shaking his head. Nesbitt just grinned. "I gotta take a dump," Nesbitt said and walked towards the men's room with his paper tucked under his arm. Waddell marvelled at the ease in which Nesbitt just assumed whatever role he required. He was the ultimate chameleon. He never looked out of place and somehow seemed to vanish whenever he needed to.

After about ten minutes, the PA system announced that the next ferry was arriving and that all vehicle passengers bound for Tsawassen should return to their vehicles. The Seabrooks, who had been sitting at their table holding hands, rose and moved towards the exit that led back to their car. Nesbitt hadn't come out of the bathroom yet. Gripped by a moment of indecision, Waddell bent down to tie his shoe and keyed his transmitter. "Targets moving back your way."

"Copy," O'Connor said. "I see them. You guys can head back."

"Copy." Waddell straightened up and stretched, producing a nice big yawn for anyone who was interested. He decided he'd wait for Nesbitt to finish up. After a few more minutes, though, he still hadn't emerged.

O'Connor came back over the transmitter. "Anytime guys. The ferry's already started to unload."

Waddell stretched again with his arms over his head. He turned into his shoulder to hide his mouth from view. "I copy. One still in the restroom."

"Get him outta there," came the terse reply. "We got no time."

"Copy." With that, Waddell headed to the men's room and entered. "Drew," he said when he came into view of the stalls. There was no response. "Drew!" he called out. There was still no reply. Awful thoughts immediately started running through his head. He instinctively fell back on his training and began sorting through the 'what if's' that a situation like this could bring. He bent down and reached into his ankle holster, bringing out his .38. The bathroom looked deserted, but there should have been at least one person still inside. He held his firearm at the ready and scanned the bathroom again. Seeing nothing, he stooped to check for feet in the stalls. The only feet visible were in the end stall against the wall. Trying to clear his head beyond the clamouring sound of his heart, he moved towards the first stall and cautiously peered around the corner. Empty. He moved forward to the next stall. He licked his dry lips as he nudged the door open. Empty. Three to go. He paused to wipe the sweat from his hands as he prepared to continue on. The next two stalls were open and empty which led him to the final stall. Knocking lightly, he stepped back and brought his gun up. Hearing nothing he quickly moved forward and kicked the stall door in. It took him a few moments for his brain to process exactly what lay before him because this was not supposed to happen. Andrew Nesbitt sat on the toilet, his pants still around his ankles, with a bullet hole through the centre of his forehead. His lifeless eyes stared unbelievingly at Waddell as a trickle of blood still seeped between them. What was left of his brain lay sprayed on the wall behind him. Clipped to the front of his shirt was the business section page with the words FUCK YOU NEWBIE as his unofficial epitaph. Waddell reached in and ripped the paper off of his partner uncovering two red splotches on his shirt in the middle of his chest. Bullet holes. *Two to the body, one to the head.*

He moved backwards in a daze. *What the hell happened?* He closed the stall door and moved for the exit, keying his transmitter as he did so.

"O'Connor," he called. There was no response. He was greeted with the sound of clicking. "O'Connor," he repeated. Again, clicking was the only reply. *Oh shit*! Just before he exited the bathroom, he remembered that he was still in a public place. He shoved his .38 in the waist of his pants and covered it with his shirt. He saw the foot passengers who had disembarked headed towards him. He quickly ducked back into the bathroom and entered the stall next to Nesbitt's. He stood on the toilet and hoisted himself up to reach over to Nesbitt's side and latched the stall door. If anyone discovered him before they were at least on the water, there would be a lot of explaining to do. Once secured, he ducked back into his own stall just as the first of the passengers entered. He quickly moved past them and headed back towards the cars, unsure of what he would find there.

Attempting to disguise himself further once outside seemed pointless so he headed straight for O'Connor. He could see the Impala in the queue just as he had left it. Only then did he realize that in the confusion, he had lost track of the Seabrooks. *Shit!* He was relieved to see that they were back in their car, waiting patiently for the loading to commence. Moving past them, he looked up to see O'Connor in the driver's seat of their vehicle. O'Connor glanced up and immediately noted the harried look on Waddell's face. Waddell's expression hardened to stone as he willed all of his thoughts to his partner's mind. O'Connor quickly glanced around as he immediately realized that something had gone horribly wrong. As soon as Waddell opened the front passenger door, O'Connor spoke.

"What happened? Why is your transmitter off?" he asked as Waddell threw himself into the seat.

"Jesus H. Fucking Christ!" Waddell exclaimed. "Nesbitt's dead. He's fucking dead!"

O'Connor, stunned by this turn of events, took a moment to take in the information being provided. "What do you mean he's dead? What the hell happened in there?" The alarm in his voice was not helping his younger partner calm down in any way.

"I dunno," Waddell answered feebly. "Jesus, I don't know."

O'Connor had begun to steady himself as his analytical mind kicked in. "Okay, Mitch. Calm down. Walk me through what happened." Waddell proceeded to give him a detailed account of everything that he had witnessed from the time he left the car to the time that he had found Nesbitt.

"Fuck. We're not alone," he reflected. "Holt was right. There is someone else on this. But why come after one of us?" he asked, half to himself. Shaking his head for clarity, he turned his focus back on to Waddell. "Okay. Who did you see enter or leave the men's room."

Waddell looked at him blankly for a moment. "What? Oh...nobody."

"You didn't see who else was in there?"

"No." Waddell could see the anger rising in O'Connor's face. "Hey! I did my job. My focus was on the Seabrooks. How the fuck was I supposed to know this would happen?"

"Your job," O'Connor exploded "is to be aware of your surroundings at all times! How the fuck are we supposed to ID anyone who contacts this piece of shit if all you're doing is *watching* them! And why the fuck didn't you call for me!"

"I tried!" Waddell shouted. "The fucking transmitter isn't working!" That immediately sent a chill down O'Connor's spine. Blocking cell phone or landline communications was one thing, but being able to block their field transmitters was another. He instantly keyed his transmitter to raise Holt. There was no response. He looked into his rear-view mirror and saw Holt just returning to his car. *Where the hell had he gone?* He tried the transmitter again, but still was greeted with silence.

"See?" Waddell interjected. "It's fucked."

"You don't know the half of it, kid." If the same people responsible for Nesbitt's death were blocking their transmitters, then that meant that they were well equipped and extremely professional. But what was there goal? Obviously they weren't trying to kill Dr. Seabrook. They could have done that at any point. Dr. Seabrook would be dealt with at the right time, but right now he was needed alive. *Their target has to be us. But how the hell did they know about us? The only people in on this were Nesbitt, Waddell, myself, Holt, and…*Holt. He looked into the mirror again and saw Holt rubbing his neck as he stretched in the front seat of his car. *Where HAD he been and why didn't he let me know he was moving?* Both legitimate questions that needed answering. But before he could figure out a way to get those answers, the line started to move as the ferry finished docking. O'Connor started the engine and waited.

"What are you doing?" Waddell asked. "We're compromised! We gotta move out of here!"

"We're not leaving this," O'Connor replied. "We have a job to do and I intend to see that it gets done. Understood?" His tone made it very clear that this point was not up for discussion.

Waddell took a deep breath. "Understood."

O'Connor looked back to see Holt following in line. "Keep your eyes on everything and trust no one."

"What about Nesbitt?" Waddell asked.

O'Connor thought about that for a moment. "Let's just hope we make it to the other side before he gets discovered. Last thing any of us need is a police welcome." It was an hour and a half ferry trip to Tsawassen. This trip would most definitely seem even longer.

CHAPTER 5

The boarding itself was uneventful. Cars were jammed into the massive bulk of the ferry like sardines. Just when you thought you couldn't fit anything more, another few cars were squeezed in. As the barricades were secured to make sure that no vehicles were able to test the depths of the Juan de Fuca Strait, the intercom came alive and encouraged all boarding passengers to leave the vehicle deck and move up to the passenger decks so that they could avail themselves of all the amenities offered to them. *In other words, we can't make more money off of you if you stay in your car.* Holt had travelled enough to know most of the sales tactics utilized around the world. The west seemed to enjoy making you feel privileged while you were being gouged. Just like the airports in North America, ferries seemed to have no concept of what things actually cost in normal retailers. It was as if they realized that as long as you had no other options for your purchases, you wouldn't care that a Bic pen cost more than the local paper you wanted for the daily crossword.

He waited for a few minutes. He could still see the Seabrooks, although they were a little further ahead due to the lane assignments in the ferry. They were probably deciding whether or not they should remain in their car or head up to the higher decks. O'Connor was nowhere to be found, but he knew he'd be close. As if summoned by his thoughts, O'Connor appeared by the stairwell and proceeded up. Robert and Anna had also reached the same decision and exited their car, heading for the stairs. Seeing as how their car was definitely not going anywhere, Holt opted to head up as well. There was no point in sitting in his car when the entire file was going to be enjoying overpriced White Spot food and 'almost' coffee. Holt moved out of his car and followed the Seabrooks once they had reached the stairs. The last thing he needed was for Dr. Seabrook to see him, but he also needed to know who he spoke to. The surveillance team was competent, but things had already progressed in a way that he did not like. Surprises were never good. Just before he reached the stairs, a hoarse whisper from the right stopped him cold.

"Pitch Black." A simple code phrase meaning that something very serious had happened. Without looking around, Holt made a quick upwards gesture with his head and proceeded up the stairs. Waddell followed closely behind. Holt had to find a suitable place to talk. Waddell definitely had something to say, but so far as anyone who could be watching knew, Holt had no connection to the surveillance team and he would like to keep it that way. The restroom was the easiest. Adjoining stalls that allowed for notes to be passed under the walls that, for some reason, never extended to the floor. He walked around the deck until he found the men's room and ducked inside. There were plenty of stalls, necessary to accommodate a ship this size. He selected one and sat down waiting. Before too long, someone entered the stall next to his. After a few moments, a note was proffered. He grabbed it and scanned the scrawl.

"It's O'Connor. Where the hell were you?" He stared at the note a moment, puzzled. He took out his pen and responded.

"When?" Simple and direct seemed to be the way to go, especially with notes.

"At the ferry line-up. I saw you get back in the car. Where did you go?" This seemed an odd question coming from O'Connor. With the apparent tone in his note and Waddell's words of warning, something drastic must have happened. His mounting apprehension would have been exacerbated if he had been able to see O'Connor's handgun aimed at him from the other side of the wall.

"Cramp. Walked it off. What happened?"

"Not here. Not safe. Meet up on mainland." These responses were not producing any answers to the questions mounting in his mind. He knew O'Connor to be cautious, but this was getting out of hand. And if Waddell and Nesbitt…His thoughts wandered back to the actual boarding of the ferry. Waddell had returned and sat down in the front passenger seat, previously occupied by Nesbitt, and then they had boarded the ferry without him. His apprehension quickly intensified to dread.

"Where's Nesbitt?" It took a few moments longer than usual for the reply to come, but when it did, Holt realized the gravity of the situation.

"He never left the terminal." With that, O'Connor left the stall and exited the men's room to find Waddell. Holt sat on the toilet running everything over in his mind. A communications block back at the Seabrook house, a phone call prompting the Seabrooks to run, a possible second surveillance team, and now a missing man. But what if it wasn't a surveillance team he was up against? What if it was something more? There were too many questions and not nearly enough answers. Waddell and O'Connor would know more, but that would clearly have to wait until the mainland. O'Connor would vanish while he and Waddell decided their next move. Any time a team lost a member the rest of them quickly rounded up the wagons and assessed their options. That was what was probably happening now. Holt saw the logic of this and decided to do the same. Just before he rose from the seat, however, a note was dropped on to the floor from the opposite stall from where O'Connor had been sitting. Holt stared at it for a moment before reaching down and opening the folded page. His chest clutched tight as he read it slowly.

"The ferry terminal was easy. You and your partner there would have been too. Lose this file. Lose the Seabrooks. Go home. You're welcome."

Holt exploded out of the stall and kicked in the door of the stall next to his. There was no one in it and, at present, no one else in the men's room. He moved quickly to the door and headed out into a sea of passengers heading to the cafeteria. He glanced around quickly, scanning the faces of everyone he could see while clutching the note in his hand. Whoever had written it had vanished. He looked around for O'Connor or Waddell, but as expected, they too had disappeared. He looked again at the note. The ferry terminal. Nesbitt missing. It wasn't hard to connect the dots. Nesbitt was dead. O'Connor and Waddell knew about it. His brain started to process the information at a rapid pace. *Nesbitt killed. O'Connor comments that I was away from my vehicle. He suspects it might be me. O'Connor didn't leave his car. Waddell did. O'Connor didn't do it. Could Waddell have? Then why warn me? No. Someone else was involved here. Someone had targeted us, eliminated Nesbitt, boarded the ferry, and was going after the Seabrooks. But why?*

Once again, Holt found himself facing a mounting array of questions. The more questions he came up with, the more he realized that he was further from the truth than before. One thing was for certain – the cost of pressing Robert Seabrook for information on Terry Philips had just risen substantially. He looked again at the note. *You're welcome.* Like some sick way of asking for thanks for sparing his life. One thing was for certain. Holt had no intention of walking away from this file now. Nesbitt's death would not be in vain. He doubted that O'Connor would give up either. Waddell was new. He might not have the stomach for this job once it got dirty. Time would have to tell. As for now, Holt went to the outside deck to get some fresh air and enjoy the scenery as the Gulf Islands glided past. Maybe there'd be a whale this time.

Anna slipped her hand into Robert's as they sat in the cafeteria. They hadn't ordered anything and hoped that their seats wouldn't be needed. So far, it looked like they would not have to move. Robert looked into his wife's eyes and saw the fear and doubt that had been there since that damn call this morning. He wished he could take that look from her and throw it into the passing water. It didn't belong on her face. What belonged there was joy and hope and wonder, not this stress. She tried to smile to assuage her own feelings of dread, but that only made her eyes seem sadder as the emotion on her face was not reflected there. Anna lived and breathed through her eyes, she always had. One look and you could tell what was wrong or what was right. At this point in time, things were definitely wrong.

"I'm sorry." He didn't really know what else to say.

"This isn't your fault, Robbie." That was true. Technically all he had done was treat a patient. But still, he couldn't help but feel responsible for the events that had led them to seek solitude on the mainland. He wasn't entirely sure where they were going, he just knew that staying in Victoria had felt like the wrong thing to do. He had contemplated going to the police, but the echoes of Holt's warning still reverberated in his head. Anna's Dad would have been the one to call. He might have some ideas about what to do. But knowing her Dad, he would insist that they fly right to him or that he come to them and that just seemed to put him in harm's way. There was no clear choice.

"I know," he said finally. "I just feel like this is all cuz of me. And I never thought in a million years that being a psychologist might put your life in danger."

"I'm okay, Robbie. We're together and we're okay." She smiled a little more convincingly as a gleam hinted at the corner of her eyes. "Besides, it's been a while since we took a trip."

That caused him to chuckle. "That's true." It had indeed been quite a while since they had gone on vacation. With his practice starting to pick up and the constant demands placed on her by the school (and the parents), there just never seemed time to get away. There still wasn't. There just wasn't any choice at present. "Wish the circumstances were different."

"If the circumstances were different, we'd probably still be home for the weekend." She smiled as she squeezed his hand. He returned the smile and took a deep breath. "So where are we going?" she asked.

He had been pondering that thought himself and still hadn't come up with anything concrete. *Just move* seemed to be a good idea. "I was thinking we'd hit the mainland and head east."

"East to where?" she whispered.

"I don't know." That was true. "I figured we'd just go til we got tired, get a hotel room, and decide from there." That seemed like a reasonably solid plan. They would be tougher to track away from their home town. There would be no 'usual hangouts' or routines to follow.

"My dad?" she asked hopefully.

"Still not sure. If this situation is dangerous, I'd like to avoid getting other people in the middle."

"But he's a cop, Robbie. A good cop. He can help us out. He will help us." Of that there was no doubt. Mark Wilson had liked Robert from the beginning which was strange from an overprotective father. He was a good cop and a good man which was why Robert wanted to keep him safe and out of this completely.

"I know he would, baby. And I'm not ruling him out. Just not yet, okay? Let's just see where this Holt guy takes this." He was about to continue when his cell phone rang. He looked at the call display. *Unknown.* He put his phone away. Looking up, he saw the questioning look in Anna's eyes. "It's nothing. It says unknown. I'll let the machine get it." After a few rings, the ringing ceased but was immediately followed by another set of rings. He looked at his phone again. *Unknown.* He glanced around as several passengers were giving him dark looks for disturbing their collective solitude with the incessant ringing of his cell phone.

"Answer it," Anna said cautiously.

Robert keyed his phone and closed his eyes. "Hello?" He was greeted by the expected hum. After a few moments, the same voice from earlier spoke into his ear.

"Dr. Seabrook. Wasn't expecting you to take a trip so early."

"Yeah, well. Things happen," he replied testily. He was getting tired of everyone apparently knowing what he did and where he was.

"Indeed. So I see you're on the ferry headed for Tsawassen. Not sure why the ferry, but..." Robert cut him off.

"Listen. I don't know who you are or what you have to do with this. But if you want me to continue having this conversation, then you'd better start explaining what the hell is going on?" A few passengers looked over at him in surprise as he realized that his voice had risen quite a bit over the span of that last sentence. He smiled sheepishly as he regained his composure. Anna squeezed his hand in reassurance.

"I understand your position, Doctor. Allow me to introduce myself. My name is Colin Vickers. I work for C.S.I.S."

"What the hell is See-sus?" Robert asked.

"It's the Canadian Security and Intelligence Service. Kinda like the C.I.A." Vickers said patiently. Acronyms were a personal annoyance for Robert and he wanted a better understanding of whom he was speaking with.

"Never heard of it," Robert lied. He had heard about C.S.I.S., but very little. One trick that he had learned from his practice was that if you feigned ignorance on a topic, it forced the other person to speak more freely about it to give you a better understanding. It also made them feel that they held the power, although in this situation that was true.

"Well that means we're doing our job. Let's face it. The only reason people discuss intelligence agencies is when something goes wrong." Vickers chuckled into the phone.

"Glad you're enjoying this," Robert added angrily. "Mind telling me a little bit more?"

"Of course. As you have probably been made aware, this all has to do with one of your patients. Mr. Terry Philips." Robert didn't speak as he waited for Vickers to continue. "We had been following Mr. Philips for a time as we had received information that he was involved in something illegal. We were closing in when he disappeared. We traced his movements back before he vanished and found you."

"And?" Robert asked. He still didn't have the information that he wanted and Vickers seemed like he was holding back.

"And then we found Holt." That name spoken again struck Robert like a lightning bolt. "Holt had contacted you so we figured we were on to something big. We contacted you. You ran. Now here we are."

Robert's mind raced as he struggled to follow along with this vein. "Who is Holt?"

Vickers paused as he looked for the best way to put it. "I don't mean to alarm you, Doctor, but Holt is a killer." The alarm that was apparently unintentional swept over his body like an early morning tide. The chill he felt went right to his hands, so much so that even Anna felt it. She moved closer to him for support. "Holt used to work with the C.I.A. He was released following an incident and, for a while, disappeared. He's been doing freelance stuff recently – mercenary work although he may be involved with a separate organization now. So far as we can tell, he's looking for Mr. Philips. Subsequently, he found you."

"Why are you telling me all of this?" Robert really didn't want to be involved with anything of this magnitude, especially when it threatened Anna.

"I'm telling you this because I need you to understand the situation you are in and I need you to take things a little more seriously, Dr. Seabrook."

"Believe me, I am," he replied.

"Not seriously enough, I'm afraid. I contacted you this morning and told you that I would call you again once we figured out a way to get to you. You ran. I didn't tell you to run, but you did anyway. This is not a game, Dr. Seabrook. You have no idea what moves to make so right now you're as effective as a blind baseball player. If you want my help you need to do as I say. Understood?" While he didn't like being admonished, Robert knew the wisdom in Vickers' words. He didn't know what to do. He had just voiced that to Anna. Vickers seemed to know and therefore should be heard.

"Understood," he said resignedly. "What should I do?"

"Good to hear it. Once you're off the ferry, you'll be on Highway 17. Do you know how to get to the Trans-Canada from there?"

"Yeah." Robert didn't know where this was leading, but at least it was heading somewhere.

"Once you hit the Trans-Canada, head east to Abbotsford. When you get to the Whatcom exit, you will see a hotel on the north side of the freeway. It's a Clarion Hotel. Go there. Go to the front desk. There will be a room waiting for you. Do not leave the room once you're there. We will come to you. Clear?"

Still not liking the tone, the message was nonetheless welcome. A plan. Something to do and a destination. It was comforting to at least have a plan to follow. He knew the Lower Mainland well enough to navigate to Abbotsford. It wasn't that hard really once you reached the Trans Canada. Plus, he would get to bypass Vancouver. Life in the big city had never been attractive to him and so he was not well suited to survive the jungle that the downtown core turned into – even on a Saturday.

"I understand," he said finally.

"Good." Vickers did not beat around the bush and Robert appreciated that fact. So many half-truths were uttered in his profession that it got to the point where one would naturally gravitate to a person who was direct. That was one of the things that had fascinated him about Anna all of these years. She never hesitated to speak what was on her mind. She never played those little 'head games' that so many men had complained about – patients and otherwise. He looked at her again and saw her eyes riveted to his face, the worry still evident. He smiled reassuringly at her and squeezed her hand. Moving the phone away from his mouth, he silently mouthed the words "we're okay" and nodded to Anna. She smiled and exhaled the breath that he hadn't noticed she had been holding. He was about to say something else to her when he realized that Vickers was trying to get his attention on the phone.

"Sorry?" he stated blankly, clearly flustered that he had let his mind wander from Vickers' conversation.

"Dr. Seabrook. I need you to focus on what I am saying. This is important"

"Sorry, Vickers. You were saying?" He hadn't meant to appear aloof, but there weren't many other conclusions Vickers could have drawn.

"I don't mean to alarm you, Dr. Seabrook, but I'm afraid there is no way to avoid that with what I am about to tell you." Robert could hear from the clinical tone that Vickers' voice had adopted that the news which was coming would indeed be bad. After a moment, the news Robert had feared without even knowing it was delivered. "Holt is on the ferry with you."

The chill that ran down his back threatened to sever his spinal column. He quickly looked about as if, by sheer will of force, Holt would materialize so that he could confirm what Vickers had just told him. This, of course, did not happen and he was left with a nagging paranoia that caused him to glance from passenger to passenger, looking for any sign of recognition.

"WHAT?!" was all he could muster.

"Holt boarded the ferry shortly after you did," Vickers said calmly. "We also know that he is not alone." That bit of news was even more disconcerting. Holt, he could recognize. If he was working together with someone else, then that could be anyone. He again scanned every face he could see. With absolutely no idea what to look for, however, he soon realized that he was wasting his time. Anna had been watching him scour the faces of the passers-by and followed suit. Realizing that she knew even less about what to look for because she was not privy to his conversation, he tapped her on the shoulder and brought her attention back to the table.

"We have been tailing Holt for a while and have tried to intercede, but so far have been unsuccessful. As I told you, he is ex-C.I.A. The agency has been very cooperative. They do not want an ex-agent running around without restrictions. This appears to be exactly what is happening now."

Robert looked at Anna again. The worry was etched on her face and her brows were furrowed. She didn't need this – any of this. She certainly didn't deserve it. Neither of them did. He made the decision to end the whole mess as soon as possible. The easiest way to do that was to follow Vickers' plan. *Let the pros take care of it.* "What do you want us to do?"

"Stay visible. Don't use the bathrooms. Don't go down to the vehicle level until you are ready to leave. Stay together. Holt is ballsy but he won't make a move in public like this. We tried to get one of our guys on board, but he didn't make it on. We will have people in place on the other side, though, to follow you to Abbotsford."

An idea struck Robert like a lightning bolt. "Wait. If you'll have people waiting, why don't you just grab Holt there?" That seemed logical and yet he knew he had overlooked something even as he said it.

"Two reasons. One, Holt is a dangerous man. If he senses that we're closing in, he might…well, let's just say there's no telling what he might do. Two, like I said, he's not alone. We don't have ID's on the other guys he's working with. We can't make any move until we know what we're up against. We're here to help, Dr. Seabrook, and we're damn good at our jobs. Just let us do them," Vickers said reassuringly.

Robert smiled ruefully as he listened to the quiet confidence coming through the line. Whoever Vickers was, he felt sure that they could handle things. He had to put his faith somewhere and here seemed as good a spot as any. "Okay. Will you be there?" Robert heard a smile on the other end.

"Yes. I'll be meeting up with you – more than likely in Abbotsford. We'll have a better idea of what resources he has at his disposal and where to go from there."

"He told me not to speak to anyone," Robert added. It seemed a little late for that, but he wanted to let that be known.

"Then don't. You don't need to," Vickers spoke smoothly. "We've contacted you and that's more than enough. Like I said, leave it to us. We have our plan. Stick to it and we'll see you and your wife safely through this."

His relief was impossible to hide. "Oh, thank you. Thank you, Mr. Vickers. You have no idea how much that means to me."

"Yeah, I do. It's kinda my job." Vickers ended the call. Robert heard the click, then lowered the phone from his ear and looked at Anna. She searched his face for some clue as to the nature of the secrets he now knew. For once, though, she could not read him. She could not discern whether what he had heard was good news or bad. She held her breath, waiting for him to speak, to say something. After what seemed like an eternity, he finally uttered the words that she, unknowingly, had been dying to hear.

"We're gonna be all right," he said to her. Tears welled up in eyes as she leaned over and hugged him tightly.

He squeezed her with equal ferocity and their embrace garnered the attention of a few spectators. She wept openly, letting the fear and anxiety of the day wash over them. He held her close to him, wishing all of his strength into her body so that her soul could be replenished. He knew what this ordeal must have done to her and was glad that they were no longer alone. "Anna," he spoke softly as he drew his hand over her hair. "Anna," he repeated.

"Yeah," she mumbled from his shoulder.

"It's not over yet, baby." He felt her stiffen as she absorbed what he had just said to her. She straightened up, releasing her hold of him, and looked him in the eyes.

"What do you mean it's not over? You said we'd be all right."

"We will." He knew he would have to be quick so that her nerves would not be shattered all over again. "The guy I just spoke with is the same guy who called earlier. His name is Vickers and he works with C.S.I.S. Do you know who they are?"

"A little. I hear about them on the news from time to time. Plus, my Dad has worked with them in the past." She eyes him warily. "What do they want with you?"

"Well, it seems they're looking for my patient as well. They contacted me and they'll be waiting for us in Tsawassen." He could see the relief once again sweep over her face as she realized that help was indeed on the way.

"Oh, thank God. I was worried we'd never find help." She looked out at the passing Gulf Islands as if noticing their beauty for the first time. Robert knew that there was no delaying what had to be said.

"Anna." She glanced at him and saw the look in his eyes. Her mood quickly darkened.

"What else? What are you not telling me?"

"It's Holt." He saw her breath catch in her throat and, for a moment, could see her pulse quicken in her neck. He figured he might as well just push through and tell her everything. He couldn't stand having anything between them. "Vickers told me that he's on this ferry. He boarded shortly after we did."

"What?!" she shouted. Anna immediately tried to rise from the table, but Robert put his hand on her arm and silently urged her to sit back down. The surrounding spectators had definitely increased in numbers, although they mostly pretended not to be watching. Robert ignored their silent admonitions and continued.

"Shhh," he pleaded. "Vickers said that we'd be fine if we stay visible. He said he tried to get one of his men on board, but couldn't so he's got guys on the other side. They know all about him and us. We'll just stay here til we cross. Okay?" She didn't seem over-convinced and he could hardly blame her. Neither of them was used to putting that much trust in anyone outside of family, let alone someone they had never met. It just seemed like there was nothing else they could do.

"So what happens when we reach Tsawassen? They gonna storm the ferry? Ride in on horseback, bugles blaring?" Her tone held a definite charge that he had never heard before. He hated that he was partly responsible for putting it there. All he wanted was to go back and live their lives as if none of this had ever happened. Could that be possible? Only time would allow that question to be answered. And time was what he hoped they had plenty of.

"No. Nothing like that. They're gonna follow us." She looked at him incredulously. He continued before she could grill him further. If he got out all the information, it might answer some of her questions. "We're supposed to drive to Abbotsford - Whatcom Road exit. There's a Clarion Hotel on the north side of the freeway. Vickers said he has a room there for us. We're supposed to check in and wait for him there."

"And this Vickers is going to meet us there?" she asked.

"That's what he said. We're just supposed to wait there. When he shows up, he'll tell us what to do from there." It seemed simple enough. But Anna still wasn't convinced.

"But why all the way out there? Why not someplace closer – like Delta or even Surrey?"

"I don't know. But, I'm not exactly in a position to question the guy's choice in venue. He says Abbotsford? Then it's Abbotsford."

"I guess. Whatcom Road? Isn't that the one by Wonderland?" She had fond memories of going to Wonderland and playing mini-golf in her youth.

"Yeah, I think so. Although, I think it's called Castle Fun Park or something now." He too had memories of the place. Go-karts, mini-golf, batting cages, and the arcade. Just thinking of them made him realize how much he had missed the mainland. Summer trips to Cultus Lake and Harrison Hot Springs, Flintstone Village / Dinotown, Alouette Lake, and fishing with his Dad by Stave Dam.

Plus, there was the hustle and bustle of Vancouver itself and the winter bliss of Whistler. He loved living on the Island, but growing up around the Fraser Valley had been wonderful. "I guess everything changes," he remarked ruefully.

She smiled as he saw the distant contemplation in his eyes. She had often thought the same thing – how everything had to change…progress no matter what the cost. But sometimes change was a good thing. It was just a matter of deciding how you were going to approach it. She was never an 'always look on the bright side of life' type of person. But she believed that things were only as bad as you were prepared to allow them to be. She squeezed his hand lovingly, bringing his attention back to her.

"Not everything," she smiled. He could see in her eyes what she was talking about and tears welled in his own eyes. A large lump filled his throat and he had to work to rid himself of it so that he could speak coherently. He hadn't realized until that moment that the thing he feared for the most wasn't losing his life; it was losing her and her love. With her assurance given, he felt the weight of the situation lift ever so gradually.

"No?" he asked.

"No." They looked longingly into each other's eyes, both trying to ease the burden that the other felt. Their attempts were thwarted by the loud speaker announcing that they were nearing Tsawassen and advising that vehicle passengers return to the vehicle deck. *Is it that time already?* they both wondered as they looked up at the loud speaker as if they could somehow see the voice behind it. They looked back down at each other, steeling themselves for the next part of this journey.

"Ready?" she asked.

"Nope," he replied. He smiled at her and together they rose and moved for the stairwell that would bring them below to their car and, hopefully, off this boat. He looked around constantly, watching for any sign of Holt. There were so many people, though, it would have been practically impossible to pick him out anyway. But still, he looked. When they reached the vehicle deck, they quickly moved to their car. Robert let Anna in first, then moved around to open his door. Movement out of the corner of his eye stopped him. He jerked up and stared towards the back of the ferry. *Was that Holt?* He only caught a glimpse and couldn't be sure. He sat down in the driver's seat and engaged the locks, gripping the wheel tightly.

"Did you see him?" Anna asked nervously.

"I'm not sure," he replied. "Might have."

"What do we do?" There wasn't really an answer that he liked for that question so he gave the only one he could.

"We wait. We wait and then we drive to Abbotsford." Nothing more could be said as they waited patiently for the ferry to dock and the cars to offload. For some reason, it took an exceptionally long time for this to be accomplished, but that always seemed to be the way of things when anticipation was strong. Finally, the rows of cars started to move and Robert eased them off the ferry and on to the mainland. Abbotsford was quite a distance to travel, but the reward that awaited them there would be worth it. He stole a quick look around to see if he could spot Vickers' men, but then thought better of it. *If they were supposed to be good enough that Holt wouldn't see them, what chance did I have?* He chuckled to himself.

"What's funny, Robbie?"

He thought about, then spoke truthfully. "I am, baby. I'm an idiot." She didn't disagree. She just smiled and patted his leg. "I know…but I love you."

"I love you too." And they headed East.

CHAPTER

6

Due to the way the cars were being discharged from the ferry, Holt actually emerged ahead of the Seabrooks. He silently cursed his misfortune as he had no idea where they might be headed. Mercifully, Highway 17 stretched for a while before any major turn-offs so he was relatively secure in his choice of general direction. The only major obstacle was if they turned South through Tsawassen itself to cross the Canada / U.S. border at Point Roberts. He was almost positive that that was not going to happen. What would be the point of going to Tsawassen and then straight South when you could just take the Clipper from Victoria to Seattle. To be on the safe side, though, he stayed in the slow lane and maintained the posted speed limit to allow them to catch up a little. Hopefully, O'Connor would be behind them so contact could be maintained. As if in response to his thoughts, his cell phone rang as O'Connor phoned him.

"Holt," he stated curtly

"It's O'Connor. Where are you?"

"Got out ahead of everyone. I'm coasting on 17 hoping you guys can catch me up. Where are you?"

O'Connor still did not trust Holt as much as he would have liked. The cramp explanation was weak at best, especially when you compared it with the timing of what had transpired back at the ferry terminal. At least Nesbitt hadn't been discovered before the trip had concluded. A police inquisition of everyone on the ferry would not have been out of the question and there were just some things he would rather not have to endure. Still, he knew he had a job to do and that job would be accomplished more easily with a second pursuit vehicle. He would have to keep an eye on Holt, though. Trust in this industry was dangerous in the best of circumstances and these were far from being the best.

"We're just coming out now. We're not too far behind them, though."

"Good," Holt replied. "Keep me posted if they turn off. I think they're gonna head towards Vancouver, but you never know."

"Will do," O'Connor said. He looked over at Mitch Waddell beside him. He was clearly still rattled by what had happened to Nesbitt. His eyes shifted as if they couldn't focus on any one particular thing and his breathing was shallow. O'Connor lightly elbowed him to get his attention. Waddell, startled, looked over at him. With a slight bow of his head in an attempt to get him to relax, O'Connor mouthed the word "breathe" to his younger partner. Waddell nodded quickly and resumed his rapid, shallow breath pattern while his leg began to vibrate and his fingers drummed a beat on his thigh. "Hold on a sec," O'Connor spoke into the hands-free device. He covered the microphone so he could focus his attention on Waddell. "Mitch," he said reassuringly. "Take a deep breath."

Waddell took that breath, exhaling quickly, and went back to fidgeting. "Waddell," he said a little more forcefully. Waddell looked over at his partner again. This time, he stopped squirming. "Take a deep breath and hold it." He nodded and took the advice proffered by O'Connor. "You're fine," he reassured. "Get a hold of yourself and you'll be fine." Waddell did and his pulse began to move back towards its regular beat. He took another deep breath and nodded his thanks, steadying himself.

"Everything all right?" Holt asked.

"We're fine," O'Connor answered. Not far from the truth really, but far enough to be considered a lie.

"So what the hell happened back there?" Holt enquired. "Your notes were... disconcerting." There wasn't really a better word to use there. He wanted to caution O'Connor about what had transpired after he had left the stall in the bathroom, but he wasn't sure if Waddell was mixed up in this. Hell, O'Connor could have had something to do with it after all. He had never left the car, sure, but that didn't mean he knew nothing about what was happening to Nesbitt. Still, he had worked with O'Connor on many occasions. He was relatively certain that he could spot a traitor even at his age and O'Connor just didn't fit the bill.

"Everything was going fine. Waddell and Nesbitt had the Seabrooks in the terminal. Nesbitt went to the bathroom. Never came out." An abbreviated version was all that was required at this point.

"Why didn't you go in?" Holt asked. "Better question – why didn't Waddell call for help?" His suspicion of Waddell was starting to rise.

"Transmitters went down." That was something Holt was not expecting to hear. Cell phones losing coverage. That he could understand, but the transmitters ran off of a radio frequency. The only way for them to go down was if the signal had been jammed. Even if Waddell or O'Connor were mixed up in this, someone else had to have jammed the frequency. They both were starting to look a little less suspicious to a now even more leery Holt.

"They were down? When?" he asked.

"Yeah they were down," O'Connor said cautiously. "Some time after Waddell left the car. That's why we had to 'Pitch Black' you. We couldn't get to you." O'Connor hesitated before he continued. He wasn't sure if he could trust Holt and didn't want to say too much. But due to the fact that his options were becoming increasingly limited, he knew he had to start somewhere. "We lost communications before we got on the ferry. It's why Waddell didn't let us know what happened in the terminal."

"Alright," Holt said, making up his mind about his two companions. "There's something else you should know. After you left the bathroom, someone in the opposite stall handed me a note as well. Basically it said to leave the Seabrooks and head home. The note also indicated that *they* were responsible for Nesbitt. 'Or else' was implied if you catch my meaning." O'Connor did.

"It's your call, Holt," O'Connor conceded. His mind was racing as he struggled to come to terms with this new development. Someone had targeted one of his team and eliminated him right under his nose. He then had the audacity to speak of it flippantly and threaten the rest of the team. Whoever this was, he was either incredibly skilled or incredibly stupid.

"We continue on," Holt said after a moment's reflection. "I've never been bullied off a file before and I'm not starting now. Hate to sound cliché, but if we quit, then Nesbitt died for nothing. Robert Seabrook is our best hope of finding Terry Philips. Philips' list of people he trusts is tiny and Seabrook is right at the top. We all need to remember what's at stake here." This was starting to turn into some kind of pep-talk, but considering the present morale it wasn't such a bad idea. "Nieto was just the tip of the iceberg. Philips is our primary concern. Seabrook is our lead to Philips. So we stay."

"Roger that," O'Connor said. It was encouraging to hear the conviction in Holt's words. They both knew what was at stake, Waddell as well. The sheer enormity of the situation was what had brought them on board in the first place. Nieto had only been part of the scenario. The next would be to find Philips.

"Watch out, though," Holt cautioned. "Whoever is on to us knows our moves – our practices. He took out Nesbitt in front of us all and they knew about Pitch Black – or at least the meeting place side of it. They're pros so we need to be at our best. You guys up for this?" Holt feared the response because he knew that his odds of closing this file alone were slim, especially if he was being hunted on top of everything else. O'Connor looked over at Waddell and asked the silent question that hung in the air between them. Waddell nodded.

"We're in," O'Connor stated just as the Seabrooks headed for a turn-off. "Shit. They're turning East on Highway 10." Holt cursed silently. He had already passed that intersection. He quickly ran through alternate routes in his mind. Luckily, there was an easy option for him.

"Okay. Stay with them. I'm gonna get on '99' and head that way. I'll probably still be ahead, but at least I'll be in the same general area." Highway 99 and Highway 10 ran parallel for a short way. Highway 10 could barely be classified as a highway at all. It was single lane traffic with stop lights. 99 was a two-lane highway that led straight to the U.S. border. *If they took Highway 10, what would be their destination? Delta? Surrey? Trans-Canada? Better keep my options open.* "I'm gonna pull off at Highway 91. That'll give me some choices when they make their next move.

"Sounds good, Holt," O'Connor said. "Be careful."

"You too." With that, Holt disconnected the call. The time to second-guess everyone had passed. He knew what his assignment was. Whatever forces were at work trying to prevent him from succeeding, they were currently out of his ability to control. Rather than spending useless hours trying to contemplate who they could be, he needed to focus on re-establishing contact with Dr. Seabrook. Whoever had spooked him had done a thorough job. The bottom line was - a scared rabbit was tougher to command. He hated the idea of someone else in control. That had to change – and fast. He drove East along Highway 99 and allowed himself a moment of calm to admire the surrounding beauty. Mt. Baker off in the distance with its rugged beauty and quiet menace (it being a volcano and sister to Mt. St. Helens). *Lord help them all if she blew.* The sun was climbing higher into the sky as it neared noon. The shadows had drawn in amongst themselves as a result. A cool breeze blew from behind him carrying the moist air from the Pacific and keeping the heat to a tolerable degree. The humidity of the Lower Mainland and Fraser Valley could be suffocating, but today it was almost perfect. *If only the Seabrooks would do something predictable* he mused.

Highway 99 bent to run parallel to Highway 10. He craned his neck to see if he could spot either his targets or O'Connor's vehicle. He knew the chances were slim as he was more than likely ahead of them, but couldn't resist the urge. As expected, they were nowhere to be seen. He'd have to trust O'Connor with this part and just wait to see where they ended up. The Seabrooks were almost definitely headed East. But without knowing their destination, trying to formulate a contingency plan seemed pointless. Canada was a big place and 99% of it was East of where they were now. He passed the overpass where Highway 10 crossed 99 and cut into the meatier part of Delta / Surrey and continued on towards 91. That highway would take him to the Alex Fraser Bridge if needed and then into New Westminster, though he doubted they would head that way. No. He figured they would try for the Trans-Canada Highway. Their options would be greatly increased from there. That highway was literally a trans-Canada highway as it stretched from coast to coast, though he doubted they were Maritime-bound.

After a few minutes along this straight stretch of highway, the turn-off for Highway 91 came into view. He took it and eased to the side of the off ramp. Luckily, there was still plenty of space for vehicles to pass by as they headed North to their respective destinations. All he had to do was wait until O'Connor called with the Seabrooks' next move. The waiting was always the hard part. Granted, it was never the part that remained with you. The nightmares, brutal images recalled from somewhere inside one's mind, and night sweats were never a result of endless hours of waiting. Those were a result of what happened when the waiting was over. Yet, in the moment, the waiting always seemed worse. Luckily for him, the wait this time was only 7 minutes. His cell phone rang.

"Holt."

"It's O'Connor. They're stickin' on 10. We just crossed 99 and we're heading into Delta." Holt closed his eyes and visualized exactly where they were. He calculated another couple of minutes and then he would head North to meet up with them on 10.

"Gotcha," Holt replied. "I'll be around 91 when you pass. We'll hook up in Surrey." Highway 10 had gone under quite the renovation over the past year or so. Once it got into Surrey and moved on to Langley, it would be a lot easier to maintain visual contact with them. That made Holt remember something that he had overlooked. "Any sign of counter-surveillance?" he asked as he looked around his own surroundings. Nothing of note had caught his eye once he had pulled over, but even he had to admit that he hadn't been paying close enough attention to rely on that.

"Not that we can see. Waddell's been pretty much wallpapering every car he can. Zip so far."

"Any sign of the RV?" Holt continued. If their transmitters were indeed being tampered with, the RV they had noted earlier would sure be a good way to camouflage a communications vehicle. At least their cell phones still worked.

"No," O'Connor responded. "One sec." Holt could hear him conferring with Waddell for a moment before he came back over the phone. "No. Waddell said there was an RV a while back, but it wasn't the same one and it pulled off at a gas station near Ladner."

"All right. Keep me posted," Holt said. "Should be re-establishing visual in a few minutes." Holt keyed off the phone and headed North on Highway 91. Highway 10 crossed almost immediately so he moved into the right lane. Up ahead, he could see the overpass and was fortunate enough to spot the Seabrooks' Camry heading East followed shortly by O'Connor. What he did not notice was that while he was moving towards the off-ramp to join the procession, a silver BMW had dipped in behind him and was closing fast.

The BMW accelerated and began to move up alongside his car as he put on his turn signal and inched towards the shoulder, preparing to exit the highway. Out of the corner of his eye, movement caused him to look out the driver's side window. What he saw made his blood run cold. The BMW had drawn even with him and instead of the passenger window, all he saw was the muzzle of a submachine gun pointed at him. The muzzle chattered as the bullets leapt from the BMW, shattering his window as he instinctively ducked and slammed on the brakes. The shards from the demolished window rained down on him and he felt a warm trickle running down the back of his neck. Sweat or blood he couldn't be sure. He could hear and feel the impact of more bullets hitting his car as his windshield exploded in a hail of glass. He wrestled with the car as his severe braking caused it to lurch to the side. Outside, he could hear the squeal of tires as the BMW driver hit his brakes hard as well.

Holt's car began making a hissing sound as steam started rising from his radiator, surely punctured during this onslaught. He nursed his crippled car to a stop and reached into his waist belt to retrieve his automatic. If the BMW had stopped, this might be more than a drive-by. He put his car in park and stole a quick glance over his dashboard to see that the BMW had indeed stopped only a few hundred feet from where he had finally ended up. He frantically looked around for alternatives. Unfortunately, his only egresses appeared to be into the highway itself or down the embankment to his right. Neither option afforded him any cover, though, as the nearest trees were quite a distance away. With no cover between him and them, he would be cut down if he even tried it. His only choice appeared to be this rental car. *Guess I won't be getting my deposit back.* Why that thought had popped into his head he wasn't sure, but he quickly dispelled it. He looked up again and saw that both the driver and the passenger who had fired at him were exiting the car. He could see the passenger reloading his firearm – an MP-5 to be precise. He surmised that the driver was likely similarly armed. He looked down at his 9mm. He knew without checking that it was fully loaded. It didn't matter. He was still heavily outgunned. He had to act now. That much was sure.

He crawled on to the floor of the passenger side and, using the only other weapon he had, reached over to press the brake and put the car back into drive. The car, leaking fluids, sputtered as he pushed down on the gas. He prayed that it could stay alive for a few more moments. No matter what the outcome, this Cobalt was beginning its final trip. The car lurched and crept forward. He pushed down on the accelerator and the crippled car slowly gathered whatever speed its dying engine could muster. Holt could hear the *thump-thump-thump* of more bullets being peppered into his car. As he had hoped, though, the shots were being concentrated on the driver's side as that was where the gunmen presumed he was. As he neared where he believed the assassins to be, he counted down. *Three….Two…One*! He popped up on the passenger side bringing his Glock up as he did so and caught the puzzled look on the face of the shooter closest to him. As he tried to sweep his MP-5 towards this new target, his forehead exploded in a mist of red as Holt's 9mm bullet found its mark. Holt quickly opened his door and leapt from the vehicle as the second shooter corrected and found his mark on the passenger side of the vehicle. Holt rolled and tumbled down the embankment at the side of the highway. Bracing his feet, he skidded to a halt and scrambled into a crouch. The Cobalt continued its doomed trip and finally shuddered to a halt amidst a hail of gunfire. Holt heard the distinctive sound of a reload in progress and sprang from his position. He raced to the top of the embankment in time to see the remaining assassin pound in the new magazine and ratchet the action. Holt brought his Glock up again and squeezed two quick rounds directly into his chest. He went down quickly and his gun fell from his hands. Holt raced towards him, his 9mm still trained on him. Other motorists slowed to see what was going on, but quickly raced away when they saw the gun.

Holt reached the downed man just as he was reaching for his radio. He kicked the walkie-talkie away and stood over him, aiming the gun at his head. Holt noticed that he was wearing a bullet-proof vest so the only injury he likely was to have was the wind being knocked out of him. He took aim and fired a shot into the gunman's knee. The man shrieked in pain. At least now he was injured. He pointed the gun back at his head.

"Who are you?" Holt commanded.

"Fuck you!" the gunman replied. Holt adjusted his aim and fired again, this time into the gunman's shoulder. Another cry of pain echoed the first.

"Who are you and who sent you?" Holt barked. "Keep in mind, I've got eight shots left and I'll use every fuckin' one of 'em." Through the pain, the man on the ground seemed to find a moment of clarity with these words.

"I was sent to take you out." That answer was simple enough. It didn't tell Holt anything, but at least he had this man convinced that he meant what he said.

"By whom?" he demanded.

"I don't know," came the reply. Holt took aim again, but the gunman continued. "No! Wait! Wait!" he pleaded. "I honestly don't know. I took the job. I don't know who hired me. I just picked up the money and came here." Holt considered this for a moment, then pressed further.

"How the hell did you know I'd be out here?" he asked.

"We didn't. We were told you'd be following this guy. Some doctor. We were told to find him and then wait for you." Another thought struck Holt.

"Where did you pick us up?" Holt could see the confusion on his face at the question. "Where have you been following us from?" The man looked indecisive so Holt moved his gun towards his other knee, making his mind up for him. In the far off distance, he could hear approaching sirens. He had a few moments, but not long.

"From the doctor's house. We've been on you since Victoria," he admitted. "But that's all I know. I swear."

"You know what?" Holt said. "I believe you." He raised his gun and pulled the trigger sending a final bullet into the forehead of the gunman lying at his feet. He reached down and fished out his wallet and keys. He grabbed the walkie-talkie and the MP-5 and ran to the final resting place of the Cobalt to gather his belongings from the trunk. He then retrieved the cell phone from the floor of the car that he had dropped at some point during the shooting and moved towards his new vehicle – at least temporarily. Holt surveyed the carnage left behind in his rear-view mirror as he moved North and was finally able to turn on to Highway 10. He doubted he would get very far in this car with the police closing in and that would have to be addressed. But first, he had to get a hold of O'Connor. If something hadn't already happened to him, it would undoubtedly be on its way. He keyed his cell phone as he pressed down on the accelerator, determined to close the gap that now existed between himself and his best chance at locating Terry Philips.

CHAPTER 7

O'Connor kept a steady distance between himself and Dr. Seabrook. With the number of traffic lights that now adorned Highway 10, it was sometimes quite a task to keep the Camry in sight. But he was being meticulous, picking his spots where it was possible to regain some of the ground lost to a particularly long red light. Luckily for him, the good doctor was not an aggressive driver. Whatever pressure that had spooked him into running in the first place had obviously been alleviated to some extent. He felt his cell phone buzz and keyed his hands-free device.

"O'Connor."

"It's Holt," came the tense reply. Something in the tone of voice coming through his earpiece told him immediately that this was not going to be a pleasant conversation. "We've got company. Watch out, they could be gunning for you."

O'Connor quickly looked over at his partner. "Heads up. There's trouble." Waddell sat up a little straighter in his seat, his eyes quickly scanning their surroundings as O'Connor gripped the wheel a little tighter. "What happened?" he asked the small microphone dangling just under his chin.

"Just traded some shots with a couple of guys on 91. If they know about me, they know about you."

"Fuck! Who the fuck is 'they'?" O'Connor asked. He was growing weary of this imposed ignorance. He didn't like not knowing what was going on. The fact that there was some person or group of people who had eliminated one of his team pretty much right under his nose was bad enough, but now they had attempted to take out the team leader as well. All of it while maintaining a strict level of secrecy. He would have been impressed had he not been on the opposite side of it all.

"I don't know," Holt replied. "But once I ditch this car, I'm gonna try and find out. Enough is enough. I got cops swinging in from all directions. I'm good for a few more minutes cuz they're probably all heading straight for 91."

"Be careful where you ditch it. Rental cars can be traced and once they find Nesbitt, they might put the two together and be able to follow our route."

"Too late for that," Holt said flatly. "Rental car's in a ditch. I'm in the shooter's 'B-mer'."

"That's no good," O'Connor observed. "The cops will trace the rental back to Victoria. Once they put that together with Nesbitt, they'll know exactly which way to head."

Holt thought about that for a moment. "True, but let's not get ahead of ourselves. We can't change what's already happened – just what will happen next. Where are you?"

"We're still on Highway 10 eastbound…approaching 152nd." Holt was dismayed at how much ground he had lost. It couldn't have been avoided and considering what he had just been through, he should have been happier to be alive than anything. But all he could think of right now was getting to O'Connor and the Seabrooks. An image of Terry Philips flashed through his mind. No. He would have to get Dr. Seabrook back under control. It was the only way to gain the information he needed.

"Alright," he spoke calmly. "I'll be in touch again when I've made up some ground. Contact me if they make a move, but I'm pretty sure they're headed for the Trans-Canada. They'll probably turn up 152nd. If they don't… if they head somewhere other than Trans-Canada, call me. If I don't hear from you, I'll assume that that's where they are."

"Uhhh…" O'Connor clearly had something on his mind, but either couldn't bring himself to say it or just couldn't find the right words.

"What?" Holt asked impatiently.

"Well," O'Connor continued. "If you think about what's just happened, there might be a different reason that I'm unable to call you." Holt thought about this for a moment, then realized what he had been alluding to. There was a chance that O'Connor and Waddell could have their own run in with a couple of shooters and things might not work out in their favour. Dead men don't make phone calls. Holt cursed himself for his lack of forethought.

"Right. Call me in 15 minutes…and be careful."

"You got it," he replied. O'Connor keyed off his phone. The windows of the car suddenly seemed to be closing in. He felt like a fish in a bowl and didn't like the feeling at all. "Mitch, I'm gonna need your best on this one. Holt just had a confrontation with a couple of shooters back on 91. He's all right, but he's a ways back. If this shit goes south…and it might…it's just us."

Waddell nodded grimly. "I won't let you down."

"Good. Keep your eyes open. Call out anything out of the ordinary. I'm gonna keep on the Seabrooks. The two men sat in silence for a while, the air between them thick with tension. They couldn't even be comforted by knowing how close they were to their destination as they didn't know where they were going. All they knew was that their target had just turned north on 152nd. It looked like Holt had been right. They were headed for the Trans-Canada. In 15 minutes, he was supposed to call Holt to update their situation. He prayed he would get that chance.

Holt found himself in a relatively affluent area of Surrey. At least the appearance of a BMW around here wouldn't attract too much attention. He knew, though, that whoever had called the police had no doubt given a description of both vehicles involved. Whether or not they had spotted the license plate was irrelevant. With the seriousness of the incident, the police would likely be stopping every silver BMW on the road.

He turned off of Highway 10 at Scott Road in search of a new vehicle. There were a lot of shopping areas here and the opportunities created were numerous. He found what he was looking for rather quickly. Pulling into an empty space, he got out and removed the license plates from the BMW. He also removed the plates from the green Caravan two rows over. He then moved further and exchanged the plates he had swiped from the minivan with the red Cavalier parked one spot over. These final plates he put back on to the Caravan. He swooped back to the BMW to gather his belongings and swiftly moved back to the Cavalier, bypassed the lock (easily enough) and punched the ignition, moving off in his new ride. The entire process had taken all of seven minutes. He was now headed east once again in a red Chevy Cavalier. If the police were looking for a silver BMW, they could have one. If the owner of the Cavalier came out and reported his car stolen, the plates wouldn't match. And to be honest, the Caravan owner wouldn't notice a thing. How often do you walk to your own vehicle and notice the license plate? It wasn't perfect, but it would provide enough of a distraction to get away from the immediate area.

He turned the radio to News 1130 to check on any developments. Aside from the usual babble, nothing of note graced the airwaves. Surely Nesbitt had been discovered by now. Either the news hadn't broken yet or it was being kept quiet. Either way, getting out of Surrey was paramount. Delta Police and the Surrey Mounties would be on high alert. His cell phone warbled and he keyed the button to accept the call.

"Holt."

"It's me." O'Connor sounded tense, but considering the situation, anything else would have been suspicious. "Looks like you were right. We're east on 104th headed for Highway 1."

"I figured. I'm too far back to even have an estimate on how long til I get up to you. You guys run into any trouble?"

"Nothing yet," O'Connor observed, emphasizing the 'yet'.

"Keep your fingers crossed. I'm gonna try and make up some time." Holt eased the gas pedal further to the floor as he calculated how much distance he had to make up. Traffic was blessedly light for a Saturday and with a shootout still resonating in the ears of the local cops, the odds of a speed trap were minimal.

"While we have a moment, I'd like to go over our plan. What do you want us to do if they stop?" the surveillance man asked. "The contingency plan we went over before revolved around them being at the house. A few things have changed since then." That was true, if not a bit of an understatement.

"Plan's still the same. We track Dr. Seabrook. Clearly we need to exert more pressure on him than we did before. Whoever got him to move pressured him with something stronger. We need to trump them. I wanna know everything he knows about Terry Philips. If he's alive, Dr. Seabrook is one of the few people he could contact. And I want Philips! If he's dead, then I want to know that too. But seeing as how he hasn't turned up yet, I find that hard to believe."

"Understood. You said trump them. How? The wife?" O'Connor asked.

"If necessary. But it's definitely an option." For a moment, Holt's vision clouded as images of 'Michelle' wandered in front of him. She still haunted him after all these years. She had been beautiful. She had been alive. Would Anna join her in his mind? Would Anna Seabrook and Michelle Thompson create an ethereal duet of torment for him? Time would have to tell. "Like I said, I want Philips. I'm done playing around with this one. It's already gone way farther than I anticipated, plus we lost a man. No. When I catch up to Dr. Seabrook, he'll cooperate quickly."

"And us?" O'Connor inquired.

"Eyes only for now. If someone tries to intercede? Shut 'em down…hard."

"Understood. I'll keep you posted if anything changes."

"Thanks, Jim," Holt said as he ended the call. He almost never used first names when on a job. The fact that he had just referred to O'Connor as Jim proved to him that the attempt on his life had rattled him more than he was currently willing to admit. His mind replayed the incident on Highway 91 and a shiver raced down his spine. He would more than likely have to manoeuvre through the minefield of post-traumatic stress once again to properly deal with his feelings, but that was becoming part of his routine. Clearly, Michelle wasn't going to leave him anytime soon. He hoped this one would.

His reverie lasted longer than he expected and before long he deftly swung his car onto 152nd Street heading north. After that, he turned left on to 104th Avenue and eventually joined up with the Trans-Canada Highway. Somewhere in the far distance, Dr. Seabrook, his wife, James O'Connor, and Mitch Waddell were playing a modified version of follow the leader. It was a game that Holt wanted to join quickly. He accelerated to 130 km/h and sped towards the Fraser Valley. His gas gauge was relatively full (a blessing) and Canada sprawled in front of him. He hoped this trip wouldn't be too far.

Robert and Anna proceeded smoothly towards their meeting in Abbotsford. They were blissfully unaware of the destruction being wrought behind them. They were also unaware of what lay ahead. Their silence was a direct result of their unease. Vickers had been a welcome addition to the day's events. His message was one of hope. And hope was what they both needed right now. Robert kept glancing over at his beautiful wife. The guilt he felt at embroiling her in all of this was tearing at his heart. After a few minutes, Anna broke the barrier that was somehow trying to establish itself between them.

"Robbie. Just say what's on your mind." Her voice held no trace of contempt or malice. No hint of accusation or exasperation. It was just…soothing.

"I'm sorry, babe." It seemed he had apologized at least ten times since they had departed their home in Victoria. "I didn't mean for any of this to happen."

"Robbie, stop. I've told you every time, you don't need to apologize. And you'd better stop before you start apologizing for apologizing so much." That caused him to laugh out loud as he had been about to do just that. She looked over at him and saw the look on his face. "You were going to, weren't you?"

"Yeah," he replied sheepishly. "Sorry," as he darted her a sideways look of mischief. She slapped him playfully on the arm.

"Look. This is almost over. Once we get to this Vickers guy, he'll give us a better understanding of where we are and what we should do." She could see her husband struggle with himself and she rested a hand of comfort on his leg. "Just be thankful that we're not alone in this anymore," as she squeezed his thigh.

He smiled at her. "I never am." He looked at her and gave her a playfully dramatic smile.

"Silly," she chided and gave his thigh a sharper squeeze. They both laughed and the burgeoning barrier between them dissipated. He took hold of her hand as they proceeded towards Abbotsford. As they approached the Sumas U.S.A. exit, he had a brief impulse to turn south and make a run for the border. Knowing that that would accomplish very little, though, he stayed on the highway. The next turn off was Whatcom Rd. As he neared it, he saw the hotel on the north side of the highway. His heart, already beating faster than normal, increased rapidly as a knot formed in the pit of his stomach. He thought he had gasped until he realized that it had been Anna. He looked over at her and saw that her placid visage had been replaced with one of pure worry. She saw the same expression on his face.

"Ready?" he asked.

"Ready as I'll ever be," came her choked reply. With that, he eased off of the highway and exited at Whatcom Rd. He turned north and they made their way to the hotel parking lot. Pulling around to the side, he slipped in to a vacant spot and turned off the ignition. They both sat there, looking straight ahead for what seemed like an eternity – neither one wanting to be the first one to move.

After a few minutes of this awkwardness, Robert turned to his wife. "I thought you said you were ready."

She smiled slightly. "I said ready as I'll ever be. Guess I'll never be ready for this," she added wryly. She curved her head towards him, her gaze penetrating deep into his soul. She didn't say anything. She didn't have to.

"I love you, too," he told her. He opened his door and stepped out, bracing for whatever might be waiting for him. If Holt was still following them, he could be anywhere. Anna also stepped out of the car and, together, they headed for the lobby. Once inside, they went straight for the front desk. Robert wasn't sure what the best way to approach the man behind the counter was. He had never asked for a room he had never reserved before. If there was no room waiting for him, he would look like a buffoon. Sometimes, though, you just had to jump in.

"Hi, there. We have a reservation," he stated confidently.

"Of course," the front desk clerk replied. He looked to be about twenty five with light brown hair and a well-maintained goatee. "And the name it's under?" he asked as his fingers began to dance on his computer keyboard.

"Seabrook." The clerk's fingers clicked away as he conjured up the necessary page information. He paused momentarily with a perplexed look on his face and appeared to restart his process. *Great*! Robert thought. *No room for us. Now what*? He thought about where he would turn if Vickers didn't show up. He was starting to panic when the clerk brought him back down to Earth.

"Yes, Mr. Seabrook. We have you in room 204." Robert tried extremely hard to stifle the shout of elation threatening to burst forth from his throat. Instead, he exhaled deeply through his nose and tried to keep his face blank. "Will you be requiring one or two keys?" he asked with a nod towards Anna.

"Ahhh…two please. Thank you." The clerk busied himself behind the counter as Robert and Anna tried to relax. After a few minutes, the clerk came back to them with their key-cards.

"There you are. Do you need help to your room?"

Robert felt like something was missing, but couldn't put his finger on it. He stammered before he realized what he had wanted to ask. "You don't need a credit card or something for the room?"

The clerk looked again at his computer screen and shook his head. "Ahhh…no. The room's already been paid for. Is there anything else you need?" Maybe things would be all right after all.

"No. Thank you." Robert took the key-cards and, hand in hand with Anna, set off to find room 204 and

Vickers. They walked hand in hand, each one of them gripping the other's hand a little tighter than normal. As if sensing this in each other at the same moment, they looked at each other and smiled.

"Things will be all right, won't they?" Anna asked as they neared Room 204. Robert gave her a reassuring smile.

"We're gonna be okay, babe. I promise." He wasn't entirely sure he believed that promise, but there just wasn't any sense in making her mood worse by verbalizing his own doubts about what their future held. To be honest, he wasn't even sure how long a future he had. If Holt was as dangerous as Vickers had led him to believe, then his future might end before the sun set. Thoughts of a setting sun brought him back to the last time he had stood upon the Breakwater waiting for Holt. *God, was that only yesterday?* So much had happened in the last 24 hours that he could scarcely believe it. He shook himself out of his reverie and focussed instead on Room 204. They had reached the door.

Pulling his key card from its sleeve, he inserted in to the slot. The light by the handle flashed from red to green and he pulled the handle. Opening the door just a crack, he glanced at Anna and gave her a brief nod. "Here we go."

He pushed open the door and the two of them stepped inside. He was fully expecting to see Vickers and at least one or two other people inside waiting. All they found was an empty room. Not empty as in there was no furniture, there was just no one inside. He paused, wondering if he had indeed found the correct room. Anna, also having the same expectation, checked the number on the door.

"Where is he?" she asked simply.

"No idea. Should we wait?" Robert started to run through their alternatives in his head. None of them seemed to be particularly appealing.

"Don't see what choice we have," Anna decided as she moved past him into the room. Robert closed the door behind her and moved to check out the full extent of their room. It wasn't extravagant by any stretch of the imagination, but they were not here for the amenities. It was a decent room in a nice hotel. He could see himself staying here with Anna the next time they came to the mainland to visit her brother Peter in Chilliwack.

Anna sat on the bed and took off her shoes. She stretched her toes luxuriously, letting a small sigh escape. She put her hands flat on the bed behind her and leaned back allowing some of the tension to leave her. "So now what?" she asked.

As if in reply, the phone beside the bed rang causing both of them to jump. She instinctively reached over to grab it, then reconsidered as she looked over her shoulder at her husband. "They'll probably want to speak with you," she said. He nodded glumly and walked the few steps to the phone. He lifted the receiver, clearing his throat as he did so.

"Hello?"

"Dr. Seabrook," came the voice over the phone. "Good to see you made it. It's Vickers." Robert stifled the urge to fire back with a snippy 'who else would it be'. He realized that it was the stress of the situation causing him to want to snap at anyone and everyone. He had even been brusque with Anna and that had been something new and abhorrent. He looked down at her beautiful face as she watched him on the phone. She smiled that smile of hers. He knew he would have to make that up to her. If given the chance, he would.

"We're here. Where are you? We expected you'd be waiting for us."

"We are," Vickers replied. I'm downstairs on my way up. I have a couple of agents with me. We waited down here to see if you were being followed."

"And are we?" Robert wasn't sure what he wanted the answer to be. Obviously, he didn't like the idea of Holt following them all the way to the Fraser Valley, but the thought of leading him into an ambush with Vickers pulling the trap shut was worth entertaining.

"No. Not as far as we could tell." *Damn*.

"Well that's good. We'll wait for you here?"

"Yes. Just stay in the room. We're almost there."

"How close are you?" Robert asked. He couldn't keep the anxiety out of his voice and he cursed himself privately for that. A knock at the door made his heart flutter.

"That close enough for you? We're right outside."

"Fantastic. Bye." He hung up the phone and started for the door. Anna grabbed his arm as he passed her.

"Who is it?" she asked.

"It's Vickers." He saw the worried look on her face and smiled reassuringly. "He's here to help, babe."

"How can you be sure it's him? Look through the peephole first."

"Babe, it's him. Besides, I don't know what he looks like. What good will looking through the peephole do?"

he asked with a smile on his face. She gave him a soft jab in the ribs.

"Just look, okay?"

"Okay." He crossed the room to the door and peered out into the hallway through the peephole. He saw four people in the hallway. They appeared to be waiting patiently. "There's 4 of 'em. One of them is a woman," he whispered. Even with his liberal views and progressive thinking, for some reason he had assumed they would all be men. Guess that mentality was still prevalent when crunch time hit. He turned to Anna. "I'm lettin' them in." She nodded her approval.

Robert opened the door for his visitors. "Dr. Seabrook?" the man at the front of this small cluster said as he extended his hand. "I'm Colin Vickers." Robert shook the man's hand and invited him in. Vickers gave a nod to the rest of his flock and they all entered the room. "It's a pleasure to finally put a face to the voice," Vickers continued.

"Likewise. This is my wife, Anna." She had risen from the bed and put her shoes back on as she moved next to her husband. She reached out her hand which Vickers shook emphatically.

"It's nice to meet you, Mrs. Seabrook, though I do wish that we were meeting under different circumstances."

"As do I," she agreed. The other individuals who had accompanied Vickers moved around the room, checking the windows, the bathroom, and possibly every nook and cranny imaginable. Anna's expression turned to one of concern as she watched this odd ballet.

"Don't worry about them," Vickers added noticing her unease. "It's standard." Anna nodded involuntarily. She would have to take his word on what was considered standard. After a few moments, each of them in turn called "Clear."

"Good," Vickers said as he clapped his hands together. "Dr. Seabrook? Mrs. Seabrook? Allow me to introduce my team. David Heath, Jeremy Olson, and Giselle Raeburn." Handshakes were exchanges all around. "Now for the tough part," he continued. "I'm going to need you both to strip."

Both Robert and Anna's eyes flew wide as they each struggled to understand what Vickers had said. Anna was the first to regain the power of speech.

"You want us to w-what?" she stammered.

"Strip. Completely."

Robert found his voice. "Listen, Vickers, I don't care what government agency you work for, but my wife is not taking off her clothes for anyone. Neither am I."

"Dr. Seabrook. I understand your feelings, but you must understand where I'm coming from. Bottom line is you've had contact with Holt. Right now, I trust you… to a point. But in order for us to continue, I need to know precisely what – if anything- was introduced to the situation."

"Introduced?" Robert asked. "I don't understand what you mean."

"Wires. Other types of recording devices. Tracking devices. See where I'm going with this?" he asked patiently. Robert did see, and once again realized how out of his element he truly was.

"Bugs," Anna interjected.

"Exactly," Vickers replied. "I knew this precaution would come up so I brought Agent Raeburn here to allow you, Mrs. Seabrook, to have a woman conduct the search. You can go in to the bathroom if you like." Robert looked from his wife to Vickers and then back again.

"Is this really necessary? Holt never touched me." *Or did he?*

"I'm afraid it is." Vickers looked over at Agent Raeburn. "Giselle, if you would be so kind?" he asked, motioning towards the bathroom door.

Agent Raeburn nodded at Anna as she passed. "It will be fine. It will hurt me more than it does you." Anna smiled at the attempt at humour, then with a shrug of resignation towards her husband, she followed Agent Raeburn into the bathroom. She had never exposed herself to a woman before (unless you counted high school change rooms). Today was a day just full of firsts.

When the door had closed, Vickers turned to Robert. "Your turn, Doc."

To say that he was uncomfortable with this was putting it mildly. No matter how hard he tried, Robert couldn't get that damned "Stripper" song out of his head as he removed his clothes. He looked at the floor rather than at the three sets of eyes he was sure were boring into him. He moved as quickly as he could in a vain effort to limit the length of humiliation. To the agents' credit, they were completely professional. Once naked, Heath got him to run his fingers through his hair, open his mouth, and show him the bottoms of his feet. He paused when Heath asked him to lift his scrotum and again when he told him to turn around and touch his toes. *Seriously?* After that, he was allowed to put his clothes back on.

"That wasn't so bad, was it?" Vickers asked.

"Says the man with his clothes on," Robert replied.

"Sorry bout that. Please, have a seat." Vickers indicated the bed as he took the chair from the small bureau the room afforded. Heath and Olson remained standing. "We need to discuss our next move."

"Sounds good," Robert agreed.

"Okay. First, I would like to get Anna out of here." Robert's blood ran cold as the thought of his wife not being by his side gripped his heart.

"What? Why?"

"Dr. Seabrook – can I call you Robert?" He nodded his approval. "Robert, I don't know how many people are following you. The bottom line is, though, they are following you. They're not following her. We need to get her away from here so she can be safe. Right now, she is your greatest strength but also your greatest weakness. If someone decides they need to make a move, she'd be an easy target. Let's face it – if someone grabbed her, I think you'd pretty much do anything to get her back, right?" Robert's face was grim, but the truth was evident.

"Right."

"So we can't let them take that chance. She's gotta go. My people will guard her and keep her safe, but I'm not going to force you…or her. I need both of you to be on board. The last thing I need is for her to make some damn fool attempt to get back to you. That'll just throw any contingency plan we have right out the window. But I need you to agree."

Robert weighed the options. Getting her out and safe was his number one concern. Whatever happened to him was irrelevant. She had to be safe. "I'll agree. She's gonna fight."

"I know," Vickers conceded. "That's why I wanted to talk to you first and alone. I'm not gonna be able to convince her. You have to. It's for her own good, but it's also for yours." Robert seemed to consider this further for a few moments before Vickers continued. "I know it's asking a lot. I can't even begin to understand what you must be feeling right now. But look at it logically. As you can see, I do not have the luxury of a large team of agents at my disposal and it takes fewer agents to protect someone at a stationary point, like a safe-house. Right now, we're very mobile. I want to put Anna in a safe-house with a couple of agents watching over her so that you and I can take care of this mess ourselves. I want her safe… and so do you."

"I'll get her to go with you," Robert said. "I'm not sure how, but I'll get her to do it." He truly had no idea how he was going to start that conversation, or end it for that matter. He had visions of having to resort to physically restraining her and heaving her into the back of a van inside a laundry bag. He'd like to avoid that…but that would be up to her. And there was the very distinct possibility that she just would not go. What his next course of action would be if that occurred was beyond his grasp. *Hope for the best.*

"Is there anything I can do to help?" Vickers asked politely.

Robert shook his head. "Not really. Although, could you wait in the hall while I talk with her? I have a feeling that your guys' presence might make it tougher."

Vickers considered this for a moment. "We can do that. We'll be right outside in the hall. Just let us know when you're ready." He motioned towards Heath and Olson who, in turn, proceeded out in to the hall. "If it will make a difference in her decision, let her know that I am willing to send Agent Raeburn with her. In my experience, women tend to feel more comfortable dealing with us when a female agent is around."

"It might. I'll let her know."

As if on cue, Anna and Agent Raeburn exited the bathroom. Anna seemed tense, but that was to be expected after having been made to strip in front of a stranger. She moved right to Robert and they embraced, holding each other tightly. Over Anna's shoulder, Robert saw Vickers whisper something to Raeburn who nodded and joined her colleagues in the hall. Vickers mouthed the words "right outside" and then he too left the room leaving Anna and Robert to themselves.

Anna felt the sense of solitude and glanced around. "Where did they go?"

"They're waiting out in the hall. Have a seat. We have something we need to discuss."

"I don't like the sound of that," Anna said as she reluctantly sat on the bed. What's going on?"

"I spoke with Vickers while you were in the bathroom…how did that go by the way?"

"Oh swimmingly," she replied. "I was thinking of getting her number in case, you know, we don't work out."

Robert smiled. "Sorry. If it makes you feel any better, I went through the same thing. And mine had an audience."

"It doesn't. The only thing that will make this feel better is for it to end. Did Vickers tell you how it will?"

"Not exactly. But he did talk to me about what our next move should be and before I tell you what it is, I must let you know that I agree with him." Robert sat down beside his wife and took her hand in his. She squeezed it tightly causing him to smile again. She was fierce, and tender.

"What's the plan?" she asked nervously.

"Holt is after me. That much we know. And we know why, well mostly. It has something to do with my patient. Whatever information Holt thinks I have, he will try to get from me." He took a deep breath before continuing. "Vickers made it very clear to me that Holt will use whatever he can to force me to co-operate with him. That includes using you to get to me."

Anna looked at him with concern. She wasn't sure exactly where he was going with this, but she didn't like the general direction. Before she could voice her worry, he continued.

"Vickers and I figure it'll be safer if they take you to a safe-house and…"

"Are you insane!?" Anna exploded. "I'm not going anywhere and I'm sure as shit not leaving your side while you go through this. How could you even suggest such a thing?"

"Vickers figures…"

"Oh, fuck Vickers!" Robert startled at her ferocity. He knew she wouldn't be thrilled about the idea being presented to her, but hadn't expected this. "Look, I appreciate him stepping in and helping us out cuz Lord knows we need it, but if he or you think that there's any chance in hell you're gonna shuttle me away to some quiet little corner you're both sadly mistaken." She crossed her arms and set her eyes hard. The bright green had turned a shade darker as she steeled herself for any attempt to persuade her further.

"Babe," he said softly. Her shoulders relaxed slightly for a moment, then resumed their rigidity. "Babe," he spoke again.

"What?"

"I don't want you to go. Hell, I prayed that you wouldn't. Vickers thinks it will be safer and he's probably right. But I need you with me. I need your strength. I can't do this on my own – even with Vickers' help." He moved closer to her and put his arms around her pulling her close. She held him tightly and breathed deeply. They rested their foreheads against each other. "I never realized how much strength I get from you til now." She smiled. "I mean I would just be so lost without you."

"You don't give yourself enough credit," she replied. "I think you'd manage."

"Maybe. But I wouldn't be happy. Let's face it. I wouldn't even know how to dress myself." That brought a small chuckle from both of them.

"You would too. Maybe not well, but you'd be clothed." Robert leaned back a little to look into her eyes. The breath-taking emerald colour had returned and replaced the hard-edged jade from earlier. They stared deep into each other's eyes, engaging in a silent conversation that words would have sullied. At the end, she voiced the simple end to the complex problem. "I'm not leaving."

"I know. But we should probably tell Vickers." Robert stood and walked to the door. One fight was over and another was about to begin. He wasn't sure if he had won or lost the first one. In his heart, he had wanted her to stay, but he had also wanted her to go. *She's here with me. No matter what else comes, that means I win.*

CHAPTER 8

Holt was satisfied with his progress so far. Traffic had been remarkably favourable and he hadn't had any run-ins with any speed traps. While he would have liked to enjoy some good music for this trip, he had been tuned to News 1130 awaiting news of the shootout or even of Nesbitt back in Swartz Bay. He was on borrowed time in this vehicle, but that was a necessary risk. He had lost too much time already. As he neared Abbotsford, he was in the middle of pondering what the Seabrooks' destination might be when his cell phone rang.

"Holt," he said once the call had connected.

"It's O'Connor." Holt let out the breath he hadn't realized he had been holding. There was no tension in O'Connor's voice. Things might actually be returning to order. "They're at the Clarion Hotel in Abbotsford by the Whatcom exit." Holt quickly visualized what he knew of the area.

"Are you set?" Holt asked.

"As well as we can be. The approach to the hotel is too open so we're by the overpass."

"What about the amusement park area?" Holt asked referring to Castle Fun Park.

"No good. The building is too far from the hotel and the parking lot is actually lower down and pretty obscured. We lucked out a little, though. There is a house by the off-ramp on the South side of the highway. Nobody's home so we're parked in the driveway. Because of the elevation of the ramp, we got a pretty good view of the hotel from here. They went in. Haven't seen anyone come out yet."

The house on the South side was fortunate for sure. One of the few breaks that had gone their way. Hopefully it would not be the last.

"Okay. Stay put and eyes on. I'm approaching Abbotsford and will be there in about 10 minutes. We'll decide on our course then."

"Sounds good," O'Connor replied.

"Any hiccups on the way?" Holt asked. Just because he sounded calm, didn't mean that he was.

"Not a one. Me and Waddell had a smooth ride all the way." That struck Holt as odd. Either the people who had tried to eliminate him didn't know about O'Connor or they knew about him and just hadn't made their move yet.

"Keep alert. Something may still be on the way." He knew he didn't have to tell them to be careful, but he did it anyway. He ended the call and pushed his car closer to 140 kp/h. Whatever the Seabrooks were planning on doing, he intended on being there.

Robert brought Vickers and his team back into the room. Vickers could tell by the look on Anna's face that the conversation had not gone the way he had hoped.

"You know I'm going to have to convince you to go," he said to Anna. She looked surprised at how easily he had read her countenance. Apparently she thought she was a better actress.

"You can try," she replied flatly. "But it won't work. I'm staying with him." Vickers looked at Robert, silently asking for assistance. But he could see that help would not be coming from him.

"I can see you're both in agreement." He exhaled deeply as he contemplated what to do next. "Honestly, I could sit here and try to turn you both around but I have a feeling that that would be a pointless endeavour." Both of them nodded together. "Of course you both have to realize the risks that you are taking."

"We understand them," Robert answered. "But the bottom line is…whatever we go through, we'd prefer to go through it together. If she was taken somewhere, I wouldn't be able to focus on anything. I'd be too worried about her."

Anna moved beside him and squeezed his hand. "Besides, if we were apart and anything were to happen to him, I don't care what government agency you work for. You'd answer to me."

Vickers studied her critically. "I believe I would," he said. He had to admit, he had underestimated Anna Seabrook. He had made the assumption that she was a woman who would stick by her guns for a time and then step aside. He had not considered her an obstacle or even a wrinkle worthy of note. He vowed to himself that he would not make that mistake again. Making up his mind, he continued. "Alright, you stay. But I do need to discuss a few things with your husband in private."

"I'm not going back in that bathroom if that's what you have in mind."

Vickers stifled a laugh. "No. No. No more bathrooms. But you must be hungry. I was thinking you could go down to the restaurant and grab some food for yourself. I believe there is a White Spot at the end of the building. I can send Raeburn and Olson with you."

Anna felt her stomach grumble at the mention of food and looked at her husband for approval. "Go ahead, babe."

"I'll bring you back something if you want," she offered.

"Won't be necessary, Mrs. Seabrook," Vickers interjected. "We'll be down to join you in a few minutes. Just get a table for all six of us."

"Okay, then," she said. "You sure?" she asked turning to Robert.

"Positive," he answered. He pulled her against him and kissed her. She patted him on the bum and headed out into the corridor with the two agents behind her.

"Good woman you have there," Vickers commented.

"The best," he replied. "So what did you want to talk to me about?" Robert moved back to the bed and sat down as Vickers took his seat at the small table provided in the room.

"Robert. It's time for you to be notified of exactly what's been going on and the people involved. You'll have a clearer picture of what's at stake and what's ahead."

"I'd appreciate that cuz I have to admit, I don't much care for being led around by the nose."

"That's understandable. Come have a seat," Vickers motioned towards the empty seat at the table. "I'll show you where we're at. Heath, hand me that pad and pen." The remaining agent handed Vickers the requested items. "I'll take you back to the beginning." Just as he was to start, though, his cell phone rang. "Damn. Excuse me." Vickers answered the phone, listened for a few minutes, then looked up at Robert. "Sorry to do this Dr. Seabrook, but I need to take this and it's private. Would you mind…" Vickers considered himself for a moment, then changed his mind. "You know what? You've been inconvenienced enough. I'm just gonna step out in the hall to take this." Robert nodded and Vickers headed out the door leaving Robert and Agent Heath alone.

"Duty calls, huh?" he asked Heath.

"Always," Heath replied.

Holt rounded the bend past the Sumas border crossing exit and the Clarion Hotel came in to view. *Still no additional word from O'Connor so the Seabrooks should still be here.* He was glad to have made up the distance that he had. Nearing the Whatcom exit, he spotted the house that O'Connor had mentioned and smiled when he saw O'Connor's car parked in the driveway. He keyed his cell phone. O'Connor answered on the first ring.

"O'Connor."

"It's me. I have you in sight. I'll be there in two." He figured he would just hop into O'Connor's car and leave this vehicle in the driveway. The owners of the house might have some questions to answer about a stolen vehicle found in their driveway, but that wasn't really his concern.

"Which car are you?" O'Connor asked.

"The Cavalier coming up the ramp now."

"Yeah, I got you. Any further trouble?" O'Connor didn't like the idea that someone was indeed gunning for them. He especially didn't like the idea that Holt might be leading any further attempts right to him. But at this point, regrouping was necessary.

"Nothin' yet. We'll talk more when I'm in the car." O'Connor watched as Holt reached the end of the ramp. Two quick rights and he was heading towards them, pulling in alongside. He quickly stepped out of the Cavalier, bringing his belongings with him and what appeared to be a firearm of some type. O'Connor popped the trunk and Holt threw in his gear and climbed into the back seat.

"Travelling light I see," O'Connor quipped. Holt shot him a look, but O'Connor continued. "Was that an MP-5 I saw?"

"Indeed. Courtesy of my welcoming committee." A small smile played at the corner of Holt's mouth. "Unfortunately, they couldn't stay."

Waddell half-turned in his seat extending his hand. "Glad you're still with us." Holt shook the proffered hand.

"You and me both. So what's the situation?"

"Like I said before," O'Connor began. "They went in. Haven't come back out. If they're meeting someone, they were either here already or they haven't arrived yet cuz there's hardly been any traffic in or out with the exception of the restaurant."

"Anything there?" Holt inquired.

"No sign of them yet if that's where they're headed. We were thinkin' it might be our way in, though. If people are lookin' for us to go for the hotel, we might be able to squeak through with a trip to the restaurant instead."

"It's not just a hotel restaurant then?" Holt asked.

"No. It's a regular White Spot that's attached to the hotel. Lots of people go there who don't stay at the hotel."

"Okay. That's how we approach then. Seeing it now, though, we should probably take the Cavalier."

Waddell took this opportunity to join the conversation. "Why is that?"

"Well," Holt explained. "I figure if whoever we're dealing with knew what I was driving when they tried to take me out, then they might know about you guys too and what you're driving. I'm pretty sure I wasn't followed when I scooped the Chevy."

"Pretty sure?" O'Connor asked dubiously.

"Yeah, like I was pretty sure when I woke up this morning that I wouldn't be dodging bullets from two fucking assassins in Delta in broad daylight. Suffice it to say, this day has been anything but routine." O'Connor thought about that for a few seconds, then relented.

"Okay. We'll take the Cavalier. Wanna grab your crap from the back?" he asked as he popped the trunk again. Waddell started packing up the few items that he and O'Connor had in their car to move over to Holt's vehicle. O'Connor stepped out and stretched while Holt retrieved the MP-5 and his bag from the trunk and shuffled it back to the Cavalier. He hadn't thought of the possible vehicle identification and cursed himself silently for the oversight. It had been caught in time, but it should have been addressed before now. With the Cavalier comfortably burdened with its extra passengers, Holt set off for the hotel.

"We'll go straight to the White Spot. There might even be an access to the hotel from inside the restaurant."

"That'd be nice," O'Connor added as he adjusted his shoulder strap that held his Beretta. Waddell in the back rechecked his Beretta, then tucked it neatly by the small of his back. Holt's Glock rested snugly near his heart... the heart that he noted had increased in tempo. *At least it still gets the old juices flowing.* The MP-5 remained in the trunk. Holt crossed the overpass and turned left at the traffic light. His pulse quickened even further as the hotel came into view. He passed Castle Fun Park and swung into the parking lot of the Ramada hotel narrowly avoiding a delivery truck that was heading out. Holt waved apologetically to him, but the driver didn't even seem to notice. *Guess he wasn't paying attention. Then again, neither was I.*

"You okay up there?" Waddell chided.

"Yeah," Holt answered ruefully. "Just eager." But as he pulled into the parking stall, he realized that it was more than that. The three of them stepped out into the cool afternoon, O'Connor pulling on a light coat to cover his shoulder holster. Holt looked around the parking lot, then studied it again. O'Connor noticed his apprehension and tensed.

"Everything all right?" he asked.

"Not sure," came the simple reply.

"Feel like we're being watched or something?" Waddell contributed. Holt thought about that for a moment.

"No. That's not it. It's something else." All three of them studied the parking lot again, looking for anything out of the ordinary. O'Connor sensed it as well. Something *was* off.

"Your call, Holt," he stated. Holt thought for a few minutes. There had been a change somewhere. If the Seabrooks were meeting people, then the meeting had either occurred or it was occurring. He could almost smell it. No. the time to move was now.

"Fuck the restaurant. We're going in." Holt strode across the parking lot with O'Connor and Waddell following right behind. All of them scanned everything that moved and all that didn't. Whoever they were dealing with had no difficulty trading shots in broad daylight so they had to be prepared for anything. They made the lobby and split up. Waddell stayed by the door while O'Connor moved to a cover position on the left. Holt headed for the front desk. The young man behind the counter smiled as he approached.

"Welcome to the Clarion Hotel. How may I help you?" he asked politely.

Holt smiled. "I'm wondering if you have a Dr. Seabrook staying here. I have a message for him." The front desk clerk looked down at his computer screen and typed in the requisite information.

"Dr. Seabrook is in fact here. If you'd like to leave the message with me, I'll be glad to make sure that he gets it." His smile was genuine. *Probably likes his job.*

"Actually I need to deliver the message personally. IF you could give me his room number, I'll just pop up and tell him myself." Holt knew that there was no way the clerk would divulge that information, but it was the song and dance that had to be performed sometimes to move people into the position you needed them in. Besides, there was the slim chance that this guy was new or unequivocally incompetent. In this case, neither was true.

"I'm sorry, sir," the clerk replied. "I can't give out that information. If you'd like, I can call his room to see if he's in and get him to come down to meet with you." The clerk reached for the phone. Holt stopped him.

"That won't be necessary." Holt looked down at the clerk's nametag. "Matt. I can't get into specifics, but it is imperative that I find Dr. Seabrook immediately. It is a security matter and the longer I take bickering with you, the more dangerous the situation becomes." Holt could see the scepticism cross the clerk's face and his own patience was starting to wear thin. He had expected this exact response from the clerk. But with the circumstances being what they were, this was going to end badly.

"Sir, that very well may be. But there is just no way…" Holt reached over the counter and grabbed Matt by the collar bringing his other hand to the back of his head. He slammed the stunned clerk's head against the counter, shattering the young man's nose. He still held his collar as the clerk struggled to right himself.

"Listen you little retard. This is not a fuckin' request. Room number. Now!" Holt heard some movement in the office behind the clerk and figured that Matt was not working alone. He motioned for O'Connor who quickly closed the distance to the counter to deal with anyone else who might want to join the fray.

Sure enough, a middle-aged woman came out from the back to see what the commotion was. What she saw was not what she had been expecting. Her co-worker, his face oozing blood, was in the clutches of a man reaching over the counter and a second man was pointing a gun at her. Her initial thought was to make a move for the panic button. *Not my first robbery.* But there was something different about this one; something that chilled her blood and caused her not to make a move. She couldn't place it at first, but then she realized what it was. There was no panic on either of the men's' faces; no indecision in their eyes. The man holding the gun motioned towards her.

"Don't try anything. I guarantee my bullet moves faster than you do."

"We don't carry much money," she uttered staring at the barrel pointed at her.

"Not interested. This isn't a robbery," Holt added. "We need information and since Matt here," he shook the clerk as he said his name "wouldn't provide it, we're gonna need you to retrieve it for me. Looks like his vision might be hampered a bit."

"What do you need?" she asked. The easiest way to survive these scenarios was to do whatever they wanted. Those stupid safety refresher courses had taught her that.

"Room number. Robert Seabrook." She moved to the computer as Holt dragged a slumping Matt to the side. She typed in a few characters. There was a panic button just by her leg, but she decided not to press it. She wanted to see her family again and felt that not pressing any alarms would offer the best chance of that happening. What she feared the most was travellers coming in or out of the lobby. Then, the dynamic would change and all bets would be off. So far, they had been lucky.

"He's in Room 204," she said flatly.

"Thank you," Holt replied. He let go of Matt who sank to the floor, his hands covering the pulpy mass that used to be his nose. "Like my partner here said, don't try anything. He'll stay and keep you company should either one of you decide to be a hero." O'Connor moved to the corner of the desk so he could best keep an eye on the two hotel workers. Holt strode quickly across the lobby heading for the stairs. "You're with me," he called, looking at Waddell. Leaving his post by the door, Waddell quickly caught up to Holt and together they moved up to the second floor.

Robert came out of the bathroom after fulfilling one of life's necessities and sat back down at the table. He looked over at Heath and smiled. The agent gave the faintest hint of a smile, then resumed his stern gaze over the room. *"This is awkward,"* he thought. *Maybe some small talk.*

"Been with C.S.I.S. long?" he asked.

Heath shrugged. "Long enough."

Cryptic. No open-ended answer to expand upon. Try an open-ended question. "What do you like best about the job?" No matter what the answer, Robert felt he could at least come up with a follow-up question.

"The silence," Heath replied tersely. So much for that follow-up question. He was just starting to summon the courage to attempt another avenue when there was a light knock on the door.

"I'll get it!" Robert shouted. He hadn't meant to shout, but the relief he felt for Vickers' return triggered the outburst. He moved to the door and opened it. He paused momentarily as his brain fought to reconfigure itself after the shock of what affronted him. Vickers was not at the door. This man was…familiar, though. The recognition was on his face as well. Then it clicked. *HOLT!* Holt smiled as he pushed Robert out of the way. He levelled the gun he had been holding at Agent Heath and pulled the trigger. The agent was reacting, but he had been expecting Vickers as well and was caught unprepared. It would be the last mistake he ever made. His head snapped back as the impact from the 9mm bullet threw him backwards. Blood splattered on the wall behind him and he fell to the ground in a heap, his own firearm slipping from his grip. Robert stumbled backwards and fell on to the bed as Holt advanced into the room. His head still echoed from the sound of the gunshot. Added to the fact that his mind was reeling from what had just transpired, he was now stampeding towards unconsciousness. A second man entered the room with his gun drawn. Both men swept the room looking for other people. The second man went to

Agent Heath's body. He picked up the fallen agent's gun and stowed it by his waist.

Robert struggled to keep his composure. He blinked furiously to try and clear the spots dancing in front of him. He wanted to scream, but couldn't seem to find the strength. He wanted to speak, but all the words in his vocabulary seemed to be as afraid as he was because they were nowhere to be found. He started to gasp as even his breath was trying to run. He saw Holt moving towards him. He tried to bolt for the door, but his legs were almost useless. He fell to the floor and began crawling for freedom. Holt was on him in moments. He jerked him off the floor and threw him back on to the bed.

"Where the hell do you think you're going?" Holt demanded.

"HELP!" Robert shouted, finally finding his voice. Holt moved again and slapped him hard across the face. Searing pain shot through Robert's head and the spots danced harder.

"Shut up, asshole. Scream again and you'll regret it." Robert shook his head to try and clear the cobwebs. Holt must have thought he was saying no because he slapped him again. "You think I'm kidding?"

Robert put his hand up. "No. No. I…I…" He was starting to lose it. "I think I'm gonna be sick." Holt looked at him disbelievingly, but changed his mind when Robert pitched off the bed and vomited on the floor.

"Jesus. What did you eat?" Holt asked with a smile in his voice.

Robert stayed on his hands and knees, swaying slightly. "What have you done? Jesus Christ what have you done?"

"Try and relax, Doctor. It was necessary. Do you have any idea what kinda shit I've had to go through to get to you?" Holt was bordering on anger as he looked back upon the day that had been.

"You killed him. You fuckin' killed him."

"Course I killed him. Trust me, he would have done the same. It's no big loss."

The callousness of that answer drove Robert to action. He leapt up and lunged at Holt, swinging wildly with all of his might. Holt deftly side-stepped the assault and dropped Robert with a solid punch to the stomach. He had never been hit so hard in his life and the breath exploded out of him as he crumpled to the floor.

"You lost your fuckin' mind?" Holt asked incredulously. "Stay down. It'll be easier for both of us." Robert gasped for air as his insides lurched. The smell of gunpowder was still in the air and the thought of what lay on the other side of the room almost made him wretch again. "Where's your wife?"

The question had Robert stumped for a moment. He then realized that he had assumed that Holt had taken her. *Thank God she's safe. Thank God Vickers got her out.* Then, his thoughts switched to Vickers. *He must certainly be dead. This bastard killed the only help we had.* He took breath, finally and managed to squeak one word. "Gone."

Robert took a deeper breath as he started to feel more human again. "I mean gone, you Fuck. She's safe and she's away from you." A smile crossed his face as he finally had something on this prick. He wanted Anna and she was out of his reach with nothing he could do about it. *Take that.* He tried to stand, but his body convinced him otherwise. Instead, he crawled back on to the bed.

"Dr. Seabrook. I recommend that you start talking… and fast."

"Or what?" he chided with mock bravado.

"Or else I'll smack you with something a lot harder than my head." Robert looked at Holt who was holding his gun by the barrel, pointing the stock at him with an evil smile on his face. Robert's head throbbed at the mere notion of what was coming. *What's the harm in telling him a little? She's out of his reach now.*

"C.S.I.S has her…and there ain't a damn thing you can do about it!"

"C.S.I.S? What the hell are they involved for?" Holt asked. He looked at his partner who merely shrugged in reply.

"Oh you don't know?" Robert asked mockingly. He was starting to like the feeling of getting one up on this Holt. "Well one of their agents contacted me after our little meeting in Victoria. He told me all about you. He told me you'd kill me." His thoughts drifted to Anna. He wanted to see her again. He wanted so badly to tell her that things would be all right and that he loved her very much. He wanted to tell her that she was the best thing that had ever entered his life. But he resigned himself to simply wishing that she knew all that. "Well. Here I am. Kill me, you bastard! And burn in hell while you're at it!"

"I'm not going to kill you, you moron. If I wanted you dead, I would have done it in Victoria. What agent?"

"Oh right. I forgot. You want to know about Terry Philips first. Well forget it. I'm not telling you anything. The only leverage you had was Anna and she's safe now so you got nothing."

"What agent?" Holt repeated.

"What?" Robert asked.

Holt was starting to get frustrated. "Open your ears, you dumb shit. I said what agent contacted you?" Robert thought about not giving him the name, but he wanted to see the look on Holt's face when he revealed the name of the agent who had bested him.

"His name was Vickers. And he beat you, you morbid son of a bitch." Robert had never cursed so much in his life, he realized. But he also knew that what he felt for this man standing before him was pure hatred. There was no reason to censor himself.

"Vickers???" The look that crossed Holt's face was not one of resignation, however. Robert noticed it was more like horror. Holt's mind began to race as he filtered everything that had happened today through his mind. This new information changed a great deal of things.

"Yes, Vickers. He's the guy you undoubtedly killed in the hall before you shot Agent Heath there," he added, pointing to the body in the corner. "Or do you even care that you just killed two federal agents?"

"What did Vickers tell you?" Holt asked, a little more patiently. Robert took this as a sign that Holt's resolve was weakening so he figured he'd show precisely how much he had been privy to.

"He told me you used to be with C.I.A. He told me you're a mercenary now, working for whoever pays you the right amount. So who hired you to kill me, huh? How much are they paying you?"

"So Vickers is C.S.I.S and I'm a mercenary. Is that right?" Holt asked.

"You bet your ass. So what now?" Robert demanded, brimming with confidence.

"What now is that it's time for you to wake up." Holt took a step forward and lowered his face to meet Robert's, eye to eye. "I'm no mercenary and I'm not ex-C.I.A. I'm current. And he is not, nor was he ever with C.S.I.S." he said with a nod to his partner. "And there was no one out in the hall. You pal Vickers is gone and by the sounds of it, he has your wife. I don't know who you thought you were dealing with, but I can guarantee one thing. Colin Vickers has never worked a day for the Canadian government."

The weight of what Holt had just said felt like a vice squeezing the life out of him. His mind started to spin and whir like some deranged machine caught up in a tornado. He looked at Holt for something, anything to focus on to avoid what was coming.

"It's time you told me everything, Dr. Seabrook." But that would have to wait. Robert's hold on consciousness slipped. The spots dancing in front of him vanished. And for the first time in his life, Dr. Robert Seabrook passed out.

CHAPTER 9

A splash of cold water forced Robert back to face the reality he would have dearly loved to avoid. This could have been one hell of a nightmare, but unfortunately his nightmare was just beginning.

"Wake up," he heard a distant voice say. He didn't want to, his head hurt too badly. Anna would give him some Tylenol and…It was the thought of her that brought everything back into focus. Victoria. Holt. The ferry. Vickers. *My God. Is this happening?*

"Doc! Wake up!" the same voice said as another cup full of water was doused over his head. He sputtered as he shook his head in a vain attempt to clear his mind.

"I'm up," he mumbled.

"Good. We don't have a lot of time." Robert opened his eyes to see Holt looking down at him. His partner had gone to the bathroom and was getting another glass of water in case it was needed.

"Where's Anna?" he asked. His only concern now was to get to her.

"I don't know," Holt replied truthfully. "But if we work together, we might be able to find out. You need to start talking."

"Talking about what?" Robert asked begrudgingly as he swung his legs over the side of the bed. It was reassuring to have his feet planted again on solid ground. It seemed like forever since he had, even though it had only been minutes.

"Vickers. Terry Philips. Everything. I need answers and I need them now."

"You need answers! What about me? I still don't know what the hell is going on and now I've lost the only person I care about! Where are my answers? Cuz I sure as shit have more at stake than you do!" Holt considered this for a moment. He tried to empathize with the man, but found himself just getting frustrated. He did have a point, though. Holt's own interest in this situation began and ended with doing a job. This was the man's life after all.

"What do you want to know?"

Robert thought quickly about all the questions he had and found the one he felt was most imperative. "Who is Vickers if he's not with C.S.I.S.?"

Holt studied him carefully before answering. "Colin Vickers *is* an intelligence operative, but he doesn't work for any government. Not for lack of trying, mind you. He applied to the C.I.A. and F.B.I. They both turned him away. So then he decided to try local law enforcement agencies: Sheriff's Department, Highway Patrol, you name it. They all said no. He was convinced that he was destined for a career in law enforcement so he headed up here to try his hand in Canada. Guess he never figured that by now his name had been black-flagged."

"Black-flagged? Is that what I think it means?" Robert interjected.

"Probably. His suitability was suspect and that was input into his file. Any background check would indicate this. He was never going to get a job with the government. He kept trying, though, in Canada. C.S.I.S., the Mounties, local police forces, Corrections, and the border guards all turned him away. But someone found him."

"What do you mean someone found him?" Robert asked, sounding confused.

"Dr. Seabrook. I have to be honest with you. We don't have a lot of time and there is a lot more that I could go in to, but the bottom line is that I just shot a firearm in a hotel room and there is a very good chance that someone heard it and called the police. Now I have the utmost respect for the R.C.M.P., well actually we're in Abbotsford so it would be Abby P.D. responding, but they have protocols to follow and we stand to be detained for several hours. If you want any chance of getting your wife back, we have to leave now."

Robert stared at him blankly, his ability for rational thought was still severely impaired. But it was the single thought "getting your wife back" that afforded him a direction. "Where do we go?" he asked simply.

"Away," Holt replied. He then turned to his partner. "Waddell. Get back down to O'Connor and tell him what's happening, then get the car and pull it around front. We'll be there in a few minutes."

"Got it," he responded, then left the room to the two men.

"Holt?"

"Yeah."

"Is Anna going to be okay?" Robert asked, fearing the answer before the question was even completed. Holt looked at him thoughtfully.

"I don't know. I wish I could give you a better answer, but I just don't know." Robert's heart sank as he thought of Anna and the fear she must be feeling right now. There was nothing he could do to comfort her. "For right now, she's safe. Vickers is a lot of things, but he's not stupid. He still needs you because he still needs Terry Philips. He knows that if he kills Anna, he loses you. Anna is his leverage and he will try to use it."

"What does Terry have to do with all of this? Better question, what do I have to do with all of this? Is it something to do with that thing in Columbia?"

Holt smiled. "Yeah. It has something to do with Columbia. Has Terry contacted you?"

Robert shook his head. "No. I haven't spoken with Terry since our last session. I take it he works for you then?"

"Not for me personally, but yes he's one of us."

"So the C.I.A. assassinated the Columbian President and now my wife has been kidnapped by people who think I have some information pertaining to it. Are you fucking kidding me? I don't know anything about this. I just figured that Terry was a client who suffered from delusions of grandeur and was a devout conspiracy theorist."

"Well nobody's perfect, Doc. Look, I'll explain more later. But for right now, we have to go." Robert nodded glumly. He had dozens more questions. Each question had the potential to sprout hundreds more. But now was not the time to ask them. Holt picked up his cell phone and dialled. He spoke briefly and told the person on the other end that they were coming down. After ending the call, he turned to Robert. "It's time," he said, motioning for the door.

Holt went out into the hallway first, his gun was firmly in his hand. Robert had never liked guns, but he was glad that this one was present. Together, they moved quickly down the hallway and descended the stairs. The lobby was almost deserted. Robert noted that there was only one person besides the two hotel staff members there. This person nodded to Holt as he approached.

"Any problems?" Holt asked him.

"None," O'Connor replied. "We had a few people come to try and check in. Told them there had been a robbery and we were just waiting for the police to arrive. Check-ins would recommence after that."

"And them?" Holt asked, tilting his head towards the staff.

"They did remarkably well. They're alive aren't they? What do you wanna do with them?" Robert did not want to know what the options were. He had witnessed a man shot to death in front of his eyes and had no desire to have that act repeated, no matter who it was.

Holt glanced out the front of the hotel. Seeing the car waiting, his mind was made up. "Leave 'em. Let's go." Holt tugged at Robert's sleeve and the three men moved through the lobby and out the front. If the police hadn't been called because of the shot, the panic button that was undoubtedly being pressed now would be bringing them quickly. O'Connor jumped into the front while Holt and Robert climbed into the back. Waddell hit the accelerator and the Cavalier leapt from its resting place and careened out on to the street.

"Where to?" Waddell called.

"Back to the house by the off-ramp," Holt answered. "We'll switch back to the other vehicle."

"Copy that." Waddell whipped the car around the corner and sped over the overpass.

Robert gripped the seat in front of him for support. "I have more questions," he pointed out.

"I'm sure you do," Holt responded. "But it will have to wait until we're clear. Believe me, we have more to discuss."

Robert was about to speak further, but another violent turn silenced him. This was followed by another jerk of the wheel and a screeching halt that left him breathless. The three men piled out of the car so he followed suit. All of them started putting their gear into the Impala parked next to them. *This must be the "other vehicle"*. After the Cavalier had been cleaned out, all four men clamoured into the new car with O'Connor behind the wheel. Holt and Robert were once again in the back.

"What do you figure?" O'Connor asked.

"Cops will be on their way and they're gonna be watching the highway and the border. Head South," Holt ordered. "We'll go through the farmland."

"You got it," O'Connor replied and swung the car on to Whatcom Rd. heading South. Sirens could be heard approaching from the West, but their primary destination would be the hotel. There would be a general alert out on the red Cavalier to be sure. But even when that car was discovered, there would be chaos trying to ascertain the direction of flight.

After a few minutes of driving in silence, Holt finally spoke. "Before you ask your questions, you need to tell us what Anna knows."

"About this?" Robert asked. "Nothing."

"Are you sure? She hasn't had any contact with Terry Philips at all. It's all through you."

"Yes, of course," Robert answered. "Why?"

"Do you trust her?" Holt asked.

"What the hell kind of question is that?" Robert bellowed. "Of course I trust her. What are you driving at?"

"It's quite simple really. Vickers is all about leverage as I told you. Right now he has her as leverage against you. If she knows anything...anything at all...he will use that to his advantage."

Robert considered this for a moment. "Anna doesn't know anything about this and even if she did, she would never tell Vickers."

"Don't be too sure. Vickers will find something that he can use against her. Everyone has an Achilles, Seabrook. It's just a matter of finding it." Robert thought about that point. His Achilles was Anna, that was for certain. Vickers knew that and exploited it. Robert had been desperate and Vickers had manipulated him beautifully. Now Anna was gone and he still had no answers.

"Is there anything or anyone you can think of that Vickers might use to make Anna cooperate?" Holt inquired. "Think quickly cuz we'll have to be fast. He has a head start already."

Robert wracked his brain as he thought of what was important in Anna's life. He thought of Victoria, friends, and family. Then it came to him. "Oh shit. Peter."

"Peter?" Holt asked, turning in his seat towards him.

"Anna's oldest brother. He lives in Chilliwack. Him and his fiancé."

"That'll be his next move," Holt stated. O'Connor and Waddell both nodded their agreement. Holt spoke next to O'Connor. "Keep to the back roads. Take us through Yarrow." The driver merely nodded. Turning back to Robert, Holt spoke again. "You need to contact him and get him away from the house - her too for that matter. Use my phone."

Holt handed him his cell phone but Robert refused it. "No. I'll have to use mine. They won't answer if it's a number they don't recognize." He pulled out his phone and punched in the number. After a few rings, it was answered.

"Hello," a female voice came over the phone.

"Hi Carrie. It's Robert. Can I speak to Peter please?"

"Hi Robert. Yeah, I'll go get him. He's in the backyard. How's life?" What a loaded question that was?

"Precious." It seemed to be the only suitable word.

"Peter!" he heard her call. "Robert's on the phone! Here he is." After a few moments, Anna's brother spoke into the phone.

"Robert! Long time no hear! What's going on? How's my sister?"

Where to begin? Anna's being held by a dangerous man who may or may not harm her and now might be after you. All of our lives are in jeopardy and it involves the C.I.A. assassinating the President of Columbia. What's going on with you? "Listen Peter. Something's come up."

"Sounds serious. Everything all right?"

"I hope so," Robert answered honestly. "What I'm about to say is going to sound strange, but I can't begin to stress to you how important it is."

A slight edge crept in to Peter's voice. "What's going on?"

"Just get him to meet you somewhere away from the house," Holt whispered to Robert.

"I can't explain it now. At least, not over the phone. I'm on my way to Chilliwack as we speak. I need you and Carrie to meet me in Cottonwood Mall right away."

"K. You're starting to spook me a little here, Rob. What the hell is going on?" he demanded.

"I'll explain it all when I get there. But go now. Don't talk to anyone. Don't answer the phone. Don't answer the door. Nothing. Just grab Carrie and get out of there." The urgency in his voice made it clear that something critical was occurring.

"Are we in danger or something here Rob?" Peter asked, still not fully convinced.

"We all are," came the reply. "Just get moving."

"What about Julie?" Peter asked. Robert had forgotten about Carrie's daughter.

"Of course Julie too. Why? She's not with you?"

"No. She was at a sleepover. We're supposed to pick her up at 6."

Robert thought about that for a moment, then turned to Holt. "Carrie has a daughter but she was at a sleepover last night. They're not due to get her until 6."

Holt considered this. "I'd like to keep her out of this if at all possible. She'll be safe at the friend's house. Anna couldn't have known about the sleepover so they'll have no way to find her. As long as we get the two of them, she's fine where she is."

Robert nodded. "Peter. Julie's fine where she is. Just get to Cottonwood A.S.A.P."

"We'll be there. And there had better be a damn good explanation for this."

"There will be. Go now. Bye."

"Bye," Peter replied and hung up.

"Good," Holt said. "Is there anyone else you might be overlooking? Family members? Friends?"

Robert shook his head. "Nothing locally. Her Mom and Dad are in Calgary and her other brother John lives in Ontario."

"That will have to do. It's possible Vickers won't make a move for Peter at all, but I'd rather not take the chance. I know how he operates and that would be a pretty standard move for him."

"So if he's not government, who does he work for?" Robert asked. "Lemme guess. *He's* actually the mercenary."

"No. Vickers is no mercenary. As I was saying earlier, he applied for almost every law enforcement job he could think of. His aptitude scores were incredibly high. It was his suitability that was the issue. He believes that he is the lone star, the one who will ride in and turn the tide of any situation just because of how incredible he is. Pathological narcissist. But he caught the eye of an organization that operates outside of the law. Spurned too often by the government, he turned his focus instead to wreaking havoc. He was gonna show everyone exactly how much they could have used him. He linked up with the G.D.M. Stands for Global Destabilization Movement – a terrorist organization working mostly in the West."

"ISIS," Robert nodded solemnly.

"No. Not ISIS. People like to believe that every terror group is linked to ISIS or Al-Qaeda following 9/11. Truth be told, there were hundreds of terrorist groups before 9/11 and they're still out there. The media just likes to group them all under the ISIS umbrella because it's easier to control people that way. You see people think they have a grasp on the idea of Islamic Fundamentalists. You say Al-Qaeda, people think 9/11. If you let them know that most of the terrorist attacks over the years have come from other distinct radical groups, you've got a panicked mass fearing attacks from their next door neighbours. Fear can control people, panic will overwhelm."

"So how does this G.D.M. factor into this and to me?" Robert asked. "I thought you said this was C.I.A. stuff."

"It is. What I'm about to tell you is highly classified. The only reason I am telling you is because you have clearance to hear it."

"Clearance?" Robert inquired. His head was starting to swim again. "I don't have clearance for anything."

"Hate to be the one to break it to you, Doc, but you do. You've already heard some of the most classified information in the world."

"How is that possible? I don't work for the C.I.A. I'm not even American." The spots appeared in front of his face again.

"You may not work directly for the C.I.A., Doc, but trust me you work with them." Robert was about to protest when Holt continued. "The C.I.A. didn't kill Nieto. The G.D.M. did. Terry Philips was undercover within the G.D.M. He went there to prevent the assassination. Obviously he failed. We figure his cover was blown. He's been on the run ever since. We tried to pull him out, but lost him just outside Bogota. We don't know where he is so we're covering any contact points he may have in North America. I was assigned you."

Robert struggled to process all of this. "But why doesn't he just contact you guys - the C.I.A.? What makes you think he might come to me?"

"His cover was blown by someone inside the Agency. He doesn't know who to trust, nor should he. He's on his own right now and he knows it. Past history has shown that one of the most common people for blown agents to contact is their shrink. It's a trust issue plus there's the whole privilege thing. They figure you can't talk."

"This is too much," Robert protested. "All I did was treat my clients. I didn't have anything to do with assassinations and intelligence agencies and crap like that." The panic was starting to build in his voice. "And neither did Anna!" he shouted. "Tell this Vickers she doesn't know anything! Hell, I don't know anything! Why is everyone so interested in me?!"

"Calm down, Doc. Roll your window down and get some air on your face." Robert did as he was instructed. The breeze that hit him did indeed help to quell those dancing spots. "Take a deep breath." Again, he did as he was told. Holt continued. "Like I said, it doesn't have anything to do with what you know. You're not the objective. It's Philips. He was deep undercover in that organization for years. The intel he has provided has saved countless lives. But there is a lot of information that he still has, particularly in regards to this whole mess in Columbia. That's what Vickers is after. Vickers is the G.D.M.'s chief intelligence operative. It's his job to make sure that people like Philips don't end up in the position he was. Now he has to clean up the mess. That makes him even more dangerous."

"How so?" Robert asked.

"Vickers will do whatever it takes to get his hands on Philips before we do. He either succeeds or he dies. A man with such drastic options will tend to take drastic measures."

"And he has my wife." Holt nodded grimly. "How do we get her back?"

"If he hasn't already, Vickers will soon know that something has gone wrong. He'll try to contact his man back at the hotel. When that doesn't work, he'll contact you directly. We'll have to wait and see what he has to say before we get too far ahead of ourselves. Vickers can be predictable, but he's also unstable."

Waddell turned around in his seat to face the two men in the back. "I just don't understand how he got past us. No one left. At least, we saw everyone who left and your wife wasn't any of them."

"It was the delivery van," O'Connor said quietly.

"Yeah," Holt agreed. Waddell had a confused look on his face, so Holt clarified. "The one I nearly side-swiped when we entered the parking lot. Something about the driver bugged me, but I couldn't place it. I just chalked it up to the fact that I was uneasy about going in to the hotel that way. But looking back, it was his face. I think it was Olson, but his hair colour was off."

The name triggered Robert's memory. "Yes. Olson. That was one of the guys with Vickers. And there was a woman too. She's the one who…strip-searched Anna. She and Olson left with her. They said they were going to get food and that they would be right back. How could I be so fucking stupid?"

"It's not stupidity, Doc. These people are experts in manipulation. You had no reason to doubt the tale they told. Gaining confidence is their trademark. Do you remember the woman's name?"

"Ray…something. Raeburn. That's it."

"I don't know her. You guys?" he asked O'Connor and Waddell. Both of them shook their heads.

"She might be newer," Waddell pointed out.

"Doubtful," Holt replied. "Vickers has too much at stake to risk bringing in newbies for this. We'll have to keep a watch for her. For now, we wait."

Robert looked out the window at the farms as they sped past. He thought of the people in the various houses and how fortunate they were to be enjoying their Saturday afternoons without much of a care in the world. Sure, they worried about bills and the economy and such. But those worries were commonplace. Closing his eyes, he wished that he could return to his life of everyday worry. He wished with all his heart that he could wake up beside Anna, her head resting on his shoulder. He wished it, and wished it, and wished it again. But then the cold hand of reality closed over his heart.

"Doc. Your phone's ringing," Holt said flatly. "It's time."

CHAPTER

10

Robert reached down and picked his cell phone out of his pocket. Suddenly, it seemed to weigh a lot more than it did before. He glanced at the screen to see the number. *"Withheld". Not like it was going to be a listed number.* He thought long and hard about precisely what he could say to the person at the other end; the person he had trusted and been betrayed by. That person now had Anna, and as far as he was concerned, held all the cards. She was most certainly his Achilles Heel and he hated himself for being responsible for her being in peril. It was now going to be up to him to get her through this. He always could rely on her strength and support whenever he needed it. Now, he had to be even stronger for her. He looked up at Holt for encouragement. Holt just nodded. It was indeed time. Robert pressed the "accept" key and nervously brought the phone to his ear.

"Hello."

"Dr. Seabrook." Vickers voice came through the phone like a steel skewer, lancing through his mind. "Would you mind explaining to me exactly what happened back at the hotel?"

Robert's mind raced as he tried to conjure up a valid response. *Could Vickers not know what had transpired? If he left, how could he? How to answer without giving anything away? Feign ignorance.* "What do you mean?"

"Don't play dumb with me, Dr. Seabrook," Vickers barked. "I think we both know we're a little past that. I tried calling Heath, but there was no answer so I called the front desk. What a surprise for me to find that they just had a police incident. So stop fucking me around and put Holt on the phone."

Robert's jaw hung loosely. He stared at Holt in desperation, not knowing what to do or say. Subterfuge seemed pointless. He just lowered the phone and reached it over to Holt. "He wants to speak with you."

Holt's face took on a look of quiet resignation as he grabbed the phone. "Hey Vickers," he said. "What's new?"

"You couldn't just leave this one alone could you, you arrogant prick. You always have to be the one who rides in and tries to fuck everything up," Vickers snarled.

"Nice to hear your voice, too," Holt joked. "And it's my job to intervene when guys like you try to pull the crap you do. If you think about it, it's actually your fault that my job exists. Something to think about."

Vickers chuckled on the other end of the line. "If it wasn't for me, you'd be out of a job? I'd say you're welcome, but I prefer to think of you suffering more than anything else."

"We could do this all day, Vickers. Get to the point. What do you want?"

"So snippy," Vickers chided. "Getting surly in your old age? Or is it the fact that even though you may have wrested that piece of shit doctor away from me, he is worthless because I have his wife."

"Something like that," Holt admitted. "Again, what do you want?"

"I want the good doctor to be reunited with his wife. Isn't that charitable of me? People say I have no heart, but what I want is for Robert and Anna Seabrook to spend some quality time in each other's company."

"You wanna imprison them both, you mean," Holt clarified. Robert looked at him worriedly. Holt settled him with a gesture of his hand.

"Such cynicism," Vickers replied. "I'm offended," he added with mock sincerity. "Consider it a supervised visit with a well connected host."

"Pass," Holt stated plainly.

"You should reconsider, Holt. I'm sure dear Dr. Seabrook would ask you to reconsider. Please put me on speaker phone so I know I have the ear of you both." Holt thought about that for a moment. He was not too keen on where this was going and didn't like the idea of having Robert involved in the call. Steps like that usually wound up somewhere unpleasant. Vickers was clearly not interested in negotiating.

Holt keyed the speaker phone and soon Vickers' voice filled the car. "That's better. Are you there Dr. Seabrook?" Vickers asked.

"I'm here," Robert answered. "Where's Anna?!" he shouted.

"In due time, doctor. Holt, you still with us?" Vickers inquired.

"Yeah, we're both here." Holt hated having control taken away. For right now, however, Vickers was correct. He had Anna, therefore he had control. Robert would do what he had to do to keep Anna safe. It was then paramount to get Anna back.

"And how about the rest of the team?" Vickers prodded. Neither Waddell nor O'Connor said a word as they continued west, driving over the Keith Wilson bridge into Sardis. "Oh come now. Don't be shy. I know there are at least two of you as Holt would never have gone into the hotel with anything less than a three person team. So I suggest you answer me or I take out my frustrations on Mrs. Seabrook."

"Answer him!" Robert bellowed.

Begrudgingly, O'Connor and Waddell both answered "Here."

"Good. Now that we're all better acquainted," Vickers remarked jovially. "I would like to take this opportunity to commend you all on making this far. Your partner never even made it out of the ferry terminal in Victoria. I guess that makes you guys the best."

"Fuck you, asshole!" Waddell snarled.

"Temper, temper," Vickers commented lightly. "Let's try and remain civil. Mr. Holt, I was particularly impressed with your survival on the highway. It seems I may have underestimated you. I don't do that very often, but I have to admit, it's been a welcome surprise." Vickers sounded genuinely grateful.

"Glad to oblige," Holt said sarcastically. "Don't suppose you'd like to reward me by giving up and walking away?"

"As tempting as that sounds, I feel there's too much at stake for me to just walk away. Besides, the Agency has tried to infiltrate our organization for years and I, up til now, have been able to thwart them. I'm not going to let the only mistake I ever made get away that easily. When I dispatch him, I may indeed quit the business; retire someplace warm."

"If the G.D.M. doesn't kill you anyway," Holt pointed out. "My offer still stands, you know. Come in. We'll protect you."

"You flatter yourself, Holt," Vickers observed. "And the C.I.A. There's more holes in that shit show intelligence agency than a sieve. Even if I did decide to turn away from my life with the G.D.M., I'd have a better chance on my own than with you. I take it then that you've told Seabrook who I am and who I work for. Not surprising. I guess my cover as a C.S.I.S. agent wouldn't last forever. Still, I rather enjoyed the ruse. Didn't like the smell though. Too much like actual government bullshit. I personally don't see how you can put up with it. I'd rather have nothing to do with any of you. I like the freedom of revolutionary action."

"You mean terrorism," Waddell added.

"Sticks and stones to me. One man's terrorist is another man's freedom fighter. History is the only judge of which is which and wars decide who gets to write the history books. Can you imagine how different our history would read if the Nazis had won World War II? D-Day would have been transformed from a heroic invasion by Allied forces in an attempt to try and gain a foothold in Europe to a minor insurrection by troublesome Jew sympathizers. Luckily, we won and history was made."

"So you're trying to make history?" Holt asked.

"Everyone makes history, Holt; even you. Everything we do makes a history in our own lives and the lives of those around us. What we are trying to accomplish is to make a future. The United States and her allies have written the history books long enough. I am merely playing my part in allowing another voice to be heard."

"Save the rhetoric, Vickers. You don't have any converts in here."

"Fair enough," Vickers replied.

"So where does that leave us?" Holt asked.

"With me in control of your man, clearly," Vickers proclaimed proudly. "Still there Dr. Seabrook? I hope we haven't been boring you with our little verbal dance of ideologies."

"I'm here," Robert said crossly. "What have you done with my wife?"

"Nothing yet, but the yet is not set in stone; goes back to that whole "who writes history" thing. My demands are very simple. I want Terry Philips delivered to me alive. Seeing as how Holt has you in his grasp, I have the next best thing. Anna. You will do as I say, or Anna will be killed." Robert's stomach lurched as the words calmly came from Vickers' mouth. The way he uttered them so flippantly chilled his blood to the bone. He knew, at that moment, that Vickers was capable of anything. Robert was about to speak, but Holt beat him to the punch.

"I'm sure it won't come to that, Vickers," he said as he laid a hand on Robert's arm to relax him. His mind whirred as he tried to formulate a plan to steer this conversation to one where the sides were a little more equal. Vickers, though, was prepared.

"Holt. Don't try my patience with your feeble mind games. Placating me is not the way to get what you want. There IS no way you can get what you want. What I want is for all of you to understand that I am completely committed to our cause. I will do whatever I have to do to protect it; including this." Footsteps could be heard coming through the phone as Vickers walked to wherever it was that he was going. They heard a light knock and a voice.

"Yes?" the unknown man said.

"It's Vickers. Open the door." A metallic thud was followed by the screeching of old hinges as an obviously heavy door swung open. "Bring her in, please."

Robert looked up at Holt, hoping to see some form of assurance in his eyes. All he saw was apprehension. "I don't like the sounds of this," Waddell muttered. After a few more moments, another door could be heard opening, followed by a sound that was both reassuring and terrifying at the same time.

"You son of a bitch!" Anna shouted. "Take me back to my husband right now! I don't know who the hell you think you are, but you can't just kidnap people like this!"

"Anna! Just do what he says!" Robert screamed.

"Save your breath. She can't hear you," Vickers advised. "I have to admit. She's quite feisty. Brave too, but we've found a way to get her to cooperate. She's been a lot more manageable since then." O'Connor looked back at Holt, who in turn nodded. The Impala shot forward as the accelerator was pushed further down. It would be a race to get to her brother now.

"I hate you," she cursed.

"Do I have your attention, gentlemen?" Vickers asked.

"Yes," Holt answered for all of them.

"Good." The unmistakeable sound of a gunshot crackled through the phone, splitting the air in the car. It was followed immediately by the piercing scream of Anna Seabrook as the bullet impacted her.

"ANNA!" Robert screamed. "ANNA!!!!!!" Waddell and Holt stared unbelievably at the phone, rendered incapable of movement at what had just transpired. O'Connor did his best to keep the vehicle on the narrow road as his thoughts raced to comprehend what had just happened. Anna was still screaming from the other end of the phone.

"You son of a bitch! I'm gonna rip your fucking head off when I get my hands on you! Do you hear me?!" Robert snarled.

"What the fuck have you done, Vickers?" Holt asked, finding his voice. "Killing her…"

"I didn't kill her Holt…and nice sentiment Dr. Seabrook. Though I doubt you will in fact rip my head off. She's been shot in the arm." The heavy door could be heard swinging shut and Anna's cries became muffled. "If my demands aren't met, she'll be shot again. The arms, the legs…anywhere I choose. She'll be patched up of course. Don't want her bleeding out. Dead wife does me no good. But how much pain she endures depends entirely upon you." Vickers continued before anyone could speak. "You have one week. It is Saturday now so I'll…..you know what? I'll be generous cuz that's just the sort of guy I am. I'll give you til next Sunday, eight days, to deliver Terry Philips to me or Anna pays with her life."

"But wait. Philips hasn't even contacted Dr. Seabrook. What if he doesn't before Sunday?" Holt asked.

"Not my problem," came the terse reply. "If he doesn't contact you, I suggest finding him. But believe me, for Anna's sake, you had better find him. I have a lot of men here. If you fail, they'll have their way with her so often that she'll be begging for death."

"You're a fucking dead man!" Robert bawled, but the line had already gone dead.

"Jesus Christ," Waddell exclaimed. "Is this guy for real?" All four men sat there for what seemed like an eternity. O'Connor was the only one even moving as he navigated through traffic approaching Vedder Road that would lead them to Cottonwood Mall. Robert looked at each of the others in turn. One of them had to say something that would make this better. It was Holt who finally broke the silence.

"He'll do everything he said he would. He doesn't bluff. We have to find Philips."

"How?" Waddell asked. "If we could find him, none of this would be happening."

Holt thought about that for a while. It was true. Finding Philips in a week when they hadn't heard from him at all was a daunting task. But the thought of leaving an innocent woman in the clutches of a man like Vickers left him with a bad taste in his mouth. *Innocent woman.* His mind drifted back to Michelle Thompson, age 31. Innocent. *Jesus, am I any different?* O'Connor snapped him out of his reverie.

"What's the plan, Holt? We still scooping the brother?"

"Yeah. No sense in giving him more ammo. Vickers commented that he found something to use against Anna. That might be the brother. We'll get him first, then figure out our next step. I gotta check in too. With any luck, somebody has a line on Philips. Maybe he's contacted someone else." Holt looked over at Robert. "Doc, you all right?"

Robert looked at him like he was from another planet. "Are you fucking serious?" he asked. "That bastard just shot my wife and told me that if my missing patient who is actually a spy doesn't turn up and get handed over to him in a week, he's going to have her raped and then executed. And you ask me if I'm all right?" The volume and pitch of his voice had risen to almost deafening levels.

"I'm sorry. That was callous." Holt looked down at the cell phone still in his hands; the phone that had carried Anna's cries of pain to their ears just minutes before. He handed it back to Robert who gingerly put it back in his pocket. Robert just stared out the window as the Sardis part of Chilliwack rolled past. He hadn't cried for a very long time, but there was no way to stop the mass of tears welling in his eyes from streaming down his face. His throat ached and he wanted to be anywhere else but in this car with these men. His only comfort with the company was that he needed them to get to Anna. He could not do it alone. He needed them to get to Anna and to free her. He needed them so he could kill Vickers. The four men rode the rest of the way to Cottonwood Mall in silence, each accompanied by their own thoughts and a desire for vengeance.

CHAPTER 11

Arriving at Cottonwood Mall, Robert instructed O'Connor to circle around the back as that was the closest entrance to the food court. O'Connor obliged and after a few minutes, pulled into a parking stall. All four men exited the car; three of them scanning the parking lot, Robert just stared at Holt.

"Something you'd like to say, Doc?" he asked without actually looking at him.

Robert, in spite of knowing Holt's capabilities, was still surprised that the man knew he had been staring. It took him a few moments before he could formulate the exact words he wanted to say. "Promise me we'll get her back." He could not hide the anguish in his voice despite his best efforts. "Promise me."

Holt lowered his gaze to meet Robert's eyes. He could see the pain residing there. He knew what the man must be going through. He even wished that he could bring himself to lie to him; to let him hear what he wanted to hear. But what good would that do? Even people in desperate situations deserved the truth. "I can't promise that, Doc." He could see the dejection on the man's face and in his shoulders. "I think, deep down, you know I can't promise it. You saw…er…heard what Vickers is capable of. All I can promise is that we'll do everything we can to get her back to you, safe and sound. Anything beyond that would just be a lie."

"How can you get her back? You don't even know where she is!" Robert exclaimed.

"No, I don't," Holt replied calmly. "But what I do know is that Vickers still needs you to get to Philips. So there will come a time when we have to meet, either with you or Philips alongside. Anna will be there so that's when we'll have to make our move."

"And if Vickers doesn't bring her? What then?"

Holt answered honestly. "I'll make sure he brings her. He may think he's in control now, but he knows he's a dead man if Philips talks. No Anna? No deal."

"You can't take a gamble like that with my wife's life. This may be a case for you, but it's everything to me. I won't allow it," he said defiantly.

Holt was starting to run out of patience. "Look, Doc, I appreciate the situation you find yourself in. But you need to stop trying to think your way through this and listen to the people around you who know what they're talking about. This isn't some closed door session where you can listen to someone rant and rave about their life and then prescribe some meds to ease the pain of living so you can go home to your happy existence. This is the kind of shit that no one likes to go through; where people live and die by what you do or don't do. What would you suggest? Don't force him to bring her? Then what? We show up with you and / or Philips, hand you over and watch as Vickers kills us all? That your plan? Cuz I sure as shit ain't doin' it?"

"Holt. That's enough," O'Connor spoke softly. Holt looked at him, the boiling blood began to cool as he regained his composure.

"Sorry," he said to everyone, and no one. "I'm just frustrated."

"We all are," Waddell chipped in. "But we have a job to do. So let's do it. Do you see Peter's car?" he asked Robert.

Robert shook his head in response. "They might still be inside, though," he added.

"Indeed," O'Connor agreed. "Let's go check it out." The four men headed for the doors, their eyes constantly surveying the area. People were coming to and fro so it was difficult to focus on everyone. Saturday afternoons were undoubtedly busy at the mall. As they moved, Robert manoeuvred closer to Holt so he could speak with him.

"Just so you know, I don't prescribe meds," he said plainly.

Holt looked at him strangely. "What?" he responded.

"I'm a psychologist, not a psychiatrist. I don't prescribe meds. I help people to figure out what is bothering them in their lives so that, if possible, they can understand it, work their way through it, and eventually become stronger because of it. Meds simply mask the pain. That's why I became a psychologist. I wanted to help people *get* better, not to make them feel like they felt better."

"Why are you telling me this?" Holt asked, studying him as he did so.

"Because I don't want you to have this notion that I see people once in a while, then wash my hands of them once they leave my office. That's not the type of person I am. I care about my clients long after they have left our sessions. It's why I do what I do. So don't think you know me, cuz you don't," Robert said with conviction.

"Fair enough," Holt conceded. Perhaps he had underestimated Dr. Seabrook. He seemed to have a little more tenacity than he had thought. *Good*, he mused. *He'll need it. Now to find Peter.*

Anna gritted her teeth as the facility doctor applied sutures to close the wound the bullet had made in her arm. She had never been shot before and didn't care for the experience at all. She was determined not to make a sound. The pain was excruciating, but she would not give these bastards the satisfaction. She had not expected the shot. She doubted that anyone had, except maybe that asshole Vickers. She had fallen for his line of bullshit hook, line, and sinker. She felt like such a fool. Her thoughts drifted to Robert. He had fallen for it too. She thought about how he must be feeling. He undoubtedly blamed himself for what had transpired. *He must be dying inside. It's not your fault, Robbie.* She knew he wouldn't be able to read her thoughts, but she hoped that he might somehow be able to sense them. *I'm okay. Take care of yourself and we will be together soon.* She didn't know if those words were true, but she had to believe in something. Hope was a dangerous thing, but hopelessness was worse. The doctor finished his ministrations and stood up. He had been surprisingly gentle, considering the situation.

"Done?" she asked sarcastically.

"Yep. I can bring you something for the pain if you like," he added.

"I doubt I'll take anything you guys give me so you just skip it," she added defiantly.

"That's understandable," he remarked. "It should heal up regardless. The pain will gradually fade without taking anything. It'd just be a faster process."

"I'm fine," she said coldly.

"Suit yourself. I must give you credit, though. I've sewn up many bullet wounds in my life. Most people make noise, but you didn't make a peep."

"I have older brothers," she replied. "You learn to take it."

The doctor grabbed his medical bag and headed for the door. Anna had a fleeting thought to make a lunge for the bag, withdraw something that could be used as a weapon, and make a break for freedom. The doctor, though, looked like he could hold his own in a fight and there was a guard stationed inside the door with them. Those odds were enough to make the gamble seem trivial.

"Why did he shoot me?" she asked the doctor before he reached the door.

He considered the question for a moment as he paused by the door. He turned back to face her. "It's not my job to ask why. I just bandage people up."

"What about preservation of human life? Didn't you take an oath or something?" she asked hopefully.

He smiled at her. "Yes I did. And I have every intention of keeping you alive. But before you run off at the mouth quoting action or inaction phrases from the oath, you should also know that I cannot control what others do, including your support team on the outside. As far as I'm concerned, you will be just fine as long as your husband does what he has to do. Therefore, it's actually your husband's inaction that could jeopardize your life. Don't try to guilt me, Mrs. Seabrook. I'm fine with what I do. Do try and stay alive, though. Death is always so messy. If you require anything further or if you change your mind about the pain meds, just ask for me…Dr. Young."

He chuckled as he left the room. The guard with him left as well and the large steel door slammed shut behind them, leaving her alone in her metal tomb. Part of her resolve weakened as she thought about what the doctor had said. *I'm fine with what I do.* She had hoped that she could appeal to his sense of decency as a medical professional. Clearly, his primary profession was something other than medicine. But he had said something else that she kept close to her heart. It was this that she clung to as the minutes turned into hours. Food trays were passed to her and, for the most part, ignored. *Do try and stay alive.* That, she had every intention of doing. Robbie would find a way to get to her. She knew he would. She wanted to see him again; to be with him again. *Their lives couldn't end like this.* Her time to act would come. She just had to figure out what was the best time. So she waited.

Peter and Carrie were sitting at a table in the food court when Robert entered with his three companions. Carrie noticed him first and motioned for Peter to look over. He turned, saw his brother-in-law, and rose quickly out of his seat, moving towards them with a concerned look on his face. He moved with astonishing speed considering he was 6'3" and about 260 lbs. Hardly any of that was fat, though, and at this moment, he appeared to be a lot larger.

"What the hell is going on, Robert?" he demanded. "And who the hell are these guys?"

"Relax, Pete. They're with me. They're here to help."

"Help with what? What's happened? Is Anna okay?" he asked as he studied the three men who had come in with Robert.

"She's fine for now," Holt replied. "What we were concerned about was you and your girlfriend."

"I don't remember asking you a god damn thing!" Peter snapped. Other patrons in the food court turned to watch the spectacle starting to form. "I don't know you from a hole in the wall." He directed his wrath back at Robert. "And if you don't start talkin', buddy, you're gonna be that hole in the wall."

"Pete," Robert started in an attempt to ease Peter's fury. "You need to calm down and listen to what these guys have to say. I'm in trouble and so is Anna. These guys are here to help. Now, would you please keep your voice down? We're already attracting attention." He smiled at the various onlookers who had become interested in their exchange. Half of them probably wanted to see a fist fight.

Pete relaxed a little, but kept an edge in his voice. "What's going on with Anna?" he asked.

"We can't talk here," Holt added. "Grab your girlfriend and we'll walk you out."

"If we can't talk here, then why the hell did you have us meet you here? We could have just met at home." Holt was about to say something rather unpleasant judging by the vein in his neck, but Robert stepped in first.

"It wasn't safe at your home, Pete." He looked into his brother-in-law's eyes intently and the blood cooled in Peter's body. "This is for real. Get Carrie and let's go." Peter nodded and moved back to gather his jacket. He spoke briefly with Carrie who then came back with him, albeit with a confused look on her face.

"What's going on Rob?" she asked.

"I'll explain it all in a bit. Right now, we just need to get going." Holt exited first, then motioned for the rest to follow. Waddell, Robert, Peter, and Carrie all filed out with O'Connor bringing up the rear.

"Where'd you park?" Holt asked Peter.

"Over there," he replied, pointing over to a nearby clump of trees. The six of them moved towards their black minivan. Once they reached it, Holt instructed Peter and Carrie to climb in.

"Is there someplace we can stop to talk close by?" Holt asked.

"What kind of place are you thinking of?" Robert asked.

"Someplace open; a lot of cars, but not that many people." They all thought about it for a moment. Carrie actually came up with the answer.

"Heritage Park? I think there's a dog show there this weekend. Should be pretty full. It's just down the road."

"Sounds like it might work. You know where it is, Doc?" Holt asked.

"Yeah. It's by the Lickman overpass," he replied.

"Good. You come with me and Waddell. O'Connor? Go with these two." Holt didn't want to spend any unnecessary time in this parking lot. There were just too many people coming and going. O'Connor climbed into the minivan just as Peter started to protest. Holt immediately thwarted that. "No arguments. Trust me, when we fill you in on some of what's going on, you'll understand why." Peter never said a word. Robert, Holt, and Waddell jogged over to the Impala and swung out of their stall. Peter fell in behind and the two vehicles headed west towards Heritage Park. Not a word was spoken in either car as they drove the three minutes down the road to their destination.

Heritage Park was a large barn-like structure where, almost every weekend, some form of exhibition was held. This weekend was no exception. An annual dog show graced the park this week and pet owners and their beloved canines descended there, vying for top prizes. Luckily for the new arrivals, the dog show was in full swing so the parking lot was packed but almost all of the patrons were already inside. Holt pulled the Impala into one of the stalls and Peter found a spot a few cars down. Everyone piled out of their respective vehicles and gathered together. Peter and Carrie exchanged a worried glance before anyone spoke. Peter was the first to break the silence.

"Can someone please tell me just what the hell is happening? What are you guys messed up in?" he asked, directing the question at Robert. "And who the hell are these guys? Somebody better start talkin' or I'm gonna fuckin' lose it?"

Robert wasn't sure exactly how much he wanted to tell Peter, or even how much he was allowed to tell him. Holt took the burden off of him, though, by fielding the questions.

"Peter, my name is Holt. Your sister and your brother-in-law here have become involved in a security matter and I have been assigned to help them out of it. The situation has become more serious than we anticipated so it was necessary that we find you to ensure your safety." The blood drained from Peter's face as the gravity of Holt's words struck him. He glanced at Carrie with a questioning look, then stared back at Robert.

"What did you do?" he asked dubiously.

"I didn't do anything, Pete. Truth be told, this just kinda sprung up. But now Anna's involved and we have to get her back."

"Back from where?" he asked. "And what the hell do you mean involved? Stop being so damned cryptic!" Carrie stepped forward and held Peter's hand. He looked down at her and relaxed a little. A good woman always seemed to have the ability to stabilize a good man. Holt again chimed in.

"Peter. A man wants information that Dr. Seabrook has. It's more of a lead to someone else and this man wants it. He grabbed Anna in an attempt to make your brother-in-law cooperate. My team and I are here to see them safely out."

"What does that have to do with us?" Carrie pointed out. "Why did you need to speak to us if this is between you guys?"

"The man we're speaking of does not like to take chances. His pattern is to use leverage against anyone to make them cooperate, like he has done with the Doc here," Holt explained. "Robert informed me that he doubted Anna would say anything…"

"That's true," Peter interjected.

"So, we had to assume that he would try to gain her compliance."

"You think he'd threaten us to get her to cooperate?" Carrie theorized.

"That would be his logical step," O'Connor added. "Well, logic the way he sees it at least."

"Well nobody has contacted us about anything except you guys, so I think we're okay," Peter noted. "Can we go now?" He shot a look at Robert who merely shrugged it off. Robert hadn't actually done anything wrong so the guilt he may have been feeling was diminished greatly.

"I think it would be in everyone's best interest if you guys disappeared for a little while, just until this thing boils over," Holt advised.

"Disappeared?" Peter asked incredulously. "And just where do you think we are supposed to go? We have lives to live; responsibilities to uphold. We can't just up and leave on a whim. Not to mention the fact that you don't seem to have any idea how long that might be."

"Just the week, Pete," Robert said. "Please. It's not safe."

"You guys are insane!" he snapped. "Why don't you just give this guy what he wants and get Anna back?" That question was posed to all of them. This one was directed to Robert alone. "What kind of a husband would let his wife stay in a situation like this? Do what he wants and get her back, ya dumb shit! What else is there to discuss?"

"He can't do that!" Waddell spoke up. Peter swung around to glare at him.

"Why not?" Peter demanded.

"Cuz I won't allow it," Holt added. "I hate to say it, but there is a lot more at stake here than the life of one woman. I'm not expecting you to understand. People in your position rarely do, but believe me when I say that if we do exactly what this man wants us to do, many more people will die including Anna. He will kill her as soon as he has what he needs." That reduced Peter to a blinking statue. Carrie slid her arm around his waist and squeezed. This broke him out of his stupor and he pulled her tighter against him.

"Now you said your daughter is safe at a sleepover?" Holt asked changing the subject.

Carrie nodded. "Yes. She's at a friend's place. We're supposed to go get her soon."

"That'll work nicely. And you said no one contacted you this morning?" Holt asked. "We may have gotten lucky."

"No one out of the ordinary," Carrie added. Holt froze.

"Who contacted you?" he asked. She saw the look in his eyes and immediately tried to put his mind at ease.

"Becky's mom called me this morning wondering if I knew what time the girls were being picked up," Carrie answered.

"And Becky is?" he asked.

"One of Julie's friends. She's at the sleepover. Don't worry, though. She just needed the address to go and pick up her daughter." Holt's eyes widened as the revelation crept over him. He looked over at O'Connor who's eyes had hardened to steel.

"You gave her the address?" Holt asked, attempting and failing to keep the dread from his voice.

"Yes," Carrie replied. She saw the look exchanged between the two men and realized where their thoughts were taking them. "Wait, you don't think…"

"Are you sure it was Becky's mom?" O'Connor asked.

"Well, yes…" she stammered. "Well, I assumed it was…Why wouldn't I?" Tears began to form in the corners of her eyes. "Oh Jesus…" she breathed. "Oh Jesus! What have I done?"

"I'm going," O'Connor spoke up quickly as he headed for the Impala.

"Me too," Waddell added following behind.

"No," Holt said, stopping both men in their tracks. "It could be a trap and if both of you go, we'll all have to go and the risk is too great. O'Connor, get over there and see what's what. We'll need the address," he said, addressing Carrie.

"No. I'm going with him," she replied, moving to O'Connor.

"It's too dangerous. I don't even like the idea of sending O'Connor, but someone has to go," Holt pointed out.

"Think it through," Carrie insisted. "Nobody there knows your man. Julie sure as hell won't know him. Unless you want a fight with a protective mother and a panic if you try to grab my daughter, I'd suggest you let me go with him." Holt considered this, then relented.

"Alright, go with him. But do exactly what he says and if things go bad, grab your daughter if you can and get outta there. He can take care of himself. What's the phone number? We'll call and make sure they don't do anything with your daughter until you get there." She gave it to him and he quickly stored it in his cell phone.

"I'm going too," Peter added striding towards Carrie.

"That I can't allow, Peter. I'm sorry. O'Connor is going to have his hands full keeping his eyes on your girlfriend and her daughter. He can't spare the attention for you as well. It's just too much to ask of one person heading into an unknown situation." Holt had no intention of letting more and more people go. The circumstances were already too unpredictable.

"Then send that other guy with us," Peter said, motioning towards Waddell.

"I can't do that either. He's needed here to help me with Dr. Seabrook. I know it's tough for you to see, but I have to focus on the fact that he is my primary responsibility. So Waddell stays, I stay, and you stay. Clear? Now we're wasting time. O'Connor, take the minivan. Their daughter will likely recognize it"

"But…" Peter started, but was cut off.

"Babe. It's fine," Carrie reassured him. "I'll be back here before you know it."

"Let me go, instead," he pleaded, taking her hands in his.

"I have to go. She's my daughter."

"She's my daughter, too" he argued. He wasn't technically her father, but he and Carrie had been dating long enough for that bond to be struck. Carrie smiled at his words.

"You're sweet," she said, reaching up to kiss him on the cheek. "Say a prayer that everything's okay?" she asked.

"I already did." With that, she turned and jogged with O'Connor to the minivan. He fired it up and they sped out of the parking lot in search of Maureen Caldwell's house. Somewhere inside of it, Angie Caldwell and Julie Thomas were playing unaware that their lives were about to take a drastic turn. Four houses down, a cube van pulled up and parked on the street. The driver knocked on the panel of the van and the three armed men in the back readied themselves for the task at hand. Snatching a girl was a pretty easy assignment, but they prepared for anything. Hope for the best, prepare for the worst. They did.

"If anything happens to Carrie, Julie, or Anna…you'll wish you were never born," Peter warned Robert. "I like you and all. You're a decent brother-in-law. But I won't hesitate in taking this out on you if this turns out bad. You understand?" He watched as the minivan disappeared from view.

"If anything like that happens, Pete. I'd welcome it," he replied. He meant it.

CHAPTER 12

Maureen Caldwell smiled to herself in the kitchen as she heard the hoots and hollers of the children who were still there following her daughter's sleepover. It had gone quite well considering that 8 "tweens" had taken over the reins of her house. The home was relatively intact and the kids had all seemed to have a blast. Three of them had gone home already leaving her daughter Angie, her best friend Becky, her "other best friend" Julie, plus the Fields Twins (Merissa and Dayton). The five of them were playing some form of game in the back. She had tried to follow the rules of the game, but all she could ascertain was that it involved a lot of shrieking. Her husband Ryan was trapped back there in the process of firing up the BBQ for dinner. She shuddered at the thought of what the decibel level would be like outside. *Poor Ryan.*

As if hearing her thought, her husband piped up. "Girls. You don't need to scream if you're standing right next to each other, right?

"Sorry, Dad," came the muffled response. The reprieve lasted approximately 11 seconds until one of the girls apparently said something uproariously funny and the shrieking resumed.

Ryan slithered through the sliding door and stood there, staring at his wife. "Whose idea was this again?" He asked with an exasperated look on his face.

"Awww, honey," Maureen replied as she moved to give her husband a consoling hug. "If you remember, we agreed that if she worked hard this summer she could have a slumber party with her friends before they all went back to school. They're going into middle school and not all of them are going to the same one. This was the last big hurrah."

"But do they have to be so loud?" he asked pleadingly. "It's like if they talk normally, they don't understand each other."

"It's pretty normal for that age, Ryan. It'll pass," she added reassuringly.

"Mmm-hmm. Were you that loud when you were 12?" he asked.

"Yes. And so were you."

"Uh-uh. If I came anywhere close to that level, my Dad would've smacked me til I stopped making noise." He looked back out the sliding door. "As a matter of fact..." he said as he started to undo his belt.

Maureen elbowed him playfully in the ribs. "Don't even think about it, Ryan."

"What?" he replied in mock sincerity. "Maybe it'd work."

"Right. How long for the food?" she asked, getting back on track.

"Not long. Chicken'll be pretty quick." They both moved away from the door and continued the food prep already underway on the counters.

"All the kids are fine to stay for dinner, though I haven't heard from Carrie yet," Maureen said.

"Really?" Ryan asked. "I thought she gave you a time for when she gonna pick Julie up."

"She did, but I tried to call her a few times today to ask her about dinner but she never got back to me. I figure we'll feed her just in case."

"Sounds good to me," he answered. He was going to say something else when the doorbell rang. "Speak of the devil, that's probably her now." He laid down the tongs he was using to toss the salad and walked to the front door. Maureen followed behind. "I think I can handle it, Mo," he chided her.

"Shut up. I have something to ask her," she replied. Ryan reached the door and opened it. He was expecting Carrie Thomas. What he saw was a man in a suit jacket and dress pants. He had dark hair and a very sombre expression on his face.

"Yes?" he asked.

"Sorry to interrupt," the man responded. "My name is Detective Marshall. I'm with the Chilliwack R.C.M.P. I was wondering if I could have a word with you." He brought out his ID and showed it to the two of them.

"What's this about?" Maureen asked.

"It's actually in regards to a young girl who we believe is here...a Julie Thomas?" Maureen's confused look was matched by her husband's.

"Yes, Julie is here. What's going on?" she inquired.

The man at the door continued. "I'm afraid I have some bad news. It seems that her mother," he flipped open a notepad and scanned it. "Carrie has been involved in a traffic accident." Maureen gasped as Ryan squeezed her shoulders.

"My God, is she all right?" Maureen feared the answer, but she had to ask.

"She's in the hospital at present. Her boyfriend asked that we come and pick her up to bring her there at once."

"Jesus," Ryan breathed. "Is it that serious?"

"Serious enough," the man answered. "Or else they wouldn't have sent me."

"I'll go get her," Maureen whispered. As she moved back through the house, the phone rang. "Ryan, can you grab that?" she called

"Uh...yeah," he stammered. "Excuse me," he said to the detective. The man nodded as Ryan moved to the hallway to answer the phone. On the third ring, he picked it up. "Hello?"

"Hello. Is this Ryan?" the voice on the phone asked.

"Yes it is," he replied. "Who's this?"

"Ryan, you don't know me but I need you to listen very carefully to what I am about to say. There may be someone coming around your house to pick up Julie Thomas. I don't care what you have to do, but do not let Julie go with anyone until her Mom gets there. Do you understand?" Ryan frowned as he tried to process this stream of information; information that flew right in the face of what he had just been told by the detective.

"Wait...Carrie's coming here?" he asked. "You mean she's okay?"

The voice on the phone paused for a moment. "Of course she's okay. Why wouldn't she be?"

Ryan looked over his shoulder at the front door. He could still glimpse the detective waiting just outside. "There's a detective here. He said she was in an accident and that he was here to bring Julie to her."

"Ryan, I don't want you to panic. But that man is no detective. He is there to abduct Julie. You cannot let that happen! Do you understand? Carrie is on her way to you right now with one of my people. I'm here with her boyfriend, Peter. Whatever you do, do not let her go with anyone!"

"This is ridiculous..." he said. Just then, Maureen popped back into the kitchen with Julie in tow. Ryan looked at them, then to the front door. He then stared at the phone for a moment, frozen by indecision. "Is this for real?" he asked.

"Life and death, Ryan," the voice replied coolly. "Life and death."

Maureen and Julie were walking towards him down the hallway when the front door burst open. The detective had a large handgun in his hand and was pointing towards the hallway. Ryan reacted immediately.

"MO! GET OUT!" he cried, dropping the phone and diving for the hallway. The first shot shattered one of the pictures hanging on the wall, barely missing him. Maureen and Julie both screamed. Maureen wrapped her arms around the frightened child and stared down at her husband as he scrambled to his feet. "MO! GET JULIE OUTTA HERE!" he shouted. Maureen, frozen with shock, stood paralyzed in the hall. Ryan moved to her and gave her a hard shove. "GET HER OUT NOW! RUN!!!" Maureen grabbed Julie's hand and raced through the kitchen. The other girls in the yard having heard the commotion, were all gathered by the sliding glass door. Their murmurs of curiosity quickly turned to cries of terror as Maureen and Julie fled towards them; a far cry from the shrieks of joy just minutes before. They burst out into the backyard.

"Girls! Come with me!" Maureen shouted as she tried to round up the terrified girls, her arms still around Julie. Merissa and Dayton clutched each other's hands as they hurried after her. Angie gripped her mother's skirt while Becky stood screaming. "BECKY!" Maureen shouted. Another round of screams echoed as the glass door shattered behind them. Maureen grabbed Becky and shoved her for the back gate. All of the girls broke into a run as panic gripped them. Maureen looked back and saw the gunman advancing down the hall. She also glimpsed Ryan hiding behind the corner of the kitchen wall with the glass salad bowl in his hand. She knew in her mind what he was trying to do, but she also knew that it was a fool's errand. If he had tried to run out the back after her, he probably would have been shot. She wished he would just hide, but in her heart she knew he wouldn't. *I love you, Ryan*.

Ryan's heart pounded in his ears as the second bullet fired burst through the patio door. He looked out and saw

Maureen trying to herd the children out the back. *I have to give her more time.* He wished he could have gone with her, but after he pushed her and Julie towards the back he had lost his balance. By the time he had his feet under him, the man with the gun was already coming down the hall. He grabbed the salad bowl and flattened himself against the cabinets by the wall. The advancing gunman would have to pass him to get outside. He had no plan in mind. There hadn't been time to formulate one. He gripped the bowl tighter as "Detective" Marshall moved towards the kitchen. Ryan saw the gun first. Marshall inched forward as he entered the room. Ryan, taking a last look out through the hole that had once been his sliding door to ensure Maureen was okay, swung the salad bowl as hard as he could. The impact to Marshall's face was devastating. The force of the blow staggered him back into the hallway. The glass bowl shattered and a few shards embedded into his eyes. Blinded, he fired several shots wildly as he went to the floor. Luckily, none of them struck Ryan as he leapt for the gun. He fell on Marshall and tried to wrestle the weapon from the stunned man's grip.

Though deprived of his sight, Marshall was still a strong man. He felt Ryan's weight on him and the frenzied attempt to grab his gun. He swung savagely with his left hand and landed a firm punch to the side of Ryan's head, knocking him against the wall. Dazed, Ryan still held the gun. He regained his position atop the other man and crashed an elbow into the bridge of Marshall's nose. The impact was enough to slam Marshall's head to the ground and loosened his grip on the gun. Ryan ripped it from his hand. Gripping it firmly, he slammed it into Marshall's face until the man under him stopped struggling. He was breathing hard and could hear nothing over the sound of his own heart. Had Marshall come alone, Ryan Caldwell would have had the chance to slow his breathing and calm his heartbeat. Instead, the only sound he was able to discern over his pulse was the two loud pops that came from the direction of the front door. Both shots from the second intruder's MP-5 submachine gun struck Ryan in the chest. He fell backwards and lay staring up at the ceiling, gasping for breath. He watched as the masked intruder swept past him heading for the backyard. He tried to get up, but found that the strength to move had left him. The pain was radiating out from his chest and starting to consume his entire body. He heard footsteps coming towards him and a second masked intruder moved past him, while another followed behind. He grabbed the third man's foot and tried to stop him from going further, but hand was easily kicked away. He lay thinking about what had happened. For some reason, he thought of the chicken on the BBQ that would surely be burnt. His thoughts drifted to the huddle of frightened girls that his wife was right now trying to escape with. And he thought of Maureen. Had she gotten away? *Run, Mo* he thought. *I'm sorry. I tried*. And he was gone.

"What happened?" Peter asked as he watched Holt's face change from concern to sheer dread.

Holt slowly shook his head. "It's happening," he said simply. "Someone's already there to grab her. I heard the shots…I have to warn O'Connor." He started to punch the numbers for O'Connor's cell phone.

"That won't do any good," Waddell pointed out. Holt looked over at Mitch with a puzzled look on his face. Waddell held a cell phone in his hand. "I have his cell phone."

"Why the hell do you have his phone?" Holt asked, exasperated.

"He dropped it when we changed vehicles," he added. "I just never got the chance to give it back to him. Tell you the truth, I kinda forgot about it."

"Oh Christ. Peter, what's your girlfriend's number. I'll call her instead." Holt readied the phone.

"She doesn't have one," he said sullenly. "We don't own a cell phone. We never thought we needed one." It was always the one time you needed something that it was never there.

"Guess you were wrong," Holt stated flatly. He considered the options and weighed the risks.

"What do we do?" Waddell asked. Holt stared at him for a moment. Waddell matched his look and, with his eyes, delivered the message *I go where you go.*

"We move. Everyone in the car. Waddell, you drive." Waddell launched himself into the driver's seat of the Impala with Holt taking the passenger's. Peter and Robert clamoured into the back.

"Please hurry," Peter said. "Do you think we'll get there in time?" he asked no one in particular. Robert simply put his hand on his brother-in-law's shoulder for support.

"We'll damn well try," Waddell answered. He slammed the car into drive and rocketed out of the parking lot. Speed limits were a non-issue this time. By the sounds of the shooting that had come through the phone, a little police presence might not be such a bad idea this time. The four men sped towards the fight knowing that there were two people ahead of them who had no idea what lay in wait. Time and distance were both against them. Mitch drove a little faster.

Maureen raced across the yards of her neighbours, screaming for help. Either no one was home or they weren't coming out. She liked the area so she hoped that most of the people were out. She hated to think that if someone was screaming for help, no one here would offer assistance. *I would*, she thought. Snapping out of her momentary side-thought, she seized upon an idea. *These people are after Julie. Get the other children away.*

"Angie," she called to her daughter. "You and Becky get everyone to her house. Becky, tell your Mom to call 911 right away." The Fields twins never broke stride as they sped towards Becky's Mom and the relative sanctuary provided there. Angie looked up at her Mom.

"What are you going to do?" she asked her. "And where's Dad?" Maureen hated to think of the whereabouts of her husband, but the question forced the thought to the front of her mind. Her voice caught as she tried to answer the simple question. She cleared her throat and tightened her grip on Julie's hand.

"Dad's gonna meet you guys at Becky's." She knew it was a lie. Even if Ryan had made it out of the house, he would not have known that they were headed for the Driver residence. But she had to make a positive statement because that was the only way to keep the children from panicking (herself as well). It was also necessary to force Angie to leave her, knowing that her daughter never would in a situation like this unless she thought Ryan would be waiting for her. What she had to do was get Julie away from everyone else. "Julie, you stay with me, okay?" They continued running as Julie looked up at her with questioning eyes.

"Mom, if Julie stays then so do I," Angie announced indignantly. Maureen searched behind her and saw the first of the gunmen exiting the alleyway and heading towards them. The others would be close behind. She had to act now.

"Angie!" she shouted causing her daughter to jump. "Don't argue with me! Go with Becky and get everyone to her house! Now!" Becky grabbed Angie's hand and yanked her towards her house.

"Come on, Angie," she cried. "Let's go." Becky succeeded in moving Angie away from her mother and they headed for Becky's house at the end of the street. The twins were already a couple of yards ahead. Maureen held Julie and raced across the street. She looked back and was relieved to see that all of the pursuers were heading for the street after her, rather than chasing the other children. *So it was definitely Julie they were after,* she thought. *Well, not if I can help it.*

Julie and Maureen ran quickly down the sidewalk. Maureen knew they were not going to win a foot race, but there was no alternative at present. She was in the process of formulating a strategy when the rear windshield of the car they were running past exploded in a shower of glass. Julie screamed and stumbled. Maureen, never letting go of the grip she had, prevented her from falling and they ran even faster. The footsteps of the pursuers were getting louder as they neared. Ahead, an intersection gave Maureen a few options. She ran through all of them quickly, but soon realized that she had no idea what to do. She looked down at the terrified face of Julie Thomas. For a moment, she pictured both of them lying dead on the street. Gunned down with no notion of why. She had no idea who these people were or how many of them there were. As soon as that thought struck, she became aware that there could be more of them ahead. What if they were running towards more of them? Maybe they had a vehicle waiting?

Her fears were confirmed when a black minivan screeched to a halt at the intersection in front of them. She and Julie skidded to a halt as the driver stepped out brandishing a rather ominous looking gun. She clutched Julie tightly, wishing her a moment of tranquility. "Close your eyes, baby," she muttered as she waited for the end. She hoped it would be quick. The first shot cracked and she fell. The shock of the sound was louder than what she had expected. Julie screamed as they both went down in a heap. Shots continued to ring out as she lay there, trying to maintain her hold on Julie. Perhaps she could shield her for a few minutes longer. She heard voices shouting as people neared her. She said a silent prayer for her, for Julie, and for Angie. Then she realized that one of the voices was female. *Funny*, she thought. *I had assumed they'd all be men.* She tried to focus on the woman's voice and quickly realized that the voice was calling her name.

"Maureen!" the female voice shouted. "Get up, quick!" Maureen lifted her head slowly and looked around. The pain that she was expecting to feel was not there. It was only the ringing in her ears that ached. Gunshots continued to go off, seemingly all around her. She looked over at the minivan waiting by the intersection. There, she saw the face belonging to the mystery voice. It was Carrie Thomas. The shock that accompanied the vision made her wretch. "Maureen! Come on!" Carrie shouted, waving to her.

She saw a man emerge from behind the car she had fallen beside. It was the same man who had come out of the minivan. He still had the gun in his hand but it was pointed over her in the direction of the men chasing her. His left hand was reaching down to grab her. "Come on, Maureen," he said to her. "Let's get you out of here." She seized his hand and gripped it tightly. Holding onto Julie, they scurried behind the car. Bullets pounded against the vehicle and some whizzed past overhead. Julie buried her head in Maureen's shoulder, weeping gently. "Miss, my name is O'Connor. I'm here with Carrie to get you guys outta here. Stay back!" he shouted at Carrie as she tried to get to her daughter. She hesitated, but a couple of bullets zipped close by her and she ducked back behind the minivan. "In a few moments, I'm gonna get you guys to run as fast as you can to the van. Carrie is there and she'll get you out."

"I can't. We'll get shot," Maureen uttered. This day was not supposed to be like this.

"I'll cover you as best I can, but you can't stay here."

"We won't make it," she repeated. "Julie's in shock. She can barely move." O'Connor looked down at the frightened child. She was shivering badly and sobbing uncontrollably. He felt genuine sympathy for this girl. He hated when children were targeted. It forced so many bad things on the minds of the young. He hated himself for what he was about to do, but he felt he had little choice. Time was working against them all. He grabbed Julie and wrested her from Maureen's grip. He sat her down and slapped her in the face, hard. The jolt made Julie cry out, but it also focussed her eyes on to his face.

"What the hell are you doing you sick son of a bitch?" Maureen demanded.

"Getting her attention," he answered. He turned his focus back to the girl. "You are gonna run with Maureen to that van," he ordered. "Your Mom is waiting there for you. Do you understand?" She nodded glumly as she massaged her cheek. She looked over at Maureen and, as if noting her presence for the first time, hugged her tightly.

"Okay," O'Connor started. "You're gonna run on the count of three. Ready? One, two,"

"Wait, wait," Maureen interrupted. "What about you? Will you be behind us?"

"I have to stay to cover you guys. I'll be okay." He wasn't sure how truthful that statement was. He wasn't even sure if he was saying it for her benefit or for his own. But Carrie had simple instructions. *Get Julie and get back to Holt.*

"There's at least three of them," she warned.

"Two, actually," he replied. "I tagged one of them when I got out of the van. The other two are over that way," he said motioning towards the direction that the bullets were coming from.

"There was another one at the house," she added. "I haven't seen him since. He's not dressed like the others. He posed as a detective.

"Thanks," O'Connor responded. That changed things considerably. An exchange with 2 armed men wearing black with balaclavas was one thing. Adding a possible third suspect to the mix dressed in civilian clothes was something else entirely. Any bystander could be a shooter. "But I'll worry about that. You just run, okay?" She nodded in reply. "Good. Ready?" She nodded again. "One, two, three." O'Connor popped up first, sighting one of the shooters trying to move closer behind the cover of a parked car across the street. He fired twice, shattering the passenger window of the car causing the shooter to dive behind the car. Maureen grabbed Julie's hand and they raced for the van. The second shooter, hidden by a tree, took aim at O'Connor and fired. The bullet struck him in the left shoulder and spun him to the ground. The second shooter adjusted his shot and fired at the fleeing woman. From the ground, O'Connor aimed carefully and squeezed off two rounds. Both of them struck the second shooter in the leg. The impact caused him to jerk and most of the bullets missed Julie and Maureen. One, however, struck Maureen in her lower back on the right side. She screamed and fell forward landing hard on the sidewalk. Julie screamed as well, stopping to kneel by Maureen.

"Julie! Keep running!" Carrie shouted as she rounded the van and headed for her daughter. O'Connor looked up and saw the second gunman taking aim at the women. He had moved out from behind the tree to free up his shot. O'Connor saw the body armour the man sported and took careful aim. He squeezed the trigger and the gun in his hand jumped with the loud report of the shot. He saw a red mist appear by the gunman's head as the fired bullet passed through his head, ending his life. O'Connor immediately switched his focus to the other shooter. He looked across the street to the car that the man had dived behind. There was no movement. He glanced back at the girls and saw that Carrie had Julie and was ushering her into the minivan. Maureen lay where she fell on the sidewalk. He could hear her whimpering in pain as she clutched her wounded side. He considered making a run for the minivan, but thought better of it. There was still at least one more shooter and if they were still here, he would be cut down for sure. He scanned the neighbourhood, but couldn't see anything. During the shooting, he had lost sight of this gunman. He hadn't seen that after the man had dived behind the car, he had gotten up and ran into the house. Therefore, he had no idea that the shooter had exited the rear of the house, proceeded down the back alley, and was right now moving towards Carrie and the minivan.

Maureen, unfortunately, was out in the open. He couldn't check on her without exposing himself. He tried calling to her, but she was either in shock or in too much pain to respond. An eerie silence descended on the suburban street. The smell of gunpowder and death filled his nostrils. He was used to the smell. It just seemed out of place here. He scanned the neighbourhood again... still nothing. He had to move because this could take a while and, undoubtedly, the police were on their way. Carrie, also noting the ceasefire sat with the minivan idling, her daughter tucked neatly in the back seat. O'Connor cautiously moved to the next parked vehicle, his eyes sweeping the street as he went. He went car by car, methodically, his heart beating heavier with each step. He made a silent prayer, then dashed for Maureen. He knelt by her side as he tried to move her. He saw the wound easily. It looked like it had gone clean through. That was a good sign. He was torn between moving her to the van or leaving her here for the paramedics. He was about to make the decision when it was made for him A startled scream punctured his mind. He looked up to see the gunman behind the minivan, his gun pointed through the window at Carrie's head. Julie screamed as well.

"Drop it!" the shooter ordered. O'Connor stared at the gunman, calculating the odds of being able to make this shot. As if the gunman heard his thoughts, he added "Don't even think about it. She'll be dead before you even got your gun up!" O'Connor knew he was right. There was no way he could gain the advantage here. He looked down at Maureen lying beside him. *You did good*, he thought. *Hang in there*. He placed his gun on the ground and put his hands up. The pain in his shoulder was excruciating, but he bore it so as not to make the situation worse. "Kick it away!" the shooter shouted. "And walk towards me." O'Connor complied. He stood up slowly and kicked his gun into the grass. Turning back to face the van, he moved forward bracing himself for the shot that was sure to come. "Stop there!" the shooter commanded. "Get down on your knees and cross your ankles! Interlock your fingers and put your hands on your head. O'Connor did as he was instructed, painfully. The gunman directed his focus to Carrie. "You try anything and you're all fucking dead." She nodded simply.

The shooter stepped out from behind the van and moved towards O'Connor. "Normally, I'd just grab the girl and the kid and bail, but you caused one hell of a clusterfuck," he spat. "You killed Frankie and Dave. So now, you're gonna pay." He fired another shot hitting O'Connor in the right elbow. O'Connor screamed in pain as he pitched towards the ground, clutching his right arm with his already wounded left one. "I didn't say get on the ground! Back on your knees!" he ordered.

"Fuck you," O'Connor hissed.

"Back on your knees or I'm gonna fuck up that bitch in the front seat - see if she likes to party. Maybe I'll take the kid for a test drive while I'm at it." O'Connor reeled as his mind went to Carrie and Julie. He might not have been able to see them safely away, but he would still try to do whatever he could to keep them from harm. Summoning all of his strength, he gritted his teeth and fought his way back up to his knees.

"There, you sick fuck," he snarled. "Leave them alone."

"That wasn't part of the deal. I just said what I'd do if you stayed down. I never said I would leave them alone if you got up." He laughed demonically as he raised the gun, aiming it at O'Connor's head. "The last thought you're gonna have is of me fucking the shit out of both of them. Take that to hell with you, you bastard."

O'Connor closed his eyes. The shot was incredibly loud. Perhaps it was because he had been expecting it. He stayed on his knees as blood ran down his face. He tried to focus his mind, but found that thoughts were escaping him. He had only one sensation that he could identify. The blood had reached his neck and was...tickling. *Shouldn't feel that*, he thought. He cautiously opened one eye. The gunman lay before him, a pool of blood spread from the gaping wound in his forehead. His eyes lay open in unabashed shock. O'Connor looked passed the fallen man and saw Holt running towards him, firearm in hand.

"O'Connor!" he shouted. "We're here. You all right?" O'Connor nodded briefly, then collapsed. It had been a very long day.

CHAPTER

13

O'Connor opened his eyes and found himself gazing up to the sky. He blinked a few times and slowly rose to his feet. He noted that he was in the middle of an open field. Cows were grazing and there was a soft breeze blowing in from the west. He felt the tall grass graze his legs. The sun was sneaking through the sparse clouds overhead as he moved across the plain. The cows seemed uninterested in his presence as they merrily chewed their cud. Up ahead, three girls were playing tag around a fallen tree. He moved towards them, smiling. They all looked up when he neared and returned his smile. As he approached further, two of the girls disappeared leaving one standing in front of him. He looked down at her and tried to speak, but no sound would come. She looked familiar to him. It was Julie Thomas. She waved and ran off towards a nearby windmill, beckoning him to follow her. He tried to run after her, but could only manage to walk slowly. As she got closer to the windmill, the skies darkened. O'Connor looked up expecting to see the sun behind a cloud, but the sun was out in the open…just dimmer. He could look right into it without any pain. He looked back towards the girl and saw that she wasn't alone. A shadowed man stood beside her, dressed in black. His eyes glowed flaming red. O'Connor tried to move, but his feet would not permit him to get any closer. He tried to scream, but his voice was gone. Julie cried out to him as her clothes were ripped away savagely by this apparition. The shadowy figure forced her to the ground and moved over her, grinning at O'Connor as he did so.

O'Connor screamed as he jolted awake; his face bathed in sweat. The sudden movement caused waves of pain to shoot through both of his injured arms causing his head to swim. He felt like he was going to pass out when a voice reached out to him, grounding him in reality.

"You're okay, Jim," the voice said. "It's over." O'Connor nodded without understanding why. He felt a hand on his wrist and a damp cloth was placed on his forehead. He lay back, grateful for the coolness now covering his face. As his mind cleared, he tried to focus on his breathing in an attempt to get that under control which in turn could slow his heart rate back to normal.

"Thanks," he croaked. His throat felt raw as he spoke, like sandpiper being dragged across gravel.

"Want some water?" the voice asked. O'Connor nodded as it was easier than speaking at this point. After a few moments, the voice returned. "Here you go."

Instinctively, O'Connor tried to reach for the glass with his right hand. His shoulder throbbed as he attempted to move it. He grimaced and tried his left hand. The pain in his elbow was much more acute. "Jesus Christ!" he exclaimed. "What the fuck?"

"If you open your eyes, you'll see there's a straw in front of you. Stop trying to move," the voice instructed. O'Connor slowly opened his eyes, expecting lights and more pain. Blissfully, the room was not well lit. What light there was was provided by a floor lamp in the corner, but the overhead light was off. "How ya feelin'?" the voice asked.

O'Connor took a sip from the proffered straw and sighed. Water had never tasted so good. "Awful," he answered truthfully. "But better now." He peered at the person who owned the voice that was stabilizing him and was relieved to see a familiar face. "Holt," he said.

"One and only," Holt replied. "Glad to have you back."

"Almost glad to be back," he answered. "I feel like shit."

"Well, you look like shit so that's a good sign," Holt remarked. "Means your mind and body are on the same page."

O'Connor chuckled briefly and painfully. "Don't make me laugh," he pleaded. He looked around the room, trying to place his location. "Where are we?"

"Someplace safe. I have a guy who owes me a few." He offered O'Connor another sip, but it was declined with a shake of his head. Holt rose and moved across the room to a desk where he returned the glass. "You did real good out there, Jim. What happened, exactly?" The memories came rushing back to him as his mind replayed the shooting. His arms throbbed as the recollection clarified.

"The girls," he said. "What happened to them?"

"They're gonna be okay," Holt reassured him. "Carrie and her daughter are back with Peter. They've agreed to take a vacation til this whole thing blows over. As for Maureen, she's gonna take a bit of time to mend. She took one in her lower back – nicked her kidney. Doctor said she's gonna be fine, though they might have to take the kidney out."

O'Connor took a deep breath. "Brave woman, that one," he said. "Risking your life like that for someone else's kid like that?"

Holt looked at him with an amused expression. "Yeah. Risking your life to protect others. Whatever does that feel like?" he quipped sardonically.

O'Connor picked up on the intended meaning. "That's different. It's part of my job. It's not part of hers. She's strong." Holt nodded in agreement.

"She's going to have to be even stronger, now," Holt pointed out. O'Connor looked at him quizzically. "Her husband didn't make it. He was pronounced dead at the scene. Looks like he was able to incapacitate one of the attackers, but there were too many of them."

"Jesus," O'Connor breathed. "Who the fuck are these guys? G.D.M. is a pain in the ass for sure, but have you ever seen them take to the streets like this?"

"No. They must be more desperate than we thought. Whatever Philips has, G.D.M. is willing to do anything and everything to make sure it doesn't fall into the wrong hands." Holt thought for a moment before continuing. "It would appear that the rules on this one are changing."

"Wait. You said that her husband incapacitated one of them. He's alive, then?"

"Yeah, but the Mounties picked him up before we even knew about him. He's under massive lock and key. I tried to get access to him, but that's not going to happen any time soon. He didn't have any ID so they're searching through fingerprints. My guess is they won't find anything. It's a safe bet they'll bring C.S.I.S. in on this one."

"Do you think they'd cooperate if we approached them?" O'Connor asked.

"We can't go through C.S.I.S." Holt replied. "How would that look? We have operatives running through your country and nobody informed you. There is a trail of bodies stretching across the Fraser Valley and onto Vancouver Island…oh and by the way…could you help us now?"

"I see your point," O'Connor agreed.

"Besides…this is my file and I want to be the one to close it."

"Did this all make the news?" O'Connor asked.

"You bet," Holt answered. "All of it. Nesbitt, the shootout on the highway, the incident at the Ramada, and this mess," he added nodding to O'Connor's bandages. "It was all covered by the late night news."

"Wait a minute," O'Connor spoke as he tried to process everything. "Late news? What time is it?" The curtains were dark and heavy in this room so he had no light reference to judge the time.

Holt checked his watch. "It's almost 3:00 am," he responded. "You've been in and out for a while there Jim."

"You stayed with me this whole time?" he asked appreciatively.

"Don't flatter yourself, Irish," Holt joked. "I heard you shouting in your sleep so I came in to check on you. That's when you woke up."

"Oh," O'Connor said. "Well, thanks all the same."

"Any time," Holt replied. "Just try not to make a habit out of it. Get some rest. I'll be back in a bit. I'm gonna try and take another run at this asshole the cops have stashed away. He might have information we need." He headed for the door. "Need anything?" O'Connor shook his head. "All right. If you change your mind, Waddell and Seabrook are out here. There's a bell on the nightstand for you. Don't try and move too much."

"Yes, Mom," O'Connor chuckled.

"Shut up," Holt answered wryly.

"Hey Holt," O'Connor added before he left. "Even if you do find a way to see this guy, there's no guarantee he's gonna talk."

"He'll talk," Holt replied. "G.D.M. wants to change the rules? Then, we'll change the rules. Get some rest." Holt left and the door closed behind him leaving O'Connor to his thoughts. Whatever pain he felt in his arms was nothing compared to what was in store for the G.D.M. man if Holt got a hold of him. That thought was with O'Connor as he drifted back to sleep. With any luck,

Julie Thomas and the shadow-demon would be nowhere to be found.

Holt emerged from the room and headed down the corridor towards the rest of the house. It was a three bedroom rancher owned by a holding company that Holt had had dealings with for years. They didn't like the idea of getting mixed up too much in espionage, but there was a debt to be paid and Holt rarely asked for favours. O'Connor was in one room resting while Robert took the master bedroom. Waddell and Holt planned to share the third room and rotate watches. Despite the house's anonymity, vigilance was still required. Holt popped his head into the master bedroom to check on Robert, who he discovered was snoring comfortably. He had lasted til about 11:30 before his body had just had enough. Holt came into the dining room area and found Waddell cleaning his gun.

"How is he?" Waddell asked, taking a small break before reassembling the firearm laid out on the table in front of him.

"He's better," Holt answered. "Looks like he's coming back to us at least." Holt took a moment to think about all that had happened today. His team was badly damaged. O'Connor was down with two bullet wounds to his arms, Nesbitt was gone, and he had barely escaped an exchange of gunfire with his life. "I was thinking," he continued. "Doesn't it strike you as odd that so much effort is being put forward on G.D.M.'s part to contact Philips through Dr. Seabrook?"

Waddell paused his ministrations. "What do you mean?"

Holt went on. "We started out as a four man team. Four because we had to cover different avenues of approach that Philips might take to come home and most of those are in the States. Yet, the response from G.D.M. has been…well…significant to say the least."

"What are you getting at?" Waddell inquired.

"I don't know. Doesn't it just seem…" Holt's thoughts muddled as he tried to find the right words. "It's almost like they *know* that Philips will contact Seabrook and I don't understand how." He sat down across the table from Waddell and set a firm gaze on his younger associate.

Waddell shrugged as he tried to conjure up an answer. "Maybe it's like this with other teams," he suggested. "Maybe there are some teams having a bigger fight than we are."

"You believe that?" Holt asked simply.

"No," Waddell admitted. "Not really, but it's possible." He finished putting his gun together and worked the action a few times, testing it out. "Smooth as silk," he commented.

"Anything's possible, I guess," Holt relented. "There's just something not sitting right with me and I can't figure out what it is." Waddell looked at him quizzically.

"Try not to think about it. You'll figure it out. My Mom used to tell me when I was younger that sometimes the easiest way to solve a problem is to not think about it. The answer usually becomes clear if you move away from the question a little bit." Holt smiled as he recalled the same advice coming from his father years ago. Parents always claimed that there was no manual for parenting, yet they all seemed to have the same lessons to teach.

"Perhaps," he admitted. He stretched and yawned and suddenly realized how fatigued he was. "You wanna hit the sack first?" he asked.

Waddell looked at him with a smile on his face as he placed his newly cleaned firearm into its holster. "By the looks of things, you could use the rest. Head down. I'll come get you at 6."

"Thanks," Holt replied. "Three hours is better than nothing," he said as he rose to his feet and headed for the third bedroom. "We'll start at 9 and figure out our next move."

"Hey, Holt," Waddell added. "How long do we have this place?" If they were going to be here a while, they were going to need supplies.

"My guy said as long as we need. With any luck, we can stay here until this whole mess is behind us." Waddell nodded and Holt went to lie down. He doubted that he would sleep much, if at all. But the attempt would be worth it. If nothing else, it would give him a chance to get off his feet for a while. He entered the room and closed the door behind him. Shuffling over to the bed, he climbed on not bothering with blankets. He rolled over onto his back and stared at the ceiling as theories and conspiracies raced through his mind. He knew he had reached the end of rational thought when he started contemplating UFO's and zombies. *That's enough for now,* he thought. He cleared his mind and focussed on more pleasant matters. A face...that cute clerk at the hotel in Victoria. *What was her name again? Trish. Maybe I'll swing by there after this is over and see if there's anything there.* He wanted to have a few more controlled thoughts, but his body had other ideas. Before he could resist further, he was asleep.

Anna tossed fitfully on the cot that had been provided for her. Her arm throbbed painfully even when she was still, but when she moved it was a thousand times worse. Not for the first time, she wished she had accepted the doctor's offer for medication. Even a Tylenol would have been welcome. *Well, maybe two...extra strength.* As it was, she had been left to her own devices. Once she was in a relatively comfortable position, she again looked around the steel room that held her. Furnishings were bare. There was a single light bulb burning in the centre of the room. Someone had thought enough to dim so she could attempt to sleep. The light it provided cast an eerie glow over the room. Not that there was much to look at, mind you. With the exception of the cot she now lay on, the only other items in the room were a metal toilet and sink in the corner and a small metal desk with two chairs. All of these were firmly bolted to the floor. There were no windows so she had no idea whether it was day or night. Her tiredness led her to believe that it was night, but there was no way to be sure and certainly no way to be accurate as far as the actual time went. The heavy steel door was just that – heavy and steel. There was a slot in the middle where food was pushed through and ignored. She knew she would have to eat at some point, but she wouldn't give them the satisfaction until it couldn't be avoided.

The only people she had seen had been the doctor, a couple of guards, and of course Vickers. She hadn't recognized anyone and had no idea where she was. She had spent the first few hours looking for any weakness in the room that she might be able to use to aid her in an escape attempt, but that had proved fruitless. She remained mindful of any opportunities that arose, but for the most part, she resigned herself to being held captive until Vickers either got what he wanted or was stopped. She thought of Vickers and the casualness he had displayed when he had shot her. He must have viewed her as some form of insect because he hadn't hesitated or even shown any remorse. A man like that was a man she truly feared. If he decided that he didn't need her anymore, she had no doubt in her mind that she would be executed. That also included if he felt that she was more trouble than she was worth. Her plan was to keep quiet and to stay under the radar until this situation came to a head. At some point, she figured, there would have to be a meeting...an exchange. She had seen enough gangster movies to know that. She would seize her opportunity then and she and Robert could leave this whole affair behind them.

Her thoughts moved to her husband. *Wherever you are, baby, rest. Our time will come. We will be together again...soon...and this will all be over. Either come for me or I will find a way to you. I promise.* Tears formed in her eyes as she fought her way to her husband's mind. He was okay. She could feel it. But he was also a long way away from her. She could feel that too. There was no way that she could reach out to him, though she wanted to desperately. She would have given anything to feel his embrace right now. What she needed was assurance. Robert would do everything he could…she knew that. She assumed he wasn't alone either. *If Vickers had lied about Holt, then perhaps Holt was with Robbie now.* She had the utmost confidence in Robert and his capabilities, but in the world where people like Vickers ran free, she had to admit that Robert was a little out of his league. She prayed that he was not alone in this. She knew what it felt like to be alone. She closed her eyes and wept softly.

Vickers sat in his office, two floors above where Anna tried in vain to sleep. He had designed this compound with the help of a few of G.D.M.'s engineers and was perfectly content to live here. He couldn't, however, as the facility was not designed to support long-term tenancy. It was more like a storage facility than anything else. The seclusion this building offered him, though, was like a drug. People, he found, always discovered ways to spoil the true beauty of solitude. Either they wanted to blather on endlessly about the trivialities in their lives or they wanted to discuss the possibilities for the future. Neither of these topics interested him in the slightest. He tolerated the G.D.M. and their mission, but wanted no part in establishing a new world with G.D.M. leading the way. In his opinion, it was just more of the same shit with a different asshole to spew it from. What the "movement" provided him, though, was access to a vast network of information, assets, and technology that he could learn to control. That was what it was all about…really. Control. He viewed the "believers" as worker ants that he could direct to accomplish his own goals. If he had to carry out a few tasks for the G.D.M. in exchange for this, it was a small price to pay. Besides, it let him practice. His idea of a new world involved one with few if any people on Earth at all. He loved the idea of returning the planet to a truly natural state so that it could be marvelled at and studied. His regard for human life (his own included) was little more than that of an insect.

But now, there was a problem. One of these insects had the power to turn on him. The G.D.M. had entrusted him to carry out a simple assassination (they had performed numerous over the past three decades) and he had succeeded. But one of the bugs he had sent to do this errand had betrayed them all…*a spy in my soup*. This insect, Philips was his name, had moved quite high in the echelon of the G.D.M. He had been privy to information that very few people had ever seen. He was made aware of future events that had been planned. He had been trusted. As head of Intelligence for the G.D.M., it had been Vickers' job to eliminate any security threats to the "movement". One had slipped through and until this particular bug was squashed, Vickers was vulnerable. He was no fool. He knew that even after he neutralized Philips, the "movement" would make quick work of eliminating him for his failure. But he had an exit strategy. All he needed was Philips' head on a platter…and for Holt to continue doing exactly what he had been doing. Vickers signed off from his computer and exited his office. He walked down the hallway and left the building. The night air was cool and clear. Tomorrow, they would have to pack up and head to one of the G.D.M.'s main holding facilities. He would much rather stay here at his 'fortress', but the decision had been made by the Assembly (the five heads of the various "Movement" organizations that comprised the G.D.M.) and their orders were never disobeyed. These same five people were the ones who planned on killing him. Once he had Philips, he would just vanish. The "Movement" would realize how insignificant their resources actually were when they attempted to locate him and he could enjoy the world the way it was meant to be enjoyed…without other people around. Ironically, to achieve that he would have to go to this holding facility first. You would have thought that going to the middle of the desert would be ideal for someone with Vickers' mindset. But unfortunately for him, this particular desert had one very large drawback. Las Vegas.

CHAPTER

14

The night passed uneventfully as the team tried to pass the time. Waddell woke Holt at six o'clock and reported that the area was quiet before he crashed for a few hours. Holt took over the watch while Waddell slept, checking in on both O'Connor and Robert throughout his shift. O'Connor was sleeping peacefully which was a relief while Robert tossed and turned, but never fully woke. At nine, Holt went in to wake Mitch. Robert was still asleep so he decided to let him get as much rest as he could. There was work to be done. After a brief discussion, Mitch left the house and drove to the local Tim Horton's donut shop and came back with an armload of goodies for the men. When he entered, he found Robert shuffling out of his room heading towards the bathroom.

"Morning, sunshine," he called which got a grumble for a response. Waddell looked over at Holt with a smirk on his face. "Not a morning person I guess."

"Cut him some slack, Mitch," Holt replied. "Remember what's going on here, okay?"

Mitch's shoulders slumped as he realized his faux pas. "Oh shit. Sorry."

Holt rose from the dining table and came over to help with the bags and coffee. "This is good. It'll get us through the morning at least. We'll do some actual shopping later."

"No luck finding food here?" Mitch asked as he walked into the small kitchen, setting down the rest of the food.

"Not much. Just some non-perishable crap. I don't feel like living off Chef Boyardee for the next week, though. No offense to the Chef, but that just doesn't sit well with me as an everyday food." Holt, over the years, had been forced to survive on a lot worse than Mini Ravioli. But if there was a way to avoid it, why not take it?

"Here's your coffee," Mitch said as he handed Holt his cup.

"Thanks," he said as he took the proffered cup from his younger partner. "You pick up anything for O'Connor?"

"Yeah. Nothin' heavy cuz I figured he might not be up for it. But there's some stuff in there for him." Mitch started rooting around in the bags and dividing up the bounty. "Dining table?" he asked.

Holt nodded in reply as he took a sip of coffee and headed for the hallway. When he reached the bathroom, he knocked gently. "Doc? There's food for you on the table when you're done." He could hear running water on the other side.

"Be out in a minute," Robert answered.

Holt went back to the dining table and found Mitch already scarfing down some form of breakfast sandwich. "Good food?" he asked as he marvelled at the speed at which Mitch was downing his breakfast.

"Mmm-hmm," came the muffled reply. "It's hot and it tastes good," he said as some bits fell from his mouth. He deftly swooped them up and fired them back into his mouth, chewing noisily.

"You're disgusting," Holt chuckled.

"I don't care," Mitch replied with a smile. "Doc coming?" he asked, eyeing Robert's portion of the food hungrily.

"Yes he is," came the abrupt reply. "So don't even think about it." As if on cue, Robert came around the corner of the dining room.

"Think about what?" he asked innocently.

"Eat your food, quick," Holt advised. "Before his mouth vacuums it up." Robert saw the grin on Mitch's face and the gleam in his eye. He realized that Holt wasn't kidding. He sat down and opened his sandwich. He hadn't known how hungry he was until the food came into sight. His stomach clenched in anticipation as he dug in.

"There's a coffee for you, too," Mitch added. "I didn't know how you took it so there's milk and sugar on the side."

"Thanks," Robert said with genuine appreciation. A coffee would be a good way to start this day. He had slept long, but not well. Visions of Anna and the events of the past day danced through his head for most of the night. Most of his dreams, thankfully, had faded to a blur. There were some lingering questions, however, that remained crystal clear. Those questions would have to be asked and answered today.

"How'd you sleep?" Mitch asked as if able to read his thoughts.

"Rough," was the simple response. "I need some answers." He directed the question directly at Holt who continued to chew, fixing Robert with a square gaze.

"Had a feeling this was coming," he replied.

Robert chuckled incredulously. "Really? What was your first clue? I'm sorry if my situation puts you in an uncomfortable position, but I seem to have a little more at stake than you do."

Holt sat back and looked Robert over, measuring him. "Tell you what. Finish your food. Allow me to finish mine. I'll check on O'Connor, then answer any questions you have." Mitch looked at Holt with a shocked expression which Holt dismissed with a wave of the hand. "He deserves to know what's truly going on," he told Mitch. Turning back to Robert, he took another bite of food and stared at him. "Deal?"

Robert eyed him warily. "Deal," he replied. "No bullshit?"

"No bullshit."

"How's O'Connor doing?" Robert asked sheepishly. He had been so consumed with his own situation that he had forgotten about the injured man in the other room. He had never seen anyone get shot before. Though technically, he still hadn't as O'Connor had been shot before they had arrived. But he had never been that close to a shooting before, either. The thought of it terrified him. He knew that O'Connor was used to being around this kind of encounter, but Anna wasn't. And they had both been shot. He couldn't help but envision Anna going through a similar experience to O'Connor's and the thought sickened him. He reluctantly took another bite of his sandwich which suddenly seemed less edible.

"He's doing better," Holt answered. "Looked like he was coming around late last night. This morning he was resting. We'll know more when he wakes up." The rest of the meal passed without much talking. They each sat with their own thoughts and sandwiches. Once the food was gone, Holt took his coffee, grabbed the juice that Mitch had bought for O'Connor, and went to see if he was awake. With a nod of the head, Mitch motioned for Robert to head into the living room. While they were waiting, Mitch turned on the TV and turned to the all news channel.

"Ready for this?" he asked. Robert looked at him quizzically, then soon understood what he had meant. News story after news story was devoted to the carnage that had been left in their wake. The reporters did not realize that all of the incidents had been connected. According to them, there had just been a bizarre number of incidents over the past 24 hours in the Fraser Valley area and Vancouver Island. Nesbitt's body had been discovered with the perfunctory "no identification has been released pending notification of next of kin" side note. The shootout on Highway 91 was touched upon with an appeal for anyone with information regarding the matter to contact police immediately. Two victims were mentioned, but again…no ID.

The shooting in Chilliwack leaving four people dead was talked about at length due to the fact that it had occurred in a residential area. There had been a few witnesses, but most people claimed to have stayed out of sight. The condition of Maureen Caldwell was listed as serious, but stable. Her husband Ryan was identified as one of the deceased. Considering that the next of kin had been there, it was obvious that Angie had been made aware. No specific mention was made of their daughter Angie. The police were no doubt keeping her under lock and key for fear of another attempt. Peter, Carrie, and Julie were not mentioned and that was a good thing. Some police representative was fielding questions about the events and asked if he felt that any of them were related. The obligatory "we are still looking into the matter" response, followed by the always present "no need for the public to be concerned at this time" line flowed freely. This was obviously not the first statement this officer had made to the press.

A few stories later, even the incident at the Ramada was talked about. The reporter called it a failed robbery attempt. That made Mitch chuckle slightly. "They've been running this all night," he stated. "So far, we've been able to keep out of the spotlight, but any detective with half a brain will start putting shit together and connecting incidents. It's best if lay low for a while," he advised.

"That's a nice sentiment," Robert answered. "But my wife doesn't have a while. She has 7 days." He glared at Mitch with sheer contempt. He was tired, yes, but he wanted these people to start doing something about the situation…something that would get Anna back. "And if she has 7 days, that means that I have 7 days cuz nothing I do after that will matter if she isn't safe."

"Then I guess we'd better get her back before then," Holt announced as he entered the room startling both men. "That's why we're still here." He sat on the couch and, grabbing the remote from Mitch, turned off the TV. "You had some questions you wanted answered?" he asked.

"Yes…" Robert faltered as the directness of the question caused him to lose his train of thought. *Probably intentional*, he thought. "How's O'Connor?"

Holt nodded. "He's good. Awake. He said thanks for the juice by the way," he added, poking Mitch in the leg. Waddell smiled. "I meant the other questions," he continued, addressing Robert again.

"Yes, I want to know exactly why this is happening. The G.D.M., whatever they are. Why do they have Anna? I Understand that it ties in with Philips and I treated Philips and all that crap. I get it. But what does an assassination in Columbia have to do with global destabilization? Has Columbia become some sort of world powerhouse or something?"

"They are about to." That answer stunned Robert into silence. "Allow me to explain. A few months ago, some local mining company just outside Bogota was doing some drilling. Trace elements of some substance…it doesn't matter. What they found was oil. A shitload of it. Possibly one of the largest concentrations in the world. How it wasn't found before, no one knows. The Columbians wanted to keep it secret cuz they knew that the minute that information came to light, every country in the world would descend on them trying to get the oil. Well, word got out. Countries started a massive bidding war to get the contract and the rights to the drilling. Nieto was no fool, though. He knew what the oil meant for his country and its economy. He had no intention of giving it to anyone. That's where the G.D.M. stepped in."

"They killed him," Robert stated.

"Precisely. We have reason to believe that the man next in line to fill Nieto's seat is either a G.D.M. operative or at the very least a sympathizer. With Nieto gone, the G.D.M. stands to gain control over one of the largest oil reserves in the West."

"So you guys sent Philips down there to prevent the assassination," Robert breathed.

"Right," Waddell answered.

"But if the C.I.A. was so concerned that this was a possibility, why send only one man? Doesn't that seem a little peculiar?" Robert asked.

"Philips wasn't alone," Holt responded. "There was a full team down there with him. Someone leaked his cover, though, and the team was wiped out. Philips has the information on Nieto's successor and the connections established to give control of the oil to the G.D.M. That's why we need him and why they want him."

"And everyone believes that he will contact me and that's why Vickers grabbed Anna?" he asked incredulously. "Give me a break. There is no possible way anyone could make that leap with any certainty. I don't care who you are."

Waddell and Holt exchanged a look, which they both in turn focussed on Robert. "It's not a hunch. C.I.A.

tracked Philips to Lima, Peru. We thought we had found him, but discovered that the G.D.M. was closer than we were. He made his escape from them, but left his computer behind. He had erased everything, naturally, but our techs were able to reconstruct some of the data from the hard drive. He was heading to Vancouver and then on to Victoria. He was coming to you." Robert's face showed more than just shock. He was struck silent with the sheer enormity of the situation.

"That's not even the worst of it," Mitch added. He looked at Holt for permission to take over the conversation and it was granted. "C.I.A. cracked the computer. C.I.A. was the only one to ascertain his destination. Vickers knew it too. Which means…?"

"Which means that someone inside the C.I.A. is working for the G.D.M." Robert remarked.

"Exactly," Holt said. "Needless to say, our team is two men down and we are in no position to manoeuvre against Vickers. I hated to do it, but I had to make the call."

"What call?" Robert asked.

"Reinforcements. They'll be here within the hour."

Robert smiled at the thought of more help coming. Both Holt and Mitch, however, looked decidedly grim. *Screw them*, Robert thought. *I don't give a crap about their wounded pride. We're coming for you, baby. Hang on. I'm coming.*

Vickers woke peacefully. He always slept well, no matter what was going on around him. Perhaps it was that he never really cared enough about anything to be stressed out by it. His life was in danger, but he did not fear death. He was in no hurry to die, however. He just welcomed death as another part of life. He stretched as he rose from his cot in the corner of his office. He had the option of an actual room within the compound, but instead chose the office as his place of rest. He hated the idea of being away from work when on assignment and he viewed personal space as a deterrent to a strong work ethic.

He moved to his computer and checked for messages or updates, and he monitored the surveillance cameras. If something out of the ordinary had happened, he had every confidence that someone would have notified him. But a good routine and diligence never hurt. As expected, all was quiet. Anna Seabrook lay on her cot and seemed to be sleeping somewhat peaceably. She occasionally turned, but didn't really stir. All of the internal and external cameras and sensors showed no signs of activity. It was just the way he liked it…isolated. But unfortunately for him, it could not stay this way. It was time to get things moving.

He picked up his phone and dialled his contact at the Vancouver International Airport. When the man on the other end picked up, Vickers said simply "My apologies, kind sir. Wrong number," and hung up. His contact now knew to expect him at some point today with cargo to be loaded without inspection. He had to admit, working with the G.D.M. had its advantages. The network of "Movement" agents, employees, and sympathizers was vast. Its largest concentration could be found in the United States, but Canada had a large number as well. G.D.M. was poised to make a substantial leap forward in their attempt to assume control of the World's economies. He inserted his flash drive into the computer to update the progress that the "Movement" was making. All five sectors were showing significant progress.

Europe was still solidly behind the Euro. The G.D.M loved the Euro because any time there was a currency exchange, fractions were left over. These fractions were harvested by the "Movement". Sure, ¾ of a penny may not sound like much. But when you're brokering trillion dollar deals between corporations from different countries, those fractions quickly built up. Rather than one transfer for the full amount, thousands of smaller transfers were completed almost instantaneously until the total amount had been transferred. The G.D.M. had computer systems in place that would precisely calculate the highest number of transactions required to produce the largest amount of residual funds. Normally, economic watchdogs would pull the plug on any such network, but the "Movement" had enough people situated within these organizations that their effectiveness was severely compromised. Add to that the usual influx of funds from arms deals, pharmaceutical kickbacks, narcotics trafficking, and prostitution, it was safe to say that the European market was a lucrative one.

Africa was even easier. With the amount of infighting between the respective governments and the warlords in any given area, the G.D.M. could pick and choose where to garner footholds. Most of the warlords in power in Central Africa were G.D.M. backed. It was a smorgasbord of money and resources. Whenever a particular government tried to crack down, aid was intercepted and pressure was applied to get them to back off. Every few years, some political idealist stepped forward to lead the charge for change. They were either convinced otherwise or removed.

Asia was similarly prosperous. With the U.S. running amuck in Afghanistan and Pakistan, the attention of the world had been drawn away from the rest of the continent. The Asian nations were producing almost too well. From drugs to guns, and from human trafficking to military hardware and other technologies, Asia was brimming with success for the G.D.M. That's why so many "Movement" people were being smuggled out to North America under the guise of Tamil refugees. The West had a very narrow view of Asia. Despite all of their propaganda about how advanced the West had become and about how racism and sexism were becoming things of the past, most westerners still couldn't tell a Sri Lankan from a Pakistani or a Thai from a Filipino. Asian was Asian. *Ignorance.*

North America, with the aid of the influx of Asian "Movement" members was starting to establish itself in another area; manpower. The sheer size of the G.D.M. in America alone was astounding. Heads of corporations, Senators, Governors, the G.D.M. had members in all sorts of high profile positions. Their attempts at keeping the economy shaky in the U.S. were proving to be highly successful. President Obama had some good ideas, but as long as the "Movement" was there to derail them, the U.S. would continue to struggle financially. When they were at their most desperate, the G.D.M. would come along as saviours and assume control of the entire economy. A huge part of that was securing the oil fields in Columbia.

South America had been the biggest trouble spot for the G.D.M. Venezuelan President Chavez had established himself securely as the leader of that nation and seemingly, the entire continent. The "Movement" had tried to get to him, but he seemed immune to their influence. Chavez did provide the necessary distraction as many international intelligence organizations focussed on Venezuela. Many other countries on the continent had been too beleaguered with corruption to allow the G.D.M. to move in. They had tried and been betrayed on more than one occasion. But when the oil had been discovered, the G.D.M. had its moment. With the elimination of President Nieto, the "Movement's" own Manuel Poveda was poised to take control of the nation. He would be able to grant control of the oil fields to the G.D.M., thus providing them a foothold in the lucrative oil market. With the U.S. spiralling economically, they would make eager trade partners with the G.D.M. and further entrench the "Movement" within the western economy.

The only person who could prevent all of this from happening was Terry Philips. He knew about Poveda and the G.D.M.'s plans. He had the names of most of the upper echelon in the organization, too. That was the information that the "Movement" was desperate to retrieve. Philips had been Vickers' man, one of his chief lieutenants. Now, Vickers had been assigned the task of getting him back. It would be his last assignment for the G.D.M. Success or failure was irrelevant. His death would come regardless. At least, that was their plan. Vickers had no intention of lying down peacefully. He bore no grudges against the G.D.M. for their rationale. It was the logical thing to do. It was what he would have done in their stead. The "Movement" had been very good to him over the years and he had no intention of leaving them to twist in the wind. His final act would be the elimination of Terry Philips. That would allow the G.D.M. to continue its mission to bring around the new world that they felt would save the planet. He would just disappear into a quiet corner of that world and disturb no one.

First thing's first, he thought. He logged off of his computer and exited the office. He summoned the drivers to the conference room to discuss their plans, then he notified the security detail of exactly what was going to happen. He preferred to leave the instructions for the team until the last minute so as to minimize the threat of a leak. It was entirely possible that he would alter the plans once they had been put in motion just to keep things even more secret. After summoning Dr. Young, the two men proceeded down to grab Anna. It was time to go.

The metal door swung open freely. Anna was sitting on the bed when they entered. "Morning, Anna," Dr. Young said warmly as he walked in. "How are we feeling today?"

"I'm fine, no thanks to you," she spat. She would have continued with a verbal attack, but she recognized the man he had brought with him. The minute her eyes saw his face, she lunged forward in an attempt to decapitate the man who had pulled the trigger. She swung wildly as she neared him. He quickly side-stepped the assault and punched her firmly in the stomach, doubling her over. She clutched her midsection and slumped to the floor, gasping for air.

"Good morning to you too," Vickers said, looking down his nose at the woman on the ground before him. "Sleep well?" he asked. Anna tried to speak, but there was still not enough air to allow a proper response. All that came was a small squeak. "I'll take that as a yes. I don't want to have any trouble with you on this trip, Anna. It's up to you how painful it is. I have no problem hurting you so try and keep that in mind before you launch any other attacks."

"Trip?" she gasped, finding a little bit of air.

"Yes. We're taking a trip, all of us," he added, motioning to the doctor. "You will be accompanying us on this trip. How you manage it will be entirely up to you."

Anna nodded feebly as she struggled to regain her composure. Her time to act would come. Her opportunity to exact revenge would be there. But for now, she would have to wait. Dr. Young moved forward and helped her back to the cot where she sat rubbing her sore stomach. He took a pill bottle from his coat pocket and popped two into his hand.

"Take these," he offered. "They'll knock you out for a while and when you wake up, we'll be at our destination." Anna looked at the pills and knocked them to the ground.

"You've gotta be kidding me if you think I'm going to take anything you guys give me," she snarled. "You all can go to Hell."

Dr. Young sighed and retrieved the pills from the floor. "Anna, I assure you. No harm shall come to you while you are sedated, but I'm afraid it is necessary."

"Your assurances are meaningless, *Doctor*," she added sarcastically. "You work for that Ape," she continued, motioning towards Vickers. "So your word is as good as his."

"I've had more than enough of you, Anna," Vickers said. "Your pathetic verbal attacks against me are matched only by your ridiculous attempts at physical battery. Just shut up and take the pills. If you don't, I'm gonna bring in a couple of guards, restrain you, and inject you with a syringe. You'll struggle, lose, and be in worse condition than you are now. Either way, you're takin' a nap. By the way, how's the arm?" he quipped.

Anna looked from Vickers to the doctor and back again. "It really is just easier this way," Dr. Young noted.

A plan started to form in Anna's mind. She would take the pills and pretend to swallow them, then pretend to fall asleep. From there, their guard would drop and she could make a break for it. "Fine," she relented. "I'll take the pills." Dr. Young slipped the pills into her hand and she popped them into her mouth. She was handed a glass of water which she dutifully drank, making sure the pills were tucked securely between her upper gums and the inside of her cheek.

"Show me," Dr. Young prompted. Anna opened her mouth and showed it empty. Satisfied, the doctor nodded and moved back to Vickers. "She'll be out soon."

"Good," Vickers replied. "See how easy cooperating can be?" he asked. Anna just turned and lay back on the cot. She wasn't sure how long she would have to pretend to still be awake. She figured if she just lay still, though, their return would give her an idea that she was supposed to be unconscious. *I might just get through this yet*, she thought. Vickers and Dr. Young left the room and the door swung shut behind them. Now, it was time to wait.

Holt's phone rang at 10:15. He looked at the number and answered it. After a brief conversation, he ended the call. "They're here," he announced. Waddell walked to the front window and peered out, confirming the arrival of the agents. He then opened the door and stood back. Five agents entered the house exchanging nods of acknowledgement. Three of them, Holt recognized. The other two were new to him.

"How ya been, Coop?" Holt asked as he stepped forward to greet the first of the agents. Jason Cooper was, in Holt's opinion, one of the best agents he had ever worked with. Standing 6'2" and weighing about 240 pounds of muscle, his physical presence was matched only by his expertise. A black man who didn't like being referred to as African-American (he always maintained that he was from Boston, not Africa), Cooper had an impressive record and an even more off the record reputation.

"Been good, Holt. You?" he asked with a friendly pat on the shoulder.

"Been better. Worse, too mind you," Holt added. "MacReady? Martinez?" he acknowledged. "Nice of you boys to drop in." MacReady was a proud Scot who specialized in security bypass. Martinez was one of the Agency's experts on South America, primarily Columbia. Both men had weary smiles on their faces. By the looks of it, the three of them had travelled most of the night to get here. The two others with them looked well rested. One was a young looking man, average build with blond hair. The other was a woman who appeared to be in her forties with jet black pulled back into a pony tail. Whoever they were, they hadn't come far. Holt's suspicions were quickly confirmed.

"Holt," Cooper said. "Allow me to introduce Agent Doyle and Agent Ballard from C.S.I.S. Doyle and Ballard? Mr. Holt and Mr. Waddell." Pleasantries were exchanged all around. "Where's O'Connor?" Cooper asked looking around.

"He's in the back, resting," Holt explained.

"Good," Cooper added. "Sorry to hear about Nesbitt." Holt nodded in response. "MacReady here pretty much demanded to come on board when he heard."

"Oh yeah," Holt replied as he made the connection. "You and Nesbitt went through training together," he said to MacReady.

"Yeah," MacReady answered with a hint of an accent. His brogue became more pronounced the more emotional he became. "I hadn't spoken with him for a few months, but we were still pretty close.

Cooper's eyes rested on Robert. "So you must be Dr. Seabrook. Not sure if I should shake your hand or punch you square in the mouth," Cooper said with a smile.

"Excuse me?" Robert replied, eyeing up Cooper's sizable hands and picturing one of his fists landing on his jaw.

"You've caused quite a bit of commotion here, Doctor," Cooper explained. "A lot of people are mobilizing cuz of this situation."

"I didn't cause this situation," Robert retorted. "And I'd much rather have nothing to do with it. But as long as that bastard has Anna, I'm not going anywhere."

"Speaking of commotion," Holt interjected. "What brought you guys in?" he asked the two C.S.I.S. agents.

"Are you kidding?" Ballard answered. "You guys run around B.C. blazing a trail of bullets and you don't think we're going to get involved? Who the fuck do you guys think you are?" Holt discovered at that moment that he was pretty old-fashioned. He didn't like to hear a woman swear.

"In our defence," Waddell chimed in. "We didn't start the shooting. We've just been defending ourselves…and him," he added pointing to Robert.

"Regardless," Doyle pointed out. "We should have been notified the minute you guys came in to the country. We could have assisted. Hell, we could have handled the entire…"

"Cut the jurisdictional outrage bullshit," Waddell fired back. "How many times has C.S.I.S. operated inside the U.S. without informing anyone? Gimme a break."

"Enough," Holt ordered. "This bickering is pointless. Both sides are guilty of it over the years. This time, it got away from us. That's all. The only argument we should be having is where do we go from here?"

"Back stateside," Cooper noted. "We have orders to bring everyone back home." The news hit hard as all of them tried to process exactly what that meant.

"Wait," Robert objected. He turned to address Holt. "You guys can't just turn and leave. What'll happen to Anna? I can't do this by myself. I don't even know where to begin."

"Nobody is abandoning the file, Doctor," Cooper assured him.

"Her name is Anna – not 'the file'," Robert snapped. Cooper looked at him with regret in his eyes.

"My apologies, Doctor. I didn't mean anything by that. Nobody is abandoning Anna. We have information that the G.D.M. will be moving her to Las Vegas. The F.B.I. is on board as well and Homeland Security has been notified, but it's doubtful they'll be caught at the border. The G.D.M. has never had any trouble crossing from Canada to the U.S. and vice versa. They have numerous connections at most North American International airports so unless we get really lucky, our next move will be Vegas."

"Why are the Feds and Homeland weighing in on this? We can handle it." Waddell didn't like the idea of other agencies getting involved.

"Cut and dry on this one," MacReady pointed out. "There was a kidnapping and now we're looking at human trafficking cuz they're bringing her over the border. She may not be a U.S. citizen, but both Homeland and Quantico want to be sure that they are informed of any developments."

"Why Las Vegas?" Robert asked. He briefly remembered that he and Anna had always talked of going to Vegas. These were hardly the circumstances that they would have considered ideal.

"G.D.M. has a large facility somewhere in the greater Las Vegas area," MacReady added. "We don't know where exactly. Its location is very closely guarded. Only a select few have access to it and we haven't been able to penetrate that yet."

"When do we go?" Holt asked.

"Five hours. We're supposed to pack you guys up and escort you to YVR where we'll make the trip to Vegas," Cooper explained.

"I'll let O'Connor know," Waddell said as he moved to towards the hall.

"O'Connor won't be coming," Cooper pointed out. Waddell stopped and stared at him, open-mouthed. He was about to say something, but Cooper continued before he could. "His injuries exclude him from this mission. He'll be taken to Seattle and tended to there before they move him back to Langley for a full debrief."

"Seriously?" Holt asked.

"No lies," Cooper responded. "Langley and Quantico have been in constant contact for the last 24 hours about this matter. That's how C.S.I.S. got involved. The three agencies are going to try and work together to sort this one out."

"Oh that'll end well," Waddell said wryly. All of the agents in the room grumbled their agreement with the statement.

"I envy them that fight," Holt added.

"Why is that?" Cooper inquired.

"Cuz I'd rather have that fight than tell O'Connor he's out." Holt took his leave and headed towards the back room. His friend and long-time partner would not take this news lightly. He hated to leave a job unfinished. Holt only hoped that his injuries would stop him from inflicting too much damage on the person who physically tried to prevent him from going to Vegas.

CHAPTER

15

Anna woke with a stiff neck and an awful taste in her mouth. She tried to move, but soon realized that her muscles ached badly. Not just some of them, all of them. She tried again to move, but decided that it was better just to lay still. Cautiously, she opened her eyes and immediately noticed that she was not in the same room she had been. Come to think of it, she hadn't even realized that she had fallen asleep. She moved her head gingerly and looked around this new room. The furnishings were sparse, much like before, but there were medical instruments and machines in with her. This was some sort of hospital. There were still no windows and the large steel door had been replaced with a regular one, though it looked particularly sturdy. There was a second door of to the side that looked equally solid. She felt light-headed as she scanned the room. Looking down at her arm, she saw an IV sticking out of the back of her hand. Her initial impulse was to rip it out, but seeing as how she had no idea what was being administered, she decided to wait. For all she knew, it was some sort of counter-agent to whatever she had been drugged with.

Drugged. But I wasn't drugged. I didn't swallow the pills. She struggled to recall what had happened to her, but could not affix her thoughts to anything in particular. She felt around her mouth for the pills, but could not locate them. *I must have drifted off and swallowed them in my sleep accidentally. Damn*! She cursed silently. She tried again to focus her mind, but was interrupted by a familiar face entering her room.

"Good afternoon, Anna," Dr. Young said jovially. "How are we feeling today?"

Why do doctors always say we when they actually mean 'you'? Do I care how the doctor is feeling? Especially this one… "What happened? Where am I?" she asked. She feared that she would not like the answer, but the question needed to be asked anyway. She had clearly been moved and apparently while she was unconscious. The thought made her blanche. Being that vulnerable in the hands of these people was disconcerting to say the least.

"You've been moved to a different facility." A flash of hope swept across Anna's face as she weighed her options for escape. Reading this, Young continued. "Don't try to escape. I assure you, this facility is even more secure than the last one. Plus you have no idea where you are so really…there is no point."

"I didn't know where I was before," she pointed out. "Why should this be any different?"

That made Dr. Young chuckle. "I guess you're right," he conceded.

"You said good afternoon. What time is it?" she asked.

"5:35. Wow. Didn't realize it had gotten so late. Guess I should have said good evening, huh?" Anna paled at the announcement. It had been early morning when she had been roused and given the pills; the ones she hadn't swallowed. Somehow she had lost at least ten hours. Again, the doctor read her expression and responded before she could talk. "That IV is administering fluids for you. We weren't sure exactly how long you'd be out."

"I didn't swallow those pills. At least, I didn't mean to," she admitted.

"I know," he replied. "And I knew you wouldn't. So I made sure that you didn't have to."

She tried to understand what he was telling her, but couldn't put it all together. "What do you mean by that?"

He smiled at her. He had a pleasant face in spite of his position within this organization. "You weren't going to swallow those pills. So I administered the toxin that knocked you out in the coating. As soon as you put them in your mouth and they came in contact with your saliva, the chemical dissolved and entered you system. You were out like a light in no time." Anna's resolve waned as she realized how easily she had been manipulated. "It's one of my own designs. Needless to say the people I work for are quite impressed with its effectiveness. I'd like to thank you for providing such a wonderful example."

"Go the Hell," she snarled.

"Now, now. Be nice," Young replied. "I could just have easily coated the pills with one of the numerous poisons we have at our disposal, but I didn't."

Anna thought about that for a moment, but then lighted on the obvious. "You can't kill me. Your pal Vickers knows that. I'm useless to you guys if I'm dead. You're after my husband and you're using me to get to him. If Vickers had wanted me dead, he would have shot me in the head, not in the arm." Just uttering those words caused a shiver to run down her spine. She had never let herself admit how closely she had come to death until now. She was truly at the whim of Vickers and Dr. Young for that matter. She had never felt so vulnerable before. She was truly alone.

"Don't cry, Anna," the doctor said. She absently wiped the tears that had begun to flow without her knowledge. "But don't overstate your importance in this matter. Truth be told, we could very easily kill you now like we could have back at the other facility. Bottom line is that your husband and the group of people he has helping him believe that you are alive. That's all we need, really. We established proof of life already. It's doubtful they'll ask it again." He paused as he checked one of the machines in the room and made a notation. "You're right, though," he added distractedly. "Vickers could have killed you when he shot you, but he didn't. There has to be a reason for that. At least, that's what Holt and his team will theorize. As long as they believe you are alive, they will act accordingly. It's one of the good parts about dealing with government officials. They're just so damned predictable." He laughed as he headed for the door.

When he reached it, he stopped at spoke over his shoulder. "If you need anything, there is a button by your right hand. Press it and I'll be here. Don't misuse it though. I have no qualms about putting you under again if I have to. Get some rest." He closed the door behind him as he left.

Anna heard the now familiar sound of a mechanical lock snapping shut and was again alone with her thoughts. Her first impulse was to push the button to get that turd to come back just so she could waste his time. That thought was quickly dismissed, however. She feared the idea of being incapacitated. To this point, nothing truly horrific had befallen her. That could easily change. Instead she turned on her side and faced away from the door. There was no window, but in her mind she could see for miles. She wiped another tear from her face, curled up on her bed, and closed her eyes. She wasn't going to rest because they wanted her to. She was going to rest because it was the only way she could be with Robbie. She hoped that he hadn't given up. She prayed that he was safe. She cried... and fell asleep.

The drive to the airport was mercifully uneventful. After the last couple of trips Holt had taken, he was glad for the rest. The small convoy of three Chevy Suburbans couldn't have been more conspicuous, but this was no longer a counter-surveillance mission. It was a show of force. Robert, Holt, Cooper, and Waddell were in the lead vehicle while Doyle, Martinez, Ballard, and Macready were second. The vehicle in the rear housed O'Connor who looked like a bomb about to detonate. He was accompanied by two other agents, one of whom had been tending to his injuries. He had argued vehemently in an attempt to stay on with the rest of the team, but inevitably had lost. The decision was clearly from higher up than Cooper or even Holt. The feeling of failure, however, was no less painful. Holt had agreed to keep him apprised of the situation as they went, but that would prove difficult. O'Connor knew that for the foreseeable future, he would be locked away in some hole somewhere answering questions about everything that had happened to this point.

Holt, meanwhile, was looking ahead to a future that was quite a bit more uncertain. He hadn't been to Las Vegas in years and had actually never been there on an assignment before. According to what he had learned from Cooper and Martinez, the G.D.M. was fully entrenched there and had their claws in practically everything. Unfortunately for this situation, that prevented bringing in local law enforcement to provide added security and intelligence. Holt rarely had use for police agencies, but in these circumstances local authorities were privy to a lot of information that agencies like the C.I.A. and F.B.I. just did not have. A lot of it was gathered through word of mouth on the street and local informants. The risk of a leak was too great.

"The Feds are gonna be waiting for us once we get to Harry Reid International," Cooper explained. "A couple of their Bureau guys are pretty well informed on the G.D.M. and their activities in Vegas. They'll be acting as our liaisons to the Bureau itself."

"I don't like it," Waddell added. "Why's the Bureau sticking their nose in this?"

"Well, what's to like?" Cooper answered. "This whole mess is hardly ideal. But we do what we can with the cards we're dealt. Langley says we cooperate with the Feds? Then we cooperate, pure and simple. Understood?" he added with a slight edge to his voice. Cooper did not like the situation either, but he liked being questioned by a junior agent even less.

"Are you sure they took her to Las Vegas?" Robert asked. "It seems to be a bit of a leap to be making such a drastic move. I mean, what if she's still here? We'd just be leaving her behind."

Waddell looked at Robert in the rear view mirror while he negotiated traffic on Marine Drive towards the airport. "A cargo plane was chartered yesterday and flew to Las Vegas this morning. No one at the airport seems to be able to recall who or what was on board…just that it left. Once we were notified, we looked into all scheduled flights out of Vancouver and Abbotsford. This one popped up cuz the payment was made using a G.D.M. dummy account. Had we known earlier, we might have been able to do something about it." He cast a sideways glance at Cooper in the passenger seat. "But by the time we discovered it, the plane had already touched down in Vegas."

"So Anna's in Las Vegas with these monsters…why? Because of some bureaucratic pissing contest between you guys?!"

"Dr. Seabrook," Cooper replied soothingly. "It's a little more complicated than that."

"No it isn't," Robert snapped. "Not to me…and not to Anna. You guys run around destroying people's lives like it's a sport of some kind and then when you actually have to play with others, you…"

"Alright, that's it!" Waddell exploded. "I've listened to just about enough of this!"

"Easy, Mitch," Holt cautioned.

"No, enough." Waddell turned to face Robert. "Yeah, I get it. You're life's been turned upside down and Anna was taken by people who aren't exactly nice guys. But none of that is our fault and I'm tired of getting blamed for it. If it hadn't been for us, you'd both be sitting with Vickers right now and trust me, your wife would be a lot worse off than she is now. The only reason she has a hope in Hell is because Vickers knows that we are with you. We may not have as much to lose as you do, but if anything that makes what we're doing that much more commendable. We're doing this cuz we want to help. We're not going to get a fuckin' parade for anything we do…ever…and we don't ask for one. But don't you dare sit there and pass judgment saying this is some kind of sport. We're risking our lives for you and your wife cuz it's our job."

"Mitch," Holt said quietly. "That's enough."

The four men sat in silence as the tension in the vehicle crept over them. In his heart, Robert knew that a lot of what the young agent had said was true. None of this was their fault and yet he found himself wanting to blame them. He had to blame somebody and they just happened to be easy targets. He was indebted to them. Waddell was right. He and Anna had walked right into Vickers' trap back in Abbotsford. If it hadn't been for them, Vickers would have had them both. Anna would have been expendable. A shiver wracked Robert's body as he completed that particular equation. He wanted to say something…to apologize. He wanted to thank them for everything they had done and continued to do. No words, though, seemed to be fitting.

"I'm sorry," he said sullenly. He looked up and saw Holt looking back at him. Robert shook his head as his eyes moistened. He couldn't find the words he wanted to use. Holt saw his struggle and knew exactly what Robert was trying to say.

Holt nodded simply as he accepted Robert's silent apology and his thanks. *It's okay*, he mouthed. *You're welcome.* The two men shared a look of understanding and respect. Then Robert looked out the window and took a deep breath. Vancouver International Airport was just over the bridge.

"This is bullshit," O'Connor protested as he was escorted away from the rest of the agents. He desperately wanted to see this one through to the end, but the decision was not his to make. Holt and Waddell had shaken his hand and Dr. Seabrook had given him a hug which hurt like hell. Now, he was on going to be on his way to Seattle and a bare room full of agents and coffee. He thought briefly of making a break for it, but that wouldn't accomplish much. Besides the fact that he still would have to endure the debrief, in his current condition he'd be lucky to outmanoeuvre a sloth with a limp.

The two agents with him guided him through the maze that seemed to engulf every major international airport and brought him to the plane that would make the short jump from Vancouver to Seattle. The plane was being held for them so it wasn't going to be a long wait. The three men boarded, took their seats, and within a few minutes began taxiing towards takeoff. He was still fuming when the wheels lifted off the ground.

Back at the airport, Robert and his swarm of agents had gathered outside of the main terminal to discuss how they were going to proceed. Robert had travelled internationally before, but he had a feeling that this would be a little different.

"There's a Gulfstream waiting to take us to Las Vegas," Cooper began. "You all know the drill," he added to all of the agents. "Dr. Seabrook, just walk confidently and follow us. You'll be fine."

"What's going on?" he asked Holt.

"We have clearance from both of our governments to make this trip so we'll be bypassing Customs and Immigration," he answered as the group entered the terminal.

"Well if we're cleared, why all the fuss?"

"Bottom line is this would have been thrown together at the last minute. Odds are pretty good that not everyone in the airport knows about it. There will be some curious looks and such and if we run into any security personnel, there could be a delay. There's always at least one moron who's seen Die Hard too many times." Holt smiled at the thought.

"I've never not passed through Customs before," Robert said with a smile and a hint of pride.

"Well here," Holt said and smacked him lightly on the forehead. "You're officially cleared to fly into the United States. Anything to declare?"

"Yeah, you're an idiot." That caused both men to laugh. "Thanks," Robert added.

"You looked like you needed a break," Holt said plainly.

"I did," Robert answered. "But what I mean is…thank you." The two men had a wordless conversation ending in a smile.

"Let's go to Vegas," Holt said finally. The seven agents accompanying Robert Seabrook grabbed their gear from the vehicles and crossed the concourse, headed for the security checkpoint. Cooper was getting ready for a battle of wills, but the fight was over before he got there. Ballard walked ahead and spoke briefly with the security officer who in turn opened the "Authorized Personnel Only" door beside the main entrance. Cooper stared at Ballard in fascination as they all passed through. She merely shrugged in response. Once through the door, they were guided by security personnel to the appropriate gate where the Gulfstream was waiting. While they waited for the gate to open, Cooper walked over to Ballard.

"How the hell did you pull that off? I was expecting trouble."

"I took the liberty of calling ahead," she answered with a smile. "I figured we'd need it."

"That was a risk you shouldn't have taken. What if the G.D.M. caught wind of it?" MacReady asked. "They could have done something to the plane."

"Sometimes you have to trust the people you work with," Ballard objected.

"That's a mistake," Cooper pointed out as the escorting security officer approached them. "No offense," he added to the man.

"None taken," he replied. "The jet is good to go. Your pilots are already on board."

"Thanks," Ballard answered. "Cooper? All of you? I'd like to introduce my brother, Chris. He's head of security here at YVR."

Cooper smiled outwardly. "Trust the people you work with, huh?"

Ballard returned the smile. "And the people you're related to. Thanks Chris," she said to her brother as the agents filed past. "You know I can't tell you what this is about," she said.

"I didn't ask," he replied feigning indignation. She laughed and gave him a kiss on the cheek. "Just be careful, okay?"

"I will. See you when I get back." Ballard followed the men as they all boarded the jet. The pilots had been fully briefed about their destination and were instructed to stay in the cockpit. Once the passengers were safely in Vegas, their services would no longer be needed and they were to continue on back to Langley. Robert and all of the accompanying agents strapped themselves in and prepared for takeoff. A trip to Vegas was not a long flight, but it would allow for some rest. They all felt that they would need it.

CHAPTER 16

Anna woke with a splitting headache. She had no idea how long she had been asleep. With a windowless room, she also had no concept of what time it might be. Her internal clock was clearly off. Perhaps it was a side effect of the drug she had been given, but she was disoriented. The ache in her body had thankfully subsided a bit, leaving her with a dull throbbing. The problem she was facing was a new one; she couldn't see properly. She was crying again. *Oh enough of this blubbering, Anna*, she cursed herself silently. *Pull yourself together and start being active by getting outta here.* She wiped at her eyes, but they were watering uncontrollably. She soon realized that she wasn't crying, but tears were flowing freely and they didn't seem like they were going to stop. She groped blindly for the button that would summon Dr. Young.

A few moments after pressing it, Young entered. *Clearly he's close to this room*, she thought. *That might come in handy.*

"You rang?" Young asked glibly.

"My eyes," she said. "They won't stop tearing up. Is there a reason?" She heard the doctor cross the room to her bed and felt a light shine in her eyes. She recoiled slightly at the intrusion that the beam caused. Clearly, she was susceptible to light as well.

"It's a common side effect of the drug I'm afraid," he explained. Though considering you're only the fourth person that it's been administered to, I could hardly call that common. But it's normal. So far, everyone has experienced an irritation of the tear ducts that has had the same result. Nothing to worry about. It will clear up in about 2 hours or so," he added reassuringly.

"Who's worried?" Anna answered sarcastically. "Why didn't you warn me about it, though? I thought I was going blind." She managed a small smile.

"To be honest, I wasn't sure it would affect you. As I said, I've only administered it three times previously. Truthfully, this particular side effect was unexpected."

Anna listened intently as he proceeded with his ministrations of her eyes. "You said particular side effect. Is there any others I should know about?"

He laughed lightly. "They've all come and gone, unless you count the fatigue. That will stay with you a bit longer, but it will diminish." He concluded his examination with a few drops of some liquid into her eyes. "There. That will help a bit. You'll still be a little teary, but you will notice a change pretty quick."

"Thank you," she said genuinely. The runny eyes were quite a pain in the ass. Besides, she couldn't very well improve her situation if she couldn't see. "Where is this place? Are we in Vancouver or something?"

"Let's just say it's something and leave it at that. You can ask all the questions you like, I won't give anything away. You're not the first person I've had to tend to over the years. And believe me, some of them were considered experts in interrogation tactics. Just lie back and wait. As long as your husband delivers our man, you and yours can go on your merry way." Anna's face fell slightly at the mention of her husband. She wished he was here… or rather that she was where he was. "Look at it this way. The less you know, the more likely you are to survive. If you don't know much about our operation, then we won't have to terminate you. So stop trying to learn more about where you are. It'll be better for you in the long run."

The logic, despite being incredibly skewed, was still pretty sound. Anna realized that the way out of here was not going to be through information. She'd have to make a move physically. *When my eyesight clears up*, she thought. *I'll know more when my eyesight clears up. I'll just have to wait until the time is right.* She had no idea what time would be right, but eventually someone would make a mistake. She just hoped she would be able to recognize it when it appeared. She might even have to make the opportunity present itself. She knew she didn't have a lot of time, but had every intention of using what time she did.

The doctor rechecked the machines before heading back to the door. She strained to watch more closely this time as he left. He used some kind of card on his belt to swipe a small panel to the left of the door. The door opened and he stepped through. Once the door closed behind him, there was the same metallic 'clunk' indicating some sort of mechanical lock in addition to the card access. *So there are two locks on these doors and...* She checked again to be sure. *No handle or doorknob on the inside. The only way to open the door from the inside is with that card. The mechanical lock must be a way to manually open the door from the outside if the card didn't work for some reason.* Did that mean that there was someone on the other side of the door? Or was the doctor locking the door once he got out? *Were there security cameras?* She rubbed her eyes to clear them of the remaining tears that had already started to dry up and looked around the room. She couldn't see any cameras, but with technology today, that was no guarantee. Almost everything could be a camera nowadays.

She made the decision. She would just have to hope for the best because she wasn't going to lie and wait to be rescued like some damsel in distress. Her first order of business was to get out of this room. What was beyond the door was a mystery, but she knew she wasn't going to garner any information from Dr. Young. He had made that very clear. The only way to discover what lay beyond the door was to see it for herself. When she regained a bit more of her strength and her eyesight was back to normal, she would summon the good doctor to the room once more. She looked around the room again for something she could use as a weapon. She was going to get that key card, and she had no intention of being polite about it.

"Once again, let's go through everything that happened," the interviewer asked.

O'Connor, exasperated, ran his hands through his hair and exhaled deeply. He looked up at the ceiling of the interview room, marvelling at the wonderful shade of green they had found to paint it. It was somewhere between pea soup and vomit, if such a realm existed. The walls were a dull grey that seemed to just absorb light. If there had been a large "mirror" on one of the walls, he would have felt like he was in a Law & Order episode. The only difference would be that he couldn't change the channel on this one. He was stuck. He had already gone through the entire ordeal twice with two different interviewers. This one had been first and had nearly put O'Connor to sleep with his droning, but he was replaced by another one who was even more infuriatingly boring. Now, number one was back to recheck his story. Such was the life of the damned who had to endure the 'debrief'.

"Everything?" O'Connor inquired.

"Everything," the interviewing agent repeated.

"Okay," O'Connor breathed. He leaned forward, resting his forearms on the table in front of him and interlaced his fingers. He lowered his head to the table, took a deep breath, and raised his gaze to lock squarely on the man sitting across from him. "From what I hear, there was this big bang that formed the universe. Or maybe it was God? To be honest I'm not sure. Either way, the world ending up being created and…"

"The more you joke with me Agent O'Connor, the longer this is going to take," Agent Miller said tiredly. He too was quite ready to find something else to do, but his job at this time was to debrief O'Connor. "I don't know about you, but I have things I would rather be doing than sitting here listening to you try to humour yourself. The sad thing is, between the two of us, I'm the only one who's actually getting paid to be here. So could you try to stay focussed if for nobody else's sake, then for your own?"

"Look, I have answered all of your questions…twice!" O'Connor snapped.

"And you'll answer them again. You know the drill. An agent is dead on a botched mission. People up the chain are going apeshit and all we have to give them so far is a colossal 'I don't know' and that's just not good enough. Now C.S.I.S. is involved, the Feds, Homeland…. If the media wasn't so goddamned incompetent, we'd be plastered all over the fucking news by now. And you're giving me shit cuz you don't feel like answering the same questions more than once? Get your head on straight cuz we ain't goin' nowhere til you and I get somewhere. Understood?"

The two men glared at each other for a few moments, but O'Connor knew that Miller was right. "What do you want to know?"

"Okay, you said that Holt met with Seabrook before any of this happened."

"Right. He contacted me and told me to get the team up and ready to move. He instructed us to go to the Breakwater where he was going to meet up with Dr. Seabrook. Our instructions were to follow him back to his house and wait for Holt there."

"And the Breakwater is…?" Miller asked.

"A wharf or jetty, whatever, that's a little south of the Inner Harbour in Victoria," O'Connor explained. "Google it if you need to."

Miller shot him a sardonic look, then continued. "Why did Holt want to meet with him?"

"You'd have to ask Holt. We were just the surveillance team. This was Holt's file. We were just there to provide support," O'Connor explained.

"What happened then?"

O'Connor took a sip of water before continuing. "We knew it was going to be an overnight surveillance cuz Holt wasn't going to meet us til the morning. We parked a ways away and curled up for the night."

"You, Waddell, and Nesbitt," Miller interjected.

"Right."

"Were you followed? Did you see anything out of the ordinary?"

O'Connor thought back to that evening. He was sure he hadn't noticed anything but replayed what he could remember just in case. "We weren't followed and I didn't notice anything. The evening went smooth. Nesbitt had attached the listening devices in the house the day before and we had the lines bugged. We were set. The night went by without a peep." O'Connor thought back to being in that cramped car. The listening devices they had placed were quite sensitive and the sounds of the Seabrooks in bed were unmistakable. Out of courtesy, he had removed his earpiece and had to smack Waddell on the side of his head to get him to do the same. "In the morning, a call came in."

"Tell me about it," Miller prompted.

"It was weird. We tapped the call the minute they picked up, but then we got scrambled. I've never seen anything like it. It was like something out of a sci-fi movie. I mean there we were with the best electronic descramblers and tracking equipment we have and we get nothing. It was like we just got locked out of our own system. Nesbitt tried to counter it, but before we knew it, the Seabrooks come racing out of the house and head for the ferry. Naturally we followed. We got a hold of Holt, updated him, and met him at the ferry."

"How did you guys come to get separated?"

O'Connor took another deep breath. This was the part of the story he hated having to go through again. "The Seabrooks went into the terminal. Whatever call came in had spooked them and made them run. Holt wanted to make sure they weren't in danger. We sent Waddell in to keep an eye on them. Nesbitt went in a bit later and Holt and I stayed to watch their car and to keep an eye out for uninvited guests. Waddell said Nesbitt went to the bathroom and didn't come back out. That's when the transmitters went down."

"Right," Miller said furtively. "That leads us to our first serious problem here, O'Connor."

"Well why don't you enlighten me?"

"I had our people check in to the transmitters you guys had been issued. According to the techs, there's no way the transmitters can be knocked out the way you described."

"Well obviously they're wrong, cuz that's exactly what happened?" O'Connor snapped back.

"Well walk me through it. Maybe there is something you've overlooked."

O'Connor shook his head in bewilderment. "I don't know what to tell you. The Seabrooks came out of the terminal and headed back to their car. Waddell comes out shortly after, comes up and jumps in the car tellin' me Nesbitt is dead. I ask him what happened. He tells me and then tells me the transmitters are down. I test mine. I can't reach anyone. An then…" the memory catches O'Connor, freezing him in mid-sentence.

"Then what?" Miller asked, sensing a possible break.

"Holt," O'Connor whispered almost inaudibly.

"What about Holt?" Miller prodded.

Shaking his head to clear it of the memory, O'Connor came back to the present. "When I looked in the mirror to see if Holt was all right, I saw him coming back to his car. I hadn't noticed he had left."

"Did you question him about it?"

"Of course," O'Connor responded. "He told me he was stretching his legs."

"And you believed that?" Miller asked incredulously.

"Look, I had my doubts at first, obviously. But when he got through that attempt on his life, I started to believe him. If he was dirty, why would they try to kill him?" O'Connor pointed out.

"Did you witness the attack?"

O'Connor thought back to the incident and realized that all he had to go on was Holt's word. "No. I was tailing Seabrook at the time."

"So all you had was his word that what he said was true."

"Listen, Miller. I know you probably think that I'm just some operative here, but one of my most attuned skills as a surveillance expert is the ability to read people. Holt was telling the truth about the shooting."

"For arguments sake, O'Connor, let's say he is telling the truth. Did it ever occur to you that the people who tried to kill Holt on the highway weren't involved in the Seabrook file? I'm sure Holt has made several enemies over the years." Miller sat back in his seat with a smug look on his face.

"Are you telling me you think this is some kind of coincidence?" O'Connor asked incredulously. "Where the hell did the Agency find you? Goodwill?"

"Try to insult me if you like, O'Connor. Bottom line is that I have an advantage that you do not. I have the objectivity to be able to look at this situation that Holt has created and try to approach it from every conceivable angle. Clearly, you lack this ability." O'Connor started to say something, but was quickly silenced as Miller continued. "I can appreciate your loyalty in this situation. Truth be told, we could use a bit more loyalty in the Agency these days. But there comes a time when loyalty has to be placed where it belongs. We have operatives heading into a situation where loyalties are going to be the least of their worries."

"If you're that concerned, why send them?" O'Connor pressed.

"I'd like to tell you that it's something as noble as saving Dr. Seabrook's wife, but I'd be lying. Truth is, we have a shot at striking a blow to the G.D.M. Vickers is a major player. We have a chance at taking him down and that's exactly what we intend to do."

"What about the Seabrooks?" O'Connor asked.

"Unfortunately, their safety is secondary on this one. Of course we'd like to see them home, but if we have to use them to draw Vickers out...we will." This revelation was not a shock to O'Connor, but it still tied his stomach in knots. He had grown to like Seabrook, or at least appreciate the man and what he was going through. Anna he had never even met, but neither of them deserved this fate. He started envisioning ways of getting to Vegas to assist, but couldn't seem to get very far. After a few moments, he realized that Miller was still talking to him.

"I'm sorry...what?" O'Connor asked.

"I said I want you to meet with our tech guys. They're waiting for you downstairs. We need to know exactly what happened with our transmitters. If the G.D.M. does indeed have the capability to disrupt our communication, then we need a new game plan...now."

"Understood," O'Connor replied. "We done here?"

"For now. I'll want to talk with you again after you meet with tech. With any luck, their questions will bring forth some new answers and likewise." Miller stood and showed O'Connor to the elevator that took him down to meet with the science gurus of the C.I.A. An agent was with O'Connor as he descended the three floors to the lab level. He was also accompanied by a lot of questions and doubts about Holt and this entire file.

When the doors opened, he was greeted by a very attractive woman in a business suit and glasses. "O'Connor, I'm Dr. Sarah Quinn. Miller told me to expect you." She extended a hand and O'Connor shook it. "Are you all right?" she asked.

O'Connor realized that he had been staring at her and quickly regained his composure. "Sorry, I just…uh…" he stammered.

"Let me guess. You are expecting a lanky man with horn-rimmed glasses? Maybe a beard?" she asked with a smile on her face.

"Something like that…sorry. Hang on a sec. You said your name was Dr. Quinn?"

"Don't bother. Trust me I've heard them all. You won't be the first and you certainly won't be the last." She turned on her heel and started sown the corridor. "Follow me, please."

Gladly, O'Connor thought. O'Connor made a concerted effort to avoid watching her as they walked down the corridor. He stole a glance now and then, though. He couldn't help it. He had always been a sucker for a woman in a business suit. It just seemed so classy. When they reached a large set of double doors, Dr. Quinn stopped and entered a code on the number pad beside it and laid her hand on a palm reader. The door hissed and opened slightly. Before she opened it, she turned and fixed O'Connor with a serious gaze.

"Two things. One, you are not allowed to discuss anything that you see or hear down here with anyone under any circumstances under penalty of treason. Clear?"

"Clear," he answered. "And the second thing?"

She smiled. "Thanks."

O'Connor furrowed his brow in confusion. "For?"

"Most guys I meet down here, especially operatives, walk the entire corridor with their eyes on my ass. You didn't."

O'Connor's face shifted to worry. *How did she know? She was ahead of me the whole time.* "What do you mean? I mean how…"

"There are cameras everywhere, O'Connor. Down here there are a lot of them."

O'Connor nodded, but then he clued in on a problem with that logic. "But even if I was on camera, how did you see it?"

Again she smiled. "You don't think I actually need these glasses do you?" She took them off and tossed them to him. He held them up and looked in, seeing an image in the upper corner of himself holding the glasses.

"Impressive," he admitted.

"Thanks again," she replied, taking the glasses back. "Now let's go find out what's wrong with those transmitters."

CHAPTER 17

The flight to Las Vegas was unremarkable. Some of the agents had passed the time by comparing war stories, some of which seemed too far-fetched to be believed. The two C.S.I.S. agents contributed to the discussion which only seemed to stoke the fire of whose agency was better. Robert listened for a while, but soon grew weary. He wondered if they would be talking of his situation at some future gathering of operatives. The flippant way they regarded some of their past endeavours made him resent them a little. He knew that they had to maintain a certain level of detachment in order to do their jobs properly, but that was a luxury that he could not afford. His thoughts turned to Anna and where she might be; what she might be feeling. There was no way he could reach out to her, though he wanted to with everything that he was. She was somewhere in Las Vegas and that was where he was heading. That made him feel a little better. With every second that passed, he was a little bit closer to her; to being reunited with her. *Holt and Cooper will get me to her. I can feel it.*

He closed his eyes and thought about Anna; the trips they were going to take, the memories that they had already shared. He imagined them walking hand in hand along the Inner Harbour back in Victoria, watching the local artists and performers ply their trades during the summer months. He imagined tourists flocking to see the next magician carve out a spot for himself on the walkway. The smell of the water mixed with the various food stands gave the area a distinct aroma. He could almost smell it as a warm breeze came in off the harbour itself. He pictured Anna standing in the rose garden by the Empress Hotel, her summer dress drifting lazily in the afternoon glow. She looked at him and smiled, those eyes so green.

He must have dozed off because before he knew it, they were descending into Las Vegas. Holt moved over beside him and put his seatbelt on.

"Have a good sleep?" he asked.

"Didn't even realize I had," Robert replied.

"It's good. You should catch some sleep whenever you can." Holt tightened his belt and sat back. "I have to admit, these Gulfstreams are pretty impressive. Ever been on one before?" Robert shook his head in response. "Me either," Holt continued. "I'm gonna have to get me one of these. Beats economy any day."

"I don't really fly that much," Robert admitted.

"You and Anna don't travel?"

The mention of her name brought an uneasy feeling that he did not like. Would they get the chance to travel?

He certainly hoped so. "Not yet. Something always came up."

"Well when this is all over, you two should take a trip somewhere. Think of it as a reward for getting through this ordeal," Holt said.

"You think we'll get that chance?" Robert asked. He hated thinking about what might happen, but there was no real way to avoid it.

"I do," Holt answered and turned towards him. "Look Robert, I know how out of control you must feel right now. Not only does Vickers have Anna, but we have no idea where Terry is either. I know it looks bleak, but we are far from powerless. Right now, our greatest ally is information. We know Vickers is in Las Vegas and that he doesn't know where Terry is either. What he doesn't know is that we are on the way there AND we have support from Langley, the Feds, and C.S.I.S. We can use all of those assets to better our chances and strengthen our position. Try not to worry," he added soothingly.

"Until Anna is safe, worry is pretty much all I'm capable of," he said with a rueful smile.

Holt patted him on the arm. "We'll get her back."

The pilots eased the Gulfstream onto the runway and taxied to the appropriate unloading area. The agents quickly disembarked and were greeted by a man with a waiting van. "Mr. Holt? My name is Agent Noel Wojanski. I'm with the F.B.I." He extended his hand and was introduced to the team. "I've been fully briefed and have been instructed to extend the full cooperation and support of the F.B.I. We have a room waiting for you guys at the Flamingo. It's centralized and won't attract much attention."

"No Caesar's Palace?," Holt asked as he tossed his gear in the back and climbed into the stretch van. The rest of the team quickly followed suit.

The young Bureau agent answered as he slid in behind the wheel. "You're fortunate we got what we did. Whole city is pretty much packed in. Gives us a nice central location on the Strip." Robert was given the front seat beside Wojanski who whisked them away from the airport.

"Have you heard anything about where she is being held? Any ideas?" Cooper asked.

"My partner is waiting for us at the hotel. She has the full file on the G.D.M. and their operations in Vegas. You can access it once we're there and she can answer any questions you have," Wojanski replied in a business-like fashion.

Holt appraised the F.B.I. agent. He seemed young. *Then again, they're all starting to look young to me.* This one, though, seemed to be a little too straight-laced. "First case?" he asked.

"Excuse me?" Wojanski replied as he looked at Holt in the rear view mirror.

"Is this your first case?" Holt reiterated as he met the young agent's gaze.

Wojanski thought about his answer for a few moments before replying. "Yes and no. I've been behind a desk for a few years and was recently promoted to field agent. This is my first case out here." He returned his focus to the traffic as they exited the airport and headed towards the famous (and infamous) Las Vegas Strip. "What gave me away?"

Now it was Holt's turn to require clarification. "Sorry?" he asked.

"How did you know it was my first case?"

"Being able to read people is practically a requirement in my kind of work," Holt answered with a hint of bravado. Cooper just rolled his eyes. Holt grinned widely.

"Don't sweat it, kid," Martinez chimed in. "It comes with experience. I was behind a desk for…God it felt like forever. Now look at me. I'm considered an expert on Columbia so I'm here in Las Vegas tracking a kidnapper. Didn't see this coming, that's for sure," he added with a smile.

That seemed to relax Agent Wojanski a little. He nodded at no one in particular and continued towards the heart of the city. Before too long, the tall spire of the Eiffel Tower at Paris came in to view. In the distance, the Stratosphere rose above the other buildings marking the far end of the Strip. The immense buildings seemed completely out of place within the confines of the surrounding desert. But that, Robert supposed, was part of Las Vegas' charm. The sun was still relatively high in the evening sky when they turned onto Las Vegas Boulevard. The lights would soon be dominating the skyline and bathing the streets with the bright glow of proposed fortune. All the places he had seen on TV were now directly in front of him. It was truly awe-inspiring. They passed the MGM Grand, New York, New York, Planet Hollywood, Bellagio, Paris. They were all here and more impressive than he had ever thought possible. For a moment, he was just another tourist dazzled by the lavishness.

Across from Caesar's Palace stood the Flamingo. Not nearly as palatial as Caesar's for sure, the Flamingo provided two things to Robert. One, it was their destination. Two, it snapped him back to the reality of why they were there. This was not a vacation. He had allowed himself to forget about his troubles for a few moments. The brilliance of the Strip had caused him to forget about Anna. He tried to swallow the large lump that had formed in his throat and choked back the tears that he felt rising to his eyes, not wanting to shed them in front of the others. He attempted to mend the hole he felt in his heart at what he considered was a betrayal of her. *How could I have let her slip from his mind for even a moment?* Wojanski swung the van around to the back of the building and disappeared inside while the rest of the team all piled out of the vehicle and retrieved their gear from the back. Doyle, from C.S.I.S., walked up to Robert and pulled him aside.

"Listen. Don't beat yourself up. You're supposed to get lost when you first see the Strip. That's what it's intended to do. It doesn't mean that she ever left your thoughts," he said reassuringly.

"How did you know?" Robert asked, barely able to contain his grief.

"You're no spy, Dr. Seabrook," Doyle added. "You haven't learned to conceal your feelings from your face. You're easier to read than a comic strip," he said with a smile. He clapped him on the shoulder and steered him towards the door that Wojanski had entered. The young agent reappeared and ushered everyone inside, leading them all up to the room.

"There's actually two rooms with a connecting door. That will serve as our base of operations. We have other rooms set up for sleeping accommodations in case this goes on for a while," Wojanski commented.

"Good," Cooper stated. "We'll get situated in the operations room and get squared away later." He looked at Holt, who nodded in agreement. The group moved quickly through the halls of the hotel. A few travellers eyed them wearily, but for the most part, they were ignored. The room was on the sixth floor and indeed connected to an adjacent room, giving the team much needed space. Wojanski entered with a key card swipe and introduced the group to his partner. "Everyone. This is Special Agent Christina Fenwick. Agent Fenwick? Everyone." The team all filed into the room and exchanged pleasantries with Agent Fenwick. She stood about 5'9" tall and had shoulder length light brown hair. Her hair was a mess and judging by the bags under her eyes, she had been up most of the night. In spite of all of this, she was still quite beautiful. She diligently shook everyone's hand and made an attempt to remember the names and which faces they belonged to. With her sleep deprivation brought on by poring over the G.D.M. file, though, she quickly lost track by the fifth person.

"Where should we drop our stuff?" one of them asked. She thought she remembered him as MacReady.

"In the next room on the beds is fine for now. You can take your kits with you when you head to your own rooms," she added, tiredly. "I'll brief you all on what we know when you are all back in here."

"Pardon me for saying this," Holt said. "I've never been good with first impressions or political correctness, but you look like crap. Been up all night?" An awkward silence descended on the team as they waited to see how Agent Fenwick reacted to Holt's straightforward approach.

She stared at him in disbelief for a few moments. He just shrugged and waited for a response. She laughed a little which broke the tension. "Yeah, I've been going over everything we have on these guys for thirty two hours straight. If it's all the same, though, I'd just like to get this over with."

"Suit yourself," Holt answered with a smile. He walked into the adjoining room and dropped his gear on the bed. He was about to go back when his cell phone rang. He took it out and looked down at the call display. Walking over to the corner of the room, he answered it while the rest of the team reassembled with Fenwick in the main area. She had several maps laid out on one of the beds in the room and numerous file folders scattered here and there.

"I don't understand why we couldn't just do this at the field office. It would have been so much easier," she stated to the people in the room.

"Easier, yes," Cooper replied. "But not more secure. The G.D.M. has people inside the Bureau…the Agency too," he added when he saw Fenwick start to react. "We're trying to keep this as quiet as possible. Too many people know already, but all of us showing up at the field office would not go unnoticed."

"If you say so," she relented. "But it's a logistical nightmare."

"Tell me about it," Cooper agreed. At this moment, Holt came back into the room, carrying his bag. "Where are you off to?" Cooper asked.

"I'm going to drop my stuff in my room. I have a meeting with an informant who has information that the Feds don't."

"Good. We'll come with you," Cooper stated.

"No," Holt answered. "I've gotta go alone. He doesn't trust anyone but me and if he sees that I'm not alone, he'll bail." Cooper remained unsympathetic. "Trust me," Holt continued. "If my guy says it's new intel, then it is."

Cooper finally relented. "Be careful. We'll fill you in on everything when you get back."

"Waddell," Holt added. "Listen to what Cooper tells you. He's on point when I'm not here. Understood?"

"Yeah," he replied.

Robert walked over to Holt as he headed out the door. "Holt. I need a minute," he said as he caught up to him in the hallway.

"I don't have a lot of time, Robert. What's up?"

"I wanna go with you," he said simply. Holt smiled a little as he regarded the good doctor.

"Doc, Cooper's good. I wouldn't leave you with him if he wasn't. But this is something I have to do on my own. There's just no other way it can be done." He could see that Robert was not fully convinced. "After I speak with this guy, I can put something in motion that might shift the tides of what's been happening here. You're just gonna have to trust me on this one."

"I still don't like it, but I guess I don't have a choice. Take care, Holt," Robert said.

"Call me Brian," Holt said. He smiled, turned, and walked down the hallway towards the main elevators that would lead him to the main lobby. Robert watched him go, then returned to the room. He tried the handle and pushed, walking solidly into the closed door. He took a step back and knocked timidly.

Cooper answered the door with a grin on his face. "Forget that the door locks, Doc?" he asked beaming with joy as Robert's face hastened towards crimson.

"Can we just forget that just happened?" he asked with a wry smile.

"Sure," Cooper answered with a meaty pat on the back. "Hey Fenwick, we might wanna see about getting a few more key cards made up." That brought a chuckle from the people in the room.

"Where'd Holt take off to?" Macready inquired. He was already rummaging through one of the file folders that Fenwick had brought up to the table.

"He said he had to meet with someone. It was something to do with Anna or the G.D.M." Robert answered. "I tried to go along with him, but he said he had to go alone."

"What's the matter? You don't like our company anymore?" Waddell added with a mock sense of despair.

Robert smiled. "I like you guys fine. I just wanna know everything that's going on."

"That's understandable," Ballard agreed. "Did he say when he was coming back?"

Robert shook his head slightly. "Only that it wouldn't take long."

"Let's get this briefing started so I can get you all caught up," Agent Fenwick interjected. "I'll also field any questions you might have and answer them to the best of my abilities. After that, Woj here," she said pointing out Agent Wojanski "will show you all to your rooms. They're all relatively close." The agents all nodded their agreement and gathered around the F.B.I. agent. "Okay. What we know for a fact, unfortunately, is not very much. We know that the G.D.M. has a facility in or around the Las Vegas area. So far we haven't been able to isolate exactly where that is. We had an informant inside, but he was burned and we lost him. The information he was able to provide before he dropped off the radar was that it was a large facility, at least 8 stories tall," she added checking her notes. "Now we have cross-referenced all of the buildings in the area against buildings of that height and gone through all of them. No luck."

"Any chance your guy was wrong? Or maybe he turned?" Cooper asked.

"Chances are slim to him being wrong. Was he turned? I can't say for sure, but all of his intel up to this point held up so we're going on the assumption that it's accurate. Which leads us to believe that the facility that we're looking for is, in fact, underground. Now because we don't know exactly how many floors this facility has and no way of ascertaining how many of those floors are actually underground, our possible buildings could be anything. Hell, it might not even have any levels aboveground. It might just be buried in the sand somewhere. So in that area, we're back to square one."

"Any suspicious movement to or from any of the casinos?" Ballard asked.

"Problem there is…what's considered suspicious in Las Vegas?" Fenwick replied. "There is always a ton of movement and we just don't have the resources to cover them all. Now, speaking of movement," she added as she picked up another file from the table. "We have it on good authority that all five members of The Assembly are either in town or are on their way. Needless to say, we are bringing our full attention to bear on this meeting as it could be a chance to seriously cripple the G.D.M."

"With all due respect," Robert pointed out. "I'm not interested in bringing down the G.D.M. I just want my wife back."

"I understand that Dr. Seabrook," Fenwick said looking directly at him. "And I did not mean to insinuate that crippling the G.D.M. was our primary motive. But the fact of the matter is that our missions might be intertwined."

"How do you mean?" Waddell asked.

"Vickers is the Head of Intelligence for the G.D.M." she elaborated. "The Assembly comes to Vegas at the same time that Vickers brings your wife here and it's all in an attempt to bring Terry Philips out of hiding, if that's indeed what he's doing. Vickers is going to want to deliver Philips to The Assembly so that they can deal with him as a collective. With Vickers' shaky tenure with the Movement, I doubt they'll want to leave it up to him anyway. Philips is far too valuable to both of them. Vickers, if he has him, can use Philips as a very powerful bargaining tool. He knows they won't keep him alive, but it might afford him the chance to escape."

"So are we here for Vickers or the G.D.M. as a whole?" MacReady asked.

"If we can determine where The Assembly is meeting, we might be able to shut them down," Fenwick explained. "If the Movement is brought down, Vickers no longer needs to find Philips and, therefore, no longer needs Mrs. Seabrook."

"Well that's a great theory," Cooper pointed out. "But what if Vickers decides that he doesn't need Anna anymore, he doesn't release her? What then? We're right back where we started except we have no bargaining position of our own."

"I hate to be blunt, but without Philips, we don't have a bargaining position now," Fenwick noted solemnly. A hush fell over the room as each person tried to formulate a plan of action. Fenwick took the opportunity to take a sip of water before continuing. "Look, our primary goal is still to get her back. We believe that Vickers is going to want to trade Mrs. Seabrook for Philips so our primary focus is finding Philips. Both the Bureau and the Agency have people on that now and I believe C.S.I.S." she added with a wave of the hand to Ballard and Doyle "are assisting north of the border." Both Doyle and Ballard nodded in agreement. "Unless Philips is in Vegas, then we need to rely on everyone else to do their jobs. What we need to focus on is finding Vickers, The Assembly, and this mystery building."

"Sounds good," Cooper added. "We're gonna split up to assist. Dr. Seabrook, myself, and Waddell will look for

Vickers. MacReady, you and Ballard see if you can find out more about this building. Start with these files and work your way out from there. Martinez and Doyle, look into The Assembly and the G.D.M. as a whole. See if you can find any direct ties to Columbia."

"Excuse me," Agent Fenwick broke in. "But at what point did you think you can just march in and give orders like that. The Bureau has done the leg work on all of this up to this point and we're not gonna be pushed aside now, or ever."

"I'm not going to get into a shoving match with the Bureau and if you will notice, I didn't give any orders to you or the rookie there," he said with a dismissive wave of his giant hand towards Wojanski. "I gave my people their orders. You and the rookie are free to do whatever you like. You said you wanted a three-pronged attack? I just gave you one." Wojanski started to protest at being spoken over, but was silenced by a menacing glare from Cooper.

"Listen up, Mr. Cooper," Fenwick answered sharply. "Not that I'm not grateful for the additional manpower in this instance, but please understand that it has been our efforts that have given us what we have. It may not be much, but if it wasn't for that, you'd all just be standing around looking at the sights. At least we have a direction to go."

"So let's go, then" MacReady said quietly with a smile on his face. "We still friends?" That eased the tension a little as chuckles were floated around the room. Cooper's cell phone rang and he walked into the other room to take the call.

"What about Holt?" Robert asked. Waddell looked at him with a quizzical look. "When he comes back, I mean."

"He'll probably join up with us," Waddell answered. "I doubt he'd walk you this far and then bolt at the end. He'll wanna be there when this comes to a head." The agents started looking thought the files and graphs on the table and the bed. There was a large map pinned on the wall showing all of the areas that had been searched without success.

After a few moments, Cooper stormed back into the room, his jaw clenched. "We have a new problem," he said tersely. "I just got a call from one of our guys in Seattle. Mitch, did you have trouble with your transmitters back in Canada?"

Waddell thought back to the ferry, and to Nesbitt. "Yeah. They went down. Why?"

"They told me Holt's responsible. We've been ordered to secure him immediately."

The shock hit hard as it swept over the room. MacReady bolted for the door. "Which way did he go?" he shouted as he ripped the door open.

"Left," Robert answered, too stunned to say anything else. What did this mean? *Is Holt part of this? Is he working with Vickers? My God! O'Connor getting shot...Nesbitt's death...dragging Waddell into the middle of it...Has he been behind this whole thing?* Doyle raced out after MacReady and the two of them took off down the hall towards the elevators.

Waddell sat down heavily on one of the beds. "What are you telling us? Holt's dirty?"

"It would seem that way," Cooper added reluctantly. He had worked with Holt for years and never had any indication that he might be a double agent. Then again, the good ones were always well hidden. "We need to find him and bring him in immediately."

"Where do we start?" Martinez asked. "He could be anywhere."

"I recommend we keep doing what we're doing. I have a feeling we'll see him again before this is over."

Anna options were limited. She had tried to pry one of the bars off of the hospital that she lay on, but that had proved unsuccessful. Aside from that, there was not much else in the room; certainly nothing she could see herself using as a weapon. Her only hope had appeared to be some sort of outlandish plot revolving around another set of those pills she had taken before they had brought her to this facility. Aside from the fact that there was no guarantee she get somehow get them into Dr. Young, there wasn't even any way to be sure she could get another dose. Why would they? She was already here. She had almost given up hope when the locks were opened on the door and a guard came in with her meal tray. Unlike the last place, this tray appeared to be metal. He placed it on the floor near the door and left the room.

Anna rose from her bed and crossed the floor quickly. Not only was the prospect of a possible weapon within her grasp, but she discovered that she was desperately hungry. She retrieved the tray and returned to her bed. She scarfed down the sandwich that had been provided with a hunger she had never felt before. It was just ham and cheese but it felt like ambrosia. There was a juice box and a banana that were both consumed with equal ferociousness. Studying the now empty tray, she tried to calculate if it would be heavy enough to do the job; to neutralize a grown man. She had no idea how much force was required, but her options weren't great. If it wasn't heavy enough, she would have to deal with those consequences when they came. She slid the tray under her pillow and climbed back into bed. With any luck, Dr. Young wouldn't be expecting an attack from someone who, up until this moment, had been relatively compliant.

She waited for what seemed an eternity, but no one came to the door. She was starting to worry that Dr. Young might not come to check on her before the guard returned to retrieve the meal tray. Her pulse started to quicken as she envisioned getting into a fight with the trained guard as opposed to the doctor. *What if the doctor is similarly trained*, she thought. *My God, I never considered that.* But it was a chance she was going to have to take. She pressed the button to summon the doctor and tried to calm her nerves. Her heart hammered in her chest and she started to breath heavily. After a few moments, Dr. Young entered her room and walked directly to her.

"What seems to be the trouble, Anna?" he asked.

She decided to tell a little truth to cover her lie; easier to have legitimate symptoms. "My heart rate is racing and I'm starting to sweat a little. I don't know why and I'm worried."

"Well here, let's have a look," Dr. Young replied. He lifted her arm to get a feel for her pulse. "You do look a little flushed," he added as he felt for the rhythm in her wrist. He started to time while he counted the beats. Anna reached gently under her pillow and gripped the tray. She silently counted to three, then wrenched her arm from Dr. Young's grasp. The unexpected movement took him by surprise and threw him off balance. Anna took hold of the tray and swung with all her might. The blow struck him squarely on the temple. The impact alone was not enough to incapacitate the doctor, but because he was off balance already, he stumbled and fell striking his temple on the small metal table beside the bed. The force of that impact caused him to lose consciousness as he slumped to the floor. Anna was stunned by the outcome of her attack, but she knew she had to act fast.

She leaped off the bed and rummaged through the doctor's pockets. She found the key card that she had seen him used earlier and grabbed it. He also had a set of keys and, to her delight, a stun gun. She grabbed all of these and headed for the door. Before she reached it, another thought struck her. She returned to the doctor and removed his lab coat. If she got out of this room and past the guard outside, she would stand a better chance of getting out of this building if she looked like she belonged there. Once properly attired, she moved back to the door and tried to quiet her nerves. *No turning back now.* She took a deep breath and swiped the key card on the panel. As expected, there followed a mechanical click on the outside and she opened the door.

Not wanting to appear timid, yet also fully aware that she had no idea what waited for her on the outside of her room, she boldly stepped through the door with the stun gun in hand. The hallway, much like the room she had just left, was quite bare. There was a small desk just to her left where a guard sat. He paid little notice to the person exiting the room, no doubt expecting it to be Dr. Young. He appeared to be engrossed in some form of puzzle book spread out in front of him. Anna bolted across to him. At the last moment, perhaps finally drawn by her sudden movement, his attention focussed on her. The surprised look on his face quickly turned to agony as the stun gun was thrust into him. He immediately tensed involuntarily before keeling over, knocking his puzzle book to the floor. Anna quickly searched the guard as her eyes swept the corridor. Nothing else seemed to be moving, but there was a single door at either end and another not far from the desk. *Which way?* She unfastened the keys on the guards belt and was about to move off when the sight of his gun caught her eye. It was a simple .38 calibre revolver and it was loaded. She weighed her options and then figured she might have use for it later. She released the gun from its holster and placed it in one of the deep pockets of the lab coat. *If I keep this up, I'll be fully armed in no time*, she thought with a half smile.

She looked around the corridor again. *Dr. Young always came to the room very soon after I pushed my button, so I can assume that this door by the desk is where he was stationed…possibly his office. I don't need an office. I need an exit.* That left her with two options. Neither way had any sort of markings or indications of an exit, so it was just a coin toss. She decided on right and walked briskly to the door, checking over her shoulder as she moved. Dr. Young and the guard would not be out for long so she had to move fast. Once she reached the door, she noticed another key card swipe machine like the one in her room. She swiped Dr. Young's card and then tried the knob. Locked. She thought about racing back to the other door, but it would more than likely be locked as well. She scrambled with the guard's keys and started trying each one. Luckily, the lock moved with the fourth key she tried. The next area contained another couple of doors, an elevator, and a stairwell going up and one going down. A grim thought filled her with despair. She didn't know if she was below ground or above it. There were no windows anywhere. She thought about again just picking one and going for (so far so good), but then was struck with an idea. She moved to the elevator and swiped the doctor's key card again, summoning the elevator. She had no intention of taking it because that would limit her movement more than ever. What she hoped to find was how many floors were in this complex and which floor she was on.

The elevator doors opened and she stepped inside. She looked at the display panel and quickly ascertained that this facility had twelve floors. According to the number that was lit, she was on the tenth floor. *Ten floors? That's an awful lot*, she thought. But then she had another idea. *What if I can get to the roof and signal for help? It's a lot less floors to cover.* She pressed the button for floor number one and stepped out of the elevator before the doors closed. If her escape was detected, hopefully they might follow the elevator down instead of where she was going. She headed for the stairs leading up and paused. She was torn between trying to blend in to her surroundings or pulling out the gun and letting it lead her away to freedom. She opted to keep it in her pocket, put kept her hand on it in case she needed it quickly. She walked up the stairs and made it to what she figured was the eleventh floor as this was the next set of doors and elevator stop. She kept heading up, hoping for a sign of freedom; a window, roof access, anything. When she reached the landing for the twelfth floor, she discovered none of these. The stairwell ended with no other way out other than the elevator and a door exactly like the one she had entered two floors ago. The elevator was clearly a step backwards, so she moved towards the door and swiped the key card again. She tried using the same key that had unlocked the tenth floor door, but it didn't fit. Panic began to set in as she faced the daunting task of trying to go back to where she had started and taking a different path. *Should I have gone the other way? Dammit!*

She fumbled with the keys as she madly tried the others in this new lock. To her amazement, one of them fit and she ripped open the door, almost falling through it as she did so. What she saw was hardly what she had been expecting. This was no roof access. It was a parking lot… and underground parking lot filled with cars. *So much for signalling from a rooftop.* The sweet freedom of fresh air would have to wait. *This entire complex is underground? Where the hell am I?* she wondered. She had no time for contemplation. She had to move…now. Her escape must surely have been discovered and any minute, guards would be swarming all over this place. She had heard no alarms, but that didn't necessarily mean anything. She raced across the parking lot, pulling Dr. Young's keys from her pocket. There was a FOB on the key ring and she pressed it madly as she ran. Her efforts were soon rewarded as the telltale "whoop-whoop" told her that his car was close. She pressed it again and the lights on a nearby BMW flashed indicating that she had found her prize. She almost let out a squeak of delight as she flew to the car and opened the door.

She jumped in and started the engine, rocketing the car forwards. Down was not the way to go. She had to go up. She sped around the corners, tires squealing as she drove. The maze of the parking lot seemed to go on forever as she made her way towards freedom. Large red painted letters reading EXIT pointed her to the left and she made the turn, barely avoiding a parked Mercedes. She saw a ramp leading up and stood on the accelerator. Before she could reach it, though, a large SUV screeched to a halt in front of her, blocking her escape route. She slammed on the brakes and the car skidded to a halt mere inches short. The passenger in the SUV jumped out brandishing a rather large looking gun that she did not recognize. Anna flipped the car into reverse, looked out the rear window, and gunned the engine. The BMW's tires squealed as she sped backwards. Her egress was again blocked by another SUV pulling swiftly up from behind. Once more, she slammed on the brakes, stopping just in time. Looking past the vehicle blocking her in the front, she made the decision to just go for it. She dropped the car into drive and was about to step on the gas when her rear windshield exploded into hundreds of tiny glass shards. She instinctively ducked as she stomped on the accelerator, hurtling her car towards the blocking vehicle. She heard a pop from behind, followed by a hissing sound as smoke started to fill her car. She coughed mightily as the gas permeated the interior. Anna tried to keep the car straight, but was quickly losing control of her senses as she started to wretch, a common reaction to the gas now filling her lungs. The BMW crashed heavily into the SUV. She wanted desperately to drive the car right through this metal monstrosity in her way, but the need to remove herself from the toxic environment she currently found herself in was overwhelming. Anna blindly scratched at the door until her fingers caught in the door latch. Lurching out of the car, she flung herself to the ground, gasping for some form of clean air.

Voices were closing in on her from all directions, but all she was trying to do was to restore her vision and clear her throat. Neither one of those tasks appeared to be possible, but she tried nonetheless. Hands grabbed at her and forced her to her feet. She doubled over in pain as something hard and metallic was rammed into her abdomen forcing all of the air from her lungs. She would have screamed had her throat not been so raw from the gas. Instead, her breath just evaporated out of her as yet another impediment to breathing was introduced. The resulting effect, however, was the need to inhale deeply which exacerbated the gas already adversely affecting her.

"Get her back downstairs!" a voice commanded. Her despair began to consume her as she was led away. She could not see where she was going as her eyes were a long way from being clear.

"Do you want us to decontaminate her?" another voice asked.

"Fuck it," the first voice replied. "She caused all this crap, she can fucking well endure it for a while." Anna didn't know what felt worse; the fact that her escape attempt had failed, or the fact that she would be suffering the effects of the tear gas for longer than she needed to. It was obvious, though. As horrible as the gas was, she knew she wasn't going to get another chance to escape. Through the tears caused by the gas, as they brought her back into the belly of this nameless tomb, she cried.

CHAPTER 18

O'Connor sat there, staring blankly at the computer screen in front of him. Dr. Quinn had already made the call to Miller upstairs and the screen backed up what she had discovered. According to the data that the techs had put together, the only way that the signals from the transmitters could have been interrupted was by attaching a scrambler to one of the units.

"Son of a bitch," he muttered.

"What's that?" Quinn asked.

"It's nothing. It's just I've worked with this guy for a long time. I can't imagine him working for the other side. I mean, what does this mean? Everything he's told us is bullshit? Have I been working for the G.D.M. without even knowing it? Christ, has everyone?"

"You can't beat yourself up over this. He's likely highly trained to be able to mask his intentions. We've always considered the possibility that the G.D.M. had people within the Agency…other organizations as well. It's the only way to explain the little amount of progress we've made in bringing them down over the years," she rationalized.

"Yeah, but we're not talking about somewhere within the Agency. This was right under my fucking nose!" he shouted, slamming his fist down on the desk causing a few papers to scatter. The movement caused a lightning bolt of pain to shoot from his wounded shoulder. It immediately reminded him of his injuries and focussed his mind for a few moments on something other than Holt. The shoulder wasn't that bad, but the elbow was throbbing. *How long has it been hurting and I didn't even realize it?* he thought. He absently tried to collect the loose sheets. "Sorry," he said trying to recreate the neat pile that had been there. His injured arms made the process clumsy and Quinn smiled at his attempt.

"Don't be. I needed to sort those anyway," she said with a laugh. She moved over and finished piling them for him.

O'Connor smiled briefly, then stopped as another thought entered his mind. "Is there any possible explanation aside from this one. I mean, what if there was another transmitter?"

"What? You mean like someone else having a transmitter besides the people on the team?" she asked.

"Yeah. We had our eyes open, watching for a chase vehicle. Maybe there was one and we just never saw it. What if they had a transmitter linked up to ours and scrambled them when they made their move?" he asked hopefully.

Quinn thought about that for a few moments. "I suppose it's possible to piggyback a signal like that, but they would have had to know not only the exact frequency, but our encryption system as well." She walked over to a different terminal and punched in some more data. "I know we have similar capabilities, but I find it hard to believe that the G.D.M. are on par with us in that regard."

"It may be hard to believe, but it's not impossible," he pointed out.

"Even if that is the case, they're still going to have to bring Holt in for questioning. He is the only one who can't account for his time when your partner was killed."

"Right." O'Connor hated to admit it, but the evidences was clearly pointing in a direction that he did not want to go in. He had known Holt for years and had worked with him on numerous assignments. He did not want to believe that it had all been a shadow; a myth created by an agent of the very organization that he had been trying to help bring down. More than that, though, was that he felt like a fool…and that did not sit well with him.

Dr. Quinn was still going over the new data that the computer was spitting out at her when her phone rang. "Quinn," she said into the receiver. She listened for a few minutes, then glanced at O'Connor with a look of quiet despair. "I understand," said quietly. "I'll let him know." She hung up the phone and took a deep breath.

"What is it?" O'Connor asked. "What happened?"

"That was Miller. He contacted Cooper right after I spoke with him and gave the order to detain Holt."

"And?" O'Connor asked anxiously as he sat forward in his seat.

"Cooper never got the chance. Holt's gone."

"What do you mean gone?" O'Connor asked incredulously as he rose quickly from the chair. The pain in his elbow made him flinch noticeably.

"He left before Cooper was notified. They're not sure where he went. They have a couple of their guys looking for him, but that's all I know."

"I need to get down there," he said flatly as he moved towards the door.

"O'Connor," Quinn. "You don't look like you're in much condition to travel, let alone get mixed up further in this at least from the field side of things."

"What does that mean?" he asked turning around.

"Miller needs your help here," she explained. "He's sending down a couple of people to escort you to a nearby medical facility so you can recoup a little. From there, you can help everyone by assisting in bringing Holt in." O'Connor started to shake his head, but Quinn persisted. "You'll be in direct contact with Cooper from there. They need you on this one, James." The unexpected use of his first name caused his conviction to falter. It wasn't a surprise that she knew his name, she had his file. It was the way she said it that made him forget that she was working for the Agency. She was a woman who wasn't trying to play some political angle or attempting to subvert him. She was truly looking out for him and his best interests. In this industry, that was rare.

"Look," he said finally. "I can see your point and I know what you're saying is probably right. I just feel like I need to do more, you know?"

"Trust me," she added, looking at his shattered elbow. "You've already done more than enough. But there is more ways than one to help and one of those is to assist Cooper from here." O'Connor finally relented and when the two agents came for him, he was ready.

"Thanks, Doc," he said to her. "For everything."

Quinn smiled. "I didn't do anything."

"You did," he explained. "You made a cynic see that there are still people out there who still give a damn…and that's a tough thing to do."

"Try and rest those arms, okay?" she added.

"I will." He turned to the two men waiting for him. "Guess it's off to save the world," he quipped. "You drive." He smiled back at Quinn and walked back through the door he had come in. He wasn't sure where he would be taken and was tired of being led around like this, but it was a necessary inconvenience. *Holt, what have you done?* he wondered. *What have you made me do?* He thought again about everything that had transpired to this point. *Where exactly were you when Nesbitt went down?* The only person who had those answers was the one they couldn't find. *My God*, he thought. *Is that why Philips can't come in? Does he know about you?* He had a million more questions, but they would all have to wait. If all he could do was to assist from Seattle, then so be it. One way or another, though, Holt would be made to answer all of them.

After what felt like an eternity, Anna was finally granted access to a shower, though access was a subjective term. She was stripped down and thrown into a small tiled area with a nozzle in the wall that dispensed cold water. Her face was on fire from the gas and she was still coughing heavily, but the water felt fantastic. She quickly realized that she was not alone and was suddenly conscious of her lack of attire. Her desire to ease the discomfort of the gas overrode her need to cover up, however. She cleared her vision enough to see that two guards watched her as she doused herself with water. "Get a good look?" she asked between coughing spells.

One of the guards stepped forward and belted her across the face. She was dazed for a moment, but soon continued her ministrations. "Don't test me, you bitch," the guard snapped as he stepped back. "There may be people here who believe you have some worth, but trust me I ain't one of them."

She tried to ignore him, but the sting of his strike still lingered. She briefly envisioned a well-placed knee to the groin, but thought better of it as the retribution possibilities danced through her head. For now, she was just content to be in one piece. "What's going to happen to me now?" she asked, fearing the answer.

"Tell you what," the guard replied. "Why don't you just shut your fuckin' mouth and focus on cleaning up? You've only got another minute left." She listened to his warning and scrubbed furiously as she tried to utilize the few precious moments of comfort the water provided. "Water off!" the guard called out. Too soon, the sprinkle ceased. She was still burning, but the effects were noticeably less. "Let's move," the guard ordered.

"What about my clothes?" Anna inquired.

"You have fresh clothes waiting in your cell," the guard responded curtly.

"And how am I supposed to get there without clothes?" she countered.

"Walking works. Now move." His tone made it very clear that there would be no negotiation on this point. Anna mustered up all the nerve she had left and stepped out into the corridor. Unlike the hallways she had seen earlier, this hall had several doors each with a small window and a food slot. This looked like a cellblock which made this a prison. She tried to cover her most private parts with her arms as she walked down the hall. A few catcalls echoed from some of the doors as she passed, making her queasy. *What kind of people are in here?* She wondered. *Could be more people like me?* she thought jokingly.

Those thoughts were quickly dismissed when one of the people shouted, "Bring her in here! I'll fix her up right!"

"Shut up!" the guard answered. Anna looked down the hall and saw that one of the doors was open. This was undoubtedly meant for her and she prayed that it was empty. Getting to the door, her fears were assuaged. The cell was tiny, but unoccupied. A set of coveralls was laid out for her on the cot. Aside from that, the only other things in the room were a metal sink, a toilet, and a single light bulb in the ceiling protected by a plastic cover. "Get dressed. Someone will be by to talk to you in a while. I don't want any shit from you. Try to pull anything like that crap earlier and I WILL throw you in with dipshit down there," he said, motioning towards the cell they had passed. "Trust me, you don't want that." Anna stepped into her cell. "Close eight!" the guard called out. The cell door slid shut and locked with a loud, metallic click.

Anna looked at her surroundings and sighed. "I think I liked the other room better," she said with a small laugh that quickly subsided into coughs. She put on the coveralls given to her, thankful to at least be covered. There was nothing else to do but wait. She climbed onto the cot and tried to sleep. She had lost track again of time, but at least she had a better idea of her surroundings. Her escape attempt had failed, but she now knew that she underground. That piece of information might be of use in the future. She didn't know how, but any information was good information.

Holt moved calmly through the casino of the Flamingo. He didn't like having to alter plans in the middle of assignment, but this was nothing new. Besides, if things worked out well here, he might actually be able to slip away into obscurity and leave this entire lifestyle behind. He hadn't realized how unhappy he was until the thought of quitting became a plausible one. He knew he wouldn't be able to just walk away, but if he played this hand well enough, he might not have to. He looked around at the patrons crowding around the various tables and slot machines, each one hoping that their hunch was right or whatever plan they had to beat the house panned out. Pathetic. Don't leave anything to chance. Make your own good fortune. Those had been lessons he had learned early on. Those same lessons he was counting on now.

As he neared the main exit to the Strip, he stole a glance back over the casino floor. At the far end, he saw MacReady and that C.S.I.S. guy sweeping through the casino. They were moving quickly, but their eyes were scanning everywhere. *Something's happened*, Holt thought. *They've been alerted.* Luckily, they hadn't seen him yet. He ducked outside and had a quick decision to make. South towards Bally's or North towards Harrah's. His plan couldn't be executed if he was made to return to the room. He headed north simply because it afforded him more options. They would be slower than he needed to be due to the fact that they were actually looking for him as opposed to just moving forward. When he reached Las Vegas Boulevard, he deftly moved through the crowd on the sidewalk and headed for Harrah's. If he could make it there undetected, he would be clear to proceed with his plans. He breezed past the numerous street 'vendors' clicking their stripper cards at him. There were a few local artists who had set up shop along the way and the crowds were a little denser around them, but he moved on despite them. Once clear, he moved a little faster, but didn't dare look back for fear of being spotted. If they saw him, they saw him. Turning around would only confirm their identification.

He ducked into Harrah's and quickly became immersed in the crowd on the casino floor. He situated himself so he could see the entrances while maintaining a low profile. He couldn't be sure if they were, in fact, looking for him, but he did not want to take that chance. Not when he was this close to finding a way out. He saw MacReady poke his head up over the crowd to try and gain a better view. Doyle was nowhere to be seen. He had probably gone South towards the Bally's or over to Caesar's. Either way, he was relatively safe. MacReady looked further north towards Casino Royale, hesitated, then went back south to the Flamingo. Holt waited a few minutes longer to ensure they weren't trying to lure him out. After a while, he grew weary of the beeps and bells of the casino floor and made his way through the casino, exiting from the north side. His contact had a room at the Palazzo. He hadn't planned on walking, but now it seemed the easiest way to avoid detection. A few blocks to the north stood the Palazzo. His contact was inside. A simple meeting was waiting, but that simple meeting would set a much larger chain of events in motion. By the end of the next day, Holt knew he would either be living in obscurity or dying in anonymity. The fact that he couldn't decide which one he was hoping for worried him. *One more day*, he assured himself. *No matter what, one more day.*

MacReady and Doyle came back empty-handed. "By the time we got to the casino floor," MacReady said. "He was nowhere to be found. That's if he even went that way. He could have gone anywhere." His brogue was more pronounced than usual. "What a pile o' shit this turned into."

"Agreed," said Martinez. "Think we're walking into a trap?" Everyone was wondering the same thing, but he was the only one who voiced it.

"We might be," Cooper admitted. "But I don't see how we can turn back now even if we wanted to. Bottom line is that no matter what that son of a bitch was working on, he still doesn't have Philips. Therefore, we still have a chance to get Mrs. Seabrook back."

"Who do you think tipped him off?" Fenwick asked.

Waddell glared at her fiercely. "What makes you think he was tipped off? You think just cuz one guy might be dirty, there are others on this who are?"

"Don't so naïve, Waddell is it?" Fenwick answered. "I don't believe in coincidences and his getting out of here mere minutes before the call comes in means that he's got someone feeding him information. Either that or he's got a bloody crystal ball up his ass."

"Maybe it was a Fed," Waddell shot back. "One of you guys might be in on whatever the hell this is." Tempers started to flare as the agents started bickering with one another. The volume was getting louder until a voice louder than all silenced them.

"STOP IT!" Robert screamed. "What the hell is wrong with you people?" The arguing ceased and all eyes turned to him. "My God, is this what you people do for a living? Run around blaming everyone else for everything? I'm not expecting you guys to take the blame for any of this, but can someone please explain to me how any of this is helping my wife? She is trapped somewhere and one of the people that had been helping me may in fact have been behind it all. Apart from that, nothing has changed. Instead of focussing on this one element, fucking go back to doing what we were doing before Holt left and find out where Anna is. I'm no expert, but if Holt is dirty as you say, then if we find her we'll find him."

The people in the room looked around at each other with sheepish expressions. This 'outsider' was right. While their egos and sensibilities had been bruised, there was still a job to do. Being duped by someone they had all trusted did leave a sour taste in their mouths, but there was still a chance to come through this successfully. Robert Seabrook was right. The key to finding Holt was to find Anna.

"You're right, Dr. Seabrook," Cooper finally said. "Again I must ask for your forgiveness."

"Just find her," he replied. "That will be all the thanks I need." Robert walked into the small bathroom and closed the door. He did not want to break down in front of anyone, especially after the oration he had just delivered. But he was truly concerned. Had Holt sold both he and Anna out? Had he been behind this whole thing? The only reason he had pegged Vickers for the bad guy was that Holt had told him so. *Holt, Waddell, and O'Connor. They would all have had to be in on it, wouldn't they?* he silently asked the mirror. *No. It would have just been Holt. Waddell is as shocked as I was when Holt bolted and O'Connor nearly got killed back in Chilliwack.* He turned on the tap and splashed some cold water on his face for clarity of thought. *Why now?* he contemplated. *Why here? Do you know where Philips is? Or are you sure that we won't find him in time? What are you up to Holt?*

He was about to press the issue further when his cell phone beeped, indicating a received text message. It hadn't so much as twitched over the last couple of days so he had completely forgotten about it. The sound actually made him jump. He retrieved the phone from his pocket and looked at the screen. The message consisted of only one word – Acropolis. *That's an odd message*, he thought. Putting his phone away, he dried his face and hands, took a deep breath to steady himself further, then went back into the room. All of the other people there had gone back to rooting through the reams of papers trying to find a lead. Cooper was in the next room talking on the phone, presumably with whomever had called to alert them about Holt. Robert offered up his text message for input as to the meaning. "Acropolis mean anything to you guys?" A couple of heads looked up at him, while the rest continued reading.

"As in Greece?" Doyle asked.

"I guess," Robert replied. "I just got a text message that said Acropolis." That caused all movement in the room to stop as all eyes now rested on Robert.

"I'll have to call you back," Cooper said flatly as he emerged from the doorway.

"Who sent you the text?" Agent Fenwick asked, rising from her chair by the table.

Robert thought about that for a moment before he replied. Something had alerted all of these people... something about this text. "I'll check." He took his phone out from his pocket again and checked the number. "It's just coming up as 'Private'."

"Let me see it," Cooper said as he moved across the room with his hand out. Robert turned over the phone, hopeful that this was relevant. Cooper entered a couple of numbers into the phone, but had no luck in determining where the text had come from. "Someone call it in," he ordered. "Get a trace and history on this cell phone. I wanna know where that text came from."

"Already on it," Waddell answered. He already had his phone out and was waiting for someone to pick up.

"What's going on?" Robert asked. "What does Acropolis mean?"

"It's a lead," Agent Fenwick answered. "The Hotel Acropolis is Vegas' newest sensation. It opened up a couple of months ago across from the Luxor. Very quickly became one of the hottest spots in town. A lot of money went in to it. We had our guys do a sweep, but they came up empty. Everything looked solid so we moved on. Now, it appears we may have missed something." The rest of the team had already focussed its attention on the Acropolis. As Fenwick had indicated, it had opened in May and was an instant success. $6.9 billion had been invested to make it one of the most expensive hotels in the world. There was significant fanfare leading up to the grand opening and it did not disappoint. The opening gala was a night of lights, music, and money with a casino that could rival any in Las Vegas. The hotel was an instant hit and catered to all walks of life. There was even a weekly show that was quickly becoming Vegas' most sought after tickets. The Luxor and the Acropolis would stage a battle pitting the armies of Greece and Egypt against one another to lay claim to historical superiority. No children were allowed due to the severity of the re-enactment, but they were already sold out for the next three months. To cater to families with children, they provided a full amusement park with shows and celebrity appearances. The Wiggles happened to be in town this week.

"Who do you figure sent the message?" Ballard asked.

"Maybe it was Holt," Robert commented hopefully. "Maybe we're wrong and he really did go to meet someone and this is what he turned up." The team considered this for a bit. Cooper finally addressed the theory.

"If that's the case, then he should be back any minute. I, personally, think that's a bit of a stretch. He would have told me more...hell he would have told me something, but he didn't. If he comes back and confirms the message, we'll take that into consideration. But he'll still have to be detained until his name is cleared in all this. Anyone else it might have been?" Cooper asked.

"Philips?" MacReady volunteered. Some of the others had thought about that remote possibility, but no one said anything. "If he's been able to make it to Vegas, he might know about the Acropolis. Does he know your cell number?" he asked Robert.

"Yes. I gave it to him just before he disappeared."

"Hold it," Waddell interrupted as he moved the phone from his face. "Did you say Philips may have sent the message?"

"That's a possibility," conceded Cooper. "Though I think about as likely as Holt, but it's all we have right now."

"I'll get them to check if any of Philips' known phones have been activated recently, particularly in Las Vegas." Waddell returned to his phone conversation.

"We also have to keep in mind that this might be meant to throw us off," contributed Martinez. "That message might have come from the G.D.M. itself to get us chasing ghosts."

"All of that is possible, but all we can deal with is what we have," Cooper admitted. "Fenwick, either you or Wojanski keep on checking out everything else in Vegas in the usual corners in case Martinez is right and this is a ruse. The other can work on digging up intel on the Acropolis. I'm going to head over to the Acropolis and check things out. Ballard, you or Doyle are welcome to come along. The other will stay here and work with Waddell and MacReady. Martinez, I want you to try and establish a connection with what's happening here in Vegas with Poveda in Columbia. I find it too much of a coincidence that this whole thing with Philips and now Holt is happening at the same time and place as the Assembly getting together. Any ties will help. We know that Poveda has the G.D.M. behind him, but without proof we're going to find it extremely difficult to move forward. All of you work together and pool your resources. Someone get on the horn with O'Connor. We'll use him as a contact away from here. He might be able to shed some light on Holt and this whole god damned mess." Waddell nodded as he would be the one to contact O'Connor. The others moved into action. Wojanski dived back into the pile of papers on Vegas and attacked them with a renewed vigour. Doyle linked up with Martinez and MacReady and approached the papers and the computers with the Acropolis as their target. "Contact your sources. Rattle some cages. I want the Acropolis either confirmed or ruled out within the hour."

Ballard walked up to Cooper. "Looks like I'm going with you," she said as the team behind her flew into action. The flurry of commotion made it hard to hear, so the two agents headed for the door.

"Good. We'll take the Monorail right to MGM and walk from there. Good luck everyone." With that, he exited the room with Ballard in tow and strode down the hallway to the elevators. This assignment was not proceeding like it was supposed to, but that was nothing new to either him or the C.S.I.S. agent with him. "You ready?" he asked as they descended in the elevator.

"Always," she replied. It was time to pay the Acropolis a visit.

CHAPTER

19

O'Connor was taken back upstairs. After leaving Dr. Quinn in her lab, he had returned to Miller, though the debrief was now over. "Welcome back," Miller said. He was standing at the back of some sort of control room. There were three large screens set up with satellite imaging and one with a topographical diagram of the Las Vegas area. Several other people were in the room attending various computers.

"Not glad to be here," O'Connor grumbled. He would much rather have stayed with Quinn downstairs. Not only was she attractive, but this Miller gave him a headache. "Were you able to reach Cooper?" he asked.

"Yes, but we weren't in time." O'Connor looked stunned as he weighed the options of what that statement meant. Seeing his concern, miller elaborated. "No, no… nothing sinister. He left before Cooper could be notified. The team lost track of him in Vegas."

"I still can't believe this is happening," O'Connor admitted.

"Well believe it," replied Miller. "We've got satellite intel coming in from Vegas as we speak and two special forces teams are en route. We might finally have the break we've been looking for and we intend to use it."

"Isn't this all a bit much for a kidnapping? I mean, I'm fond of Dr. Seabrook and all and I hope things turn out well on this for him and his wife, but I haven't seen mobilization like this in years."

"This transcends the Seabrooks, I'm afraid," said Miller. "For the first time, we have a chance to move on the G.D.M. and hard. If the Assembly is in fact in Las Vegas, we can deliver a crippling blow to the 'Movement'. Finally a chance to shut these guys down."

"What about Robert and Anna?" O'Connor asked, leery of the answer.

"Robert and Anna? I think it's time you gained some perspective, O'Connor. Like you said, I hope things work out for them, but weighing their happiness against the danger that the G.D.M poses to thousands, maybe millions, of people is simply ludicrous. You need to take a look at the big picture and realize the opportunity that has been presented to us here."

O'Connor started to protest, but in his heart he knew that Miller spoke the truth. He really did like Dr. Seabrook and while he had never met Anna, he described her as a wonderful person. Still, how do you compare the lives of two people you knew versus the lives of thousands of strangers. Up until a few days ago, Robert and Anna had been strangers too.

"Look," Miller continued. "I understand where you're coming from. We've all been there, but these are the calls that have to be made. We're not abandoning them…not at all. Cooper and the rest of the team will still be focussing on getting Mrs. Seabrook back safely, but the rest of us need to focus on bringing the G.D.M. to its knees."

"Right," O'Connor agreed reluctantly. "What do you have so far?"

"Not much as of yet," Miller admitted. "MacReady's on the horn with Munroe right now." Miller motioned to one of the computers. Chad Munroe had been an intelligence specialist for 24 years. His knowledge of computer systems and satellites was legendary. Clearly, the Agency felt that the opportunity to close in on the 'Movement' was clear enough to send the very best. He was furiously scribbling down everything being spoken to him through the phone, occasionally interrupting for clarification.

After a few minutes, he put the phone down and spoke to the control room. "Everyone if I can have your attention," he announced. "Target for surveillance is the Acropolis Hotel and Casino, Las Vegas Boulevard. I need SAT-SCAN A.S.A.P. and an E.T.A. on the special forces. Also, I need any tracking available on Brian Holt. Last known location was the Flamingo. He is considered a person of interest at this time so I just wanna know where he is. Check out his contacts, places of interest, and his associates in the area. We'll proceed from there when the time comes. Call in any favours you are owed. This is the big one."

Miller motioned for Munroe to cross over to him. "E.T.A. on the spec forces is 23 minutes," an anonymous voice called out.

"Good," Monroe replied as he manoeuvred through the chaos of the control room. "Let me know when they're 'wheels down'."

"Copy that," the voice replied. Munroe had served as one of the chief satellite intelligence operators for the past seven years. As such, he was burdened with a great deal of stress in his occupation and it showed. The stress lines that adorned his once handsome face now made him look a lot older than his 51 years. But his eyes were sharp and a brilliant blue. He always came alive when there was a fish to be caught. Today was such a day.

"How goes it, Miller?" Munroe asked as he greeted the man with a firm handshake.

"Not bad. You?"

"Same old story. Terrorism, rogue agents, Vegas… just another day in paradise," he added with a chuckle. "Who's this?"

"Chad Munroe? May I introduce James O'Connor. He's helping us out with the G.D.M."

"You the guy who took two shots?" Munroe asked, clearly sizing the man up.

"That's me," O'Connor admitted. "News travels fast."

"In this line of work, almost too fast. I'm surprised I didn't hear about it before you got shot." Munroe laughed a little harder this time. He definitely seemed to enjoy his work, despite the stress.

"Yeah, well I'm just glad I'm still around to be able to tell anyone about it," O'Connor noted dourly. The pain in his arms throbbed any time someone mentioned the shooting. The pain, in fact, was always there but just seemed to make its presence more pronounced when it was mentioned directly.

"He's a surveillance nut like you," Miller added helpfully. That seemed to pique Munroe's interest.

"Surveillance, huh? Didn't anyone tell you that surveillance is a behind the scenes arena? You found yourself on the wrong side of the camera."

"Couldn't be avoided," O'Connor defended. "Plus it all worked out for the best."

"You say so." Munroe turned his focus back to the control room. "Anything yet on Acropolis," he called out.

"Coming up now," another anonymous voice called. Moments later, the center screen lit up with a history of the Acropolis while the building schematics scrolled past on one of the other monitors. "SAT-SCAN will be in position in seven minutes."

"SAT-SCAN?" O'Connor inquired.

"Oh, it's a beaut. There are three of them. We can move them pretty much wherever we want in a matter of hours," Munroe explained. "Their orbit is highly classified. They're almost completely undetectable and give us a real-time image with minimal lag."

"Isn't that what most spy satellites can do?" O'Connor asked.

"Indeed, but this one can defend itself and can give us additional strength on the ground. She can tap into any number of encrypted signals and transmissions and can even mess them up."

"How so?" O'Connor was not one to be impressed with technologies. His experience with the transmitters earlier was one of the reasons why. But something had this expert buzzing and O'Connor found himself eagerly awaiting his response.

"I'm not sure I should be telling you this, but what the hell. If you tell anyone outside this room I'll just have you killed," he said with a smile. O'Connor wasn't sure if he was joking or not. "Say you have a team heading towards an urban objective and you need to get there unnoticed. This baby can send a scrambling signal to completely neutralize your targets surveillance equipment. Cameras, wires, bugs, motion sensors, everything…gone. You can't fight if you can't see," he concluded.

O'Connor thought about the possibilities of this technological marvel and was chilled at some of the possible ramifications. Then a thought occurred to him. "How is it able to do this?"

Munroe beamed with pride as he embraced the question. "It's actually a simple concept. The satellite can detect surveillance and counter-surveillance devices and ascertain their frequencies. At the necessary time, it can shut them down rendering your target blind as a bat… without radar," he added with a laugh.

"You say it can detect the devices themselves?" Munroe nodded in reply. "Well why didn't you just move the satellite over to Vegas as soon as this came up? If this toy of yours is as good as you say, it would have detected the hell out of the Acropolis and could have saved a bunch of time."

"Detect surveillance equipment? In a Las Vegas hotel and casino?" Munroe asked sarcastically. "My God, why didn't I think of that? Clearly the Acropolis is the only casino in the entire city to be loaded to the gills with surveillance. Gimme a break. We're not rookies here. Without a location, we would have just been spinning our wheels and to put it bluntly, this thing costs a shitload of money to reposition and use."

"Right," O'Connor answered apologetically. "So what happens next?"

"We coordinate. With the SAT-SCAN's attention from above, we work to get our teams in place. With a little bit of luck, the Assembly will make an appearance and we'll be ready for them. Cooper's group will have to act quickly, though, cuz if the Assembly shows its ugly head we're gonna have to act immediately."

"And if the Assembly doesn't show?" O'Connor asked.

"Then we wait," Miller interrupted. "We wait and gather intelligence on the Acropolis and its patrons. Examine the workforce. Run it through the ringer. If the Acropolis is indeed a front for the G.D.M. or is even owned by them, we're gonna know every detail about everything in that building."

"Amen," Munroe agreed. "Now come on," he said to O'Connor. "We have a little time before the team lands. Let's go and see what SAT-SCAN can do."

―⸺―

A loud banging roused Anna from a surprisingly deep sleep. She obviously hadn't realized how drained she was, but felt it now. Her joints ached and her stomach felt like a lead balloon. She opened her eyes slowly and looked towards the cell door. An unfamiliar face was peering back at her. "Time to get up," the man announced. "Doctor's here to see you."

Dread filled her body as the thought of being confronted by Dr. Young consumed her. *Would he understand that it was nothing personal? That she was just trying to escape? How do you apologize for cracking someone over the head?* The mechanical door slid open and a young man in a lab coat stepped inside. This was not Dr. Young and not what Anna had been expecting.

"How are we feeling today? Planning on attacking anyone else or should I just go ahead and call for help now?" His smile was definitely fake. She could see the hatred in his eyes. They bore into her like daggers.

"Where's Dr. Young?" she asked. "I hope he wasn't hurt too badly." She genuinely wished that he would be okay. Apart from being on the wrong side of this situation, he had treated rather humanely for the most part. She doubted this new doctor would extend her the same courtesy.

"He's dead," the new doctor said simply, glaring at her.

The force of his words caught Anna squarely in the chest. She had never intended on killing anyone. She just wanted to be free. She had hit him hard, yes, but the force shouldn't have been enough to kill him. *Unless he fell awkwardly. Yes, he had hit his head going down. My God! What have I done?* "I didn't mean to kill him," she said as her eyes filled with tears. The thought that her hand had brought the end to a man's life was just too much for her to bear.

"Don't flatter yourself, Anna," another voice said from behind the new doctor. "You didn't kill him." Vickers stepped into the room brandishing a semi-automatic pistol. "I killed him."

"You killed him?" she asked incredulously.

"Yes I did," he replied simply. "Well actually this gun killed him." Anna looked from this madman's face to the gun he held, now pointing directly at her. "More specifically, one of the bullets inside this gun killed him. But I'll gladly take the credit for pulling the trigger."

Anna closed her eyes and said a silent prayer for herself and for Dr. Young. She had never been a particularly religious person, but like most people faced with a life or death situation, prayer just came naturally. "Why did you do that?"

"The why was easy," Vickers explained. "He let himself be overpowered by a prisoner in his care and then exacerbated his screw up by having his keys on him. The key card I can understand. He needed that to move around the facility. But having his personal keys on him? That's a level of carelessness that I will just not tolerate. Had you gotten away, you would have jeopardized everything…this facility, our location. No. Killing him was a formality."

Anna was nauseated at the way this man could describe someone's death so flippantly. He clearly had no respect for human life other than his own and that made him even more dangerous than even she had realized. "What happens now?" she asked fearfully.

"My position hasn't changed, Anna. I don't want to kill you, but I have no difficulty shooting you." She braced herself for the impact, but it didn't come. "You still have value to me. That is the only reason you continue to be alive. But don't test my patience again. Understood?" She nodded meekly. "Good. I will leave her in your capable hands, Doctor." With that, Vickers drifted into the hall and was gone.

"I'm not going to give you anything for the pain cuz frankly, I'm glad you're suffering. As you may notice, there is no paging button to press to get me to come. You have a button there on the wall," he indicated with his finger. "You can press that if you require assistance, but that will bring guards…not me. Press it for non-emergency purposes and you'll be tossed into a cell with a couple of the guards and no cameras. Clear?" She nodded again, disgusted at the thought of what her fate could be. My name is Dr. Shelby. I will do rounds twice a day…in the morning and again at night. If you have questions, ask me then. If not, keep quiet."

He quickly left the room and the door slid shut behind him. The metallic clunk sounded a little louder this time, but that was just her isolation and frustration making things seem more vivid. Anna's only consolation was that this new doctor had given away a little detail that she doubted he had intended to. If he came around in the morning and again at night, she might be able to estimate what time it was. It was not valuable information, but at least it was a way to find something to occupy her mind. It was a better alternative than reflecting on her surroundings. *Wherever you are, Dr. Young, I'm sorry. Wherever you are, Robbie, we'll see each other soon.* She had to believe that because time was running out.

The Monorail was crowded, as to be expected on any given day in Las Vegas. Because the strip was so long and so many people had more than they had expected to drink, the Monorail was a preferred mode of transportation for many of Las Vegas' visitors. There were numerous such people on board tonight. Cooper wasn't one to refuse the occasional drink, but he had never understood the desire to get so drunk as to be rendered ineffective not just for assignments, but for living. One young guy in the corner of the car looked like he was preparing to churn out whatever lay in his stomach. Cooper watched him as the car eased to a stop behind Paris and, as if on cue, the man pitched forward and introduced his stomach contents to the floor by the passengers attempting to embark. Most of them retreated quickly while a few brave souls just stepped over the pool of vomit. *Regulars*, Cooper thought. The man's buddies were screeching with laughter as he tried to retain some of his dignity, straightening up and trying to smooth his rumpled clothing. The attempt just made him look more pathetic.

"Charming," Ballard muttered.

"Just wait til the smell hits us," Cooper pointed out. The two agents focussed their attention elsewhere as bystanders started weighing in on this breach in transit etiquette. They had a job to do and had no intention of being dragged into some sort of drunken scuffle. They both got up and moved as far away from the commotion as the Monorail would allow. It moved off, finally, and continued on its way towards the MGM. A lot of the people in the car had moved to get a better view of what could easily turn into a brawl as voices started to rise. The distraction gave Cooper and Ballard a chance to talk.

"What are you hoping to find?" Ballard asked. She didn't know Cooper's intentions for the Acropolis and wanted to be prepared for what he had in mind.

"Proof would be nice," he answered. "Proof that the G.D.M. is indeed behind the Acropolis. But that's unlikely. Mainly, I'm going to get a sense of the place. I wanna see what kind of security we're dealing with, the layout.." Ballard started to say something, but Cooper continued, answering her question. "I know I could get the layout from photos and blueprints, but that's not how I work. I like to be inside where I can…it's hard to explain," he finally admitted.

"I know exactly what you mean," Ballard said. "All that two-dimensional crap will do will give you a layout of where the walls are. When buildings are occupied, they come to life. That's what we're going to see isn't it?" she asked. "How this building breathes?"

Cooper stared at her in amazement. In all the years he had been working for the government, no one had ever known what he had meant. They had all thought he was eccentric. Not only did Ballard know, but she used the same words that he did. The buildings did breathe. They had a pulse and they had emotions. You couldn't get any of that from pictures or schematics. "I'm impressed," he admitted. "I didn't really think C.S.I.S. would be the place I would find my soul mate."

Ballard smiled. "I'm not interested in dating government types," she pointed out.

Cooper, suddenly flustered, tried to explain. "No, I didn't mean that...I just meant..."

"Relax, Cooper," she assured him. "I know what you meant." She smiled politely before continuing, refocusing on the task at hand. "Do you think everyone who works there is G.D.M.?" she asked.

"It's possible, but I doubt it. More likely just the higher-ups, maybe the security and the shipping and loading guys. The casino people and the actual hotel staff are probably just workers. That's what makes this so damn difficult. If it was all 'Movement' people, we could just take 'em. But with so many possible civilian workers, there's no telling who on the inside is dirty."

The level of noise inside the car had increased to the point that it was becoming uncomfortable. Security would undoubtedly be waiting at the next stop. It was time to get moving anyway. The train stopped at MGM and Ballard and Cooper got off just as security entered to try and quell the fight that had broken out inside the train. *God bless alcohol.* They moved smoothly through the casino floor. MGM was massive and it took a while before they emerged on to Las Vegas Boulevard. New York, New York was directly ahead of them. Shrieks from the elated passengers aboard the Coney Island roller coaster replica mingled with the hustle and bustle of life on the Strip. They both surveyed their surroundings. To their left was the Tropicana. Behind it, stood the immaculate architectural wonder known as the Acropolis. Seeing it for the first time in person caused them both to gawk openly. It truly was a marvel. The hotel was designed to look like the Acropolis, including the Parthenon. There was an arena off to the side where the Greek-Egyptian war took place. The amusement park couldn't be seen from their vantage point with the exception of the very top of the Ferris wheel.

"Wow," Ballard muttered.

"You said it," Cooper agreed. "But remember what's at stake here. If this lead is legit, then there is a very good chance that Mrs. Seabrook is somewhere inside. With a place that big, she could be anywhere."

"Well Fenwick did say that her source confirmed the facility is huge. This definitely fits the bill. Guess it's not underground after all."

"Don't rule that out yet," Cooper cautioned. "Just because of the size of this place, that doesn't mean that there's nothing under it. For all we know, this thing is an iceberg." That thought made them realize exactly how large this complex could be and it humbled them both.

"We're gonna need a bigger boat," Ballard quipped as they strolled towards the walkway that would carry them over traffic to the Acropolis.

"Not necessarily. This might not be the right place," Cooper pointed out.

"Do you believe that?" prodded Ballard. "What sense are you getting from this place?"

Cooper stared at the giant structure before them. He took a deep breath and calmed his emotions. "No. This is the place. She's here." They crossed over to the other side of the street and made their way down the long drive that led to the main entrance of the hotel and casino. "Now let's go find out a little bit more about this place."

CHAPTER

20

Vickers was staring at his computer screen analyzing numbers and trends. He had a lot of money put away for his retirement, but still he wanted more. Besides, after a lifetime of stress and espionage, the thought of attempting to live a normal life was disgusting. At least by playing the stock market, it afforded him the chance to introduce some much needed stress to his soon to be stress-free life. The last thing he wanted was to drop dead of a heart attack in six months because his body simply couldn't adjust to relaxing. A knock on his office door drew his attention away from the screen.

"Come in," he called. One of his subordinates popped his head in the door.

"Sir? We have a problem that needs your attention." He stood in the doorway, unsure of whether or not he should enter. Vickers had a reputation of being very particular about who was granted access to his office. He was relieved when Vickers motioned him in.

"What seems to be the trouble?" Vickers asked smugly. He was sure there was nothing that couldn't be dealt with.

"It's the C.I.A., sir." That simple statement got Vickers' attention. The young man decided to just get it out as quick as possible to make this as painless as he could. "We just received word that there is a team of operatives in Las Vegas and that they're focussing their attention here."

"What do you mean 'here'?" Vickers asked as alarm bells started to go off in his head.

"The Acropolis, sir." The young man took a step back as Vickers rose from his chair.

"How is that possible? Even if they followed us to Vegas, how could they know about this place already?" His mind whirred into action running through every conceivable scenario. None of them seemed to fit.

"I'm not sure, sir, but our information is solid. What should we do?"

Vickers glared at the young man standing before him. He wanted desperately to wring his neck, but that was just the frustration talking. It wasn't the messenger he was upset with…it was the message. "Get out," he ordered. "And get Raeburn in here."

"Yes sir," the young man said as he headed for the door, relieved to have been granted this reprieve.

Vickers watched as he scurried from the room like newly illuminated cockroach. "Weakling," he muttered. He sat down at terminal and quickly did away with the stock market estimates. His portfolio would have to wait. He called up his encrypted messaging service and grabbed the remote control from the top drawer. Using it, a panel opened up on his wall showing the surveillance screens from around the complex. Ruling out the lower levels, he assigned the images of the casino floor to the screens in front of him. He quickly studied them, but saw nothing that appeared to be out of the ordinary. He was about to go through them again when another knock on the door interrupted him. "Enter," he called.

Amanda Raeburn stepped into the office and immediately started to apologize. This was summarily dismissed with a wave of Vickers' hand. "Do not trouble yourself with this. I didn't see it coming so I can't very well be upset with anyone else now can I." The logic seemed sound, but Raeburn was still leery of the man. He had been known to eliminate people he had felt had let him down in the past. She did not want to be a new statistic for his file.

She looked over the screens on the wall. "See anything?" she asked.

"Not yet," he admitted. "But I will. What do we know for sure?"

"The information just came in. There are four field operatives along with an expert on Columbia, two C.S.I.S. operatives, and two F.B.I. field agents. They're with Dr. Seabrook and have apparently identified the Acropolis as a point of interest."

"Where are they?" he asked.

"The Flamingo. Room 612," she added, pleased to be able to sound like she was on top of things. "I have Olson gathering a team in case you want to move on these guys."

"Good. Let me know when they're ready." He paused for a moment as his thoughts began piling on top of each other. "How the hell did they figure out that this was where we were?" he asked, more to the air than anyone else.

"We're still looking into that. I'll have an answer within fifteen minutes."

"Don't bother. Bottom line is, they know we're here so they'll be coming. Knowing the way those assholes operate, there are probably special forces teams on route as we speak."

"Should we go on alert?" she asked.

He thought about that for a moment. "No. Not yet. They're getting ready, but they won't want to make a move. They'll probably try for our guest downstairs first." He had to allow for the possibility that there was a leak somewhere within the organization so the fewer people who knew that they were alerted, the better. "Get your team ready to move. You and Olson will lead it. Strike them in the Flamingo before they make their move against us. Once we've eliminated them, we'll alert everyone to prepare for the Special Forces teams."

"What about Philips?" she inquired. "Dr. Seabrook is still our best bet at finding him." Vickers smiled. Raeburn didn't have to worry about whether or not Philips was found. It wasn't her neck on the line, it was his. If anything, he'd have figured that she would have wanted Philips to remain hidden. The Assembly would kill him for failing and she would move up a notch in the hierarchy of the G.D.M. But she actually seemed to care. He didn't know if he viewed that as a strength or a weakness.

"If they had Philips, we would have known about it by now. If he's dead, then this entire operation is basically moot and we continue as planned. I have a feeling, however, that Philips is alive and well and possibly in Las Vegas. If I'm correct, then he will show himself when he's ready. For now, ready your team and swat those bugs at the Flamingo for me. How the rest of this plays out will be determined after they have been neutralized."

"Will do, sir. Thank you, sir," she said before she left the office.

She's loyal, he admitted to himself. *She'll see this through to the end. Now let's find out who they decided to send on recon,* he thought as he returned his focus to the bank of surveillance screens. If this team wanted to investigate the Acropolis, their first order of business would be to send a small surveillance team…two or three people at most to scout around. It didn't take long to spot them. Camera six had them strolling through the casino. It wasn't that uncommon to see a black man walking arm in arm with a white woman. It hadn't always been that way, though, but in the world of today there was nothing wrong with it. This particular couple, however, were not interested in each other at all. They were too busy studying the layout of the building and the people who worked there. The casual observer would never have noticed it. They were quite good in their subterfuge. But Vickers was no casual observer. He knew what to look for and recognized it when he saw it. He picked up the phone on his desk. "Security? Camera six. The interracial couple. Track them and keep me posted on what they do and where they go. Use the transmitters. I'm coming down." He hung up and left his office. It was not a long trip to get to the casino level, but he wanted to be there as quickly as he could. It was time to welcome these people to the Hotel Acropolis.

Ballard clung to Cooper's arm as they moved through the casino. "I'm not seeing anything out of the ordinary. You?"

Cooper kind of shrugged. "Not particularly. Security is tight, but that's to be expected from a new mega-casino like this one. There are cameras everywhere, but the staff all look pretty typical. I have a feeling that most of them don't even realize who their true employer is. Makes an assault unlikely."

"Would you even risk an assault with this number of civilians?" she asked looking around at the swarm of gamblers trying their luck at the various parlour games.

"It wouldn't be a direct assault. We'd probably go in through the parking area and straight into the heart of this beast. But that's in a perfect world. Too much bureaucracy now. The Agency would never green light something like that unless there was a nuke or something inside."

"I don't think an assault is the right way to go anyway. Too many risks for civilian casualties." She looked around again at the people playing the slots.

"What would you suggest? Standing outside and calling them out like some ridiculous game of Red Rover? Trust me, you wouldn't want to see what they'd send out."

She laughed at the visual that that image conjured up. "Hardly. I just think there are more subtle ways of doing things."

"Perhaps," Cooper admitted. "But I've never been one for subtlety. You wanna head downstairs and scope out the parking area?"

"Can we access it?" she asked.

"Only one way to find out," he said, nudging her towards a bank of elevators situated in the corner of the casino. They moved through the last few rows of slot machines and down the small row of shops that catered to all manner of souvenirs and overpriced clothing. There were six elevators at the end of the promenade…three per side. "Any preference?" he asked.

"Honestly, I don't think elevators are a good move right now; no escape. I say we look for stairs. They should be close."

"Good point," he admitted. "Look around. I'll head this way." Ballard walked around the corner and went back along the promenade in search of another way down while Cooper tried some of the doors surrounding the elevators. A few patrons cast curious glances at him, but continued on their way. A young couple who had clearly had a little too much to drink stumbled past Cooper and summoned one of the elevators. They started kissing heavily as they waited. Cooper thought the display was a little over the top, but what the hell…they're young. As the elevator doors opened, Cooper sensed a shift in the air around him. Something was wrong. He turned around and saw that the young couple were no longer kissing, but had turned to face him and had been joined by a man coming off of the elevator. Alarm bells instantly rang in his mind as he quickly sized up the situation and assessed his options. None of them looked appealing.

"Good evening, Mr. Cooper," the man from the elevator said calmly. That was not a good sign. "And what may I ask brings you to my hotel today?"

"Cut the formalities, Vickers," Cooper replied. "You know what brings me here. Why don't you make this easy on everyone and just hand her over?"

"Her? Whoever do you mean? Have you lost someone?" Vickers asked with a smug grin.

"Knock off the act, Vickers. We both know why I'm here." Cooper started to edge his way towards the promenade. Vickers saw the slight movement, though and positioned himself to block his path.

"Don't bother trying to leave. You're a guest of the Acropolis now. I wouldn't want you to feel we short-changed you on your stay here." The young couple moved to stand on either side of Cooper while Vickers stood in front of him. "Please bring Mr. Cooper down for a tour of our facility," he said to the woman at Cooper's side.

"Lay a hand on me and you'll regret it," Cooper warned. "You wouldn't want a scene in your precious new monstrosity would you?"

"Oh please," Vickers replied. "Do you think I'm worried about that? Security dealt with a belligerent black man in an upscale Las Vegas casino. Flip to page 48 for details. Gimme a break. As long as we don't use any racial slurs, we'll probably get some awards for it." He laughed menacingly as he nodded to his pair of security personnel. "Take him."

The young woman put her hand on Cooper's shoulder as her partner grabbed for his other elbow. Cooper quickly snapped his elbow up into the young man's chin sending his head flying backwards. Cooper balled his fist, spun, and drove it straight into the woman's sternum causing her to lose her breath. She doubled over in agony as her partner tried to re-establish his balance. Cooper looked up in time to see Vickers reaching for his gun inside his shoulder holster. He closed the distance in less than two strides and grabbed him by the head, spinning him around and sending him tumbling into his bleary eyed cohort. The two men went sprawling to the floor by the elevators. Cooper did not wait for an invitation. He took off for the casino to find Ballard.

Vickers keyed his transmitter as Cooper fled. "Security. Close the exits. Bring them down now!" he shouted.

In the casino, the patrons were oblivious to what was going on just a short distance away. They were too focussed on their hopes for a turn of a friendly card or a nice bounce with the dice. Security, however, was on the move. He saw a couple of them heading for the main exit and a couple more heading straight for him. "Time to cause a scene," he muttered. He walked directly towards the closest security guard and, before the guard could properly react, delivered a straight kick to that man's chest, dropping him. A few startled bystanders screamed as another security guard drew a baton and lunged at Cooper. He deftly avoided the guard's first strike and slammed his fist into the man's throat. He, too, dropped to the ground. Panic started to set in among the gamblers and a few of them headed for the exits. *Good*, Cooper thought. *Try and stop them all.*

A plain clothes security officer ran up behind Cooper and tried to pin his arms, but he was just too big to subdue that way. Cooper bent forward and took a step back, lifting the man off of his feet. He then spun around and sent him crashing over a blackjack table. Cooper moved further towards the exit, trying to gain some cover with the fleeing civilians. He did not see the security guard off to his left taking aim at him with a 9mm handgun. The shot rang out, deafening in the confines of the casino, but penetrated harmlessly into the ceiling. Screams were even louder as people pushed and trampled one another in an effort to flee. Cooper spun to face the shooter, but only saw the reason why the shot had gone awry. Ballard now had the man's gun and was in the process of driving it strongly into the bridge of his nose. He crumpled behind a row of slot machines.

"Thanks," Cooper called out.

"Not a problem," she replied. "Shall we?" she asked motioning for the exit.

"Way ahead of you." Cooper ran for the doors as Ballard dropped in behind him. There were three security guards attempting to withstand the onrush of people while keeping their focus on the two operatives heading towards them. Cooper noted that none of them had guns...at least that were visible. Ballard fired two rapid shots into the glass door beside the guards causing two of them to dive for cover. The third stood his ground, either from a sense of duty or fear. Cooper ran into him headlong, hoisted him up, and propelled him through the shattering door behind him. Once outside, Cooper dropped the man he had just used as a battering ram, grabbed Ballard, and headed down the driveway towards Las Vegas Boulevard with the rest of the panicked mob from the casino. Ballard stuffed the gun in her blouse and the two of them blended in with the crowd as police began arriving. There were too many people for the cops to even try and sort through so they just went straight to the casino to try and regain some semblance of order.

"Monorail?" Ballard asked.

"No. It'll be a zoo. Let's catch a cab." The panic was everywhere, though, and it was clear that they weren't going to have any luck on this side. They figured it would be more likely to be able to get a cab away from the action so they trotted across the Strip to New York, New York. Sure enough, a few cabs were waiting on that side of the road.

"Where to?" the cabbie inquired as they climbed into the back.

"Flamingo!" Cooper shouted. "And faster than you've ever gone in your life." The cabbie grinned in response and swung into traffic.

"You think there's trouble there?" she asked.

"I ran into Vickers. He knew who I was. That means he knows we're here." He picked out his cell phone and dialled Waddell. The call would not complete. He tried again, but with the same result. "Shit," he cursed. "Call your partner." Ballard took her own phone out and tried to call Doyle. Her result was no better.

"Nothing," she said. "How can that be?"

"Cuz they're the next target. Cabbie! Step on it!"

"I have a possible in with the Acropolis," Martinez announced to the room. All heads turned and looked at him expectantly. "One of my informants has a brother who works as a valet at the hotel."

"How do you know he will help us?" Fenwick asked. "If he's G.D.M., he'd just flip over on us."

"He's not G.D.M. The entire family is a lot of things, but they aren't G.D.M. My informant and his brother follow Zeitgeist."

"Like the ghost?" Waddell asked curiously. That brought a few chuckles from the people in the room.

"That's poltergeist," MacReady corrected him with a smile. "But thanks for trying." Waddell gave him the finger which MacReady shrugged off.

"No. Zeitgeist is a movement of its own." The heads turned back to Martinez, so he continued. "Basically they believe that the way society is set up right now is not working. They want to see the abolition of the monetary system and the implementation of a barter system. Governments right now are misusing resources. Zeitgeist believes that there are enough natural resources in the world for everyone to be self-sufficient. Basically feed everyone without the politics."

"Is that it? Sounds like something the G.D.M. would be behind," Wojanski interjected.

"Not really. Zeitgeist isn't about terrorism. I think they're wanting a social awakening of some kind for the betterment of mankind. The G.D.M. wants to be a superpower. Both groups feel that the current global community isn't set up right, but the G.D.M. plans on installing themselves as master to a world full of underlings. Zeitgeist is more about equality."

"You turning hippie on us, Martinez?" MacReady chided.

"Nothing wrong with equality," Martinez pointed out.

"Can we use this Zeitgeist to get to your guy?" Doyle inquired. "Sounds like it might be a starting point at least."

"It's possible. A lot of people know about the G.D.M., but think their activists and shit. If we opened his eyes to the truth, he'd probably help us out. I don't know too many 'Zeitgeisters' who'd condone what the G.D.M. is doing."

"That's a pretty big gamble for 'possible'," Fenwick added. "We'd need to talk to him first, feel him out to see if he'll assist us. What's his name? I'll run it through our system."

"Rafael Castillo. Here's his address." Martinez walked over and handed her a sheet with the information he had on Mr. Castillo. Martinez turned and looked at Robert who had a grim look on his face, so he headed over to him. "You okay, Doc?" he asked.

"I just…it's nothing."

"Frustrated, huh?" he asked. Robert simply nodded as Martinez clapped him on the shoulder. "This part of it is…always. The good news is that we believe Anna is at the Acropolis and we might have a way of getting in there, but these things take time. We're making progress, though. We'll find her." Robert nodded again and took a deep breath.

"Thanks," he said.

"Anytime," Martinez replied with a smile. "Any word from Cooper?" he asked the other people in the room.

"Nothing yet," Wojanski answered.

"Listen up," Fenwick called out sharply. All noise in the room quickly dissipated. "Just got word from Quantico. There's been reports of an attempted robbery at the Acropolis. Shots were fired." Mumbling rose from the people in the room and Robert stepped forward. "Details are sketchy right now as police are just arriving on scene now. I think we all could agree that the timing for this is suspicious. We should treat this as a possible hostile move by the G.D.M. against us."

"Someone get a hold of Cooper," Waddell called out as he ran to the adjoining room to get his gear ready. Martinez and MacReady followed suit along with Doyle and Wojanski. Fenwick went back to the computer to monitor the communications between the Feds and the local authorities. Robert stood, transfixed on the F.B.I. agent as she went back to work.

"What's happening?" he asked.

"Dr. Seabrook, we have some of the best people working on this situation as we speak. Believe me we are doing everything we can for your wife. At this point and time, though, we need to find our colleagues and get them back safely. Please, let us do our jobs."

Again, he simply nodded and wandered into the next room. He had no real purpose, he was just too dazed to stand still. The need for movement...any movement... was hard to resist. The five men in this room were all donning bullet-proof vests and readying their sidearms. The C.I.A. men also brought out MP-5's which Wojanski eyed enviously.

"You guys came prepared," he noted.

"We always do," MacReady replied.

"You don't think they'll come here do you?" Robert asked, suddenly apprehensive. He felt particularly vulnerable right now, possibly due to the fact that he was the only person in the room without a gun.

"I doubt it," Waddell answered. "We're just getting our shit together so we can move quickly."

"No luck raising Cooper or Doyle," Agent Fenwick called from the other room.

"Try again," Waddell answered. "Now we gotta go get 'em." The men finished their final touches and checked each other over to make sure everything was secure. Wojanski put on his suit jacket to conceal his body armour and shoulder holster. The rest of them donned large jackets. "Here, Robert. Put this on." Waddell handed him a vest and helped him put in on. Robert looked into his eyes, worriedly. "It's just precaution," Waddell said.

"I don't have a gun," Robert pointed out.

"You're not authorized to carry one," Wojanski piped up. Robert looked at the young agent, then back at Waddell.

"He's right. Besides, do you even know how to use one?" Waddell asked.

"Point and shoot?"

Waddell smiled. "Something like that. We ready?" he asked his associates. They all nodded in agreement.

Agent Fenwick stuck her head into the room. "I've got two SUV's on their way to the parking level to get you guys. Head down when you're ready." She went back to her makeshift office to continue monitoring the situation.

"Alright, we take the stairs. Get down to the parking level and meet up with our rides. We'll head to the Acropolis and try and track down Cooper and Ballard. Once we've done that, we'll reassess and go from there. Agreed?"

"Agreed," came the collective response.

"Good. Let's move." MacReady moved over to Robert and quietly handed him a revolver. "Here," he said. "It's not much, but it'll do the job. It's a .38, loaded. Just point and shoot."

"I'm not authorized," he objected mildly.

"Yeah well we don't always follow the rules," MacReady added with a smile.

"Thanks," Robert said as he put the revolver in his pocket.

"Hopefully you won't have to use it," MacReady pointed out before entering the hallway.

Waddell pulled Robert aside. "You okay?" he asked.

"Been better," he replied with a shrug. "I don't like all this. I just want to get Anna and go home. I never wanted any of this."

"It won't be much longer. Everything will work itself out," he added reassuringly.

Martinez and Wojanski were waiting at the door to the stairway. MacReady and Doyle took the lead and went through first.

"Come on," Martinez called out, before disappearing through the door. Wojanski waited until Mitch and Robert joined him, then the three of them entered the stairwell. MacReady and Doyle were already two floors beneath them, completely unaware that Raeburn's G.D.M. team was just a little further down and already on its way up.

CHAPTER 21

O'Connor stared at the monitors in front of him. Despite the sheer number of people in the office with him, there was a deathly silence that hung over everyone. "What the hell just happened?" he asked, watching the satellite images as hundreds of people came racing out of the Acropolis.

Chad Munroe was the next to say anything. "Alright people, listen up," he called. "There has clearly been an incident at the Acropolis. I want intel on everything happening in Vegas right now. I want reports on everything. I don't care how inconsequential it may seem. I want police calls, security alarms, fire, ambulance, anything. Get in touch with Cooper. Find out what the hell is going on?" The others in the room had already started making their calls and getting their computers on task to their new assignment. "Who is our F.B.I. liaison down there again?" Munroe asked.

"Fenwick, sir," an anonymous voice answered.

"Get her too. I wanna know that all our people are safe. I want a sit-rep in five minutes."

"What do you think is going on?" O'Connor asked.

Munroe looked up at the images that SAT-SCAN was providing and processed as much as he could. "Either this thing is coming apart or it's about to." Just then he had another idea. "Anyone got eyes on Holt yet?" Silence was his only answer. "If it's a negative, I still need to hear it!" he barked.

"Negative, sir," one of the analysts replied. "We are still waiting to hear back from a couple of contacts, but as of right now…he's gone."

"Dammit," he cursed. "That son of a bitch is probably neck deep in this shit." O'Connor still struggled to believe that Holt could be working for the other side. He had to admit, though, that the timing was suspicious to say the least. Still, speculation would do no one any good right now. What they all needed was information and that was in limited supply. "Any luck reaching Cooper or Fenwick?"

"No, sir. All of our attempts are being blocked."

"What the hell do you mean blocked?" Munroe demanded.

"None of the phones are receiving. It's like they all just stopped working."

"Like the transmitters," O'Connor breathed.

"What transmitters?" Munroe asked. "You know something about this?"

"Possibly," O'Connor answered. "Back in Victoria, when my partner was killed, our transmitters stopped working. They wouldn't send or receive anything. Cell phone jammers are one thing. We have had those for quite a while. But the ability to jam transmitters is something new. I was discussing that with Dr. Quinn downstairs earlier…trying to figure out if it was possible that the G.D.M. had this kind of technology."

"Clearly they do. Alright," he called out to the people in the room. "There is a possibility of jammers being used to block cell phones and transmitters. Start calling the hotels directly. Use the landlines and get someone talking to us."

"Yes, sir," came the reply.

"With any luck, they haven't blocked everything." Both he and O'Connor wished that that were true.

Holt walked into the restaurant at the Palazzo and found his contact quickly enough. "Good to see you, John," he said as they exchanged handshakes. "It's been a while."

"Too long," his contact replied. "Wish it was under better circumstances."

"Is it ever?" Holt replied with a smile. "Were you successful?"

"It took some convincing, but yeah…I got em. You wanna see?"

"They're here?" Holt asked.

Now it was the contact's turn to smile. "Yeah. They're here. Follow me." The two men rose from the table. John deposited some money on the table to cover the food that he had barely touched. They left the restaurant and headed into the hotel itself. "You sure you need to do this?" John asked.

"Unfortunately, yes. I don't like the way this one is playing out. Neither side is doing what I'd like them to do so I need to play my hand properly. Best way to do that is to stack the deck. If I can do that successfully, then this will be the last move I ever have to make. I can retire."

"Well maybe I shouldn't help you, then," John admitted. "You're one of the best and I'd hate to lose you."

"Good thing I know you're joking," Holt added. "No, this is it for me. I want out and this is the best way for me to do it."

"Still getting the nightmares?" John asked. Holt simply nodded. "Still the same woman?" Holt nodded again. "I hope you know what you're doing, my friend."

"So do I."

"We're here," John said as they stopped by a hotel room door. "You're sure? You can still back out."

"I'm sure," Holt replied. John opened the door and the two men entered. Inside the room, two men were standing by the door and two other men were seated in the corner. It was the two men in the corner that Holt was interested in. He moved passed the two sentries and walked over to the table. "Dr. Al Hicks and Dr. Scott Miller. So glad to finally meet you. I've heard a lot about you both. Tell me," he asked as he pulled out a chair and sat down. "What's it been like working with Robert Seabrook?"

Doyle and MacReady moved smoothly down the stairs. Neither of them was in a particular hurry as they did not want to get to far ahead of the rest of the men behind them. Each of them assumed the role of scout and were eager to make sure that the SUV's were where they were supposed to be.

"What do you think happened?" Doyle asked.

"Cooper probably found something," MacReady replied. "He's good at sniffing out trouble…has a knack for it."

Doyle's thoughts turned to Lisa Ballard. They hadn't been working together long. She had transferred from a different department only six months prior, but he felt a certain kinship with her as he did with all C.S.I.S. operatives. "I hope Ballard's all right."

"Try not to think about it. If she wasn't capable of handling herself, she wouldn't have been sent here, right?" MacReady pointed out.

"True," Doyle admitted. "Even so, you have to agree that…" MacReady's hand on Doyle's arm silenced him. "What?"

"Did you hear something?" MacReady asked, his head cocked to the side with his eyes closed, straining to hear.

Doyle tried to listen, but could hear nothing. "What was it?"

"Sounded like a radio being keyed off." They peered further down to the next floor. "Might have been my imagination." Both men drew their sidearms as a precaution. Neither one of them was able to raise them before the first volley of bullets leapt up towards them from below. The first few rounds struck Doyle squarely in the chest, throwing him back against the wall. MacReady instinctively ducked and threw himself back to the landing just behind him. He could hear several bullets whizzing past his head as he scrambled for whatever cover he could find. He flung open his bag and ripped out his MP-5. Doyle, dazed by the impact, said a silent prayer for his body armour as he crawled to the landing to join MacReady. More shots followed and ricocheted around them. The sound was deafening due to the enclosed space of the stairwell and the smell of the discharged rounds wafted up towards them.

"Jesus Christ, you all right?" MacReady called as he started to return fire down the stairwell. Unable to respond verbally due to the wind being knocked out of him, Doyle just gave the 'okay' sign with his hand as he grabbed his own automatic from his bag. He struggled to find his breath as he pulled back on the charging slide and joined the fight.

"Reloading," MacReady called out as he retreated to his bag to remove more magazines. Doyle moved into his spot at the corner of the landing and started to fire down the stairwell. MacReady was back by his side a few moments later and tapped him on the shoulder. Once Doyle had exhausted his magazine, they switched places again and Doyle was able to grab more ammunition for the fight.

"This is no good!" MacReady shouted over the roar of the firing in the stairs. "We have to move. When the others get here, we'll regroup somewhere where we have room to manoeuvre."

"You got it," Doyle replied as he loaded as much ammunition as he could carry into the various pockets and pouches that his vest afforded him.

"Coming down!" shouted a voice from above. It startled Doyle, but he quickly recovered when he remembered that there were more people of his coming down the stairs.

"Clear to four!" he called back, indicating that the passage was clear to the fourth floor landing where he and MacReady were entrenched. Martinez was the first to appear, already brandishing his MP-5.

"What's the sit-rep?" Martinez asked over the noise.

"We started taking fire from the floor below. We're holding here for now til you guys catch up with us, then we're gonna move out where we have more room."

"Sounds good. The others should be here any second," he answered. As if on cue, Waddell, Wojanski, and Robert came down the stairs a moment later. Robert covered his ears as he tried to get accustomed to the decibel level his senses now encountered. Wojanski pushed him back against the wall and stood in front of him with his 9mm out and ready. Doyle repeated his update to Waddell before he went to relieve MacReady.

"We're pulling out," Martinez informed everyone as he went to the doorway leading to the fourth floor hallway. This stairwell was clearly no longer an option, so they had to find another way out. Martinez cracked the door and peered out. Seeing nothing, he smoothly moved into the hallway, weapon ready. He motioned for the others to join him as he moved south towards the elevators. Wojanski grabbed Robert and pulled him along into the corridor with Waddell close behind. A few nervous heads poked out into the hallway from several of the rooms close by, attracted by the noise from the stairwell.

"F.B.I. Everyone stay in your rooms!" Wojanski called out. The heads vanished and the slams of all the doors quickly followed.

"We're gonna have to move quick once Doyle and MacReady pull outta there," Waddell pointed out. "It won't take them long to figure out we've moved on."

"What do you suggest?" Martinez asked as he kept his focus on the south corridor while Waddell monitored the north.

"What about the elevators?" Robert asked. The men pondered that option. It was a risk due to the ease at which elevator movement could be monitored. In addition, it would not allow any mobility at all should they become trapped. But the truth of the matter was there was no way to know what awaited them in any of the other stairwells.

"It's an option, but I'd rather stick to the stairs. The last thing we need is to get boxed in," Martinez said.

"Agreed," Waddell replied. "Do you think we should split up?"

Martinez thought about that for a moment, then realized that it was too late for that. "Oh shit. Fenwick. She's still back in the room." He keyed his transmitter to contact her. "Fenwick." There was no reply. "Agent Fenwick." Still nothing. He looked over at Wojanski. "You give it a try," he ordered.

Wojanski keyed his transmitter, but the result was the same. "I'm not getting anything," he answered.

"It's worse than that," Martinez pointed out. "I didn't even hear your transmission. Theses fucking things aren't working."

"Jesus Christ," Waddell breathed. "Alright, I'll go get her. You guys link up with Doyle and MacReady. Head to the south stairwell. I'll grab Fenwick and meet you there. Be sure to clear the stairwell up to six as well before we head down cuz we're gonna be coming fast."

"Sounds good," Martinez replied just as MacReady and Doyle joined them in the hallway trailing smoke from the smoke grenades they had just deployed. Waddell ducked back into the stairwell and raced up towards the sixth floor. With any luck, whomever was coming up from below would be advancing cautiously affording him enough time to make it.

"MacReady, Doyle, cover the rear. We're heading for the south stairwell. We're gonna link up with Waddell and Fenwick there and move down," Martinez advised them.

"Copy that," MacReady replied. "Make it quick. The smoke won't last forever." Martinez readied his MP-5 and headed south towards the other stairwell. Wojanski fell in behind him tugging Robert along while MacReady and Doyle backed down the hallway ready to shoot anything that poked its head out. Robert found it difficult to breathe and his ears were still ringing from the shooting earlier. It was almost surreal for him. He felt lighter than air as he glided down the corridor behind the young F.B.I agent. He realized that he was close to losing consciousness again and that was the last thing he could afford to do. He slapped himself in the face to try and regain some of his faculties.

"You all right, Doc?" Wojanski asked as Martinez made it to the door.

"Just a little light headed," he answered. Wojanski reached into his pocket and brought out a small can.

"Here," he said, offering it to him. "Suck that down. It will clear your head."

"What is it?" Robert asked.

"Energy shot," he replied with a smile. "Perk you right up in an instant." Robert thanked him and downed the shot. It indeed worked quite quickly as he shook himself awake. Martinez entered the stairwell and braced himself against the corner of the wall covering their descent. Wojanski waited until Doyle and MacReady joined them before heading up to clear up to six.

"Any sign of nasties?" MacReady asked.

"Nothing," Martinez replied. "Looks clear. You?"

"Nothin' came out by the time we got here. So far so good."

"Good. We wait here five minutes for Fenwick and Waddell. If they're not here by then, we move on without them." It was not an easy decision to make, but one that had to be made nonetheless. Fenwick and Waddell had five minutes to get to them or they would be on their own.

Chad Munroe and O'Connor were poring over every bit of information they had in front of them. No matter how much of it there was it didn't seem like enough because they did not have any answers.

"Sir, we have reports coming in from the Flamingo. There are several rooms reporting loud noises coming from the halls…possibly gunfire."

"Shit," Munroe grumbled.

"How soon til special forces can make it there?" O'Connor asked.

"Not for another twenty minutes," came the response. "They just touched down and are loading into their vehicles now."

"Dammit," Munroe said as he slammed his fist onto the desk sending a few papers flying. "Why the fuck can't we reach anybody?"

"Sir, SAT-SCAN is reading some sort of energy spike at the Flamingo and the Acropolis. It might be what's preventing communications."

"What sort of spike?" he asked.

"Looks like some form of jammer, but I've never seen anything like it." Munroe moved over to where the technician was monitoring SAT-SCAN. "Right there," the tech pointed out. "It's high-powered, but incredibly focussed."

An idea quickly sprang to Munroe's mind. "Can SAT-SCAN cut through it?" he asked.

"Yes, sir. That's what she's designed for."

"Good. Establish communications with our team through the satellite. They might not be able to respond to each other, but we should be able to at least talk to them and let them know what we know."

Other technicians came over to assist in redirecting SAT-SCAN's function from observation to communication. It would take a few minutes to accomplish, but time was a commodity that they were low on. Munroe prayed they had enough.

Waddell reached the sixth floor and stepped into the hallway. There was a couple waiting by the elevator, but other than that, it was empty. He moved swiftly down the hall in the other direction towards the room that had acted as a command post just a few minutes before. Once he reached the room, he used his key card to open the door. He opened it and stepped to the side before peering in. Fenwick looked up from her desk, confused as to why he was there. Clearly she had no idea what had transpired just two floors below.

"What are you doing back up here?" she asked. "Forget something?"

"You could say that," Waddell answered as he stepped through the door and placed a well aimed shot through the F.B.I agent's head with his 9mm handgun. She fell backwards over her chair and collapsed in a heap against the wall. Her brain had already stopped functioning before she hit the floor. The only movement left in her was the blood making its final exit from her wound as it darkened the carpet around her head. Waddell entered the room and closed the door behind him. He made a quick scan of the rest of the room, then took out his second cell phone and pressed 3. "It's me," he said when the call was answered.

"You better have good news for me," Vickers said simply into the phone.

"Your team was late. They were already on the way down when you guys finally showed up. They got caught up in a goddamned firefight in the fucking stairwell. I thought you said you had this under control!" Waddell snapped.

"Don't forget who you're talking to, Waddell," Vickers cautioned. "I appreciate you're in a bit of a mess, but things are well in hand. What's happened so far?"

"I killed one of the Feds. The rest of the team is over in the south stairwell. They're going to be heading down to the parking level where they're supposed to be meeting with two vehicles to escort them out of here."

"Where are you?" Vickers asked.

"I'm back up at the room. I'm supposed to meet up with them and head down."

"Any sign of Philips?" Vickers inquired.

"Possibly," Waddell replied. "Dr. Seabrook received a text message from someone. That's how they were alerted to the Acropolis. It might have been Philips."

"Indeed," Vickers said, contemplating the situation.

"I'd like to get out of here," Waddell pointed out.

Vickers thought about that for a moment, but decided otherwise. "No. You are to stay with them. Tell the rest of them that the F.B.I. agent was gone and so were the files. Put the suspicion on her. They're so preoccupied with Raeburn's team that they'll believe it without question. If Philips sent that text, I need to know it. He may be trying to contact Dr. Seabrook. I knew he was in Vegas," he added absently.

"What if they don't believe me?" Waddell asked.

"Then take them out and bring me Seabrook. He and his wife can die together. Any sign of Holt?"

"Not a peep since he took off," Waddell answered.

"Well keep your eyes and ears open. I don't like not knowing where everyone is. I have a feeling we haven't seen the last of that maggot. At least when he was with you I knew where he was. Now, he could be anywhere and he's just the type of fly that I don't need."

"You don't think he took off?"

"Holt? Never. Knowing him, he's got another angle he is pursuing and I'll be damned if I'm going to let him get in my way again."

"I should have killed him when I had the chance," Waddell said matter-of-factly.

"You'll get your chance again," Vickers said.

"How can you be sure? No one knows where he is."

"Simple. We'll get the C.I.A. to find him for us," he said with a laugh. "Just leave that part to me. You get back to the team and stick to the cover story I laid out for you. I'll instruct Raeburn to move to the south stairwell and try to take as many of them out as she can. Contact me again once you are clear."

"Yes, sir," Waddell replied.

"Mitch, you've done a great job for us so far. Your contribution to the 'Movement' will not go unnoticed. Keep at it and you will see the fruits of your labour."

"Thank you, sir," he answered filled with pride. Vickers ended the call while Waddell gathered up whatever supplies had been left behind that he could carry. He cast a last look around the room, his glance resting on the body of Special Agent Christina Fenwick. He smiled to himself and went to rejoin the team in the south stairwell.

Vickers, meanwhile, keyed his transmitter so that he could speak with Raeburn. "Alpha Two this is Alpha One."

"Alpha Two go ahead," came the muted response.

"Be advised…you are clear to six. Targets have moved to the south stairwell. Send three up to the room to gather intel…reassemble the rest of your team accordingly."

"Alpha Two, copy," Raeburn answered. Vickers had complete confidence in her abilities in the field, so he put the matter largely out of his mind. With both her and Waddell working towards a common end, he could redirect his focus to the more pressing matter of finding Philips. None of his sources had turned up anything and it was getting frustrating. The Assembly was set to convene in less than 48 hours and if he had any chance of staying alive, Philips had to be terminated. Time was running out.

CHAPTER

22

Holt left the room at the Palazzo and went down to the casino floor. What he had in mind was risky, but it was clear to him that some chances were going to have to be made. A meeting with Vickers was going to have to happen soon, with or without Philips. Obviously, he would prefer to have Philips there or at least know his whereabouts, but that did not appear to be the way this going to play itself out. He would have to initiate the meeting and pretend to have Philips in hand. As long as Vickers believed it and showed up with Anna, there was room to manoeuvre. The tricky part was going to be finding who on the team was dirty. Vickers and the G.D.M. were just too well informed and always one step ahead of them. Even back in Victoria, Holt had felt he had been playing catch up from the start and he hated being behind in anything. No. There was a leak somewhere and it needed to be plugged. He had his suspicions, but unfortunately that was all that they were. He looked around and noticed that the street was not nearly as crowded as it should have been. His senses picked it up before his brain did. Something was wrong. He noticed that the majority of vehicles and pedestrians were heading south towards the main part of the strip and that very little traffic was coming north.

"What's happening?" he asked one of the passers-by.

"Some incident at the Acropolis. It's all over the news," he replied.

Oh shit, he thought. He immediately tried his transmitter, but there was nothing on the other end. He ripped out his cell phone as he attempted to hail a cab. He tried Cooper, Waddell, MacReady, and Fenwick, but received nothing. *Shit.* Fuck the Acropolis. He had to get back to the Flamingo.

He successfully wrangled a cab and ordered him to the hotel. "Take the back roads. The Boulevard is gonna be a log jam." He sat back in his seat as the cabbie swung east and headed for the back route to the Flamingo. His planning had taken him away from the team when they needed him most. He cursed himself silently and prayed that he wasn't too late.

Cooper and Ballard leapt from the cab before it had even come to a complete stop. They hit the ground running and raced down the short alcove of a parking entrance to the Flamingo Casino. "See anything?" Ballard called out.

"Nothing," Cooper replied. "But that might mean that they're already on their way up." He tried his transmitter again and still got nothing. "Communications are still down."

"What about the hard lines?" Ballard suggested as she motioned towards the concierge desk of to the left. Cooper nodded and the two of them pushed through the small line up of people to the front of the line. There were a couple of protests starting to well up, but they were quickly silenced by a menacing look from Cooper. "I need you to raise room 612."

"Excuse me, miss, but there is a line up here and I will get to you the minute I am done dealing with these guests," the concierge said politely. He attempted to re-establish dialogue with the man Ballard had pushed aside, but was met with an even more determined C.S.I.S. operative.

"I don't think you understand. This is not a request. Raise room 612 on the phone immediately. It's a government matter," she added a little more sternly.

"Ma'am," the concierge continued. "If you don't lower your voice, I'll have to call security."

At this point, Cooper had had enough. "Listen, dipshit. Call security. You're likely going to need them. But either you call room 612 right now or I'm going to break your fucking arm and call it for you! Understand that?" The concierge stared blankly at the large man's face. It was clear that he was not joking and that the fate of his arm was indeed in jeopardy. He reached down and pressed the alarm to summon security as he picked up the phone to dial room 612. Cooper snatched the phone from the man's hand and listened intently, but the call went unanswered. "Shit," he grumbled.

"Anything?" Ballard asked as she watched for approaching security personnel.

Cooper shook his head. He gave the phone back to the concierge. "Keep dialling it every two minutes until I answer is. Is that understood?" The concierge nodded just as the first of the security officers arrived at the desk.

"Sir, I'm going to have to ask you to step away from the desk," the security officer advised.

Ballard removed her identification from her pocket and tossed it to the young officer. "My name is Lisa Ballard. I'm with C.S.I.S. This is Jason Cooper with…"

"Another agency," Cooper interjected as he turned around to face the young man. "You need to get on the horn and get your head of security over here right now. There may be a major incident going on right now in the hotel and you guys are gonna assist."

The officer looked over the ID and compared it to the woman who had tossed it. He was clearly out of his league and he knew it, but he kept his professionalism. "Wait right here and don't move." He keyed his radio and informed his colleagues of the developments as more officers began to arrive.

"Good," Cooper said. "The more the merrier. You guys are gonna be responsible for the well-being of the guests of this hotel. I have a feeling that they're going to need your help before this is over."

After a few moments, an older gentleman wearing a rather expensive suit came over to the desk. He had on an earpiece and was holding a radio. "My name is Tyson

Renzo. I'm head of security here at the Flamingo. What seems to be the trouble?"

"Have you had any reports of trouble on the sixth floor? Particularly Room 612?" Cooper asked.

Renzo hesitated a moment before speaking. "We haven't had any reports from 612 or the sixth floor. Who are you again?"

"You paused," Ballard observed. "You've had reports of trouble from somewhere else?"

"I'm not in a position to discuss our security matters with people who might be a security matter themselves. Would you mind explaining to me exactly what you guys are doing here?" he asked pointing to the concierge who was listening intently.

"Call the room again," Cooper told him, then directed his focus back to Renzo. "There are lives at stake here. What reports did you receive?"

Renzo sized the man up. One of his best resources at his disposal was his ability to ascertain the quality of a person by his or her eyes. He saw no deception in this man and acted upon that. "We receive a few complaints from some of our guests on the fourth floor. Something about loud noises coming from the stairwell…possibly shooting. I've sent a couple of my officers up to investigate. One sec," he added as he pressed his earpiece a little tighter. Cooper watched the man swallow heavily. "We just received a number of calls of men on the fourth floor with guns."

"Call your people back. They're in over their heads," Cooper advised. "Wait a minute. Your transmitters are working?"

"Yes of course they are. Why?" Cooper's mind raced as he contemplated his options. *If their communications aren't affected and neither are the land lines, then it's just our devices being jammed. That must mean that whoever is jamming it has to have access to one of our communication devices.* With the information he had, he drew only one conclusion. "It's gotta be Holt. Keep an eye out for him," he advised Ballard. She nodded as Cooper went back to speaking with Renzo. "We need to borrow some of your transmitters. Ours are being jammed. We're gonna head up and see if we can't neutralize the situation."

"We should really wait for the police," Renzo pointed out. One of his men was already calling it in.

"In a perfect world we could, but we've got people up there who need help now. Those transmitters?" Renzo hesitated a little more. Giving this man some leeway when it came to stories was one thing. Handing over security equipment was something else entirely. He, after all, had a hotel and casino to run. "Look I'm not interested in the workings of your casino. Those things have multiple channels?" Renzo nodded. "Good. Pick the channel you want us to stay on and you can monitor us as we go. Either way, we're going now."

"Carlson. Biggs. Give them your radios." Both men reluctantly handed over their equipment. Ballard and Cooper scooped them up, inserting the earpiece into their ears. "Channel six is open. You guys stay on that. If you flip channels even for a second, I'll shut em both down. Clear?"

"Got it," Cooper answered. "Thanks."

"I'll be monitoring on six as well. Good luck. I hope you can get your people out."

"Thank you again," Ballard added. "If you can do it quietly, try and get some of these people out of the casino." Cooper and Ballard headed for the elevator at a trot.

"Sir," Security Officer Carlson said. "We should be going with them. If they're right, they will need all the help they can get."

"Look, son," Renzo replied. "I understand how you feel. God knows I'd like to go with them. But if they are right about what's going on, I'm going to need everyone single person I have to make sure our guests get out of here safely. Our priority is to them and this hotel. If they are right and this things turns bad, we're gonna have a full fledged panic on our hands. I want a security meeting in five minutes in the north boardroom. We need an action plan."

Cooper and Ballard made it to the elevators. Thankfully, there was no one else waiting. They got in and stared at the number bank. "What do you figure? Four or six?" Ballard asked.

Cooper thought about that for a moment. "Well, if they left six and shots were heard on four, they might try to head back up to six to regroup. Plus the last thing we need is to open the door into a firefight. I say six."

"Agreed," Ballard said as she pressed the button for the sixth floor. She drew the sidearm that she had wrested from the Acropolis guard and checked her rounds. She had eleven left. Not for the first time, Cooper cursed himself for not having brought a gun. Ballard dropped to one knee at the side of the elevator door and waited for them to open. Cooper tried to make himself as small as he could on the other side of the doors. Neither of them knew what to expect, but both had to be ready for anything.

Waddell raced down the hallway towards the south stairwell. He wanted to be sure he was out of breath by the time he got there. Wojanski was waiting for him when he reached the door.

"Where's Agent Fenwick?" he asked looking back down the hall.

"She's fucking gone!" Waddell announced as he started down the stairs towards the others.

"Wait! What do you mean gone?" Wojanski called as he followed him down. Waddell was already nearing the rest of the team before Wojanski finally caught up with him.

"Fenwick's gone," Waddell repeated. "She took off. All the files…everything. She's fucking gone."

"Jesus Christ," MacReady breathed.

"No wonder they knew where we were," Martinez said aloud. "What the fuck do we do now? She led us right into a goddamned trap. 'There'll be SUV's in the parking area'. Fuck!"

"No way!" Wojanski protested. "She'd never do that."

"Oh yeah?" Waddell replied. "How the fuck do we know you're not involved in this too?" The weight of that statement resonated throughout the small space. Each of the men turned their attention to the young Federal agent.

"What do you say, Wojanski?" MacReady asked. "Anything you'd like to add?"

Wojanski, quick to see where this was going, tried to distance himself from Fenwick. "Look, I can't speak to Fenwick. All I know is that I'm in this with you guys. If she was dirty, we'll get her for it. But come guys, you gotta believe me. I had nothing to do with this."

"It's irrelevant," Robert said loudly enough to be heard over the volume of the men in the stairwell. They all stopped and looked over at him. "It doesn't matter now. If she was dirty, they knew we were heading to the other stairwell. They don't know where we are now. But the longer we stay in one place, the more likely they are to figure it out. Let's just work on getting out of here. We can deal with him later," he said with a nod to Wojanski.

"What if he is with them and they can track him?" Doyle pointed out.

"Well then they already know where we are and it's been nice knowing you. Let's just get moving."

"He's right," MacReady agreed. "We make for the casino floor. Fuck the parking level. We'll get out with the rest of the guests when they evacuate. Everyone gear down. Autos, vests, everything except your sidearms. Take off your jackets too," he added as he started taking his gear off.

"Are you insane?" Martinez asked incredulously. "I'm not taking off my shit. Besides, why the hell would the hotel be evacuated?"

"Simple," MacReady said. He reached over and pulled the fire alarm. The bell started ringing immediately and people throughout the hotel reacted to the unwelcome sound. A few unscrupulous gamblers tried to make a move by scooping a bunch of chips from the tables and making a run for it. Renzo and his team had spread out for what was coming. They hadn't expected a fire alarm, but were prepared nonetheless. Biggs and two of the other officers dealt with the would-be thieves as Renzo started to organize the evacuation of the casino.

Back in the stairs, Waddell and the other operatives followed MacReady's lead and were soon down to their shirts and pants. Each member put their sidearm in one of their pockets, including Robert who was still grateful to Mitch for providing him with a revolver. "We good?" MacReady asked. All of them answered positively. "All right, this stairwell is one of the evacuation routes. When the guests start heading down, we blend in with them and get outta here. Agreed?" They all nodded. "Martinez, you take lead." MacReady stepped to the side bringing Doyle with him. He leaned forward and spoke in his ear. "You watch Wojanski. He steps out of line…you drop him. Clear?"

Doyle nodded, and then whispered back. "What about Waddell? Something just doesn't feel right about any of this."

"I know. I'll watch him. You sensing something?"

"Might be nothing," he added as hotel guests started filing into the stairwell. They were too focussed on exiting the building to notice the small pile of firearms and body armour in the corner. "Might just be the situation."

"Well, keep your eyes open," MacReady advised. Martinez was already moving downstairs with the other guests. Wojanski went next, followed by Doyle. Robert and Waddell waited for a few more people to go down before joining the procession. Finally, MacReady joined the throng and the team moved towards the casino floor. With luck, they would all be mistaken for hotel guests and left alone.

The fire alarm sounded just as Cooper and Ballard exited the elevator. "Shit. Talk about bad timing," Ballard muttered.

"I doubt it's a coincidence," Cooper said. "It's probably being used as a distraction. We should hurry." The two of them moved quickly towards Room 612. The only movement in the corridor was that of hotel guests moving towards the evacuation route. "If we hurry, we might be able to slip out with the rest of them." Cooper hugged the wall as Ballard led the way down the corridor towards the room. She held her gun low so as not to attract too much attention from hotel guests, but it was ready. A couple of people cast worried glances at her, but she shooed them away with a wave of her hand.

Having reached the room, Ballard kept watch over the hall while Cooper took out his key card and went to swipe in. That was when he noticed that the door was ajar. He tapped Ballard on the shoulder and directed her attention to the problem. She nodded in understanding and swung around to face the door. Cooper was about to kick in the door when Ballard stopped him. He shot her a confused look, but soon realized what she was getting at when she motioned towards the door to Room 614…the adjoining room. Cooper made his way to the other door and pressed his ear against it. He could hear muffled sounds coming from within. He waited a few moments and counted at least three distinct voices. He indicated that to Ballard with his fingers. She moved towards him and they met between the two rooms.

"I'll let myself in to 614," Ballard suggested. "When I do, kick the door in to 612 and get out of the way cuz they're gonna be firing. Tell me over the transmitters when you are gonna make your move. When I hear the shots, I'll move in and cut em down."

Cooper looked worried. "Maybe I should go in with the gun," he said.

"This is no time for misplaced chivalry, Cooper," Ballard spoke flatly. "I'm trained for this kind of job too. Besides, if one of them makes a break for the door, he'll have a lot more to contend with if you're waiting for him than if I was." Cooper reluctantly agreed and took his position by the door to 612. Ballard moved back to 614 and carefully inserted the appropriate key card. The lock released and she slowly opened the door. Leading with her gun, she cautiously peeked into the room. The three voices were all coming from 612. She crept forward towards the doorway joining the two rooms. He heart hammered in her ears loudly enough that she was worried they might be able to hear it. She took a deep breath to steel her nerves and waited. In her earpiece, she heard Cooper's voice.

"Three...two...one..." Cooper struck out with his foot and kicked the door open forcefully, causing it to slam against the wall. He quickly ducked from the doorway as the three men inside all opened fire with automatic weapons. With all of their attention on the intrusion, they lost focus on the second room. Ballard came to the edge of the doorway and saw one of the men by the window. He was wearing body armour so she had to be accurate. She aimed for his head and squeezed the trigger. Blood from the bullet impact splattered the window behind him as he went limp and collapsed to the floor. Ballard moved a little further in and sighted on the second man. He said seen his companion go down and was swinging his submachine gun towards Ballard, firing as he turned. She fired two quick shots. The first one hit him high on the shoulder, causing him to spray his shots wildly. The second found its mark on the man's head. He fell backwards onto the bed, his lifeless eyes staring up at the ceiling.

The third man was now focussed on the doorway shielding Ballard. He fired into the wall she was hiding behind with a silenced Uzi. Cooper used this change in focus to act. He burst through the door of Room 612 and closed the distance between himself and the shooter before he could react. He grabbed the gun and ripped it out of the man's hands. Shock registered on his face at the loss of his gun momentarily until the expression was replaced with a grimace of pain as the gun he had just been holding was driven into the bridge of his nose by the sizable attacker. He fell backwards to the floor as Cooper descended on him, grabbing his head and twisting it violently to the side. He was rewarded with the sound of breaking bone as the man surrendered his life to the C.I.A. operative pressing down on him. Cooper quickly gathered up the Uzi he had just used as a club and scanned the room for anyone other visitors. The only other person he saw was the body of Agent Fenwick in the corner of the room. He grimaced slightly as he resumed his scan of the area. Once he was sure the room was clear, he called out to Ballard. There was no response. He moved quickly, and quietly, to the doorway to 614 and peered in. Agent Ballard lay on the floor, blood seeping from two wounds she had sustained when the bullets passed through the wall she had been using for cover. One was in her arm, the other in her chest. She was not moving.

"Shit, shit, shit," Cooper muttered as he went down to his temporary partner, placing the Uzi to the side. "Ballard," he called as he checked for a pulse. It was there, but it was weak. "Ballard, come back to me." He checked her breathing which was shallow. He keyed his transmitter. "Renzo! Renzo!" he shouted. "You there?"

"Yeah, I'm here," Renzo answered.

"I need emergency medical up here in 614. As soon as the ambulances start arriving, send one of the crews up here." He ripped open Ballard's blouse and saw the exit wound. There were no air bubbles so it didn't appear that her lungs had been punctured. He felt under her and found the entrance wound in her right shoulder blade. Luckily, it had missed her heart as well.

"I've got a crew here right now. I'm sending them up. What happened?" Renzo asked.

"Let them know that there is a federal agent down, one gunshot to the left arm and one in the back. Both appear to be through-and-throughs. Breathing is shallow and her pulse is thin. I'll stay with her til they arrive."

"I'm coming up too," Renzo added. "Sounds like you could use any help you can get right now."

Cooper turned Ballard over into the recovery position and applied direct pressure to both the entrance and exit wounds. The one in her arm was not life-threatening, so he left it for now. He still had to be mindful of his surroundings. He thought about moving her to a different room entirely in case other G.D.M. shooters were on the way. In the end, though, he felt that it might do more harm than good to move her. If there were more people coming, he would see to it that they regretted ever trying to set foot in this room.

After what seemed like an eternity, there was a knock at the door. "It's Renzo."

Cooper reached down and grabbed Ballard's sidearm and aimed it at the door. "Come in," he called. Renzo poked his head around the door, saw the gun pointed at him, and quickly ducked back.

"I've got EMT's here, Cooper. Let em in." One of the EMT's dangled an equipment bag through the doorway. Cooper lowered the gun.

"You're clear," Cooper called out. Renzo came back around the door, saw that Cooper had lowered the gun, and ushered the EMT's into the room. Cooper stepped aside as the paramedics began to work on Ballard. He motioned for Renzo to follow him into the next room. Renzo did and was struck by the carnage left in Room 612.

"Jesus Christ! What the hell happened in here?" he asked as he surveyed the bodies of Agent Fenwick and the three gunmen.

"Never mind any of that," Cooper dismissed with a wave of his hand. "Listen, I have to go and try to track down the rest of my team. They are still in danger. What is your security detail up to?"

"They're all occupied with the evacuation down in the casino. I've got a couple of officers heading up to assist guests to the exits, but that's about it."

"I need someone to stay with Ballard. Even when the paramedics take her. I would, but I can't."

"I'll stay with her til they get her downstairs. I can't leave the building, but I'll get one of my best people to go with her," Renzo offered.

"Thanks," Cooper said. Then he had a brainstorm. This fire alarm was no coincidence. *I wonder if MacReady is using it as a distraction to get out of here.* "Question. Can you tell where the alarm was pulled?"

"Yeah, of course. Do you need to know?" Renzo asked.

"It might be important."

Renzo switched his transmitter channel. "Hatfield, it's Renzo. Can you tell me where the alarm was pulled?" Renzo listened to the response and nodded. "South stairwell, fifth floor landing," he said. "It's part of the evacuation route."

That's where they are. "Does it lead straight to the casino?" he asked.

"No," Renzo replied. "That evacuation route only goes to two. You have to go down a couple of hallways to get to the escalator to bring you down to the casino level."

"Tell your security detail to get some people over to that escalator. There might be trouble coming their way." He moved back to Ballard and removed her transmitter that she had received from Renzo, gathered up the Uzi and her handgun, and made his way to the central stairwell.

"Hey Cooper," Renzo called after him in the hall. Cooper turned before he went into the stairs. "She's in good hands. Don't worry about her."

"Thanks," he said, and moved into the smoky stairwell. *Shit. Maybe there is a fire*, he thought. But this smoke was not from a fire. He could tell the difference. Someone had deployed a smoke grenade in here. He hoped that whoever had been waiting down below was gone. He had some ground to make up and four floors to cover. With that thought, he plunged into the darkened stairwell, prepared to meet his maker.

Vickers radioed Raeburn once more. "Alpha Two, this is Alpha One."

"Alpha Two, go."

"I have the evacuation plan for the Flamingo Hotel. If they are indeed following it from the south stairwell, they will emerge on two and have to get to the escalators to get out. You can intercept them there."

"Copy," Raeburn replied. "We are already in position."

"Good. Remember, we need the doctor alive. Everyone else is expendable. One, out." Vickers sat back with a satisfied grin. He enjoyed being in control of things. He also enjoyed having competent people working for him. The G.D.M. had its advantages and its drawbacks, but they seemed to weed out a lot of incompetence. He could appreciate that. He turned to his security monitor and saw Anna sleeping on her bunk. *Maybe when this is over, I'll take you with me,* he thought. *It would be an interesting way to spend my retirement.* The thought aroused him, momentarily, before he refocused on the situation at hand. *That can wait.*

Munroe received the news he had been waiting for. SAT-SCAN was ready to contact his people. The satellite had also been able to listen in to the transmissions of not only the Flamingo, but the G.D.M. team as well. O'Connor sat at the console armed with the knowledge that Cooper was on his way down, one of the agents had been shot and was being tended to by paramedics, the G.D.M. had a death squad waiting for the team, and the team was heading right towards them.

"You're on," Munroe said. "Remember, they can hear you but can't respond to you until SAT-SCAN can set up an isolated signal."

O'Connor nodded and keyed the terminal. "Flamingo Team. Flamingo Team. Codename Breakwater. Hold your positions immediately." The members of the team in the stairwell all stopped abruptly as the receivers in their ears spoke for the first time in a while. "This is O'Connor," he continued. "Be advised. G.D.M. aware of your location and are lying in wait. Suggest alternate route."

In the stairwell, Waddell cursed silently. *Codename Breakwater? That had to be O'Connor! How the hell did he get to be a part of this?* He keyed his transmitter, but found that it wasn't working. For a moment, he panicked and thought that they had learned the truth about him and had cut him off, but MacReady soon caught up with him and had the same problem.

The voice in their ears continued. "Meet up on third floor landing. Discuss options. Will advise from this end as we go. Still no sign of Holt. If spotted, treat him as hostile until we know more." Martinez reached the third floor landing first and waited for the rest to arrive. It didn't take long. Doyle and Wojanski arrived next.

"What the fuck was that all about?" Doyle asked. Wojanski shrugged.

"Sounds to me like we have some help from outside," Martinez suggested. "At this point, I'll take anything I can get. But if he's right, how the hell did the G.D.M. know where we are?"

"I'm telling you, they're tracking us," Doyle said. "It's the only explanation." He turned his focus over to Wojanski. "Aren't they?"

"I told you I don't have anything to do with this," Wojanski answered. "I have no idea how they know, but it's not me." Robert, Waddell, and MacReady joined them on the landing.

"What's our plan?" Martinez asked.

"Well it would seem our exit strategy has been compromised," MacReady pointed out. "I say we get out here on three and move to a different evacuation route."

"Sounds good to me," Robert admitted. The other men all nodded in agreement. Waddell didn't like it as he had no way of alerting Vickers of the change, but there was little he could do about it. The plan was simple enough. Head down the halls of the third floor until they reached the central or north stairwell, go down to the second floor and use the other escalator to reach the rear of the casino. The problem with their intelligence was that despite SAT-SCAN's advanced technology, it could not account for orders given face to face. Raeburn was meticulous. She did not want her ambush to be flanked so she had sent Olson and a small squad up to the third floor to lie in wait and to act as back up should the need arise. Little did anyone know that Martinez was coming out of the stairwell and heading straight for Olson's team.

CHAPTER 23

Holt had heard O'Connor's message. *Treat him as hostile.* It was clear that he couldn't go back to the Flamingo now. Even if he tried to assist, one of his own team could shoot him dead. No. Their reunion would have to wait. He hoped it would end well for everyone involved. But now it was time to put his plan in motion. The phone rang at the front desk of the Acropolis Hotel. The scene was still chaotic as police and security personnel tried to regain control of the area. At first, no one reacted to the ringing phone. The hotel was a mess and no one was thinking about future reservations at present. After a few tries, someone finally answered.

"Hotel Acropolis," came the terse response.

"Yes. I'd like to speak with Colin Vickers, please," Holt said evenly. The clerk on the other end clearly hesitated before responding.

"We don't have a Colin Vickers here, sir," he replied.

"I know," Holt agreed. "Get him. Page him. Whatever you have to do. Tell him it's Holt. He'll pick up." Holt smiled a little as he thought of Vickers' face when he was informed that Holt was calling *him*.

"I'll put you on hold." *Thought so.*

After a few minutes, Vickers picked up the transferred call. "Mr. Holt. What do I owe for the honour? Did I win an award?" he chuckled.

"Hardly," Holt answered. "I'm not interested in small talk. I have what you're looking for…or should I say who. I'm willing to trade him for Anna."

Vickers laughed out loud. "Oh come now, Holt. You expect me to believe that after all this running around, you just stumbled across Philips and are willing to hand him over just like that? How stupid do you think I am?"

"I don't think you're stupid at all, Vickers. I think you're tired." The silence from the other end of the phone indicated that Vickers had not been expecting that. "You're tired of the game and truth be told, so am I. I've watched you operate over the years, Vickers, and I know what's at stake for you. You and I both know that when you turn Philips over to the 'Movement', you're a dead man. So I asked myself, why is he doing it? Then I figured it out. You want out. You wanna clean up the last bit of unfinished business you have and leave it all behind you. Well guess what, I want out too. I give you Philips, you give me Anna. You can do what you want from there."

"And I'm supposed to believe you because you say so? I doubt that, Holt," he snarled into the phone.

"Believe what you want, Vickers, but I will be waiting for you at 10 o'clock tonight. I will send you the coordinates. If you want Philips, bring Anna there and we'll trade." Holt terminated the call before Vickers could reply. There was a chance that Vickers would not show up. What Holt was counting on was Vickers' survival instinct. Without Philips, he had no chance of survival. The mere chance that he might be able to get him might be enough to get him to the exchange. Now it was just a matter of getting everyone else there.

Olson squeezed the grip on his SMG automatic. He was stationed just inside the door of Room 347. He had a clear view of the man exiting the stairwell. He could have been a guest, but he showed a little too much hesitation. The other guests had been in a hurry to get out of the building. This man appeared to be cautious. Olson had him pegged as an operative almost immediately. He slowly keyed his transmitter. "I have movement on three," he spoke softly. "Target coming through door from south stairwell. Bravo Two and Four move up." Two of his squad moved to positions a little further away. There was a corridor that ran east to west about halfway along the one that Martinez was currently walking down. The two men took up positions there. "Bravo Three, stay at the north stairwell. We may still need you there." Olson peered around his corner and saw that the man had now been joined by three others. He recognized Waddell as the fourth man. *If our intel is correct, that leaves two still in the stairwell.* His orders were clear. Eliminate as many of them as you can. Waddell was considered expendable. *Happy hunting, men.*

"Bravo Two and Four, weapons free…engage."

Three of the first four shots struck Martinez in the chest. The fourth struck him in mid-thigh. He fell in the hall with a thud as the intense noise of gunfire filled the cramped hall. With no real way to go, it was like a shooting gallery for the gunmen. Wojanski was hit next as he was spun around when a shot shattered his left arm. He screamed in pain as he fell. Doyle made a dive for one of the room doors and was lucky to find one that had not been closed properly by a fleeing guest. Two shots ripped the door jamb apart as he fell headlong into the room. One bullet had grazed his right shoulder, but besides that he was uninjured.

Out in the hall, Waddell hit the floor as bullets whizzed past inches over his head. "Jesus Christ!" he shouted. The hall was quickly filling with the acrid smell of cordite and spilled blood. MacReady reached through the doorway and grabbed Waddell, tugging him back towards the stairs. Martinez, though gravely injured, still tried to raise his gun in a final attempt to aid his team. For his efforts, he was silenced before he could get a shot off. Wojanski rose to one knee and fired down the hall with his Beretta as many times as he could before another volley from the unseen shooters tore through him and sent him backwards, ending his brief career as a field agent.

"Get back!" MacReady shouted to Robert as he dragged Waddell back into the relative sanctuary of the stairwell. Robert did as instructed and retreated to the stairs leading up. Waddell slithered the last few feet and kicked the door closed. "What about the others?" MacReady asked him as he prepared to open the door again. Waddell braced his foot against it, preventing him from heading back out.

"Martinez and Wojanski are gone," he answered. "Didn't see what happened to Doyle."

"You all right?" Robert asked him from the stairs.

Waddell did a quick check and was relieved to find that he hadn't been hit. *What the hell were those guys thinking? They knew I was with the team and that I was leading them right to them. Did they not see me? Did they miss on purpose?* Mitch had a lot of questions and very little answers. From the start, things had not gone according to the plan that Vickers had laid out for him. Nesbitt was not supposed to have been killed. The woman was not supposed to have been kidnapped. For certain, he wasn't supposed to be dodging bullets from other G.D.M. operatives. *Vickers would have some explaining to do…if I make it that far.* His thoughts were interrupted by Robert.

"What do we do now?" he asked. "We're trapped. They were waiting for us on three and there will undoubtedly be more of them waiting below."

"Okay here's the plan," MacReady said. "We get back up to our equipment. Clearly we can't slip out with the guests. We gear up and push for the roof. We'll try and get a signal to O'Connor and he can send a chopper to get us."

"That's it? That's your plan?" Waddell was incredulous. "Right now we have no way to even be certain that that is actually O'Connor. Even if it is, we have no way to signal him because our communications aren't working yet. All we can do is listen." Mitch didn't like the idea of heading up at all. If, for some reason, they decided to return to their room, Agent Fenwick's body would give him away. He would have to kill them all and then report that everything had been lost. None of his options were looking good at the moment.

"We make for our gear, then the roof. Clear?" MacReady was in no mood for a debate.

"What about Doyle?" Robert asked. "You can't just leave him."

MacReady looked at him with grim determination. "I don't like the idea any more than you do, Dr. Seabrook. But at this point and time, my primary responsibility is you. I don't know if Doyle is alive or not, but I can't risk sticking around to find out. I've gotta get you out of here and right now, that means staying mobile. Let's go," he said as he tugged Robert along with him up the stairs. Waddell followed behind, constantly looking back over his shoulder for anyone moving towards them. Sadly for him, it didn't seem to matter which side they were on, anyone could be trying to kill him.

Doyle braced himself against the door. He blessed his good fortune that this door had been unsecure when the shooting had started or he would have been cut down in the hall like his team members had been. He listened intently as the echoes from the shooting trailed off. Glancing quickly around the room, he ascertained that he was inside a standard room, not much different than the one the team had first assembled in. There was no adjoining room which was a relief. As it stood, he only had to concern himself with the one entrance. He moved away from the door and placed himself behind the only real cover this room would afford…the corner of the wall which housed the bathroom. He checked his ammunition and confirmed that he was fully loaded, though now he wished he still had his submachine gun at his side. He rechecked his shoulder wound and saw that it would need a couple of stitches, but shouldn't pose a problem. He dropped to one knee and pointed his firearm at the door, ready to punish anyone who tried to rush in.

Cooper heard the shooting from the landing of the fourth floor in the stairwell. He tensed momentarily as he thought the firing might have been directed at him and braced for the impact. There was none and he was able to determine the approximate distance that the shooting was coming from. He placed his sidearm back in its holster and readied the Uzi he had taken from the fallen shooter. Poking his head around the corner leading down to the third floor landing, he observed a man crouched at the door leading to the hallway. He was dressed all in black with full body armour on. He was speaking quietly into a headset as the shooting tapered off. Cooper strained to hear what was being said.

"Nice work, Bravo Two and Three. Bravo Four, move up to reinforce. Two and Three, when he arrives, sweep forward and clean up." The man stood up and was preparing to leave when he stopped and adjusted his headset. "Go ahead Alpha Two." *So there is a second team*, Cooper thought. The man with the headset listened for a few more moments before responding. "Copy that. Team confirms two down. Redeploying now. Will contact again with any changes. Bravo One, out."

Cooper had heard enough. He raised the silenced Uzi and aimed it at the back of the man's head. He pressed the trigger and fired off a short three round burst that tore through his skull and sent him flying into the wall in front of him. Cooper quickly swept down the stairs and took the headset off the corpse as he checked the hall for any sign of activity. Seeing none, he stuffed the communicator he had with him in his pocket and donned the headset. He could hear the chatter between the other members of the team.

"Bravo One this is Bravo Two. Four is with us, we are moving forward. Confirming two dead in the hall. A third made it to one of the rooms on the right. We are moving now to engage."

Cooper didn't have long to act. He didn't know which one it was, but one of his team was about to be ambushed. He cautiously opened the door and peered into the corridor. What he saw caused his blood to boil. Lying dead in the hallway was Martinez and Wojanski. There was a shooter at the corner just ahead of him and two more shooters preparing to enter a room on the right with their weapons drawn. Cooper said a silent prayer and stepped out into the hall. He moved quickly and quietly as he closed on the man he assumed to be Bravo Four.

Knowing that Bravo One was behind him, 'Four' never thought to watch his blind side. His final thought as the bullets passed through him was 'how the hell am I getting shot?' Cooper dispatched him quickly and continued firing down the hall at the two remaining shooters who now found themselves the victims in the very same ambush they had just executed. One of them turned to return fire while the other made for the door. Neither plan was successful. The one who stayed in the hall had no real cover and was soon taken out by the sustained fire from Cooper. The man who entered the room had focussed all of his thoughts to getting out of the line of fire. He had completely forgotten that on the other side of this particular door was a man with a gun whom he had just tried to kill. He made it two steps into the room before Doyle placed a well aimed shot into his forehead.

Silence descended once again in the hall as Doyle tried to make sense out of what had just happened. The door to the room lay open and he saw the body of another enemy lying motionless just outside. *It's gotta be one of us*, he thought. He moved to the door, but didn't dare stick his head out in case he was mistaken. Instead, he called out. "Ho."

"Who's there?" came the reply.

"Fuck you. Who are you?" Doyle wasn't about to give away anything about who he was.

"This could take a while," the voice answered.

Doyle cursed silently. One of them would have to give first. *What the hell*, he thought. *It's not like they don't already know exactly where I am.* "It's Doyle. Who are you?"

"Doyle, it's Cooper. You okay?"

God Damn what a relief. "Yeah. Just grazed. Where you been?"

"Just got back," Cooper answered. "I'm coming to you." Doyle again retreated to his corner in the room and waited with his gun aimed at the hall. After a few moments, a small Kleenex was dangled around the corner of the doorway and waved. Doyle smiled slightly as Cooper's head appeared shortly after.

"Fuck are you a sight for sore eyes," Doyle breathed as he rose to his feet.

Cooper entered the room and slapped a large hand thankfully on to the Canadian's uninjured shoulder. "I could say the same thing about you. Where is everybody else?"

Doyle shook his head, partly to respond negatively and partly to clear his senses. "Didn't see. When the shooting started, I just bailed in here. If they're not in the hall, they must have headed back into the stairs."

"Well hopefully they didn't go down. There's a second team waiting down there for them," he added.

"You know that for sure?" he asked curiously.

Cooper nodded. "I've been listening." He motioned towards the headset of the shooter at their feet. Doyle knelt and scooped the headset from him. "Ballard with you?" he asked. Cooper didn't answer right away which caused Doyle a moment of anguish. He stopped what he was doing and stole a glance at him. "Cooper?" He could read in the man's face that something had gone wrong. The gnawing of dread started to eat at his stomach.

"She got hit, Doyle. Back at the room. EMT's are with her now and I've got the head of hotel security with her." He wished there was more he could add, but at that moment, he just didn't know more.

"Shit," muttered Doyle, as he resumed his work to get the headset off the man at his feet. "Did you get the message from O'Connor?" he asked.

"O'Connor. How does he figure into this?"

"Guess that's a no. He's been able to contact us through our communicators, but we haven't been able to respond yet. Should be soon though." Doyle readied his new headset and grabbed the Uzi from the man's hands. "What do you figure?"

Before he could respond, their newly acquired headsets snapped into action. "Alpha Two this is Alpha One." Cooper put his finger to his lips to silence Doyle. The two men listened intently as the conversation continued.

"Alpha Two here. Go ahead Alpha One."

"Change in plans. Pull your team back and regroup at primary rally point."

"Alpha Two, copy. What about the target?"

"New developments. Will explain at the rally point. Alpha One, out."

Cooper and Doyle shared a look as they tried to formulate a plan. Neither of them knew where the rally point was or who Alpha One was, but they wished they could be there to greet him. Their personal reveries were interrupted by another radio burst.

"Bravo One, this is Alpha Two."

Cooper pointed to his headset and showed Doyle one finger to indicate that this headset had belonged to Bravo One.

"Bravo One, this is Alpha Two. Respond." At the other end of the transmission, Raeburn began to get a very uneasy feeling. "Bravo Team, from Alpha Two." The silence was deafening as she began to gather her primary unit on the second floor. She was relieved when the radio crackled to life. Her relief was short-lived.

"Alpha Two. This used to be Bravo One. He and the rest of Bravo Team are dead. Recommend you do as Alpha One says and retreat to the rally point. We'll meet you there." Cooper clicked off his headset and smiled. "There. That should give them something to mull over."

Doyle smiled as well. "I gotta get back to Ballard. You said she was back at the room?"

"Yeah…though she might already be moving to the ambulance by now. Take the elevator. It was clear when we came up."

"Thanks," Doyle replied. "What are you gonna do?"

"I'm gonna see if I can track down Dr. Seabrook and the others. Once that's accomplished, we'll have to start a massive clean-up. I'll have to coordinate with the F.B.I. on that one. I'm sure they'll want Wojanski and Fenwick returned for proper burial."

Doyle looked up at him sharply. "Fenwick! You killed her?" he asked incredulously.

Cooper was taken aback. "I didn't kill her. She was dead when we got there."

"Got where?" Doyle asked with a confused look on his face. None of this was making any sense. "We were told she took off. We figured she sold us out and bailed with all the files. Must have been working with the G.D.M. all along."

"She didn't take off. I found her in the room. She's dead. Three shooters were in the process of going through the files when Ballard and I showed up. We took them out, but one of them hit Ballard." Both men stared at each other as the gravity of his words sunk in. "Who the hell said she had taken off?"

"Waddell. He went back up to the room and came back saying she was gone."

"Son-of-a-bitch," Cooper breathed. It only took the seasoned veteran a few moments to piece together exactly what had transpired. Waddell was working for the G.D.M. He had to have been doing so right from the start…since before Cooper was even asked to provide assistance to Holt in this matter. Did that mean that Holt was innocent? Or were they working together? Unfortunately, the revelation of Waddell's involvement only seemed to add more questions than it answered. "I'd better find him. Get to Ballard. Take this," he said as he handed him the communicator that was tied in with Renzo. "See her safely to the hospital. Stay with her there. I'll be in touch as soon as I know more."

Doyle nodded. "What are you gonna do?"

Cooper was already heading out the door to go after Waddell. He stopped and turned around. "I'm going to go and plug our leak."

Vickers hated not being in complete control. In fact, there were few things in the world that he hated more. Holt's phone call had been unexpected to say the least.

Did he actually have Terry Philips? It wasn't out of the question. In his opinion, Holt didn't possess many traits that he admired, but he was definitely resourceful. If he did have Philips, how much had Philips talked? How much did Holt now know about the inner workings of the G.D.M. and the Assembly? Whether Holt was telling the truth or not, one thing became crystal clear. It was too dangerous for Holt to survive the night. The situation at The Flamingo had gone haywire. According to his last conversation with Raeburn, Olson was likely dead and whatever containment they had enjoyed was evaporating. Pulling the rest of the team out had been the only plausible alternative. Today was not supposed to be going like this.

Vickers picked up his office phone and punched in the appropriate entry. After two rings, the call was answered. "Dr. Shelby, here."

"Shelby, it's Vickers. I need you to get the Seabrook woman ready for transport in fifteen minutes. Round up two of your guards to go with her. I will meet you all in the loading area. If you get there first, have three vehicles readied. I will be there as soon as I can."

"Yes, sir," came the reply. "Am I to accompany you all as well?" Shelby inquired.

"Yes, you'll be coming along. Your primary concern will be her."

"As you wish, sir. Do you want her to be drugged for the trip?"

Vickers thought long and hard about that. How many times in those ridiculous Hollywood action movies had the 'damsel in distress' somehow managed to interfere with the sinister plans of the villain? He had always thought to himself that they were idiotic not to just be rid of her once and for all. But now, faced with a similar scenario, he found himself actually needing her to be lucid. What chance would he have for Holt to turn over Philips if Anna appeared to be dead or was absent entirely? Not for the first time since this whole affair began, Vickers cursed himself silently. *If this is the price I must pay for my freedom, then I pay it gladly.*

"No. I need her to be coherent. Just get her ready. No restraints. Just put her in the lead vehicle."

"Understood."

Vickers ended the communication. Now it was on to other matters. He had Anna, but he wanted to strengthen his position any way he could. He tried to get a mental image of exactly what had gone down at the Flamingo. *According to Raeburn, she and her team had been lying in wait on the second floor with Olson on the third. Olson and his team had been eliminated but there was no way of knowing how many people (if any) he had been able to neutralize. Somehow they had gotten word that there was another team in place waiting. They couldn't go down anymore. There were too many unknowns and Raeburn had reported nothing out of the ordinary. So if they can't go down, they go up?* he asked himself. *The roof.* He grabbed his communicator and spoke briefly to the man at the other end. He smiled as he visualized the trap he was setting springing shut. Another idea came to him that he hadn't considered until now. If Holt did indeed have Philips, then Dr. Seabrook was no longer vital to Holt. He could, however, prove most valuable to Vickers. He took out his cellular phone and dialled a now familiar number. After a couple of rings, it was answered.

"Hello?" the voice asked cautiously.

"Dr. Seabrook, it's Vickers. I was wondering if I could have a few moments of your time."

Robert put a hand on MacReady's arm to stop his progress. MacReady stared at him with a perplexed look on his face. "We've gotta keep moving," he said.

"It's Vickers," Robert replied. "What do you want, Vickers?" MacReady took out his own mobile phone and checked to see if it was working yet…it wasn't.

"I called to tell you some good news, Dr. Seabrook. It would appear that your man Holt has found Mr. Philips." Robert was barely able to stifle a gasp as he considered the ramifications of what this man was telling him. The thought that Holt was working against him swept through his mind and he visualized Holt and Vickers laughing together and patting each other on the back as they drove away with Anna. His nightmare was thankfully short-lived as Vickers continued. "My deal is still good. I trade your wife for Philips. Holt has set up a time and place for the switch. I assume that you know where it is?"

Robert stared at the floor for a few moments. Clearly, Vickers still believed that Holt and Robert were on the same side. That gave at least a glimmer of hope that Holt had in fact not abandoned him. If Holt was working with Vickers, the two of them would have been long gone once Phillips had been found. *So I still have an ally in Holt. Thank God.* He wasn't sure what Holt and Vickers had discussed, but there didn't seem to be any point in lying to anyone right now. "No. I haven't spoken with him in a while."

"Well, we'll have to make sure you guys end up in the same place then," Vickers replied with a chuckle. "Keep your phone with you. I will contact you again with more information."

Before he could respond, the line went dead. "What the hell was that about?" MacReady asked just as Waddell joined them.

"That was Vickers. He said that Holt contacted him and that he has Philips and is willing to make the trade." Robert couldn't contain his smile any longer. The idea that this entire nightmare could be over in a matter of hours seemed almost too good to be true.

MacReady returned the smile, but also added a caution. "Don't get too far ahead of yourself there, Robert. There's still a lot that can go wrong." MacReady turned to Mitch. "Holt has Philips. There's gonna be an exchange."

Mitch let out an audible sigh. He didn't have to act on that one. If there was going to be an exchange, he might still have a chance to escape this whole ordeal. "Well that's some good news," he said as he clapped Robert on the back. "But we had better keep moving." The two other men nodded and moved on towards their gear. Mitch and MacReady quickly donned their vests. MacReady tossed Martinez' to Robert.

"Here. Put this on." Robert hesitated as the thought of putting the vest on. His thoughts drifted to the man now laying dead just a few floors below. It seemed somehow sacrilegious to even contemplate wearing it. He had died trying to help him just a few minutes before. MacReady correctly read his thoughts as they burned across his face. "Doc. He would have wanted you to wear it. If you end up dead, then this entire mess was a waste of time. Let's face it, the G.D.M. needed you to find Philips. If Holt has him, they might just decide that you are now expendable. From what you told me Vickers said, Holt is trading Philips for Anna. Amazingly, you are now the one who's in the most danger."

The shock of his words resonated deep within Robert's soul. From the moment Anna had been taken, he had been so consumed with worry for her well-being that he had never stopped to worry about his own. Now that Anna was apparently being brought to an exchange, the thought of being eliminated this close to being with her again was like some sort of cruel hoax. To have endured all of this only to end up failing was a prospect that he hated to consider. Suddenly, his own mortality stepped to the forefront of his mind and he started to put on the body armour.

MacReady helped him as it was clear he had absolutely no idea what he was doing. Mitch suited up and grabbed his MP-5. Somehow, it seemed heavier. MacReady readied his automatic as well and the three men resumed their climb to the roof. They had no idea that just a few floors beneath them, Raeburn and her team were already exiting the building dressed as paramedics. They were still running under the assumption that heading down was a trap and that Special Agent Fenwick of the F.B.I. had sold them out and taken off. They had no idea that Cooper was heading after them with the crucial information regarding whom the traitor actually was. Mitch kept nervously checking over his shoulder.

CHAPTER 24

Doyle used the security radio to contact Renzo. After identities had been verified, Renzo informed him that he had Ballard and was just getting to the elevator to get her down to the casino floor. "Good. I'll meet you," Doyle replied gratefully. "I'm on three." He jogged down the hall and waited by the elevator doors. After a few moments, the doors opened and he was face to face with a rather massive looking sidearm. Beyond that, which occupied most of his mind, he could barely make out the forms of a couple of paramedics, a stretcher, and the man holding the hand cannon.

Doyle raised his hands in surrender. "It's Doyle. You must be Renzo." The men locked eyes and Renzo lowered his gun.

"Get in," he commanded. Doyle didn't hesitate as he squeezed inside the already cramped elevator. "Sorry about the welcome, but under the circumstances…"

Doyle waved him off as the doors closed. "Don't mention it." He keyed the elevator into motion again and they resumed their downward journey to the casino floor and Renzo's waiting personnel. "How is she?" Doyle asked, turning his attention to Ballard and the paramedics. Ballard looked incredibly pale. She was bandaged and had an oxygen mask over her mouth and nose.

"She's lost a lot of blood," one of the medics reported. "We've got her stable enough to move her, but we need to get her to a hospital a.s.a.p."

Renzo put a hand reassuringly on to Doyle's shoulder. "I've got security personnel waiting for us on the floor plus a police escort waiting to accompany you guys to University Medical Center. She'll be okay."

"Thanks," replied Doyle. He wasn't sure he could allow himself to believe him just yet, but it was nice to hear it nonetheless. He leaned down to his partner's side and whispered in her ear as he grabbed her hand for support. "Ballard, it's Doyle. Can you hear me?" He felt the tiniest of squeezes as her hand tightened on his. His breath caught in his throat as he gently squeezed her hand. "I've got you. We're gonna get you to the hospital, but you gotta hang in there, okay?" He felt another squeeze, this time just a little bit stronger.

The doors opened to the chaos that the Flamingo casino had deteriorated into. Renzo's security detail was there, however, and whisked Ballard and Doyle through the mess and out to the ambulance. The police escort was waiting and more police cars were arriving. Nobody paid attention to the ambulance that was already pulling out on to Las Vegas Boulevard. Nobody noticed that that ambulance did not turn towards U.M.C., but instead headed for the Hotel Acropolis. Raeburn and her team had successfully made their escape.

Ballard was loaded into the back of the ambulance and Doyle climbed in with one of the EMT's as the other one went around to handle the driving. Renzo shook Doyle's hand before the doors closed. "Good luck," he said.

"Thanks for everything," Doyle replied. He sat back as Renzo shut the doors and the small convoy of emergency vehicles began their trek to the hospital. Doyle thought fleetingly of his injured shoulder. He had forgotten about it. He would have to remind himself to get it checked when they reached the hospital. He'd do it only after he was sure Ballard would be okay.

Cooper made it to the small pile of supplies discarded by the team from earlier. Not much was left, but he quickly sifted through and retrieved a flashlight, radio, and amazingly a magazine full of ammunition that someone had clearly overlooked. He tried the radio, but still had no luck. *Come on O'Connor. A little intel would be good right now.* He didn't know how much of a lead Waddell and the others had on him, or even exactly which way they had gone. *Why would they head up?* he wondered. *They wouldn't go back to the room. What else could they hope to achieve by going up?* And then the thought hit him. *The roof! They're heading for the roof.* He broke into a run and leaped up the stairs. *Hang on, MacReady. I'm on my way.* He prayed he wasn't too late.

Mitch, Robert, and MacReady finally made it to the top floor and found the roof access. As expected, it was locked. It appeared to be a pretty standard automated lock probably controlled by the security system somewhere in the depths of the hotel.

"What now?" Robert asked.

"Don't suppose you brought any C-4?" Mitch asked, referring to the plastic explosive.

MacReady smiled. "Even better," he replied. He reached into his hip pocket and pulled out a small tool that looked like a large set of pliers. He jammed the edge of the instrument into the corner of the doorway by the lock. He then reached into another pocket and retrieved a second device that looked more like a thick calculator. He attached this device to the end of the device protruding from the door. He bent down and entered a few numbers into the second device's number pad and stood back. "Check this out," he said with the enthusiasm of a small child on Christmas. The two other men looked on in amazement as the 'pliers' part of MacReady's contraption began to spread apart, forcing the locking mechanism on the door to lose its grip. After a few moments, the lock gave way and the door popped open.

"Impressive," Robert said as he watched MacReady retrieve his toy.

MacReady grinned. "Way less of a nuisance than explosives. You just type in how far you want the tines to expand and it does the rest."

"Where the hell did you pick that up?" Mitch asked enviously.

"Around," MacReady answered. "And that's all you need to know," he added with a chuckle. "Shall we?" He motioned for them to head out to the roof. Only then did they hear the unmistakable sound of helicopter rotors.

Waddell opened the door and peered out onto the roof. There was indeed a helicopter about to touch down on the roof. He ducked back inside and turned to the others. "There's a chopper landing."

"Is it for us?" Robert asked hopefully. Mitch wasn't sure which answer to that question he was hoping for. It could be an assault team, a rescue effort, medical personnel, C.I.A., F.B.I., G.D.M.? The possibilities were endless. There was just no other way to turn. This helicopter was arriving and with it came the next twist. Mitch resigned himself to his fate and stepped out onto the roof.

He was relieved when bullets did not pass through him as the helicopter set down on the roof. It was a standard AH-10 transport, a 'Huey'. He looked towards the large chopper and saw the pilot give him a thumbs-up and then started gesturing for them to hurry. Mitch recognized the pilot and suddenly, his world started to look a little more optimistic. The pilot was G.D.M. He had flown with him before, but couldn't place his name. *So, Vickers figured we'd head for the roof and sent us a helicopter. I'm impressed*, he thought. *Now, how to get rid of MacReady?* The idea came to him almost immediately.

"MacReady, we have to be careful out there. There might be snipers. I'll go to the chopper first. I'll find out who they are and I'll get them to get us outta here. When I'm set, I'll signal and you and Robert follow while I cover you."

"No way. I'll go. You stay here with him. You've been here since the beginning," MacReady pointed out.

Mitch flashed him a warm smile. He actually liked MacReady. It was a pity things had to turn out like this for him, but he had to look after himself first. "Let me take the risk on this one, then. Keep me covered." Before MacReady could respond, Mitch was out the door and racing for the helicopter. MacReady braced himself in the doorframe and covered his run. He scanned the vicinity, but could see nothing of note. Waddell made the chopper and ripped open the side door. He climbed in and positioned himself in the door, motioning for the others to follow. MacReady didn't notice that he never spoke to anyone in the Huey to find out who they were. He was too focussed on keeping everyone alive.

He grabbed Robert and brought him close so he could speak to him over the whoop-whoop of the blades. "Stay close to me and you'll be fine!" he shouted. MacReady stepped out onto the roof tugging Robert behind him. They moved steadily across the rooftop towards the sanctuary that the helicopter provided. MacReady kept his eyes moving from side to side as they reached the halfway point. It was then that he locked eyes with Waddell and knew that something was wrong. Waddell was looking behind them and motioning for them to get down. *Shit, there's someone behind us*, he thought. MacReady forced

Robert to the ground and spun around, raising his gun in an attempt to ward off this latest attack. He braced for the impact of the bullets he knew would be coming as he put himself between Robert and whoever was coming up behind them. There was no impact. There was no one there. MacReady stared at the empty doorway they had just come through wondering exactly what was going on. He never saw Waddell levelling the gun sights to line up with the back of his head. He never saw the hint of regret in Mitch's eyes as he pulled the trigger. All he saw was the brilliant flash of light that blinded him and the following darkness that descended upon him for all of eternity.

Robert felt MacReady fall to the ground beside him. He didn't see where the shot had come from because he had covered his head with his hands in a vain attempt to shield himself. He looked over at the C.I.A. and saw that he was dead. Robert waited for death too. *Here it would end. On the roof of the fucking Flamingo. Who would ever have thought?* His mind drifted to Anna. For some reason, he thought of the day they had met. His memory became particularly vivid. He saw every hair, every pore, every twitch of the muscles beside her mouth when she was about to smile. He wished he could have seen her again, but he was glad that he was able to envision her now. In many ways, he considered the day they met the first day of his life. It was only fitting that she was here with him now.

His reverie was harshly interrupted by a vice-like grip on his bulletproof vest pulling him to his feet. He cast a bewildered look at the face confronting him. It was Mitch and he seemed to be saying something. No…shouting something.

"I said move your ass!" Mitch yelled over the deafening roar of the Huey's rotors. He shoved Robert towards the waiting chopper.

Robert snapped out of his daze and remembered where he was. He stammered towards the helicopter, aided by the C.I.A. man beside him. He looked back at the figure who had fallen protecting him. *My God, how many people are going to suffer for me before this nightmare is over?* he wondered. He was almost to the Huey, still looking back at MacReady, when movement in the doorway caught his eye. At first, he thought it was whoever had shot MacReady coming to finish the job. He was relieved to see that it was Cooper. *Thank God he is all right.* He could see that Cooper was yelling something, but he could not make out what it was. He tapped Mitch on the arm and pointed towards Cooper.

As Mitch turned to see, he saw the look on Cooper's face and realized right away that he knew. Cooper had figured it out and had come here to stop him. Mitch pitch forked Robert into the helicopter and whirled around to face Cooper. He fired three quick shots at the large man, but none of them found their mark. Cooper dived to the side and rolled quickly back to one knee as he returned fire. His first shot zinged off of the Huey while the second shot hit Mitch squarely in the chest. The vest prevented the shot from penetrating, but the impact knocked Mitch back against the helicopter and stole his breath away. He struggled for air at the doorway and tried to realign his target. Cooper was just a little quicker and fired another two shots: one hit him again in the chest while the other hit him in the left shoulder where the vest was not providing protection. He spun around and fell into the helicopter, pulling himself the last few feet with his uninjured arm.

"Take off!" he screamed. The pilot didn't need to be told as he was already increasing the power and pulling back on the cyclic control, lifting the transport off the roof.

Robert was scrambling around to see if Cooper was all right as Mitch slammed the sliding door shut. "What the hell were shooting at him for? He's on our side!" he exclaimed.

He was silenced by a severe right cross that sent him reeling to the floor of the helicopter. He landed with a thud loud enough to be audible over the noise from the engine. Bright lights danced in front of his eyes and a high-pitched whine dominated his hearing. His jaw throbbed as he struggled to stay conscious. He turned over and stared horrified at the man now standing over him.

"Do me a favour, Robert. Just shut the fuck up," Mitch snapped. His shoulder was killing him and he was in no mood. "If it was up to me, I'd just throw you out of this fucking bird right now and be done with you."

Robert wasn't used to the strategies involved in intelligence work, but he quickly put together what was happening. His mind started piecing it all together and the picture that was being created sickened him. "It was you," he breathed. "It's been you this entire time. Right back from Victoria. You've been behind everything!" he shouted as his emotions began to take over. Mitch just sat there with a smirk on his face as he held his injured shoulder. "It wasn't Holt who was working against us! It was you! You fucking piece of shit!" he screamed as he lunged at the C.I.A. man before him.

Injured or not, Mitch was still a trained man. He fired a punch into Robert's chest sending him stumbling backwards against the door. The vest bore the brunt of the blow, but Mitch was strong enough to make the punch count. He gasped as his lungs tried to recapture the air that had just escaped. Mitch moved forward quickly and struck Robert in the temple with the back of his fist, sending him sprawling to the floor again. "Stay down or I'll put you down," Mitch warned as he sat down in the rear-facing seat behind the pilot.

Back on the roof, Cooper took careful aim at the rotors of the ascending helicopter. He drew his breath in and held it, steadying his aim as his grip on his gun tightened. Visions of a helicopter crashing into a very crowded Las Vegas Boulevard prevented him from pulling the trigger. He blinked, let out his breath, and lowered his gun. "Fuck," he murmured. He replaced the gun back into his holster and walked towards MacReady's body. There was no need to rush. Even from a distance, Cooper could tell that his colleague was dead. He knelt down beside him, reached down and closed his eyes. "Rest, brother," he said quietly followed by a silent prayer.

The sound of his cell phone ringing shocked him. He hadn't thought about it in a while and the sudden chime made him jump. He reached into his pocket and retrieved the device. "Cooper," he said into it when the call came through.

"Cooper, it's O'Connor. Good news. We've been able to re-establish communications. At least, we think we have.

We've been trying to raise people on their communicators, but we aren't having any luck. At least we have phones. What's the situation?"

Cooper wanted to scream, not at O'Connor, but at the world. Ten minutes. Maybe even five minutes sooner. Things might have turned out differently. "You're too late. They're gone," he said finally.

"Gone? What do you mean gone? What's happened?" O'Connor asked. The strain in his voice was evident. Though he didn't know the particulars, he knew enough to realize that things had gone terribly wrong.

Cooper filled him in as best as he could. He also added what he had learned from Doyle and the truth about Waddell. "Ballard and Doyle should be on their way to the hospital by now. Still no sign of Holt."

"Jesus Fucking Christ," O'Connor muttered as he struggled to come to terms with the information being relayed to him. Munroe and the rest of the team in the room with him were listening as well. A few people cried as they felt they had failed. They would be counselled and put back to work. For now, the focus still needed to be on getting the rest of their people out. "I'll have a detail sent to the hospital to watch over Ballard and Doyle. As for Holt, he actually contacted me." That news surprised Cooper. "He's going to try and get Anna out. He wouldn't tell me how or where so they're effectively on their own. As for you, get down to the parking level. We'll have a team there for you in five minutes."

"No," Cooper replied as he sat down next to MacReady. "If you speak with Holt again, you might want to let him know that they have Robert too. I'm just gonna stay up here for a while and sit with MacReady for a bit."

O'Connor could here in the big man's voice that this was non-negotiable. "Alright, Cooper. We'll send them up to meet you. You can escort MacReady down if you like."

"Thanks," Cooper said. He disconnected the call and sat staring across the Boulevard at Caesar's Palace. Even from this distance, he could see dozens of people in the windows watching the goings-on at the Flamingo. He wondered distantly if they could see him and finally decided that he didn't care. "Sorry I wasn't quicker, Mac," he said softly as he buried his head in his hands.

Robert crawled to the back of the compartment. Summoning his strength he hoisted himself up on to one of the seats there and turned to stare at Mitch. There were so many questions to ask…so much he wanted to say. He couldn't even begin to fathom how he could begin. The one question he kept coming back to finally left his lips. "Why?"

Before Mitch could answer, the pilot turned around and spoke to Mitch. "You check him for weapons?" Robert felt the lump of the .38 revolver MacReady had given him back at the hotel. He tried to figure out if he had enough time to draw it and fire. *'Point and shoot'*, MacReady had said. He hated the thought of losing the only advantage he had.

Luckily, Mitch was unaware that MacReady had given him the gun because he shook his head. "No. He's clean." Robert considered pulling out the revolver and showing this asshole exactly how "unclean" he was, but no matter what his views on Mitch Waddell were, Anna may very well be waiting for him at the end of this flight. So he waited.

Mitch turned his head to face him once more. Again, Robert asked the question. "Why?"

Mitch studied the battered man sitting across from him. He had endured a lot to be sure, but he felt he owed him nothing. "I don't have to answer to you, Robert. What I do and why is my own business." His shoulder ached like a son-of-a-bitch so he laid his arm across his lap to lessen the strain.

"Is it money?" Robert persisted. "Is that why you sold us out? All of us?" he added, referring to the team of C.I.A. and F.B.I. personnel who had sacrificed their lives and well-being in an attempt to thwart the plans of a terrorist organization.

"Just to shut you up, I'll tell you. The money is good. Don't get me wrong. But that's not why I work for the Movement. I do it cuz I believe in what they stand for. I believe that the U.S. has had its run of the west for far too long. Now, it's time for a new power to emerge and establish a new west. One free from the tyranny of the largest terrorist organization in the world...the United States Government."

Robert couldn't believe his ears. "But you work for the goddamned government! What does that make you? How the hell did you slip past the screening process?"

Mitch laughed. "I didn't join the Movement until after I was in the C.I.A. After I had been in for a couple of years, I was approached by a guy who said he wanted to have a chat. Lo and behold, he introduced me to the Movement and my eyes were opened."

"Yeah, but your brain shut down," Robert fired back. "You have a duty to the people of the United States to bring groups like the G.D.M. to justice."

Mitch laughed. "Spare me the God Bless America rhetoric. Trust me, if you knew half the shit I've learned over the years, you'd be running for the fuckin' exits. And I'm not just talking about the stuff the G.D.M. has done to fight the U.S., I'm talking about the shit the U.S. has done throughout the world. It would turn you inside out." Robert started to speak, but Mitch cut him off. "Just sit back and shut up. I seriously doubt you'll be able to change my mind considering all that I have invested in this already. Just enjoy the flight. Apparently you'll be reunited with your wife soon. So don't make me open this door and turn you into the messiest Rorschach test in Las Vegas."

Robert was still furious, but the thought of seeing Anna again and having her in his arms was enough to silence him. He looked out the window of the Huey as they angled west. Dusk had taken hold of the Nevada horizon which would bring evening close on its tail. The lights of Las Vegas began to dominate the twilight and their brilliance seemed to hide the devastation left in the wake of all that had transpired. That was what Las Vegas did, though. It hid all the evils of men under the glimmer of opulence. It was like magic.

CHAPTER

25

Anna was awake and sitting on her bunk when she heard the customary clunk of her door about to be opened. It was the only interruption in her day so whether or not it was an unpleasant experience, it was still better than the isolation and boredom she found herself living with. The door swung open and Dr. Shelby entered the room. He seemed rather perturbed by something. She didn't care enough to wonder what it could be.

"Get up!" he barked. "You're leaving." Anna sat for a few moments, blinking at him. She had heard the words, but couldn't seem to make sense of what he was saying to her. Was she free to go? Moving to another cell? "I said get up," he reiterated as he advanced on her. For a moment, she thought he was going to hit her. Instead, he reached down and pulled her to her feet, shoving her towards the door. Her legs ached from lack of use, but she kept her footing as she was marched out into the corridor. There were two guards accompanying Shelby. Both of them looked like they had been the love child of a Rottweiler and a cement mixer.

"Do you want her cuffed?" one of the hulks asked.

"No," Shelby replied. "I'd actually preferred it if she tried something. Then I could say that her death was justified." So they weren't planning on killing her. That was a positive. "Is everything ready?" he asked.

The second behemoth answered this time. "The vehicles are primed and ready. Each has a driver and a guard. You two will be riding in the second one." He swiped his ID card through the reader and the door leaving the cell block swung open. There was another corridor on the other side that ran perpendicular to the cell block. They turned right and headed toward another security door. After another swipe, they entered a small foyer with a single elevator door. Both guards produced keys and put them into keyholes on either side of the door. Simultaneously, they turned the keys and the doors opened. All four of them stepped inside and their ascent began.

"Where are you taking me?" Anna asked. None of the men answered. They all just stared straight ahead. *Even here of all places, people just stare straight ahead in elevators.* The thought made her chuckle in spite of her circumstances.

"Something amuse you?" Shelby sneered.

"Nothing," she replied. She really didn't see the use in trying to explain it. "I'm just tired." That seemed to be enough for Shelby because he did not pursue the matter further. The rest of the elevator trip passed uneventfully.

The doors opened to yet another foyer with a security door. After passing through that and down two more halls and one more door, they finally arrived at a shipping and receiving area. Waiting in a row were three GMC Tahoes. Two men were positioned beside each of them and Anna could see that they were armed to the teeth. "Oh, Jesus," she mumbled.

"Thank you, gentlemen," Shelby said. "We'll take it from here." The two escorting guards nodded and disappeared back into the depths of the building from whence they had come. Shelby grabbed Anna by the arm and shoved her forward. "Let's go." She was tempted to fire off a harsh retort, but found she just didn't have the energy.

As they neared the vehicles, a familiar face stepped out from behind the lead car. Her energy was enriched by her adrenaline as she raced towards Vickers, hell bent on splitting his head open. Before she could reach him, he pulled out a stun gun and pointed it at her. Despite her rage, she was still feeling the effects of her treatment earlier and her body had no desire to undergo unnecessary pains. She skidded to a halt ten feet away from him with Dr. Shelby close behind.

"Pretty tough guy aren't you, you piece of shit. Why don't you try your luck without the gun?" Her fists clenched as she visualized thrashing the man standing in front of her. Her arm still ached from where he had shot her earlier. The pain was a reminder that no matter what happened, she still owed him one for that.

He merely smiled. "As much fun as the idea of beating the crap of you is right now, I have more pressing needs.

Put her in back," he ordered as he motioned towards the second SUV. Shelby shoved again. This time she shoved back.

"I'm getting pretty sick and tired of being manhandled by you, you prick. I know how to walk." Shelby was about to slap her when Vickers stopped him.

"Just open the door for her, Doctor. I'm sure she can manage." Shelby nodded his acquiescence. He wanted to wipe the defiant look off of her face so badly, but he knew that that would have to wait for another time. He opened the rear door of the second SUV and Anna climbed in.

"Asshole," she muttered as she sat down on the seat. Shelby slammed the door shut and went back to speak with Vickers.

"I still think drugging her would be wiser. She's tougher than I gave her credit for."

"I know she is, but we have an exchange to make. Plus, I have a feeling she'll be a little more agreeable when she discovers that we have her husband." Vickers smiled at the idea of having an ace in the hole. This was Vegas after all.

"When did this happen?" Shelby asked.

"Not long ago. I just received word from our source that had been accompanying him. They will meet us at the coordinates Holt set up. This is working out better than I could have imagined." Vickers looked around at the large loading area for the grand Hotel Acropolis. He hated to admit it, but he would miss the opulence of this life once he stepped away from the G.D.M. He had no intention of roughing it, but there were just some luxuries that had to be eliminated if one wanted to maintain a low profile. After he had delivered Philips to the Assembly, the plan was to disappear into the night, find a little quiet corner of the world to call his own, and to never again worry about the stresses of intelligence work. The most troubling thing he intended on tackling was the crossword of whatever local paper he happened to frequent.

There were a couple of loose ends to finish up with first and one of them just drove into the loading bay area. The ambulance pulled to a stop in front of him. Raeburn stepped out and came around to greet him while the remainder of the team climbed out of the back. "Glad I made it. Thought you guys might have gone without me," she said as she shook hands with Vickers.

"Nice to see you made it back in one piece," he said with a smile. "You get everyone else out?" Raeburn had already told him about the Bravo Team so she knew he was just referring to the rest of Alpha.

"Everyone else is accounted for," she added sombrely. She hated losing people, but to do so on an assignment like this was a particularly tough pill to swallow. She hoped it wouldn't reflect too badly on her in the eyes of the Movement.

"Pity about Olson," Vickers said quietly. "He was a good man."

Raeburn thought she might have heard a slight emphasis on the word man, but she decided to shrug it off. If Vickers had a problem with her because she was a woman, he should have said something long before now. *Besides, without sounding too insensitive, between me and Olson who's standing here...me or him?* "Yes he was," she replied coolly. "So where are we off to?"

"You won't be coming with us, I'm afraid. You've been re-designated."

She had never heard of that before and didn't like the sound of it at all. Had someone higher up heard about the misfortune at the Flamingo? Was she being pulled off of active assignment? "Re-designated? What does that mean?"

Vickers shrugged. "To be honest, I'm not entirely sure. Just before I came up here I received a call from the Surgeon. Apparently, you are supposed to go to your office and contact him at once. Here's the number," he said, handing her a slip of paper. She gingerly reached out her hand and tired to grasp it but her fingers were trembling. The Surgeon was notorious within the G.D.M. Brought on as a hired gun, he acted as the finger of God for the Movement. If Vickers was the head of Intelligence, the Surgeon was the head of Operations. One tried to go through a career without ever meeting him. But when summoned, you had better be available.

Raeburn took the slip of paper and stared at it. It had a 212 area code which meant New York. But in all honesty, the way the Movement operated, that number could be from just about anywhere in the world. She looked up at Vickers to see if he knew anything about what the Surgeon wanted, though she had a sinking feeling that she knew. Failure was not looked upon lightly in the eyes of the G.D.M. Vickers almost looked pleased. *Son of a bitch. What did he tell them? You set me up for them, didn't you. You fed me to the lions.* She hid her feelings deep down inside. There would be no point in fighting for it now. The damage had been done by this lug. After all she had sacrificed for him over the years. To be so casually discarded like this was almost too much to bear. Her only choice was to place the call and hear what the Surgeon had to say. She might even be permitted to argue for her survival. No matter what, her fate was now out of her hands.

"Thank you," she said curtly. "She summoned all of her dignity and walked towards the elevator that would take her to the area of the Acropolis where her office sat. She shed not a tear, though she felt like she might.

Vickers watched her go. With Olson gone, she was the last of the team that had started this to still be alive. After the Surgeon took care of her, there would be no witness to the events that took place leading up to their move to Las Vegas. He could end this chapter and begin life anew with a fresh start. *Maybe Canada,* he thought. "Let's move," he ordered as he climbed into the first vehicle. The drivers and their guards all climbed into their respective vehicles. Dr. Shelby climbed into the rear of the second car with Anna already inside. He was fully expecting some form of attack, but she was just sitting still looking straight ahead. He sat down and noticed the reason she was not causing a fuss. The guard in the front passenger seat was turned around in his seat and pointing a handgun directly at her from over the seat. Shelby looked at him with a quizzical expression.

"I heard she could be a handful," he said simply.

"Fair enough," Shelby replied as he sat back to enjoy a peaceful ride.

Holt sat in the driver's seat of the van he had obtained from one of his contacts in Las Vegas. He sat patiently at the coordinates he had given Vickers, methodically working through a Sudoku puzzle. He checked his watch for the hundredth time. 9:26. This part of the desert wasn't too hard to find. It was away from the frenzy of the Strip, but not too far out to be considered desolate. The road, if it could be called that, that he was sitting on cut through the desert and ran south from a little burg west of downtown Las Vegas called Searchlight. More precisely, it started a couple of klicks west of Searchlight off of Nipton Rd. The path ran south from and wound through the desert towards the Nevada/California border. It was actually more like a set of tracks in the sand that more than one person had used. Holt had arranged a few transfers here over the years and he knew the area well.

He reached behind him and slid open the small window that allowed access to the back of the van and turned on the light back there. Al Hicks and Scott Miller sat with their backs to each other in the middle of the cargo van. Each had tape over their mouths. "How are you guys holding up back there?" Holt asked with a smile.

"*Puck* you. It stinks back here," Al replied through the tape. At least, it sounded like 'puck'. Holt figured he actually said something else.

"Well, try not to fart," Holt replied with a derisive laugh. He closed the window and turned off the light as he ignored the increased objection from the back. He set down the puzzle book and got out of the van to stretch his legs. It was time to get ready anyway. He was parked on the 'road' facing north towards Nipton Rd. He knew he didn't have long to wait. There was even a good chance that Vickers would be early.

The pilot set the helicopter down well outside of the city. Even if there were interested parties tracking their route, they would be long gone by the time a land vehicle showed up. There was a car waiting for them with a driver. Mitch slid the door to the chopper open and motioned for Robert to exit. Robert hopped down with Mitch right behind him and they both moved to the car. The chopper kept its rotors turning and soon lifted off again, disappearing into the evening sky.

As the sound faded into oblivion, Robert turned to Mitch. "Before this is over, there will be a reckoning and you will be made to answer for what you've done here." He said it with such certainty that he forced himself to believe it.

"We'll see about that," Mitch replied with a shrug. "We all have to pay for it some time. I'm planning on having some fun in the sun before that happens though so lemme know how that whole revenge thing works out for you." He opened the rear door of the car for him. "Get in," he said.

Robert weighed his options again. Run for it, try the gun, punch him. None of them would bring him to Anna. Once he had her back, he could make his move. Until then, as hard as it was, he had to do what this man said. He climbed into the back seat and Mitch closed the door before walking around and getting into the front passenger seat. "You know where you're headed?" he asked the driver.

"I have the coordinates right here. I know the place. We'll be there in fifteen minutes," the driver replied as he put the car in gear and moved off.

"Good. Hear that Doc? Be there in fifteen minutes. You and your wife can be together. Told you I'd get you to her," he added with a laugh. Robert said nothing. He sat back and looked west as the sunlight strained to hold on to the darkening sky. In fifteen minutes he would be with Anna again. If today were to be the day he died, he could think of no other person he would rather be with in those final moments. He closed his eyes and dreamed of her face.

Vickers received confirmation from the driver he had sent that Dr. Seabrook and Waddell were en route. Good. According to their estimates, they would be arriving at approximately the same time. He turned to his own driver. "When you get to the turn-off that leads south away from the town, just pull over. We'll wait for the others there and proceed together."

"Sounds good," The driver replied.

Vickers did the calculation again. He had three drivers, three guards, himself, Dr. Shelby, and Anna. Aside from the last two, that gave him seven shooters to face Holt and Philips. When you added Waddell and the driver accompanying him, that made it nine. He liked those odds just fine.

Raeburn entered her office cautiously. Part of her expected it to explode when she stepped inside, but no blast was forthcoming. She was sweating noticeably and her heart was pounding inside of her chest so loudly that she could hear little else. She thought she had done an admirable job working for the G.D.M. She couldn't believe that all of her efforts meant nothing because of one assignment that had none gone according to plan. She had heard, however, of people being 'removed' for far less. She cursed herself for failing and she cursed Olson as well. She sat down at her desk and looked for something to do that would delay the call she knew she had to make. She tried to log on to her computer, but the screen explained to her that her password was no longer valid. She swallowed hard as she stared at the flashing red "Access Denied" that lit up her screen. *So that's it*, she thought. *Just like that.* She turned her monitor off, picked up the receiver, and dialled the number on the slip of paper. After two rings, the line clicked on.

"Yes?" the man on the other end of the line said. His voice was heavily distorted due to some form of voice modulator.

"This is Giselle Raeburn. I was told to call this number." Her voice sounded distant, even to her.

"Indeed," the voice said. "And call it you have. It would seem that you and I need to have a little chat."

Raeburn reached over and opened the top drawer of her desk and pulled out a small address book she kept in there. She opened it and took out a picture of her mother. She hadn't seen her in quite a while and yet she found her face the only comfort she wanted right at that moment. They weren't allowed to keep any pictures in their office, but this one she kept hidden. She stared at it while the Surgeon said what he had to say.

The three SUV's were parked along the side of the road when Waddell's car pulled up to them. Vickers was standing by the first vehicle and waved Waddell forward. Mitch stepped out and came over to Vickers.

"Son. You've done one hell of a job," Vickers said as he approached Mitch and extended his hand. Mitch slapped it away.

"Don't even start with me, Vickers," Mitch stated angrily. "What the hell was that bullshit back at the Flamingo. Your little fucking goon squad nearly blew my head off. If I hadn't reacted quickly enough, I'd be dead. I've worked with you guys enough to know that your tactical teams don't do anything without orders. So would you mind explaining why I was a target?"

Vickers eyes the man warily. While he could tell he was upset, he didn't get the sense that he was willing to do anything about it. There was a hint of fear hiding behind those eyes that attempted to appear enraged. "Mitch. If I had ordered you to be killed, you'd be dead. Even if I had given that order and the team had failed, why would

I not have had you killed before you stood before me now. As I said, you did a good job. If my team was a little overzealous, then I apologize."

"And what about Nesbitt?" Mitch prodded. He wasn't ready to move on just yet. "Why wasn't I informed about that? I don't like being kept in the dark on matters especially when I am the one most illuminated by the situation."

"I understand, Mitch," Vickers send as he tried to console his mole. The last thing he needed was this a soap opera like this just before the exchange. "But you handled yourself admirably. Sometimes, people on the front lines have to be kept in the dark for their own sake. I'm sure your years in the C.I.A. have taught you that. It's not always comforting, but it is sometimes necessary." Mitch's shoulders relaxed as the words reached out to him. What Vickers was saying did make sense. "Your dedication to the Movement has been exemplary. Keep this up and you will have a long and illustrious career."

"Thank you, sir. It wasn't easy." Mitch was on the verge of gushing at the praise from Vickers. His reputation within the Movement was legendary, but so was his temper. Adulation rarely flowed from his lips, but here it was and Mitch was bathing in it.

"I can imagine. But you made it and that's all that counts. He in the back?" Vickers asked with a nod of his head. He was glad that he had been able to appease this idiot's ranting.

"Yeah. He's none too happy either."

"Well his wife is here so that should shut him up."

"How do you want to proceed?" Mitch asked. He hoped he would still get to play an integral part in how this played out. Seeing it come this far, it would be only fitting to see it to its conclusion.

"We're gonna head south to meet Holt. He'll probably want us to send over the woman as he sends us Philips. Once we have him, we take them down. I don't want any loose ends on this one."

Mitch liked the sound of that. He didn't care about Holt one way or another. Whether he lived or died was irrelevant. He had served a purpose – to get Mitch into a position where he could become of value to the Movement – but beyond that, he was expendable. That thought, however, triggered another memory; one that Mitch had almost forgotten about. He had barely survived the ambush in the hallway of the Flamingo. Someone had deemed him to be expendable. That someone was more than likely talking with him right now. *Maybe after we take out Holt and Anna, I take you out*, he thought. "What about the Dr. Seabrook?" he asked instead.

"What do you mean?" Vickers inquired.

"Well you mentioned that the exchange was Anna for Philips. What about Dr. Seabrook? Does Holt even know that we have him?"

Vickers thought about that for a moment. It was possible that Holt had been in contact with someone who knew that Robert had been captured. Then again, Holt might be even more ignorant than Vickers had hoped. "It doesn't matter whether he knows or not. We can use Dr. Seabrook to our advantage if Holt decides to play by a different set of rules. We'll deal with the Seabrooks at the same time." Mitch nodded in agreement and went back to his car. Vickers climbed back in to his SUV and the small convoy began making its way south into the desert.

Ten minutes south of their position, Holt waited in the front seat of his cargo van with his two 'guests' tied up in the back. He prayed that he would be able to pull this off. He tried to consider all of the possibilities that lay ahead of him. Sadly, most of them did not end well. The most important thing for him right now was getting Anna out of there and home safe.

As he sat there, his phone buzzed. He looked down at it and saw that it was a text message from O'Connor. *Be advised. Vickers has Robert. Does this change anything?* Holt stared at the phone for a few seconds. Did it change anything? Or was it just one more person he had to try and get out safely. It didn't really matter. He could see the approaching headlights from the north. Not for the first time today, he wished he had more time.

CHAPTER 26

Holt shielded his eyes as the vehicles approached. The last thing he needed right now was to be blinded. He flashed his own lights in response to let them know exactly where he was. He didn't want them to get too close and he doubted they wanted that either. As expected. The lead vehicle slowed to a stop about fifty yards away. Two more vehicles pulled up on either side. Holt was hoping they might try to use some form of intimidation stance like this. In their attempt to appear as a large mass, all they had accomplished was to mire two of their vehicles in sand rather than have them remaining on the existing flattened tracks. The two flanking vehicles killed their lights so only the ones on the tracks remained illuminated. Holt could hear a fourth vehicle pulling up behind. He logged than in his memory.

The passenger door of the first vehicle opened and Vickers stepped out. Holt did likewise, making sure to not take his eyes off of him. "Holt!" Vickers called out. "Glad you could make it!"

"Wouldn't have missed it for the world!" he replied. "You look like shit!"

"As do you!" Vickers responded. "But enough of the pleasantries. Show me Philips." Vickers could hear Holt laugh.

"You're kidding right? Until I see both Anna and Robert, Philips will remain out of sight."

Vickers did not like that Holt already knew about Robert. That had just happened which meant that Holt had been in contact with someone who knew this as well. "I have a better idea," Vickers said evenly. "Why don't we just rush you and take him. We keep the doctor and his wife and use them both for target practice. I doubt you could stop us all."

Holt laughed again. "Do you think I'd be foolish enough to have Philips with me for this?"

Vickers' tone grew menacing. "We had a deal, Holt. Philips for Anna. I'm willing to throw in Robert in the exchange as well. But if you're telling me that Philips isn't even here, then I'm afraid you've run out of bargaining tools."

"Philips is here," Holt said reassuringly. "He's just a little further away. He will be brought to me when I see that Anna and Robert are safe."

"You expect me to hand them over without seeing Philips first? You're dumber than I remember."

"You don't have to hand them over. I just need to see that they're okay. Once that has been established, I'll make the call to get Philips here. We'll make the exchange at the same time."

Vickers smiled to himself. Holt was a worthy adversary, but at times he could be so predictable. Of course the exchange would occur at the same time. Philips and the Seabrooks would pass each other at some point between the two cars. Once Vickers had Philips, his team would open fire and cut them all down. Vickers turned and nodded to one of the vehicles. Dr. Shelby opened the door and climbed out, followed by a reluctant Anna. He grabbed her arm and marched her to the front to stand in the glow of the headlights. Holt was glad to see she was still standing.

"And Robert?" he asked.

"He's coming," Vickers replied. Anna looked around expectantly as Dr. Shelby withdrew back to the shadows. There was some movement from behind the vehicles, but Holt could not see what was transpiring. He adjusted his stance and felt the weight of his Glock at the small of his back.

Holt didn't need to see that it was Robert, though. Anna did that for him. When the figure rounded the vehicle, Anna raced for him and wrapped her arms tightly around his neck. He hugged her just as fiercely as she had and lifted her off the ground. Despite the gravity of the situation, Holt allowed himself a smile. He was glad they were together again. Now the trick was to get them out.

Anna and Robert kissed passionately as their combined grief and despair flowed between them like a raging river. The tears flowed freely down their faces as all of the pent-up emotion of the past week exploded out of them in uncontrollable waves.

"My God! Anna, are you all right?" Robert asked when they broke apart.

"I'm fine. What about you? I can't believe you're here."

"Where else would I be?" he replied. "I couldn't leave you…not ever." The two of them began to talk over each other as each of them tried to say everything that they had wanted to say to each other, but couldn't. To an spectator, it would have been impossible to make out anything that was being said because it was simultaneous and so full of emotion. The two of them, though, heard every word and their love and appreciation for each other and what they had been through grew with each passing moment. Vickers had finally had enough when he came up and forcibly separated them.

"There! They're alive, Holt. Now bring me Philips." For the first time, Robert noticed the vehicle in front of them. He had been so consumed with the sight of his beloved wife, he hadn't even noticed that there was anyone else around, let alone that Holt was now here in the desert with him. He took Anna's hand and they stepped back to the front of the vehicle, facing Holt.

Holt pulled out his radio, keyed it, and spoke softly into it. "He'll be here in five minutes," he called out.

"Five minutes?!" Vickers responded angrily. "What the hell are we supposed to do for the next five minutes? Get to know one another?"

"No," Holt replied. "I have something else in mind. Dr. Seabrook, I have something of value you might be interested in." Robert squinted at Holt, but couldn't quite make his face out. He looked over at Anna, but she was as confused as he was.

"What game are you playing Holt?" Vickers countered. "We're not interested in whatever it is you have. Philips is my only concern."

"That may be true, Vickers. But as in most things in life, this doesn't just concern you. There are other people who stand to lose in this." Holt stepped back behind the scope of the headlights and was partially obscured for a moment.

"Don't try anything stupid!" Vickers called out as he pulled out his gun from its holster. He pointed it at the back of Robert's head. The rest of his drivers and guards took this as their cue to emerge from their vehicles and stand at the ready. Mitch remained in the back. Vickers could see the back of the cargo van open and after a couple of minutes, Holt returned tugging two people behind him. Their hands were behind their backs and they looked like they had been worked over a bit. Holt pushed them down to their knees in front of his van and stood behind them brandishing a submachine gun of some kind. He pointed it at the backs of their heads. Vickers was about to ask who the hell these people were, but Robert answered the question for him.

"Jesus Christ, Holt! What the hell have you done?" Robert asked. "They don't have anything to do with this! Scott? Al? You guys all right?" They did not answer.

"Who are they?" Vickers asked. Variables being introduced like this was never a good thing. The only thing he could do was to find out as much information as he could in the next five minutes so he had a chance and being ready for what was to come.

"I work with them," Robert replied. He turned and saw the gun pointed at him. "They're not involved. Holt must be using them to get to me."

"What do you mean 'get to you'? I thought you two were on the same side."

"I thought he might be working against us. With him having kidnapped my colleagues, I'm starting to think that maybe I was right. If he's not working for you, and he's against me, there must be a third party involved. He must be working with somebody else."

To Vickers, this sounded all too surreal. But as he thought more about it, it did start to make a little bit of sense. Was there something he had overlooked? There were double agents everywhere. Could Holt be a triple agent? If he was, it could be anyone. Vickers started going through a list of suspects in his mind. He quickly brought this to a halt. He could spend the better part of a month running through suspects and scenarios and still have no answers. In the end, he would have to push all of that aside and concentrate on the job in front of him. He had to secure Philips. Everything else was secondary.

"Dr. Seabrook," Holt called. "I thought you might like to witness the consequences of what happens when people cross me. I don't have your wife, but I figured if I grabbed these two pieces of shit, you might realize how easily I can invade your life and fuck with it as I please."

Robert's mind was spinning as he struggled to comprehend exactly Holt thought he could accomplish by threatening the lives of Al and Scott. "Holt. Please. They have nothing to do with any of this."

"Don't kid yourself, Robert. I found these two snooping around your files, particularly the ones containing information about Terry. I brought them here for two reasons: to find out how long they've been working for Vickers, and if they're not G.D.M., then to find out how long all of you have been working against me."

Robert shot a look over to Vickers to gauge his reaction, but he seemed as confused as Robert was. "Kill them!" Vickers shouted. "I don't care who they are!" Holt raised his gun to the back of Miller's head.

"Wait! Whatever it is you're planning, Holt. Please don't do it," Robert pleaded. "I don't know what you think you know, but I never crossed you. It was Mitch."

That news came as a shock to Holt. He had figured somebody on the inside had been working against them, but he hadn't suspected Mitch Waddell. As he thought about it, though, things started to fall into place. The transmitter breakdown in Victoria that led to Nesbitt's death could have been caused by attaching a scrambler to one of the radios tied into the network. Waddell was the one who inexplicably had O'Connor's cell phone when he was heading into an ambush back in Chilliwack.

His thoughts were interrupted by a commotion over by Robert. Waddell had stepped out from behind the vehicles and slapped Robert in the face and sent him to the ground. Vickers ordered him to step back while Anna helped her husband back to his feet. Waddell followed instruction and stepped aside. *So it was true. Waddell was the rat.*

"What's going on, Mitch?" Holt asked mockingly. "You forget which country you fight for?"

"Fuck you, Holt. My country quit fighting the good fight years ago."

Holt just shook his head. This was a wrinkle, but one that could be ironed out. "You're a piece of shit, Mitch. I'm going to enjoy killing you."

Mitch was about to reply, but Vickers stopped him. "Enough of this. Holt, I don't hear any cars approaching. Philips should be here any moment. I have a feeling you're full of shit."

"I never said he was being driven. He's coming on foot. Don't bother trying to flank around and scoop him. He knows to bolt if anyone approaches him." Holt stepped up and pushed both of the kneeling men down in front of him.

"Holt!" Robert shouted. "Don't! They're innocent. They are doctors like me. They have nothing to do with this."

"Don't be naïve, Robert. No one is innocent." Holt raised his gun and pointed it again at the back of Scott Miller's head. Robert turned his head and pulled Anna to him. He did not want her to see what was coming. She knew Scott and Al and she had suffered enough already. He pulled her face into his shoulder and closed his eyes. The shot rang out, startling Robert with its volume that pierced the night. What Robert hadn't planned on was hearing the groan from beside him as Vickers went down. Robert snapped his head up as more shots rang out. He looked across the short space between where he was and where Holt was standing. Holt was firing well aimed shots at the G.D.M. vehicles and shooters. Al Hicks and Scott Miller had taken up firing stances on one knee and were shooting as well. Holt started to advance and was yelling for them to get out of there.

Robert, stunned momentarily, grabbed Anna by the hand and raced across the sand into the darkness outside of the glow of the headlights. Mitch, protected from the bullets by the vehicles, saw them go and took off after them. Vickers clutched his right side where Holt's bullet had struck. He should have been prepared for something like this, but his desire to get his hands on Philips had clouded his judgment. He dragged himself behind the SUV and returned fire. Judging by the sound of firing, he still had around five shooters left. Against one man like he had been expecting, five would have been plenty. But against three? The odds were suddenly not as good as he had once hoped. *Who the hell were those guys and where did they come from?* He stole a glance around the SUV and saw that neither Holt nor his two comrades were visible. They had obviously taken off into the darkness to improve their chances. It was time for Vickers to do the same. Wherever Philips may have been, it was clear that he would not be making an appearance tonight. It was time to go.

He looked around and saw that Waddell's car was still waiting there. He gathered his strength and made his way across the sand towards it. "Kill 'em all!" he called out to his remaining shooters. They could either succeed at eliminating Holt and the other two or they could die covering his own escape. He no longer cared. He was officially retired from the G.D.M. If they found him, he was a dead man. He made it to the car and slid into the driver's seat. The keys were inside and he started it up. He heard a knock at the door and jerked his head up to see the panicked face of Dr. Shelby.

"Let me in," he said. "Don't leave me here." Vickers assessed the man, then nodded towards the passenger side. Shelby ran around the car and opened the door. Vickers fired one shot into the man's head. Dr. Shelby dropped to the ground with one foot in the car, his blood darkening the sand around him. Slamming the car into reverse, he headed back to the road. If the helicopter pilot had done what he was instructed to do, he would be waiting and fully fuelled at the Searchlight Airport. Once Vickers made it there, he could begin his life as a contented retiree. He looked back to the fight in the sand that he was moving away from. He thought of all of the fights he had endured over the years. He thought about the thankless work he had put in for the G.D.M. and all of the people who would continue the fight even after he was gone. He would not miss any of it.

Hicks and Miller swept to either side of the vehicles. Holt stayed with the van and continued to fire at the remaining G.D.M. shooters to keep their attention on him. Hicks spotted two of the shooters by their muzzle flashes. The other three would be on Miller's side. Hicks moved forward, his approach covered by the dark. The headlights provided an eerie cone of illumination in an otherwise dark desert. Holt had successfully knocked out the SUV's headlights so the only lights remaining were trained on to the G.D.M. vehicles. Hicks was deathly silent, the sound of his footsteps masked by the Nevada sand. The first shooter he encountered didn't stand a chance. His focus was still on Holt. He never felt the bullet that entered the back of his head. He dropped without making a sound. The second shooter on Hicks' side saw his partner go down and whirled to find where the shot had come from. He caught a glimpse of movement in the darkness and fired wildly at it. This, however, allowed Holt to sight in his picture more accurately and a short burst from his MP-5 slimmed the enemy's number down to three.

Miller was having a little bit more difficulty with the three men on his side. Each of them had abandoned their vehicles and headed into the darkness. Miller couldn't be sure where they were, so had situated himself behind a small dune and maintained surveillance over the area in front of him. Visibility was extremely low as night placed a strangle-hold on the desert floor. Miller steadied his breathing as his eyes swept the ground for signs of movement. There was none. He smiled slightly when the sounds of the other two shooters were silenced. Hicks had definitely enjoyed more success than he had. He thought he saw movement just off to his left, but couldn't be sure. Even if he was correct and fired, his position would be marked and he would likely be gunned down by the other two. His options appeared bleak.

An eerie silence crept over the area. He strained to hear any sounds that might indicate where his targets had fled to, but sand was not a very helpful substance when it came to making noise. He could see Hicks moving between the vehicles as he searched for survivors. Holt was nowhere to be seen, but he knew he was somewhere behind him. He heard a small thump ahead of him and braced for whatever was coming his way.

"Cover up!" Holt shouted from behind him. He instinctively closed his eyes and covered his ears just as a flash-bang grenade detonated twenty yards in front of him. The concussion swept through him like a wave. His chest felt heavy and the wind was knocked out of him. He heard the shooting before his other senses kicked in. Shaking himself back into focus, he opened his eyes to see one of the shooters fall to his knees a mere fifteen feet from where he was lying. He raised his own gun and fired a shot into the man's head, finishing him off. Holt had already turned his attention to the second shooter and dropped him with a quick burst from his MP-5. The third shooter attempted to make a run back to the vehicles. Hicks stepped out and fired a well aimed shot into the man's right leg. He went down with a thump, shrieking in pain. Hicks moved to him quickly and kicked his weapon away. He flipped him over and secured his wrists with a zap strap.

"Miller. You all right?" Holt asked in the dark.

"Yeah, I'm good. Thanks for the last second warning."

Miller heard Holt laugh. "I almost didn't say anything at all. Get back to Hicks. I'm going after Waddell."

"Roger that," Miller replied. "Take him out." He said that to the night sky, though. Holt was already gone.

Robert and Anna never broke stride as they raced through the night. Luckily, the direction they had chosen was relatively flat so footing was not an issue. Even so, running over unfamiliar terrain in the dark was never a good idea. Both of them were in good shape, but sand really was not an ideal running surface. After a couple of slips, they began to slow their pace. They were breathing hard, but they didn't dare stop.

"You're a dead man, Seabrook!" Mitch called out from somewhere behind them. Robert stole a look over his shoulder, but could see nothing. He pulled Anna to the side slid to the ground behind a small rise. They tried to muffle their breathing as they lay in the sand, attempting to become one with the ground. They could hear the rhythmic thump-thump of the footsteps approaching them. There were no lights out here of any kind, but because they weren't really behind any cover, they felt as exposed as they could be.

Anna gripped his hand hard and squeezed. Robert pulled her to him and kissed her. "We're gonna be okay," he whispered.

"I don't care what happens," she whispered in return. "I'm just glad to be with you again." He smiled in the night and pulled her even tighter against him. Anna giggled in spite of the situation.

"What's so funny?" he whispered. He couldn't believe she somehow had the energy to find anything even slightly amusing.

"I'm sorry," she replied. "I guess some things never change."

"What do you mean?" he asked quietly.

"Is that a gun in your pocket or are you just really happy to see me?"

Holy shit, the gun. He had forgotten all about it. He shifted positions and pulled the .38 from his pocket. "You're a life saver," he murmured. Anna felt the gun in his hands. In any other circumstance, she would have been upset that he wasn't aroused being this close to her. Here, in this desert, she said a silent prayer of thanks that it was in fact a gun.

"Where did you get that?" she whispered.

"From a friend," he replied. His thoughts turned back to the rooftop of the Flamingo. MacReady had given this gun to him in case he needed it. He had given his life trying to protect him, only to be betrayed by one of his own. Now, in the middle of nowhere, he was still protecting him. Robert lay flat on his stomach with the gun out in front of him. He used the ground to steady his aim. He couldn't see anything yet, but when he did, he did not plan on hesitating. *'Point and shoot'*, MacReady had said. That was just what he intended to do.

"Robert!" a voice called out from the dark. The thumping footsteps had stopped. There wasn't a sound in the air. The voice chilled his blood. It seemed to be coming from everywhere at once. "Robert!" the voice called again. "When I find you, I'm gonna kill you nice and slow. I should have killed you a long time ago, but I was under orders." Robert wanted to scream at Waddell, but he knew that that was exactly what Mitch wanted. "After I'm done with you, I'm gonna take that pretty little bitch of a wife of yours and show her what a real man can do."

Anna cringed beside him. She hated the sound of this man's voice. She wanted to rip the gun out of her husband's hand and pull the trigger for him. Robert reached over and patted her shoulder reassuringly. "Ssssh," he whispered. "He's desperate." Anna scanned the darkness to see if she could see anything, but there was nothing to be seen.

"Robert!" Mitch continued. "Your wife is gonna scream if you don't show yourself. She's gonna scream for you, but you won't be there. Give yourself up. It's the only way to save her the pain."

Robert clenched his jaw tightly in a vain attempt to block out the images that Mitch's words were conjuring in his mind. He knew, though, that if he gave himself up Anna would be spared nothing. So he waited.

The silence of the night was destroyed by the ear-shattering sound of a single gunshot. The shot came from close by. The muzzle flash gave away Mitch's position, but to Robert's horror, the flash also illuminated their position.

"Gotcha," Mitch said. Robert fired twice in the direction of the muzzle flash. Mitch hadn't expected the shots but reflex made him hit the ground. The first shot passed by wildly, but the second would have hit him had he not reacted. *So you have a gun*, he thought.

"We have to move," Robert said as he grabbed Anna. The two of them scrambled to their feet and raced off again.

This time, though, Mitch was close behind. He didn't want to run the risk of losing them in the night, so he fired one shot that hit Robert in the right shoulder blade. Robert screamed in pain and pitched forward into the sand. Anna screamed as well and flung herself on top of her husband in an attempt to shield him. *Touching*, Mitch thought as he raised his weapon and took aim at the back of Anna's head. *Well at least you can die together.* Mitch never took into account that the muzzle flash from the shot that struck Robert would give his positioning away because he didn't consider that someone might be after him. He had been too focussed on catching the Seabrooks.

Holt had heard the screams from both Robert and Anna so he knew that the muzzle blast had to be Waddell. He went down to one knee and fired repeatedly at the spot he had seen the muzzle blast. He sprayed his shots over a small area because he couldn't be certain of exactly where Waddell had been. He heard the grunt and subsequent groan that signified that at least one of his shots had found its mark. He withdrew his emptied magazine and slammed a fresh one in. If Waddell had been injured, he was still a definite threat. He approached cautiously, unsure of what to expect. What he encountered was a frenzied volley from Waddell that echoed across the desert. His shots were wild as he didn't know where the shooter had been. A wild shot could still kill with impunity. Holt dived to the ground to avoid the bullets.

Waddell had stopped firing just as he hit the ground. The sound had alerted Waddell to his location. Mitch rose slowly to his feet and advanced on Holt's position. He limped severely as one of Holt's shot had entered his left thigh, but he was determined to finish him once and for all. Holt rose quickly and pulled the trigger to end this battle once and for all. There was no sound except for a click. He tried again, but to no avail. His MP-5 had become jammed with sand. Mitch fired close to where he was standing.

"Goodbye, Holt" he said as he took aim at the C.I.A. man in front of him. Holt braced himself and heard the sound of a .38 revolver going off. He watched as Waddell spun around from the impact and faced his attacker. Anna stepped forward and fired three more shots into Mitch's chest, emptying the .38 of its remaining rounds. Mitch stared dumbfounded as he dropped to his knees in the darkness. Blood started streaming out of his mouth as he tried to raise his weapon to kill this woman whom appeared out of the night like some kind of wraith. His brain would not cooperate, though, as it was too busy trying to keep his body alive. The effort was in vain. His heart had been punctured by one of the shots and the blood that his body needed to survive was flowing too quickly into the Nevada desert under him. He fell forward and his vital organs surrendered their fight.

Anna wept as she lowered the gun; the events of the past week had finally culminated to this point and she had reached her emotional limit. She turned and headed back to her husband who lay clutching his shoulder.

"My God, baby. Are you okay?" she asked. She knew it seemed like a stupid question considering all that had just happened, but she had to get a sense of how bad he was.

"It hurts like a mother, but it's all right." She kissed him on the forehead and tried to help him any way she could.

"Robert!" Holt called out. "Where are you? You guys okay?"

"Who is that?" Anna asked as she squeezed the gun in her hand. She remembered that it was empty, but if there was someone else out there, they might not know that.

"It's okay," Robert said quietly. "He's here to help. We're over here, Holt!" he called.

"I can't see shit," Holt replied. "Could you be more specific?"

Robert smiled in spite of the pain. "Marco!"

"Are you kidding?" Holt replied. When he didn't hear a response, he smiled and shrugged. "Polo!" After a minute, Holt found the couple in the desert. "You're hit. You okay?"

"Get me to a hospital and I'll live," he said simply.

Holt smiled again. "I can do that." He pulled out a small radio and clicked in on. "Miller, Hicks, you guys there?"

"Yeah we're here," Miller replied. "Where are you?"

"Southwest of you about eight hundred meters or so."

"We're already on our way. We heard the shots. You guys all right?"

"Robert took one in the shoulder. Doesn't look too bad, but we should get him to the hospital to be safe."

"Roger that," Miller answered. "I'll get a chopper to come. We'll guide them right to you."

"Copy. Thanks." Holt turned back to the Seabrooks. They sat staring up at him.

"Would you mind explaining all of this to me? What the hell are Al and Scott doing here and what have they got to do with all of this?" Robert asked.

"Dr. Seabrook. In all honesty, I'm sure there are a million questions you have about all of this, but let's just worry about getting you fixed up first. We'll deal with the Q & A later." Robert started to protest, but Anna squeezed her hand on his shoulder.

"Baby, later," she said. Robert looked at her and saw how tired she was. It wasn't even that she was tired. She was shattered. He pulled her to him with his good arm and looked back up at Holt.

"Promise me?" he asked.

"I promise. I'll tell you everything you wanna know." Robert nodded. That would have to do for now. "That was some nice shooting back there, Anna. I owe you my life."

She just shrugged it off. "I did what I had to do," she replied. "I suppose I should thank you as well. If you hadn't shown up when you did, we probably wouldn't be having this conversation. It's nice to finally have a face to go with the name that's been floating around for the past few days."

"Just doing my job," he answered with a smile. "Where'd you learn to shoot like that?" he inquired.

It was Anna's turn to smile. "Like I always said, I have older brothers. They're both shooters and figured that a 'girl' should know how to handle a gun. I always thought the mentality was borderline Neanderthal, but I guess I owe them a thanks, too," she added wryly.

"Give them my thanks as well." Holt and Anna tended to Robert's shoulder while they waited for Hicks, Miller, and the Medivac helicopter that would take them all from this place and back to civilization. Robert's life would hopefully start returning to normal. This whole affair might actually be behind him. More important, he had Anna back with him. Despite being shot, Robert had never been happier.

Vickers manoeuvred his car down the road towards the Searchlight Airport. Had there been a police car anywhere in sight, he would have been pulled over for suspicion of drunk driving because he was having great difficulty staying on the road. Holt's bullet had done extensive damage, but he had no intention of letting that get in the way of his retirement. He finally made it to the airport and made his way to the south side where his pilot should have cut a hole in the fence allowing him to sneak to small helipad where the chopper should be waiting. He was relieved to see that everything was in place. He climbed through the fence and moved towards the helicopter. He had made it. The pilot stepped down from the cockpit when he saw Vickers approaching. Vickers waved as he stumbled towards him. The pilot removed his helmet and Vickers stopped cold.

How did I miscalculate this badly? What did I overlook? Why didn't I leave earlier when I had the chance? All of these questions circled his mind as four bullets from Raeburn's sidearm penetrated his body. He fell backwards and wound up laying on his back, staring up at the night sky. There would be no retirement…at least not the type he had envisioned. He tried to focus on the stars. They seemed to be moving, but his vision was clouding over. His final sight was Raeburn standing over him, obscuring the constellations from his view. She raised her gun and fired a single shot into his forehead.

She calmly stepped away from him and walked over to the gap in the fence that he had entered, just as a sedan pulled up outside. She got into the passenger seat and the driver sped away, heading back to Las Vegas. She reached into her pocket and pulled out her cell phone. "It's done," she said when the call was answered.

"He's dead?" the Surgeon inquired.

"Yes," she replied. "What would you like me to do now?" She wasn't sure she was going to like the answer to that question, but she knew that she needed to follow his instructions closely…no matter what they were."

"Take some time off. You've done well. Find a beach somewhere and catch some down time. You're going to need the rest."

"Thank you, sir," she replied gratefully. She could use some R & R.

"Congratulations on your promotion, Raeburn. Don't let me down."

"I won't, sir. Thank you." The Surgeon disconnected the call and Raeburn sat back in her seat, letting out a deep sigh.

"Where to?" the driver asked.

Raeburn thought of all the possible destinations she could go. She had a new lease on life and had just been given the chance to take a vacation; the first one she had ever taken since joining the G.D.M. She wasn't exactly sure where she wanted to go, but she knew where she had to go to get her there.

"Harry Reid Airport, please." She smiled inwardly as she rested her head back and tried to enjoy the start of her first day as Chief Intelligence Officer for the G.D.M.

CHAPTER

27

Robert lay in his hospital bed, his shoulder was heavily bandaged and the pain medication he had been given was working marvellously. Anna was beside him, holding his hand and Holt was standing at the foot of the bed. There were flowers all over the room. Anna had been busy making sure that everything was the way she felt it should be. Robert smiled. While he never would have thought of any of it, the room looked and smelled quite wonderful.

"Doctor says you're gonna make a full recovery," Holt said.

"Yeah. He said that nothing major was damaged so it'll just be some physio time and stuff. I thought I knew a physiotherapist, but it turns out he works for the C.I.A. or something. Weird how longs work out?" Robert and Anna both stared at Holt. Holt returned their gaze. He had made them a promise, after all.

"You wanted the truth, so I'll tell you. Ask away."

Robert figured the direct approach would be the best one. "How did Al and Scott get mixed up in this? Are they spies?"

"Are you asking me if they work for the Agency?" Holt asked.

"Sure. Let's start with that."

"Yes they do. Both Al Hicks and Scott Miller have been working for the Agency for about eight years. Scott Miller is a physiotherapist and Al Hicks is a psychologist." The Seabrooks looked at each other like they had seen a ghost. Who were these people Robert had been working with and befriending over the years.

"So they are paid by the C.I.A.?" Robert asked for clarification.

"Yes," Holt replied. "But then again, so are you," he added. This caught Robert completely off guard. He had never once been approached to work for the C.I.A. or any other government agency. The mere idea was ludicrous.

"I don't work for the C.I.A.," Robert pointed out.

"I hate to argue with anyone in a hospital bed, Robert. But the truth of the matter is…you do. You've been working for the Agency for about two and a half years now."

"Holt. You said you would tell me the truth if I asked. Now you're just making things up."

"I'm not, Robert. Would you like me to explain?" Robert gestured with his hands for Holt to proceed. "Most of the clients you've been counselling since you set up your practice have been Agency operatives. Years ago, the C.I.A. realized that their agents were burning out at an alarming rate. None of it was physical, it was psychological. The Agency decided to set up counselling sessions with psychologists so that the operatives could find ways to deal with the problems they face in their jobs. The psychologists were sworn to secrecy due to the doctor/patient privilege so we didn't have to worry about security. In addition, the psychologists would treat the stories they were told as some form of delusion or something. Most of the patients were deemed as being narcissistic with delusions of grandeur or they suffered from some form of paranoia. It was a nearly flawless system."

Robert stared in disbelief at the man standing a few feet away from him. How could this be true? Sure, some of his patients told outlandish tales, but surely there had to be a more plausible explanation than this. "Did that include Terry Philips?"

"Yes. He was one of our operatives. He had infiltrated deep into the G.D.M., due in part to his ability to talk with you. It allowed him to release a lot of the burden he was under."

"What happened to him?" Robert asked. He desperately wanted to know.

"The truth is, I don't know. We kept hoping he would establish contact with someone, but he never did. In Vegas, when I realized that it was unlikely he was going to appear, I split from you guys and got things in motion to flush Vickers out into the open."

"But why didn't you clue anybody in? After you left, we started thinking that you had set us up. They might have been able to help."

Holt thought back to the decision he had had to make at the Flamingo. It was not one he had made lightly, but looking back it had been the correct one. "I didn't know if I could trust everyone there. I had a feeling that there was a leak somewhere within the team. Vickers just seemed to know a little too much about what we were up to. I didn't know it was Waddell, but thinking about it now, it seems pretty obvious. Twenty-twenty hindsight and all that," he said with a shrug.

"Wait a minute," Anna interjected. "Something doesn't add up here. You said that Robbie, Al, and Scott all worked for the C.I.A. Yet why is it that Robbie was the only one who didn't know it? Al and Scott both showed up in the desert, Lord knows how, and they were ready for a fight. If what you're telling us is true, then why didn't we know any of it?" Robert nodded in agreement. He hadn't thought of that, but now that Anna had mentioned it, it did seem quite peculiar.

"It's actually pretty standard for what the Agency has set up. Let me ask you something, Robert. Did you believe the stories that Terry told you?"

Robert thought about that for a few moments. He remembered back to the sessions he had had with Terry. Some of those stories were just too impossible to be true. "No. I didn't believe him. I thought that he was making them up to make himself feel more important than he actually was. I wanted to find out what he felt he was lacking in his real life that made him create this fictitious one he claimed to live."

"Exactly. It allowed you to remain completely neutral and objective. But more importantly, it kept you from being swept up into the politics of the assignments. You could give clear, unbiased advice and provide a safe environment for our operatives to talk about the problems they were dealing with."

"And the others?" Robert asked.

"Scott is physio. It's a lot tougher to explain away why a patient is recovering from a bullet wound or multiple fractures. The physical side had to be notified because otherwise, they could contact the authorities if the injuries were suspicious. Psychologists, like yourself, tend not to believe what they are being told so there is very little to report. As for Al, he never saw patients. His job was to oversee you; to make sure that the program was running smoothly."

"Jesus," Robert breathed. His mind raced as he tried to piece all of this together. He thought he and Anna had lived such a normal life. Now, it was apparent that their lives had been anything but ordinary.

"They're out in the hall if you'd like to see them. They wanted me to speak to you first," Holt explained. Robert looked to Anna for guidance. She met his gaze firmly.

"It's your call, Robbie, but they did save our lives."

Robert looked back to Holt and nodded for them to be brought in. Holt stepped out into the hall and came back a few seconds later with Al Hicks and Scott Miller in tow. Anna, unsure of how she was going to react when she saw them again, walked towards them and threw her arms around them both. Scott had braced for a slap when he saw her come towards them, but was relieved when it did not come. She squeezed them both tightly as the tears of relief streamed down her face. Even though they had not been completely forthcoming with who they were, they had been friends for years. What they had done in the desert, what they had risked for them, more than made up for any deception on their part. Both men hugged her tightly. Robert fought back his own tears as a large lump formed in his throat. Whatever Al and Scott were, they had helped them out of friendship. What more needed to be said? Anna brought them over to the bed to speak with Robert. He, Anna, Al, and Scott began the long process of talking about everything that had happened from the start. Holt took this as his opportunity to slip out of the room. While he would have loved to stay and assist in filling in the blanks of all that had transpired, he had been summoned back to Langley. There were questions that needed answering there, too.

After a long plane trip that seemed even longer due to the fact that he really didn't want to be taking it, Holt endured the escort from the airport to C.I.A. Headquarters in Langley, Virginia. He had a feeling that the coming debrief would be longer than the flight itself and was not looking forward to it. He was brought to one of the numerous interview rooms and told to wait. The room was furnished with a long table in the center of the room with numerous chairs arranged around it. White fluorescent lights dotted the ceiling giving it a well-lit, yet not too bright appearance. The floor and walls were grey and dull. The only missing was the giant two-way mirror on the wall. In its place was numerous cameras covering the entire room. Ten minutes after he sat down, he was joined by three people; two men and a woman.

He recognized one of the men and was surprised that this had reached all the way to his desk. The three people entering the room took their seats across the table from Holt. The man Holt recognized took out a large file folder and started going through it. The woman started writing in her notepad while the third member of this committee just sat with his pen at the ready.

"Mr. Holt, I'm Deputy Director of the National Clandestine Service Ryan Aldridge. This is Tyler Ramsey. He is head of the Psychological Wellness Initiative and to my left is Dr. Allycia Bidon. I won't beat around the bush, but she is here to assess you as we go." Nods of acknowledgement were made all around before the D/NCS continued. "I'm sure you figured this out already, but I would be remiss if I didn't state that these proceedings are being recorded and while everything said here will remain confidential, it will be accessible for reference in the future by those with clearance."

"I understand," Holt replied. That was pretty standard. With the loss of life so great on one assignment, it was understandable.

"First, before we begin," Aldridge said. "Is there anything you would like to say to this committee regarding the incidents in British Columbia and/or in Las Vegas?"

"No, sir," Holt replied. He had plenty of questions that needed answering and he was sure that they did as well. All of it would come to light in its own time.

"Very well. Mr. Holt, I would like to say first and foremost that I'm glad you made it back. We've been following this assignment closely and it would seem that many aspects did not go as we would have hoped. We have already met with Mr. O'Connor and Mr. Cooper. They have provided a lot of information about what transpired out there. I'd like to hear your take on what happened and what went wrong."

"Director Aldridge. I take full responsibility for what happened out there. I could have handled things differently and approached some aspects in a different way. Perhaps things would have worked out better."

"Holt, I appreciate the gesture but the time to fall on your sword is passed. I need to know what happened."

Holt nodded. At least he had taken accountability for the mess. Director Aldridge clearly wanted the truth. "Waddell was a big part of it," Holt said flatly. "It's damned near impossible to lead a successful assignment when one of your team is actively working for the other side."

"Very true," Aldridge replied.

"How did he slip past the screening process?" Holt inquired. It seemed inconceivable that the Agency had put him on a G.D.M. assignment without knowing he was a G.D.M. operative.

"He didn't join the Movement until after he was in the C.I.A." Aldridge explained.

"What? You don't do follow-ups?" This was ridiculous.

"We do. We actually used to a lot more than we do now. Budget cutbacks have severely hampered our ability to successfully track the development of all our operatives. Ask yourself this: when was the last time you were interviewed or tested?"

Holt had to admit that he couldn't even remember the last time that had happened. "So you just let us all loose in the world and hope for the best?" Holt hadn't meant it to sound as snide as it did, but that's how it came across. Aldridge sloughed it off.

"We monitor as many as we can, but the numbers are just too great. That's why we started the P.W.I. in the first place. We rely on the assessments of the heads of each office. It's really the only way we can maintain any form of control of our operatives."

"What happened to the others?" Holt feared the worst as he hadn't had contact with the team in quite a while.

"Well, like I said, we have spoken with O'Connor and Cooper. O'Connor is still nursing that arm of his and Cooper is having some trouble getting though it. Fenwick and Wojanski are both dead. By the sounds of it, Waddell was the one who pulled the trigger on Fenwick. Needless to say, the Feds are losing their minds over that one. It will be a while before relations are back to normal with them. Wojanski went down in the shootout. We lost Martinez there, plus MacReady up on the roof. Again, Waddell appears to have been the trigger on MacReady. Then, of course, there's Nesbitt. We're still not sure if Waddell took him out or if someone else did. Surveillance footage is spotty at best, but it doesn't look like he did it. Ballard and Doyle were both wounded. Ballard more significantly than Doyle, but both of them are expected to recover fully. They're still at U.M.C., but they'll be transported back to Canada when Ballard's well enough to move. Probably by tomorrow. C.S.I.S. has a shitload of questions too, but at least they're getting their people back."

"Civilians?" Holt asked. He always hated the collateral damage aspect of the damage. He knew first-hand how devastating the loss of life can be, especially to the innocent people who never signed on to inherit the risks of government service.

Aldridge checked the file and leafed through his notes. "Couple people were wounded in Vegas, mostly from the panic of the evacuation. Up in Canada, that couple with the kids got shot up, but you already knew that. He didn't make it. Hell of a mess."

"I'd like to contribute something to them…the family I mean. The dad is dead and the mother is in hospital, I'd like to help them out somehow."

Aldridge waved his hand in the air. "It's being taken care of. The Agency is making a large donation to the fund that's being created for the Caldwell's in Chilliwack. I believe the Mounties are kicking in some money as well. She and her daughter are being looked after."

"What about Anna's brother Peter and his family?"

"They're doing okay. We haven't really heard too much from them so it's hard to know for sure, but we'll probably get the police up there to do a follow-up with a counsellor to make sure they're coping. I'd like to switch the focus back to the assignment itself. There is always going to be collateral damage on a file like this. I have reviewed a lot of the actions taken by everyone involved, but there are a couple of things that aren't clear. Would you be willing to clarify them?"

"I'll do my best," Holt answered simply. He still had a lot of questions, but there would be time. This interview looked like it was going to take a while. Over the next few hours, D/NCS Aldridge and Tyler Ramsey combed over every aspect of the assignment; from Holt's initial involvement back in Victoria, right up to and including the conversation he had had with the Seabrooks in the hospital room just before he made his way back to Langley. He wasn't entirely sure how they knew about that so quickly, but chalked it up to the wonders of the C.I.A. Through it all, Dr. Bidon sat and took notes.

"What made you think you had the authority to divulge that much information to Dr. Seabrook and his wife?" Ramsey asked. "Neither one of them had clearance to hear anything you told them. If Seabrook decides not to continue on in his capacity as counsellor to some of our operatives, then we have a major security leak within the P.W.I. department. And that's what I get to deal with."

"With all due respect, sir, the Seabrooks had just survived a particularly harrowing situation during which two of the people they considered friends popped up out of nowhere and began shooting people alongside C.I.A. field operatives. I don't think a simple 'nothing to see here'," making the air quotes with his hands, "would have sufficed."

"There were alternatives to laying out the entire operation for them, Holt. When you let this kind of information out, you jeopardize the lives of everyone in the P.W.I. The whole point of the department is that nobody on the outside knows of its existence."

"Then I guess we should bring the Seabrooks on the inside. Then, there won't be a problem."

"And if he doesn't want to?" Ramsey asked. He was getting more aggravated as the conversation wore on. "We can't exactly force people to do so."

Holt didn't want to antagonize anyone, but there didn't seem to be a way out of it. He was about to launch into a verbal offensive, but Director Aldridge stepped in.

"There's no point in arguing about this now. It's already happened. Tyler, talk to Dr. Seabrook and find out what he intends to do. If he's in, we have no problem. Holt, I can appreciate what you went through with Dr. Seabrook out there. I was in the field for fourteen years, so I get it. But don't ever do that again. I'm a pretty reasonable person, but there are some lines that can't be stepped over without consequences. Are we clear?"

"Crystal," Holt answered. He could feel Ramsey glowering at him, but he wasn't going to be goaded into resuming a scrap. "What happened to Vickers?"

"We're not entirely sure," Aldridge replied. "We're getting reports that a body turned up at the Searchlight Airport. It matches Vickers' description, but we'll have to wait for a positive ID."

"He must have bled out," Holt surmised. "I didn't think I hit him as nicely as I had hoped."

"You didn't. If it is Vickers, it would appear someone else finished him off. The body they found had five bullet wounds in him. With your one, that means another shooter put four more into him. We're not going to get our hopes up til we know for sure, but it would appear that the G.D.M. had had enough and decided to silence him. Good riddance if you ask me."

"What happened to Terry Philips?" Holt asked. Director Aldridge stopped, looked down at his files, and took a breath. He looked back up at Holt.

"Terry Philips was shot and killed two days ago by the U.S. Border Patrol as he tried to enter Texas from Mexico. He was mistaken for an illegal. When he refused to stop, they opened fire."

Holt watched the Director's eyes for any sign of deception. "Is that the official story or is it the truth?"

"It is what it is, Mr. Holt."

"I see. And what's happening in Columbia? What was the fallout from the assassination?"

Aldridge grimaced a little. "That's where it gets confusing. As expected, Manuel Poveda was named President successor to Nieto. We believed that Poveda was G.D.M. and that this was all a ploy to give the G.D.M. control of the oil fields. Turns out we were half right. Poveda's first official act as President was to sign a declaration that the oil collected from the fields would be used primarily to improve the quality of life for Columbians. They will sell the oil to, basically the highest bidder, and then use that money to build a better infrastructure for the Columbian citizens. That move doesn't seem to benefit the G.D.M so we're a little surprised."

"Noble, but do you believe it?" Holt asked.

"Normally I wouldn't, but I actually do. He's even asked the United Nations to oversee the process and has asked the World Bank to ensure that everything is conducted legally and equitably. I'm not really sure what to believe. Regardless, we'll be monitoring the situation closely."

"It's the military," Holt said.

"Excuse me?" Aldridge replied.

"The President of Columbia, much like the President of the United States, is the head of the military. With the drug trade so prevalent in that country, the military has gradually been increased over the last few years. It's used to maintain order in a lot of the country and is also a key in the war on drugs. If the G.D.M. controls the military, they can utilize it any way they deem appropriate. The soldiers themselves may not even be aware of it, but the G.D.M. just got their hands on an army and Poveda appears to the world as a saint."

"If you're right, this is going to get a lot worse before it gets better," Aldridge conceded. "For all our sakes, I hope you're wrong."

"I'm not. It's what I would do. It's what you would do as well," Holt added as he looked across the table at Director Aldridge. He only nodded pensively. "So what happens to me now?"

"For that, I will be consulting a few people on how best your skills can be utilized," Aldridge said.

"I'd like to get right back out there. Columbia is still unstable, but that won't last. We need cleanup crews in Victoria and Las Vegas. I'm here if you need me." Holt hated sitting around. He would much rather be doing something, even if it was tedious.

"That's one of the reasons I asked Dr. Bidon along with me today," Aldridge admitted. "Her assessment of you is one of the items I need to look at to figure out where you're abilities will best be suited. Dr. Bidon?" he said as he gave her the floor.

"My recommendation is simple. I have reviewed his file and been over the reports from this past assignment and I believe Mr. Holt has held up remarkably well considering what has happened. The loss of a colleague can be devastating and the betrayal of another can be equally destructive. Having taken all of that into consideration, however, it is my recommendation that Mr. Holt be removed from active duty and placed on leave for a minimum of four weeks where he should get counselling and find some time to uncoil."

"That's ridiculous," Holt objected. "I don't need time to relax. I'm perfectly fine."

"Is that so?" Dr. Nolan asked.

"Yes, that's so."

"How are you sleeping, Mr. Holt?" Holt hated to admit it, but it had been far too long since he had enjoyed would could be described as a good night's sleep. His mind was always racing and many times he woke up sweating and breathing heavily.

"Just fine," he answered. It sounded lame even to his own ears.

"Michelle Thompson been around lately?" The name struck Holt like a lightning bolt. She had invaded his dreams on numerous occasions and would sometimes appear to him while he was awake. She was popping up more and more lately. She had never really gone away.

"That was a long time ago," he commented quietly.

"And yet you still carry her with you. That says a lot. Take the time off. Try and get your head clear. If things are going to get as bad as we think they are, the C.I.A. is going to need you to be at your best."

Holt looked from Dr. Bidon to Director Aldridge who just sat there watching him. "If I refuse?" Holt asked him.

"Then I'll make it an order. But I have a feeling that that won't be necessary."

Holt stared blankly at the table in front of him. Maybe he did need to take some time off? Maybe the years of assignments were finally starting to take its toll? Holt nodded sullenly as he agreed to the down time. Immediately, though, he felt the weight on his shoulders lift ever so slightly. Perhaps it wouldn't be so bad after all.

EPILOGUE

Despite a valiant effort on the part of the public relations department of the Acropolis Hotel and Casino, the numbers just couldn't be ignored. Since word started spreading about their involvement with what had transpired in the preceding days, people started distancing themselves from the newest "jewel" on the Strip. After a few months of hemorrhaging money, the decision was made to sell the Acropolis. The MGM Group jumped on the opportunity to re-acquire the site at a remarkably reduced rate and promptly levelled the area. The Flamingo, however, benefitted from a relative boom following the event in question. The security detail was commended for their response and handling of the situation with exceptional praise being focussed on the team's evacuation protocols. Tyson Renzo became a minor celebrity for a short while and was featured on CNN. He hated every minute of it.

The FBI and CIA were dragged through the mud for a while, but that was to be expected. Conspiracy theorists launched their usual diatribe of "what is the government not telling us" and "Big Brother". Once they started in with their rants about Roswell, Area 51, and mass government enforced sterilization, the nation had already moved on.

One of the most amazing things about Western civilization is how quickly it can recover. The events that took place in British Columbia and Nevada would soon be overtaken by hearsay and rumour. The return to normality was surprisingly swift. Only the people who went through it would remember it the way it actually happened. For them, normal would never quite be the same again.

Three weeks after the events in Las Vegas occurred, Robert's shoulder was almost completely healed. He noticed that as he lifted his beer with his right hand and found that there was hardly any pain. The physiotherapist had said that it would be around this time so that was encouraging. He looked around Peter's backyard at the people that had gathered for this BBQ. It was likely going to be the last one of the year as autumn was rounding the corner at full speed. The sun shone brightly today, however, blessing this reunion with a brilliantly blue sky.

Anna was hugging Peter for the hundredth time, but he didn't seem to mind it at all. He was glad she had decided to take some time off from work. It may have seemed selfish, but he didn't want to share with anyone, especially losing her to the demands of being a teacher. Carrie and her daughter Julie were in the kitchen preparing some cold drinks for everyone. Julie was thrilled to be invited to this party. Normally she would have been sent away to play with the children, but today she got to stay and hang out with the adults. She was dying to help out any way she could. Anna's parents, Mark and Gail, had both shown up and her other brother John had made the trip too. Robert's mom Kathy was standing with them asking about the latest developments in everyone's lives. She was well loved and was genuinely interested in how her extended family was doing. Robert had the sense that it stemmed from loneliness. Not for the first time, he wished his dad was still alive. His mom was a rock, though. She had pushed on and become an important member of this circle he saw forming in his brother-in-law's yard.

"Robert, can you give us a hand bringing these out?" Carrie called out.

"Sure," he said as he set his beer down. He walked into the kitchen and saw Carrie and Julie trying to balance way too many drinks on to not enough tray. He smiled as he crossed over to them. "Here, I'll grab some."

"Thanks," Carrie said. "I just had a vision of a cascade of lemonade washing the party away." They both laughed.

"Do you think we made enough for everyone?" Julie asked. Robert couldn't tell if she was hoping the answer was yes for a job well done, or no for the excuse to keep making more.

"I think it looks just about right," he said and gave the 'tween' a kiss on the forehead. "Let's go find out."

The three of them came out onto the back porch and were greeted to cheers at their arrival. Robert had a feeling that they were making a slightly bigger deal of the lemonade for Julie's sake. It worked because she was absolutely beaming with pride. The drinks were passed out and the conversation was lively. The music was a good volume blasting out Steppenwolf's "Magic Carpet Ride" which made Peter believe that it was time to show off his air guitar routine. This brought laughter to everyone as Peter really started getting into it.

Carrie thought she heard the doorbell so she ducked inside to see who it was. When she opened the door, there was no one there. She stepped out and looked towards the street, but she could see nothing. *Must have been my imagination*, she thought. She was about to close it when something caught her attention out of the corner of her eye. It was an envelope taped to the front door. Three words were handwritten on it: *Robert and Anna*. She took it down and brought it with her to the backyard. She smiled when she saw that John had now joined his brother with some air drums and the two of them were rocking out to "Paradise City". Julie was howling with laughter. Carrie saw Robert and Anna sitting off to the side holding hands. She avoided John's flailing limbs and made her way over to them.

"This came for you guys," she said, handing them the envelope. Both of them looked at it with a confused expression.

"Where from?" Anna asked as she flipped it over in her hands. There was no postmark or return address.

"It was stuck to the front door."

A moment of panic swept through Robert as he thought about what could be inside. He quickly dismissed those thoughts. If someone had wanted to harm them, it wasn't exactly hard to find them with the amount of noise that Guns & Roses were currently supplying. Robert met Anna's gaze and together, they opened the envelope. Inside was a letter and another envelope. Robert handed Anna the second envelope and read the letter.

Dear Robert and Anna,

I wasn't sure if you even wanted to hear from me, but I just wanted to take the time to personally thank you for all that you endured over the past month. I'm sorry that any of this was brought to your door, but you both handled yourselves amazingly well and should be proud of the bond you have. I am in your debt because you have shown me that there can be beauty in a world where most of what I see is ugly. You showed me that there can be goodness even in the face of evil... love in the face of hate. Your efforts did not go unnoticed. As for me, I was able to take some much needed time off. I couldn't go away completely, though. I had to keep tabs on what was going on. Robert, I'm glad you decided to stay on in your position. I'm sure you will help a lot of people in the future. Anna, while I didn't get to meet with you for long, I want you to know that I consider it an honour to have met you and I wish that the two of you have a long and wonderful life together. I sent you a little present inside the other envelope. I don't want to hear any buts (though considering you have no way of finding me, that will hardly be an issue). Enjoy it. You both deserve it. I'll be in touch.

Holt

"Wow," Robert said. "Didn't expect that." He handed Anna the letter to read.

When she was done, she looked at Robert and smiled. "Could be worse, I suppose. Having someone like that in your corner."

"Indeed. Open it up," he said, nodding towards the second envelope. Carrie moved off to leave them be while Anna carefully opened the present that Holt had sent. She took it out and stared for a long time at what she held in her hands.

"Babe, what is it?" Robert asked.

She looked up at him then, tears gathered at the corners of her eyes. Robert was starting to get worried when a few of them lost their grip on her eye lashes and rolled down her cheek, but the smile that started to spread across her face assuaged his fears. She handed the present to him and watched as he read what he held. After he realized what it was, he returned her gaze. An unspoken conversation took place between their eyes as the realization that it would finally happen swept over them both. They were going on a cruise and, for the first time in their lives, they would get to see the Mediterranean Sea. They hugged each other tightly. Words seemed trivial at the moment. Then they rose together and rejoined the party. It was turning out to be one hell of a day.

At 8:41 on Monday morning, Dr. Gus Foley was sitting behind his office desk in downtown Lansing, Michigan. He had had a wonderful weekend boating on

Lake Superior and was fully recharged for the coming weeks. He had a pretty light schedule, purposefully set up that way so that he could ease his way back into the grind of a work week. He had a couple of new patients to contend with, but for the most part it was shaping up to be a rather ordinary day. He was just stretching the last of his neck muscles out when his intercom buzzed.

"Yes, Anika?" he said into the machine.

"Dr. Foley, your 9:00 appointment is here. Would you like him to wait?" Anika replied. She knew that Gus liked to start and end his appointments precisely at the allotted time. This was a new client so he obviously wasn't yet aware that the doctor didn't see people early. After his glorious weekend, though, he was surprisingly flexible.

"That's okay, Anika. Send him in."

The door to the office opened, and a middle-aged man entered the room. He appeared confident and walked straight over to the desk, extending his hand. Dr. Foley stood and shook the man's hand.

"Hello. It's a pleasure to meet you. My name is Dr. Foley. Please have a seat."

The man sat down and gave the room a quick once over before returning his focus to the doctor now sitting across from him. "It's a pleasure to meet you too," the potential client replied. "You'll have to forgive me. I'm a little nervous. How do we start?"

The doctor smiled warmly. "Why don't we start with your name and go from there?"

The client smiled.

"Sounds good. My name is Terry Philips."

CPSIA information can be obtained
at www.ICGtesting.com
Printed in the USA
LVHW040725080623
748726LV00001B/1